Rival Hearts

W. Million

Stomill Books

Little Falls Series

Reading Order

Book 1 – Rival Hearts

Book 2 – Mending Hearts

Additional content: First Date Challenge by Wendy Million (novella about Kai and Mckenna who appear in Book 3)

Book 3 – Healing Hearts

Book 4 – Guarded Hearts

All books in this series have bonus content. You can check for that here: https://wendymillion.com/bonus-content/

To anyone who's ever wished for a second chance

Chapter One
Maggie

I opened the door to the karaoke bar one town over from Little Falls, the June breeze blowing in behind. I was probably the last one to arrive, but Mrs. Smith was a talker, and she'd walked me out of the pharmacy to her car to gripe about small-town politics. Dispensing medications was my first job and listening to the people in my town was my second.

"Ahhh! Maggie!" Lila, my best friend, cried from the bar as soon as she caught sight of me at the entrance. "I love you for closing up early," she said when she reached me. With her glossy black hair cascading over her shoulders, she looked like she belonged in a commercial for hair products.

"Like I'd miss this!" I grinned and enveloped Lila in a hug. "Besides, I gave my customers lots of notice. It's your birthday. Welcome to the dirty thirties. Is there anyone in Little Falls who doesn't know it's your big day?" Once I learned they'd planned an open mic night instead of singing karaoke, the decision to attend was easier.

Not that I would have said 'no,' even if Lila signed me up for a solo performance. Earplugs might have been a necessity for everyone else, though. Neither of us could carry a tune if our lives depended on it, but Lila loved to marvel at the talent of others. I suffered through her addiction to pop star-wannabe television shows like *The Voice* and *American Idol* because there was no friend in the world I loved more than Lila Wang.

"It's not usually the paying customers who keep you away." Lila looped her arm with mine and sauntered past the sports memorabilia dotting the walls toward the long table at the back of the bar. Her table was closest to the stage, of course. "It's those customers who come into your pharmacy looking for the mayor who are the real time suck."

"You enjoy my mayor status." I gave Lila a sideways glance. "It helps while we're in the urban renewal meetings and we function like one brain." I tapped Lila's temple.

"There's still no one registered to run against you?" With her fingers crossed, she squeezed her eyes closed. She mouthed, *please say 'no.'*

"No one yet. The deadline is tomorrow." Up ahead at the heavy wooden table, my older brother and sister, Tyler and Emily, were laughing, probably at some inside joke no one else understood. Other friends were gathered around, celebratory drinks in hand.

"Four more years, baby!" Lila released me and threw up her hands. "Did you tell anyone else yet?"

I glanced around, hoping no one heard Lila's enthusiastic cheer. While the likelihood of someone springing up at the last minute to run against me was slim, I didn't like to make proclamations until I was sure they'd come true. "Tomorrow night," I said. "When it's definite."

"Anyone with eyes knows what a great job you've been doing for our town. In four years, you've managed to revitalize the downtown core."

A small smile rose at her claim. It was true, sort of. There was still lots of work to be done to create the Little Falls of my vision. The fact we traveled to the next town over for this event made me feel like a traitor. I should have insisted on doing something locally to support the downtown core I'd so painstakingly cultivated. But our small town of four thousand hadn't quite established a nightlife.

And I'd never been able to say no to Lila. Ever since we met on the playground when we were five, we'd been best friends. Lila's family emigrated from China and, even though we didn't speak the same language at first, it felt like our hearts strained toward one another, seeking something only each other could provide. We often called ourselves sisters by choice. My family accepted Lila as one of our own. According to Lila, she hadn't felt like an only child since she'd met us. Sometimes, Lila said, she forgot she was one.

"Lila's in the house!" Tyler stood up and saluted us with a sloshy beer. He owned a thrift shop in town and followed fashion with the same passion I devoted to medications and innovations in medical treatments. Although he was wearing jeans and a T-shirt like the rest of the people at the table, the cut of his clothes was more flattering, as though he'd told his outfit to behave, and it had listened.

Lila laughed at Tyler's theatrics as she plopped down beside him. Her lilac dress billowed around her knees. Without waiting for an invitation, she grabbed his beer from his hand, tipped it back, and downed the rest. I couldn't help a grimace. If there was one thing we sometimes bickered about, it was that I no longer let loose with alcohol.

For a while, we'd been united in our drunken ways. Perhaps if I was able to control my wayward thoughts and actions when I had one drink too many, I'd be able to indulge. I no longer trusted myself where alcohol was concerned.

"Where are the shots?" Lila scanned the table, searching for willing participants. "Jell-O shooters? It's my birthday!" She threw up her hands and let out another whoop, drawing everyone's attention toward the table.

Tyler signaled the waitress while I found a chair near the end of the group, facing the stage. They'd all be getting drunk, and at least this way, I wouldn't feel excluded for one part of the evening. By the time everyone needed a ride home, I'd be the most popular person there. I preferred being on the fringes, but I had learned to be adaptable. Being the outgoing, social butterfly was needed to perform my mayoral duties, and I could embrace that persona when I had to.

Top 40 tunes blared from the speakers, and I ordered water from the waitress when she made her next pass. Fernando, one of Lila's work colleagues, leaned into my shoulder and put his lips close to my ear.

"What time does this start?"

I shifted toward him so my voice would travel over the buzz of the crowd. "In a minute or two." I checked my watch. The first performer should have started five minutes ago. Running behind for some reason? Or fashionably late? Maybe the potential performers were intimidated by the large audience? I'd been here before with Lila for an open mic night, and the bar hadn't been this packed.

The yellow curtain on the stage stirred. Kareena, the owner, burst through the gap to the small bit of stage in front. She looked flushed and too excited for a simple open mic night. "Ladies and Gentlemen." She waited for everyone to quiet down.

I sat straighter in my chair. The place hummed with an unusual energy.

"Tonight, as some of you know—news like this spreads like wildfire—we have the privilege of a very special guest." Kareena glanced behind her, her brown cheeks rosy. "Oh gosh, I am *so* excited." She giggled and covered her mouth.

I frowned and eyed everyone in our party who looked equally confused. Other people in the crowd whooped and hollered as though they, too, knew the secret. What could be so special about some singer at open mic in a town barely bigger than Little Falls?

"I was going to do this big, long spiel about our guest, but he asked me to keep it simple since his appearance is last-minute. So, maybe I'll let it be a surprise to those of you who don't know yet." Her grin was broad enough to split her face. "Enjoy the night, everyone!" With a flourish, she threw back the curtains and disappeared.

"That was weird," Fernando muttered. "The only person I know who has ever inspired that kind of weirdness is—"

The curtain peeled back, and the chords of a familiar song started. My breath caught in my throat.

Grady Castillo.

I never uttered his name. Hadn't spoken it in years. He'd burst onto the music scene with his stint on *Center Stage*, the talent discovery program, when I was at college in Florida. Lila had told me how crazy my town went over one of our own winning the top spot. A heap of money and a recording contract. When he only produced one successful album and then largely disappeared, *I* was thrilled.

"Well, I'll be damned," Fernando called over the familiar beat of the song. "I wonder what he's doing back here."

I braced myself for the lyrics. I didn't want to look at him, but I couldn't tear my gaze away.

He'd aged well, which caused a spike of irrational anger. His brown hair was artfully tousled, and his brown eyes, even from here, had the same soulful expression. They hinted at so much emotional depth, just under the surface. Those eyes probably fooled many women into thinking he was a decent guy. His skin was a light shade of brown, a color I used to envy because my pale, freckled skin could never achieve it. Those impossibly long, muscular legs were bent, and his boot-clad feet rested on the rungs of the stool he was perched on while he strummed his guitar.

This song, more than any of the others on his album, boiled my rage. The song was a lie. Whenever it came on the radio, I turned it off. If someone started singing it, I had to grit my teeth. Everyone in our little town knew this song was about Grady's brother, Trent, and his stint in jail. It was also about me. What cut the deepest was that some people believed Trent had gone to jail protecting me.

Nothing could be further from the truth.

But we'd created our lies together, and I wasn't one to break a promise. The experience taught me to be more careful about who I got into bed with. I suppose we all learn that particular lesson at some point, but for me, that lesson was layered.

Lila, who was the only person in the world other than Trent who knew *most* of the truth, wrapped her arms around my shoulders. She pressed her cool cheek to mine with the hint of barley floating around us.

"If you want to get out of here," Lila whispered in my ear, "just say the word."

I tilted my head back but couldn't quite make eye contact. "I'm not ruining your birthday because Grady decided to grace us with his presence."

Before I'd admitted some of the truth, Lila was a puddle at Grady's feet like the majority of the town. He'd made it into the final *Center Stage* show, and everyone rooted for him. Then, he won the top prize. Around here, Grady was a golden boy, even if his fame didn't stick anywhere else.

The sound of the guitar rose, spreading out across the bar, and the room came alive with the crowd bursting into the chorus. A rousing anthem about brotherly love and the betrayal of a woman. Every word cut me like the sharpest knife. I gritted my teeth, determined to ride his performance out. Surely, Grady wouldn't be the sole singer on stage. Other people would perform. He'd sing a few songs and disappear. I could suffer through his brief appearance for Lila.

She gave me a squeeze and eased off my shoulders to wander back to Tyler and her seat beside him. I had fled to Florida for college, telling everyone who asked that my move was for a warmer climate. The truth and a lie, all rolled into one.

After Trent was arrested, I needed some distance from this place, from these people, from the jackass on stage who blamed me for his brother's harsh sentence. Throughout it all, I hadn't told anyone the truth. When Lila visited me in Florida, I had finally broken down and told her almost everything. All the lies had been shameful, but for some reason the truth had felt worse.

Song after song I sat with my arms crossed, wishing I could be any-where but here. He didn't bother to speak between songs, to work the crowd. Other people in the bar clapped, sang along, sighed wistfully at the sheer magnetic presence of Grady Castillo, while I fumed. Each lyric was another needle pricking me. As much as I hated him, his album proved he felt exactly the same.

Our relationship hadn't always been bitter. In high school, when I'd gone to Sunday dinner at Trent's house, I caught Grady staring at me as though he couldn't figure me out. His curiosity made me happy, ignited something in me too. *Let him stew. Let him wonder.* Then, the fuse I'd lit blew up in my face.

"I need a drink," I muttered to Fernando before standing and smoothing my skirt. Water wasn't going to be enough. Shoulders back, I headed toward the bar. There was a long line, and I stood tapping my foot out of sync with the musician on stage. I was almost at the front when the music stopped, and I sighed with relief. Did I still need a drink? If this ordeal was over, there was no need to give into a bad habit. Turning on my heel, I plowed into a very solid, very broad chest.

The soft fabric of his shirt, the tangy smell of him assaulted my senses with a flurry of punches, almost knocking me out. The simple navy round neck slithered across his muscles underneath. Part of me hated that I knew about his muscles, but beneath my hatred was a frisson of lust, familiar, unwanted.

My body was a traitor. I'd spent the last hour staring at the center of his chest instead of his stupid chiseled face, not giving him the satisfaction of making eye contact. What would I see in Grady's eyes when I glanced up? Twelve years ago, we'd been this close, closer, and those eyes stole a piece of my soul. I couldn't afford to give any more away.

With a deep breath, I stepped back and stared at him. He was stupidly tall and broad. I couldn't remember exactly how tall. Six foot five, maybe? Enough to hurt my neck if I was too close, barefoot, and looked up for too long. I squared my shoulders and gave him a sugary smile. "You must be thirsty." My tone was so sweet it dripped syrup. "All that singing would be hell on your voice. No need to speak." I held up a hand in the direction of his face. "I wouldn't want you to strain your precious vocal cords."

Grady's brown eyes scanned me, and I tried to decipher the emotion behind them. Amusement and something else I couldn't place. He chuckled and raised his bottle of water. "No need to worry, Maggie May. I don't make a living off my voice anymore, so I can let it get as rough as it needs to be."

The familiar timbre sent an unexpected jolt through me. I hadn't heard his voice in person since that night. Goose bumps rose on my arms, and I yanked my sweater tighter. "My middle name isn't May."

His lips quirked up, unrepentant, and he didn't respond. Someone tried to get his attention. He shook his head and gave them an apologetic smile, gesturing toward me. "We're catching up." The crowd around him thinned back.

"No, we're not," I muttered.

His lips quirked again, but he didn't say anything.

"You're back in town, then? Trying to make something of your life?" I jutted out my chin and crossed my arms. Any sense of playing nice disappeared. The goose bumps on my skin were from disgust, nothing else. I hated him.

He scanned the crowded bar. "Seems to be a few people who think I've already made something of myself." He shrugged. "But they're probably easily impressed—give them a glossy surface and they'll root for anyone." He directed his pointed gaze at me and sipped his bottle of water. "I heard you'd graduated from ruining one man's life to taking down a whole town. Little Falls still standing, or have you demolished it as well?"

His mother lived in Little Falls on the opposite side of town to my family. Penny Castillo had put my sign on her lawn during the previous election. Of all the conflicts I had helped to settle over the last four years as mayor, none of them caused my blood to boil like Grady was doing right now. He knew nothing about anything.

Leaning forward on my toes, I said, "I've spent the last four years looking after the people you abandoned while you chased fame and fortune." I raised my eyebrows in a challenge. I'd been the one to help Penny Castillo fix her garage when a windstorm had taken off half the roof; I'd been the one who picked up Trent from jail when he was finally released; I'd been the one to find his brother a job a few towns over when no one else wanted to hire him. What had Grady done? Won a singing contest and disappeared.

"Only four years?" His intensity drilled into me. "What was Trent's sentence again?"

I hated the heat creeping into my face.

Rage.

The heat was from rage and not humiliation. "It'll be me looking after them for another four years twenty-four hours from now."

"What are you talking about?" His sharp gaze turned curious, thoughtful.

My jaw ached from holding back the diatribe threatening to explode out. "I'm running uncontested for another term as mayor of Little Falls."

Grady pinched the bridge of his nose and then looked toward the ceiling. "Uncontested?"

"That's right. Uncontested," Lila said, appearing out of nowhere to throw her arm around my shoulders. Her words were slurred, but I was so glad for the backup, her level of drunkenness didn't matter. "It's because she's the best fucking mayor in any town anywhere."

Throwing back his head, Grady laughed. "In any town anywhere?"

With a frown, Lila used one finger and pressed it into his broad chest. "Yes! God. Why do you have to be such a hot prick?"

I clamped my hand over Lila's mouth. In the morning, Lila would regret those words. "She meant the prick part. The hot part is the Jell-O shots talking. Everyone in this bar is hot to her right now."

"What makes you so sure no one is going to run against you at the last minute?" Grady's eyebrows lifted, and he raised his bottle to his lips again.

Lila laughed through my hand and removed it from her face. "Because they'd have to own property in town, get enough supporters or file as an independent, and they'd have to think they could beat Maggie. No one is that dumb or that desperate." Considering how drunk Lila appeared to be, I was impressed with how smoothly her little speech spilled out of her. "And," Lila added, holding up her finger, "we know everyone who fits the criteria, and they're not running." She cocked an eyebrow at Grady and flicked out a hip. "Maggie's got it in the bag."

On instinct, I wanted to correct Lila, but the expression on Grady's face made me hold my tongue. Technically, Lila wasn't wrong, but I didn't like the way Grady's gaze turned calculating as it dragged across us. He chuckled to himself, and a hint of amusement lit his face.

A Hispanic woman I didn't recognize appeared at the edge of our circle. "Sorry to bother you, Mr. Castillo. But we were hoping to get a selfie and an autograph? You're like the biggest celebrity around here."

"Sure." Grady half turned toward his fan. The smile on his face had faded at the request. "Ladies." Grady pointed his water bottle at us. "I'll be seeing you around. I bought some prime real estate in Little Falls. Looks like we'll be neighbors." He backed away from us and then trailed the woman to her group.

"Neighbors?" Lila squeaked out. "Grady Castillo is coming back to Little Falls for good?"

That's what it sounded like. My heart thumped wildly in response. Did that mean I'd have to see him all the time?

Turns out I definitely needed that drink after all.

Chapter Two

Grady

I laid on the king size mattress in the middle of the living room. I purchased the run-down colonial style house on a whim a few weeks ago. The ceiling above me was cracked and more gray than white. I wasn't sure yet what had lured me back to Little Falls. Something had called me home. Maybe Mom getting older or that Trent rarely talked to me anymore, or maybe I was done with drifting.

Not that the reason mattered. The trip was already worth every penny I poured into returning. After running into Kareena in Utica, she'd taken advantage of our former high school friendship to get me to play a set at the open mic night.

As soon as the curtains had drawn back on the stage and I saw Maggie Sullivan sitting with a stick up her ass a few rows back, her auburn hair illuminated by the edge of the stage lights, a fire lit inside. On instinct, my fingers strummed the opening chords to the song I wrote about Trent and Maggie. Very few people understood the song, all the things said, the even greater number of things left unsaid. For years, I pictured Maggie's face while I played it. Last night, I'd gotten my wish, and for a brief moment, before she'd closed herself off, I'd seen what I wanted.

Guilt.

How did my town elect Maggie Sullivan as mayor? Made no sense. She was as fake as a person could be and still be somewhat human. A liar. A skilled one for sure, but were so many people in town fooled by her pretty face?

Beside me, my phone buzzed. Blindly, I reached for it and squinted at the name. Kelvin Brown, one of my best friends from high school, was calling. I silenced it and set it on my chest. Hite and Zeus, my two large, mixed-breed dogs stirred beside me. As I returned my focus to the ceiling, I gave them their morning scratch. Animals were preferable to people. They didn't pretend. They didn't complain. Hite and Zeus had traveled the world with me and never questioned any of my choices or decisions. The perfect companions.

My fingers dug into the thick fur at Hite's neck. Maggie's comment last night about chasing fame and fortune instead of looking after my family stung. When I'd scored an audition for *Center Stage*, taking the chance was a no-brainer. At twelve, my father had died without life insurance, and I'd stepped into his shoes. The odd jobs I picked up when I finished high school had barely kept all of us afloat. Who wouldn't have gone after money and fame when the other options kept my family in poverty forever?

Sitting up, I stretched and sighed. Maggie probably had no idea what I'd done after winning *Center Stage*. Most people didn't. I didn't intend to explain my choices to someone like her. No matter how wary and surprised her brown eyes had been when they'd looked up into mine last night, the truth remained.

At one time she'd been a mystery I puzzled over, but that was solved the minute Trent was arrested. Maggie showed her true character in the days, weeks, and months afterward. Pretty, glossy surface. No substance. Not worth a second thought or even one sleepless night.

Something banged against my front door—likely a fist. The dogs stirred around me but didn't bark. I grabbed the worn jeans off the floor next to my mattress and yanked them on. The pounding continued, and I held in another sigh. Could only be one person. That level of annoying persistence was special.

Opening my door, I leaned my bare shoulder into the edge and waved Kelvin into the house. Stepping past me, Kelvin glanced around the run-down entrance while Hite and Zeus circled him.

"I called you."

"I know."

"You should have answered." Kelvin sounded pissed, but when he half turned to look at me, his white teeth flashed in his brown face, taking the edge off his words.

I should have answered, but I couldn't get my head wrapped around seeing Maggie again. I'd known we'd run into each other eventually. Inevitable, given how small the town was. Last night had been unexpected, but I couldn't decide if it was unwelcome. "I was getting my head on straight."

"It's always a little crooked. Why should today be any different?" Kelvin turned around in the foyer taking in all the decay. "You dozing this place to the ground or what? You're probably getting a lung disease sleeping in here."

I chuckled and shrugged. "I've slept in worse places. Why are you here so early?" I squinted into the bright sunlight before closing the door.

"You called me last night and said you were running for mayor and needed a wingman."

A deeper, stronger laugh escaped. "I did what?"

"Yeah, man. You said stick-up-her-ass-Maggie couldn't get a second term without having to work for it."

I shook my head. I shouldn't have done those shots with Sabrina, my ex-girlfriend from high school. At least I hadn't brought her home. Not that she didn't try. Not that I didn't consider it.

For a moment, my mind rewound to Sabrina's hand sliding up my leg, massaging my inner thigh. I'd looked at her and thought, *Should I?* Then, she gave a high-pitched drunken giggle, and I decided I should not. Sober Grady was very happy drunk Grady led with the right head. I didn't come to Little Falls to slip into old habits. None of those habits had brought me any happiness the first time around. Anger. Depression. The one lick of happiness was forever tainted.

"Let me grab a shirt, and we can get breakfast." A pack of gum sat on the landing of the chipped wooden stairs that divided the house, and I grabbed it, tossing a piece into my mouth. "Want one?"

"You're going to brush your teeth, right? I'm a fucking dentist. You're not going to do this to me, are you?"

I grinned and chewed a little louder, rolling the piece of gum around my mouth, pretending to coat my teeth with it. "No running water at the moment. I need to buy more bottled water today. Used the last bottle for the dog dish." True, but it was also fun to fuck with Kelvin a little—he'd become too uptight for his own good.

"You need to bulldoze this place."

"The house was a good deal." Crossing into the living room, I threw my shirt over my head and called back to Kelvin. "Breakfast?"

"Man, I'm on my lunch hour. It's lunch."

"Whatever." Sometimes I forgot other people worried about keeping track of their day. In all the years I'd traveled, I'd worked on whatever schedule suited me. From the minute I left Little Falls after winning *Center Stage*, I'd drifted. Buying this house was the first time I dropped anchor. "Is that a yes?"

"Only if we walk past the office and I can grab you a toothbrush and toothpaste. I cannot sit across from you knowing you've got all that bacteria and shit coating your teeth."

"You and Maggie could make little stick children with all your rules. I imagine you don't have much competition for her."

"I'm gay, Grady. Remember?"

I squinted at Kelvin in mock surprise and then grinned. "I'm just fucking with you. I was the first person you told. Always considered that an honor." I slapped him on the back. We'd been drunk during our last year of high school when Kelvin had burst out with his sexual orientation. I'd suspected long before Kelvin told me, which was why I'd never given him a hard time about dating girls, or who he'd slept with, or any of the other shit most of the guys in our circle had been preoccupied with at the time. With my index finger, I banished the dogs back to the mattress and walked out the door in front of Kelvin. "Lead the way Mr. OCD. The toothbrush awaits no man."

"You can be a real prick sometimes." Kelvin slipped out the door behind me. "You locking this?"

"No. That mattress is heavy. If some robber can get it out the door, they earned it. Besides, I've heard from a few people Hite and Zeus are intimidating when I'm not around."

"They are big mutts—got some husky or German shepherd in there somewhere," Kelvin agreed.

The two of us walked in silence for a minute before I said, "Maggie's little friend called me that last night."

"She called you a mutt?"

"No, a prick." My mind ticked through the night before. "What *is* her name? I kept looking at her, and it was driving me nuts. I don't remember a cute Asian girl hanging around Maggie in high school."

"That's Lila. Local architect. Been here since she was a little kid. Speaks Mandarin and a couple other languages—Spanish? French? I can't remember. Sits on a few committees with Maggie." He gave me the side-eye. "Sometimes I wonder how you lived in this town for twenty-five years before you left and can't remember anyone."

I shrugged. "It's a gift." I'd moved around to so many places that everyone I ran into in town felt both familiar and foreign, like I couldn't place where I'd met them. Embarrassing, sometimes, especially when so many remembered me. Shoving my hands in my pockets, I added, "When you've moved as much as I have in the last few years, everyone looks like someone you should know and like a complete stranger. Too many places. Too many faces."

"You'd be a shitty mayor. That's one of the most important things—connecting with people."

A slow grin broke out onto my face. "So, you don't think I should run?"

"If the only reason you're running," Kelvin said unlocking and opening the glass door to his office, "is to fuck with Maggie Sullivan, then you should keep your dick in your pants. She's more man than you are."

"It wouldn't be the only reason." I took the toothbrush and toothpaste from Kelvin's outstretched hand and disappeared into the bathroom. Was it the only reason? I hadn't even remembered our conversation this morning when I'd woken up, and I'd never thought about being the mayor of Little Falls before. For a minute, I stared at myself in the mirror. Did I have the fortitude to do the job? As I brushed my teeth, I tried to talk myself out of this bright idea.

When I finished, I shoved the toothbrush and toothpaste back into the bag, and I stuffed the parcel into my back pocket.

"So, what's the other reason?" Kelvin asked as soon as I emerged from the all-white bathroom into the all-white office.

The temptation to run a finger along the ridges of the textured white wallpaper was tempting. We'd never leave the office if Kelvin thought I dirtied his walls. Wasn't worth the risk.

"Maybe there isn't one. Does it matter if I run to fuck with her?" I opened the office door.

"Maggie is the darling of Little Falls. She'll kill you. You'll get destroyed." Kelvin relocked the door.

"Darling Maggie could do with being taken down a peg or two. After what she did to Trent—" I shoved my hands in my front pockets, shoulders hunched.

"Your brother never pointed so much as his baby finger at her, man. Maybe you should let it go. Do you even know she was involved for sure?"

In the minutes it had taken Kelvin to try to talk me out of running, the idea of challenging her for mayor had become greater than any obstacle. Whenever anyone told me something couldn't be done, I balked. For me, a challenge made was a challenge met. I'd jump off that cliff, call that person, sleep in that place, take on that impossible job. Now, I supposed, I would run for mayor. "What if I don't care if I win? What if I run for fun?"

"How is being such a big dick fun? Why do it?" Kelvin raised his eyebrows. "You don't have better things to do? That house you bought is a disaster. Campaigns cost money. You need supporters, signs, debates… Not something you can do on a whim."

"Watch me." I turned to walk backward so I could look at Kelvin, who I figured should have been wearing scrubs but was dressed in jeans and a T-shirt instead. "Come on. What's the harm?"

"We'll make a mockery of democracy."

"If I was threatening to piss all over your office, I could see you getting upset. But this? This'll be *fun*."

"You gotta take it at least somewhat seriously, or I'm out. I run a business in this town. You might be passing through, but for some of us, this is our life." Kelvin stopped walking and threw up his hands. "This town is my life."

I paused in the middle of the sidewalk and stared at Kelvin, letting his words sink in. Some of his speech was valid. I'd never intentionally embarrass Kelvin, who had stuck with me through all my crazy stunts over the years. Turning to face the shops across the steady main street traffic, I nodded. "I don't want to win. So, I'm not trying too hard, okay? But I won't make a fool out of you or anyone else except Maggie. Deal?"

"This is a stupid idea."

"The last idea of mine you called stupid—"

"Yeah, yeah. You won the whole damn thing on national television. You're such a smug fucker sometimes." Kelvin paused in front of a sandwich shop and gestured toward the door. "First we eat, then we plan for someone's downfall."

"Excellent." I rubbed my hands together as I stepped into Kathy's Café ahead of Kelvin. Anticipation made my heart beat a little faster. There were few things I loved more than rising to a challenge.

"I didn't say whose downfall. 'Cause I'm pretty sure it's going to end up being yours." Kelvin's laugh almost sounded evil to my ears as the door clicked closed behind us.

Chapter Three
Maggie

I held the city hall internal phone away from my ear and stared at it, disbelief running through my veins like ice. I returned the handset to my ear, took a deep breath, and said, "What? I didn't catch that, Ruth. Can you say that again?"

My secretary cleared her throat. "Grady Castillo registered himself as an independent candidate for mayor."

"An independent candidate?" I spent one day a week in the mayor's office, and this week I'd decided on Friday. Mayor of Little Falls wasn't a full-time salaried job, which meant I was constantly juggling my pharmacy business with the interest of the town. There were few advantages in being a politician on such a small scale, which is why I'd expected to be declared mayor for another four years. Avoiding proclamations out loud didn't mean I didn't say them in my head. Right now, my brain was having trouble processing this turn of events. The calculating look Grady had given me last night made a lot more sense. "Does Grady even have a job?"

"Do you want me to come in there?" Ruth asked, and the scrape of the chair legs on the wooden floor as she rose from her seat was clear through the phone and the thick oak door. Instead of waiting for an answer, there was a click in my ear, and Ruth popped her head into the office.

"What in the world?" I set down the handset and rocked back in my leather chair. The mayor's desk, big, wide, and older than me, was laid out between us. I smoothed my hands along the grainy surface hoping, like a genie in a bottle, it would magically restore logic and order to my life. Grady Castillo returning to town unannounced and then running against me for mayor was insane.

"I know." Ruth nodded. "Absolute lunacy. Why would he want to run against you?"

"Why would he want to run at all?" I raised bewildered eyes to Ruth. "Does he even own property in town?"

Ruth inspected the piece of paper in her hand. "Looks like he bought the old Whittaker place."

"The Whittaker place?" I shook my head. "The mold penetrated his brain, that's what's happened."

With a small laugh, Ruth shrugged her shoulders. "Looks like we have ourselves a race for mayor."

"Seriously? What job did he list?" I rounded the desk, my heels muted by the gray carpet, and snatched the paper out of Ruth's hands. "Musician? That's what he put down?" Last night he'd told me he didn't make his living off his voice anymore. So, what was this? A lie?

"Technically, probably true. The cash prize and then the royalties off his hit album."

"One hit album," I reminded her. "One."

Ruth smoothed her chin-length salt-and-pepper hair. She was old enough to retire and had been for a few years. But when I had gotten into office, Ruth had agreed to stay on for my first term. Everyone had been counting on a second.

"There's no way Grady wants to be mayor." I thrust the paper at Ruth and spun on my heel to return to my desk. "You've met him? Grady Castillo can't remember anyone's name, ever. He and Trent were banned from the pawn shop when we were kids. Banned!" On the tip of my tongue was the reminder that Trent was a convicted felon, but I caught myself in time. I never talked about him like that, and I wasn't going to let my temper get the best of me now. Grady had always brought out the worst in me. "He would be a terrible mayor. I bet he doesn't even have a plan or a platform or anything."

"He has managed to get you quite worked up."

"A loophole." I picked up the phone and dialed the former mayor, who'd retired when I took over. "There must be some reason Grady can't run, right?"

Ruth shook her head. "I checked through everything I had on file to see if he was even allowed to run. It seems his candidacy as an independent is perfectly legal." She worried her bottom lip for a moment in silence. "If the house he bought and the career he listed is any indication, he probably doesn't have much money."

I narrowed my eyes in thought. "And you need money when you're an independent." My fingers drummed on the desk as I waited for Bill to pick up. Thoughts swirled around my head as I tried to make sense of this new development. This week marked the end of June. I had until November to wage a campaign so strong I'd leave Grady choking in my wake. After what felt like the five hundredth ring, I set down the phone. Who didn't have voicemail? I rested my chin on my open palm. "I can beat him, I think."

"You sure can."

I'd defeated Roger Gallagher four years ago to take this job. The campaign had been long and tough. My win had been earned. Already, something about the way this campaign was unfolding was unsettling instead of energizing.

"Who do you think he has helping him?" The Grady I remembered from years ago couldn't have organized a drinking contest at a brewery. Creative, intelligent, but scattered, and disorganized. Not mayor material. Not campaign material.

Ruth glanced down at the sheet in her hand. "Kelvin Brown signed as a witness when he declared his candidacy."

I took a deep breath and released it in a huff. I stood up. I sat back down. "I don't like that. Kelvin could run a half-decent campaign with markers and masking tape. Do you know him, Ruth? We went to high school together. Sort of. He's older than me. Tyler and Grady's age. God." I put my head in my hands and then flopped back in my chair, totally discombobulated.

"What makes you think he'd be so good? He's a dentist in town, isn't he?"

I nodded and hummed while I considered how to phrase it. "Kelvin cares about how other people perceive him. So, he always puts his best self out into the world."

"He's like you," Ruth said with a smile.

"He is." I pressed my fingers into my temple. "See my point?"

"Grady alone might not be a problem. But with Kelvin by his side, they'll give you a run for your fancy chair."

A knock on the doorframe behind Ruth made us both jump. We'd forgotten to close the door. Lila stood in the entrance with dark glasses perched on her nose. Her appearance almost made me smile. There was no sun streaming into city hall, so Lila was feeling the echoes of her birthday celebration.

"Four more years?" Lila held up her phone with the time prominently displayed. "It's closing time."

"I'll let you two talk." Ruth slipped past Lila to her desk.

"Close the door," I said. As soon as it clicked, I didn't wait for Lila to turn around. "Grady Castillo registered against me."

"Shut the front door!" Lila spun on her heel and then pressed her fingers to her temples, groaning. "I shouldn't have gone to work today." Gingerly, she removed her glasses. "I'm too hungover. I thought you said Grady Castillo declared himself a candidate for mayor, which would mean I'm in the twilight zone." Lila gave me a thoughtful look. "Or I'm still drunk. Am I still drunk?"

"Doubtful. It's more likely we've entered the tenth circle of hell."

"How many circles were there before Grady showed up in town?"

"Nine."

"Right."

We stared at each other for a moment before Lila sank into the gray leather chair on the other side of my oversized desk. With her fingers pressed into her temples, Lila winced. "Why would he run for mayor?"

"Who knows?"

"Do you think..." Lila shifted in her chair. "I sort of remember bragging about you being uncontested last night."

"You did."

"Is that why he decided to run? Did my big mouth ruin your slam dunk?"

I shook my head and sighed. "I don't know. But if you being proud of me set him off, there's not much we can do about that. Grady is

Grady. He's always been hard to figure out." That was the truth. The whole time I'd been with Trent my final year of high school, I'd had my eyes on Grady. We'd spent weeks, months sparing over this topic or that at Sunday dinners. Despite our bickering, there'd always been a cool aloofness in the way he'd challenged me. For a brief moment, that coolness had burned bright.

Then Trent got arrested, I went to college in Florida, and Grady won a national talent competition.

Now, we were rivals for the mayor of Little Falls. Every time reality entered my mind, the top of my head threatened to pop off. I'd thought he was gone for good.

"Are you worried?" Lila drew me back to the present.

"I can't decide. I wasn't that worried until I found out Kelvin Brown witnessed his candidate application."

Lila leaned back in her chair and crossed her legs. "Geez. Kelvin?" She took a bottle of aspirin out of her purse, shook out two pills, and popped them into her mouth.

"Yep."

"He cleans my teeth. I'm looking for a new dentist." Lila grabbed her phone, and her fingers flew over the keyboard. "All right, all joking aside. We need a game plan. I'll round up Emily, Tyler, your parents, and get in touch with anyone else who was part of your campaign four years ago. Sound good?"

"Yes. Thank you. I know we need to spring into action, but I feel like I got hit by a semi. If Kelvin wasn't involved, I'd say there was no way Grady was going to take this seriously."

"But he is, so we have to assume..."

"I'll get the lawn signs ordered and start talking to the people who did my pharmacy commercials and ads about mocking up some political ones."

"Are we all set for the Fourth of July? Fireworks are ordered? Parade is under control? We need to kill it this year."

"Yes. At least it's all set. We were already planning on going all out there, so no changes are needed."

Lila headed toward the door, an aura of determination around her. With her hand on the knob, she shifted her shoulders and hesitated for a beat. "Part of me thinks I shouldn't say this, but then another part of me thinks you might not have considered it."

"What's that?"

"The town loves Grady. They spent weeks rooting for him on *Center Stage*. It was years ago, but still. I know you were away, but it was a really big deal. Huge. Now, he's back and running for mayor." Lila's dark eyes filled with worry. "He might not know everyone, but they know him. They'll feel like they *really* know him. We have to consider the loyalty vote for some people might not lie with you."

Lila was right. I'd been remembering Grady as the man-boy I once knew at the end of my high school career. Back then, he'd been a twenty-something handyman who couldn't figure out how to do life. Why would I ever take that guy seriously? But time had passed, and Grady had found some success both in Little Falls and beyond. So instead of Lila's warning giving me a shot of panic, it centered me. I knew how to run a campaign against a worthy adversary and win. There were rules of play, strategy.

Grady Castillo was going to have his ass handed to him, and I'd take great pleasure in being the one to do it.

Chapter Four

Grady

Kelvin took a beer out of the cooler in what should have been my kitchen. "How do you expect people to vote for you when you don't even have a house that works? Who doesn't have a fridge?"

"To recap, I don't expect people to vote for me. Or not many people." I took a swig of my beer and hauled out one of the lawn chairs I'd bought that day for Kelvin to sit in. Flicking my wrist, the chair opened up and I pushed down in the middle so it wouldn't collapse when Kelvin sat down.

"And lawn chairs in your house? This is the first and last planning meeting here if this is where I have to sit." He took a sip of his beer and then held it away from his face so he could read the label. "And what is with this beer?"

"It's Korean. Like my dog, Hite. I like it."

"Hite is Korean?"

"Yep. Zeus is Greek."

"Right. Yeah. I forgot you collected them along your travels." He glanced at the two behemoths lying at my feet. "Seriously, though, when are you starting work on this place?" Kelvin picked at the label on his bottle as he took in the cracked walls and stained carpet in the living room. "You should have moved in with your mom."

I took a long drink of my beer. "I'm thirty-four. Who the fuck moves back in with their mother at thirty-four?"

"Someone who can only afford a house that'll cause headaches, asthma, and who knows what other respiratory illnesses."

"You searched this up last night, didn't you?"

"Of course. Google Doctor *is* good for some things. We're very close."

"Like developing a hypochondriac disorder?" I took another swig of beer and squinted at Kelvin. One of the things we'd had in common was a thirst for knowledge. Kelvin had excelled in high school in every subject. School hadn't been as big of a deal to me, but I'd loved to read, anything and everything. "What about Google Dentist?"

"Utter bullshit." Kelvin laughed. "Half of the crap on there is just plain wrong."

Not surprising, and I grinned. The thing was, I could have afforded a better house. But there'd been something about this place, like the town itself, that had drawn me in. I'd come home for the anniversary of my dad's death, and this house had been for sale. I'd toured through it with the real estate agent, and a feeling of rightness had seeped into my blood. Maybe the sensation that it was time I stayed, the desire to lay down roots, was simply nostalgia. This place, old man Whittaker's house, had been the last handyman job I'd done before going to my audition nine years ago.

Everything after that had been a whirlwind, sweeping me up and carrying me off. I'd felt hopeful my last day here, like maybe there was more to life than this town and shitty-paying jobs. I chuckled to myself. Now, I was running for mayor. What was wrong with me? Did the town even pay a salary?

"You're thinking about it, aren't you? About how dumb all this is? Are we quitting? Maybe we should quit. Did you see Maggie already has signs up everywhere?" Kelvin heaved himself out of the lawn chair and went over to the curtainless windows to point across the road to the signs dotting my neighbors' lawns. "Did you pick one of those slogans I sent you? We're already behind schedule."

"Take some deep breaths, Kelvin, or else I'm going to start hyperventilating for you. We're fine. It's been a week. The election isn't until November. I don't want to win. I want to make it harder for Maggie."

"So far, your plan for making it harder seems to be doing nothing but walking your dogs and registering as an independent."

"I like walking my dogs. It helps me think."

"About what? You haven't picked a slogan. You have no plan. No platform. Probably most of the town doesn't even know you're running."

"I can't put all my good ideas out there at once. Who would do that?" I gave Kelvin an amused look. Kelvin scowled. "Besides, I still have my real-life job that needs to get done. And you said I needed money for this campaign, so I took on some work I wouldn't normally consider, much less complete." I looked up at the ceiling. "Thinking is half the paycheck."

"I wouldn't want to stunt your intellectual process." Kelvin's voice dripped with skepticism. "But you made a promise to me I wouldn't be embarrassed by being associated with your campaign."

"I don't care about the slogan or the platform or any of that stuff. Put down whatever sounds good to you. I can talk bullshit all day long. I've been doing it for years. The platform and slogan aren't going to matter because I'm not going to win." I stood and walked back to the cooler in the not-quite-a-kitchen and grabbed another beer. Hite and Zeus were close at my heels.

"Every day I wake up and remember I agreed to this, I want to stop being your friend." Kelvin's voice echoed around the empty house.

"That's fine." I walked back into the living room and passed Kelvin another beer. Kelvin didn't mean it. We'd pulled all sorts of pranks in high school, and when I went to visit Kelvin in college before *Center Stage*, we'd spent many wild nights making choices worse than this. "But you'll still be my campaign manager. That contract was binding."

"At least tell me you're going to show up at the Fourth of July parade and fireworks. We can announce your run for mayor there."

"Sounds like a plan." The cap of my bottle was being stubborn, and I put it on the edge of the window and leveraged it open. "That must make you happy. I used the word 'plan' in a sentence."

"As long as our plans are the same."

"Doubtful." I tipped the beer back. "Fourth of July must be some sort of big PR deal for Maggie, right?"

Kelvin's nod was slow to come.

"We'll announce my candidacy and use the celebration to launch our first political move."

"And what'll that be?"

"No idea." I shrugged. "But I'm sure I'll figure it out on my next walk." I reached down and scratched both dogs idly.

"One last thing," Kelvin said. "Once we announce, you're going to need people to help organize things—distribution of signs, word of mouth PR, maybe run a few ads."

"I've been gone for nine years." Kelvin was the only person I'd stayed friends with. Any time I came back to Little Falls, which hadn't been very often, I'd slipped into town for a day or a weekend with my mom, a quick beer with Kelvin, and then I'd disappear again. Being here had filled me with complicated feelings, ones I didn't want to examine too closely.

"There must be some people," Kelvin said, but I could tell by the look on his face both of us knew that wasn't true. "Maybe play your famous card?"

"I'll find some." I made a circling motion with my beer. "I'll round them up."

"Okay, good. Look, I gotta get going." Kelvin passed his second unopened beer back. "I've got a date in Utica tonight."

"A date?"

"Yeah, this guy I met on a dating app. We've been chatting for a while, so I'm hoping dinner goes well."

At the mention of Utica, I thought of at least one person I could convince to help with my campaign. 'Campaign' sent a chill across my heart. Why was I doing this? Why couldn't I let it go as Kelvin had suggested? Maggie hadn't paid any price for what had happened to Trent. Being inconvenienced a few times during a local election was minuscule in comparison. I could do this.

"All right, man. Good luck tonight. I'll catch you later."

As soon as Kelvin was out the door, I hooked my two dogs to their leashes and decided to take a long walk. Eight o'clock at night was prime thinking time. A brisk wind ruffled my hair and stirred up the fur on the backs of the dogs as I wandered down tree-lined streets. I'd covered almost every neighborhood in town at some point in the last couple of weeks. Kelvin was right—I did a lot of walking. So many areas of the town had become run-down. Shockingly so. Little Falls needed something to jump-start it back to its former glory.

In my mind, this town had always been small but full of life. Now, it was tired and beat-up. Perhaps if I'd stayed, that was how I'd feel too. Was it possible to make a life here? I'd never been able to settle anywhere for more than a year since I'd left. Something in me kept pushing me forward, away, on to the next thing.

Without realizing it, I'd ended up in Maggie's parents' neighborhood. I'd avoided this area of town thus far. Her parents were small-town royalty, her mother a lawyer and her father a doctor. There were few families who could compare. This was the most expensive part of town with bigger lots, bigger houses, and bigger opportunities.

Out on the front lawn, Maggie and her father, Jim, were talking and laughing. At the corner of the street, I hovered with Hite and Zeus, and they whined, eager to continue. I couldn't tear my gaze away from the scene playing out in front of me. Behind the pair was a massive wooden sign emblazoned with, *Margaret Sullivan for Mayor–Building our Future, Together.* It looked a little weathered. Jim patted the corner, and Maggie laughed again, shaking her head. They hugged, and Maggie's sigh was almost audible from where I stood.

Watching them together was a muscle memory. If I closed my eyes, I could remember what a hug from a dad felt like. Every day since my father had died, I'd missed him. My feelings toward Maggie were questionable, but a part of me had loved Jim Sullivan for years.

As our family doctor, Jim had been in my life for as long as I could remember. When my father died in a drunk driving accident, Jim had been the doctor at the hospital to give us the news that my father wasn't going to wake up. While my brother and mother had been saying goodbye to our comatose father, Jim had sat in the waiting room with me. Even now, years later, the words Jim said to me that day felt as fresh, as new as when they first hovered between us.

"Losing a parent is awful," he'd said. "It'll be awful for a long time, maybe forever. We never quite get over the loss. But someday, maybe when you're a parent, it'll make you love your kids a little harder. Or at least it did with me. Out of the darkness, there's a bright spot, even if we can't see it yet. If you ever need to talk, I've been there. I know what it's like. And I'm always happy to listen."

We had talked a lot over the years, in the office, on the street, while I was cleaning Jim's gutters, but never about my dad. The topic had been too big, too impossible to broach even with someone as warm and approachable as Jim. Watching him with Maggie made my chest ache for that bond, the closeness, lost in an instant.

Back when Trent and Maggie had been dating, if that was even what had been going on, I had been jealous of the time Trent got to spend time with Maggie's family. Jealousy evaporated the night Trent was arrested. Before I'd gotten the phone call, Maggie had declared *'It's not what you think'* about her relationship with my younger brother. In my mind, if they hadn't been dating, Maggie wouldn't have been mixed up in my brother's dirty deals.

Truthfully, her as the mastermind made more sense than them dating. Trent as the muscle. Maggie as the brains.

With that thought at the forefront of my mind, I headed toward Maggie and her father. They broke apart at my approach, and Jim smiled, but there was a strain at the edges I hadn't seen before. Around town, I'd experienced many moments like this since I'd returned, where time had taken its toll on someone, and I could see it stamped all over their face, their body, in the color of their hair. Sometimes the change was so great I didn't recognize them. Jim had aged, but there was still a dignified air to his aging, his hair still mostly dark, his face still largely unlined, as though time had decided to be gentle with him.

"Grady Castillo!" Jim came forward with his hand outstretched. "Maggie tells me you're running for mayor against her. May the best woman win."

I couldn't hold back a grin, even as I focused on Maggie with her arms crossed tight around her. Hite and Zeus strained on the leash, eager to get to Jim or Maggie. Once Jim shook my hand, he crouched down and ruffled the dogs' fur.

"Beautiful beasts," Jim murmured as I scanned Maggie, who was studiously avoiding my gaze.

"Nice sign, Maggie May."

"Thank you." A façade draped over her as she loosened her arms and wandered over to crouch beside her father. "I've loved all your signs around town too. What's your slogan again? I can't quite remember. I've read your campaign platform somewhere, right? My father would love to make an informed choice, if you could give him your spiel." Her fingers massaged Hite's neck before she looked up at me, a wicked gleam in her brown eyes.

I smothered a grin at her obvious attempt to get under my skin. "I'm not a seasoned politician like you, Mags. I'm taking my time putting together something memorable."

She pursed her lips and tried to stifle a laugh. Whatever. Her laughter was fine. She had no idea what I was doing. Needling her was my goal, not winning the election. If she was stewing over any aspect of this race, that was a win.

"Still," she hedged. "There must have been something about the town that pushed you to run. To make you feel like you'd be good for the residents of Little Falls as their leader after having been absent from everyone's lives for so long."

I clenched my jaw. There she went again with that absentee nonsense. I'd come home whenever I was needed.

"Now, Margaret." Jim rose. "We're not getting into a political debate on the sidewalk. Did you want to come in? Coffee? We have a little shitpoo in there, but she's fairly well behaved, at least with other dogs."

"Dad, it's shih-poo."

"Yes, well, it shits and poos wherever it wants. If I didn't love your mother so much, it would have gotten a one-way ticket to the vet years ago. How hard is it to housetrain a dog?" Jim gave my two an appraising look. "Unusual-looking dogs. What are they?"

"Strays I picked up on my travels." I smiled, and I ruffled their soft fur on instinct.

Jim looked me in the eyes. "Takes a lot of commitment to cart two large dogs around from country to country."

"Not cheap, either." I enjoyed their company and their enthusiasm for any person, any environment. While you might have to win over people, you rarely had to win over a dog. I tightened my grip on the leashes when Maggie rose, and the dogs strained toward her. "Worth it, though."

"A constant captive audience," Maggie mumbled and flashed me a sardonic smile.

"Loyal. Trustworthy. A dog doesn't lie."

Maggie flushed, and I felt a surge of satisfaction.

"Coffee?" Jim asked even as his gaze shifted between me and Maggie. His jaw hardened for the briefest moment.

"Not tonight," I said. "I should get home. I've got some work to do." The words left my lips before I could reconsider.

"Oh." Maggie perked up. "You've got a job?"

A slow smile spread across my face. "I'm sure you looked at my candidate information. My job was listed there."

Her cheeks rosy, Maggie didn't deny the accusation. "Musician."

"Yep."

"Another album coming out?" Jim asked, a slight frown creasing his brow. "That first one was such a hit."

And more than one song blatantly about your daughter. Had Jim never realized? Noticed the subtle references? He'd probably heard more of my songs on the radio than he realized.

"No new album for me," I said. "Just odds and ends I still do for people I know."

"Well," Jim said, "like the rest of the town, I was pretty proud of you when you won *Center Stage.*"

My heart sank at the realization that screwing with Maggie's mayor race might damage my relationship with Jim. A loss I hadn't considered. I'd always been this way. Dive headfirst into something and then assess the fallout. Unfortunately, Trent had also been like that. After our dad died, we'd run wild around the town for a couple years. Grief stamped us all in different ways. In some respects, I was amazed the people of Little Falls had voted for me the first time. Now, in theory, I was asking them to do it again.

"The experience definitely opened a lot of doors for me. It was nice catching up with you, Jim." I stepped around them and started down the street. Not far down the sidewalk, I stopped and turned back. "Oh, and Maggie May—I'll see you at the Fourth of July celebrations. I have a good feeling about them this year."

Maggie smirked and crossed her arms. "I have a good feeling about everything that's going to happen between now and November. Campaigns are so much fun. Let me know when you start yours."

I laughed and turned around, my brain ticking through all the ideas circling. A sense of competition had been lit in me by the smug look on her face. If these ideas starting to form were any indication, she might wish she hadn't looked at me with such certainty.

Chapter Five
Maggie

I had finished taking Tyler and Emily through all the ways I needed their help for the celebrations when Ruth knocked on the partially open door. I glanced up from the parade planning, Tyler and Emily flanking me at the desk.

"What are you doing here, Ruth? It's Saturday."

"I know." Ruth came forward with a sheet of paper outstretched in her hand. "Kelvin Brown dropped this off at the close of business yesterday, and I forgot to put it on your desk. Seems he and Grady Castillo put together a little float."

I found the ends of my long auburn hair as I read through the dimensions of their parade idea. "This is bigger than the finale at the very end."

"I know. I told Kelvin I wasn't sure it would get approved. He hauled out the parade regulations and said their float didn't contradict any of them." Ruth backed out the door. "I have to go meet my family to get the perfect spot. Have a good day, everyone!" She waved and then drew the door closed behind her.

"Kelvin would know." Tyler held out his hand for the application and drew a lollipop out of his pocket. "Where's Lila? I thought she'd be here." He ripped off the wrapper and stuck it into his cheek.

I frowned and shuffled papers on my desk until I located my phone. There on the screen was a message from Lila. "Running late. As always."

"Once again, I'm really sorry my real estate agency sold him the Whittaker place."

"You didn't sell it to him, someone who works for you did." I shrugged. No one could have predicted how events would unfold from there.

"I know, but…" Emily frowned and rubbed her forehead before seeming to gather herself. "The parade starts in two hours. You can't deny Grady's request without people thinking you're trying to prevent him from getting votes."

"Oh," I said, dragging out the word. "I'm fairly convinced Grady will do a fine job of not getting any votes without my interference. The campaign has been running for almost two weeks. No signs. No platform. People keep asking me why I have signs up everywhere when I'm going to be declared the mayor. No one knows he's running. I sure as hell am not spreading the word."

Tyler's shoulders hunched, and he ran a hand through his dark-blond hair, tinged with red. He removed the lollipop from his cheek and gave her a sheepish look. "There is a chance I've told a few people." When I glared at him, he continued, "I didn't want people thinking you were so starved for attention you were advertising yourself when you didn't need to."

Emily, her campaign manager, raised her hand. "I told a few people too."

"Great. My campaign is doing more work for Grady than he is." I gave a snort of disgust. "I thought with Kelvin involved Grady might be a bit of a challenge. But he's the same guy he's always been."

"Knock, knock." Lila opened the door, her knuckles grazing the dark wood. "Did you guys get the text from Pete? Sabrina Kim filed a noise violation complaint about tonight's fireworks."

"You've got to be kidding me." I closed my eyes.

Tyler chuckled to himself, the lollipop clicking against his teeth.

"What's so funny?" I snapped.

"Uh…" Tyler looked around at them, waving the lollipop in the air. "Isn't Sabrina Kim Grady's old high school girlfriend?"

Lila gasped. "Grady's playing dirty."

I collapsed into my chair. Sabrina had been at the open mic night a few weeks ago, and I'd seen her getting cozy with Grady at the bar.

"She used to get noise violations all the time in high school for the parties she threw," Tyler continued. "I smell a rat."

"What time are the fireworks slated to end?" Emily came around the desk to peer over my shoulder.

"Eleven fifteen," I confirmed. "We didn't publish the finish time, only the start."

Lila bit her lip. "The Little Falls bylaw starts at eleven, right?"

"Yep," I said. "I have to talk to Pete." Rising, I gathered all the parade papers together and handed them to Lila. "Can you please keep this organized while I figure out how to fix our timing problem?"

"Can she file a complaint about something that hasn't happened? And about the Fourth of July Fireworks no less?" Emily tightened her strawberry-blond ponytail, readying herself for battle.

"I don't know," I admitted. "Pete will know. Sabrina or Grady or whoever must have gotten the idea from someone." I grabbed my purse off the table near the door and scooped my keys out of the front pocket. "Text or call with any other problems."

"Got it," Lila called after me as I shut the door.

****

At the warehouse, I stared at the boxes beside Pete. In my head, I counted them again. Then, out loud, I counted them a third time.

"Pete," I said carefully. "There aren't enough fireworks here."

"I realize that."

"Why didn't you tell me yesterday or, I don't know, any other day we'd been shortchanged?"

"I didn't know. Our summer students counted the boxes."

I eased my hands down my face and crouched so my knees almost touched my chin. "I suppose the only good news is the noise complaint is a nonstarter. We will barely have enough fireworks to light up the sky for five minutes, let alone finishing late."

"I can make some calls and see if any other towns have extra we can buy off them."

I closed my eyes and let Pete's voice wash over me. There had always been something about the way Pete spoke that I found comforting. His slow, careful drawl was different than the way most people spoke in Little Falls, and the rhythm calmed my anxiety enough for me to focus. He was an implant, a Southerner who'd moved here because his wife had fallen in love with Little Falls as a kid. Right now, I was grateful he was the one delivering this second blow to my day.

"Take photos of all of this. We'll have to go after the shipping company or the supplier later." I rose and rubbed my face one more time before squaring my shoulders. "If we do get them, what about Sabrina's noise complaint?"

"I was duty bound to tell you, but she can't make her complaint until it actually happens. She raised quite a stink on the phone with me today, talking about how the noise would wake up her sleeping children."

"She has three, right?"

"Yep, all by different daddies."

"Not so lucky in love."

"Or birth control."

"Pete!"

"I'm just saying, she didn't even know the rule was a bylaw when she called. When I explained to her there was an amendment in the bylaw for the Fourth of July and other civic holidays involving fireworks, she told me she didn't know what any of those words were, but she'd raise hell if we went past eleven."

I stifled a laugh. "Sounds like she needed a better complaint coach too."

"Must have been Grady. Kelvin would have tattooed the words and definitions on her skin."

"Grady's like her. He probably doesn't even know what those words mean." An unkind statement. Grady was smarter than he let most people see, but he'd seemed to enjoy his slacker image in high school and beyond. I'd never understood why he and Sabrina Kim, who was not faking her lack of intelligence, had spent so much time together.

"Seems odd to me, him running for mayor against you. You reckon that's got anything to do with what happened with you and Trent?"

With anyone else, I would have bristled at the implication there had been something foul about me and Trent. But with Pete, he was simply trying to puzzle Grady's motivation out, not being malicious. There might be other people in town who'd come to this conclusion, too, and wouldn't have the guts to ask.

"You mean about Trent going to jail?"

"Yeah, and a certain faction of the public who thought maybe Trent wasn't capable of what he was convicted of doing."

"I didn't have anything to do with Trent cooking meth and selling it. That's a schedule two narcotic. It carries, as we all now know, a mandatory sentence in New York State. I wouldn't have gone anywhere near that."

"Sorry, Mags, I didn't mean to imply you did. Only wondered if Grady might've thought Trent wasn't clever enough to do it on his own."

And he hadn't been, of that I was sure, but I hadn't willingly helped Trent either. Thinking about what happened back then caused a rush of anger. The fallout had been such a debacle, and I hadn't seen any of it coming. In hindsight, I'd been naïve. Forgiving myself had taken a while, but I'd only been seventeen. The things that don't occur to you at seventeen are endless.

"One of the things I like most about you, Pete, is your bluntness." I smiled and then picked my words carefully. "Trent was the mastermind of that scheme, not me."

"What do you reckon Grady thinks?"

Unbidden, the look on Grady's face after Trent was arrested entered my mind—disgust, betrayal, and underneath it all, like me, the guilt over something we'd never speak of. "He doesn't like me. I'm certain of that." If I'd had any doubts, Grady's behavior since he'd returned made his feelings clear.

"He's running out of spite."

I gave the tiniest shrug and head shake. "Who knows? Grady probably doesn't know. He's a drifter. Even if he wins, he won't stay."

"You don't think so?"

"Four years in one place? According to Penny, since he left here, he's spent a year at most anywhere before moving on."

"What's she think of him running?"

"She's his mom." When my phone buzzed, I dragged it out of my pocket. "The parade starts in half an hour. I have to go."

"I'll see what I can do about getting us more fireworks."

A deep sigh escaped. So far, today wasn't going as I'd expected. It could only get better, right?

Chapter Six
Grady

The horrified look on Kelvin's face told me I hadn't quite hit the mark. "You don't like it?" I stared at the sign on my float. The wind kicked up for a moment, reminding me we were out in the country surrounded by open fields.

"Taste the new, quit the old," Kelvin said the words slowly, as though that might make them different.

"Yeah. Maggie is old. I'm new."

Kelvin narrowed his eyes and tilted his head. "Aren't you supposed to be good at this?"

"At coming up with a slogan? Nope. That's got nothing to do with my job."

"No, I mean at arranging words."

"Well, it was either this or 'The new game in town.' I thought you'd like this better. Sabrina said you'd like this better." I wasn't quite as baffled as I was making it sound. Yes, I'd let Sabrina pick my campaign slogan, and I knew it wasn't a good one. I'd had to give her something in exchange for helping me, and the slogan was it. I wasn't taking the chance of sleeping with her now that I knew she had three kids.

"I mean." Kelvin scratched the back of his head. "You're inviting the town to eat you."

"Yeah," I said, nodding. "There is that." We stared at the incredibly large words emblazoned on the float for another minute. "I thought about going with 'If Bush can do it, God knows I can too,' but it seemed a little long."

Kelvin rubbed his face with his hand. "You promised. I even gave you a list to choose from."

"It's a fucking slogan. I could have put up there—This time, Vote Castillo for Mayor." I gestured to the large decals. "At least this is memorable."

"Sure, if you were a high school senior obsessed with eating things."

I grimaced. Sabrina had labeled all of Kelvin's suggestions as too boring. So, I had let Sabrina pick from a website devoted to student council slogans. Those options had seemed as good as anything else I could find on the internet. "You told me I needed people on my team. I got people."

Most of my team were women. I'd tried to talk some of my old buddies from high school into helping, but they'd laughed at me in a good-natured way. Run against Maggie Sullivan? Fat chance. They wanted to save themselves the embarrassment. So, I'd approached their sisters and mothers instead. They'd been more agreeable. One of the benefits of my short stint with fame was my ability to switch on the charm. I lived in someone else's skin when I slipped the charming mask on, a persona *Center Stage* cultivated and taught. Helpful, for sure, but it always felt a little slimy too.

"I was hoping—I don't know what I was hoping for—but it wasn't this." Kelvin sighed and pulled himself onto the float.

A pang of regret pierced my chest. "Look, Kelvin. This is going to work. I promise. Today will be better than you expect. If there's one thing I learned, it's how to put on a show. It'll be fine. Is it a shitty slogan? Sure. But when I'm done, it won't matter. You gotta trust me." I hopped onto the float beside Kelvin, and we stood staring at the rolling countryside. I didn't want the float to be in town until the last minute. For that, I figured Kelvin was probably grateful. Everything about the float was loud, designed to be noticed, to shake things up.

Kelvin walked around the bed of the truck, surveying all the details. I hadn't skimped on them. Lights, neon colors, huge lettering for my name and slogan. The stage would raise and lower as the float went down the town streets depending on the song I was singing. There were bubble machines, and some of my female helpers would pass out badges with my campaign slogan on them. My crew agreed to meet the float in town.

"What's in these boxes?" Kelvin gently kicked one with his foot.

"Fireworks." I also managed to recruit the summer students working at city hall with Pete. Both of them were in their early twenties, aspiring musicians looking for input into the industry. Talking them into borrowing the fireworks to give back at the end of the parade had been too easy. Technically, the two boys had stolen the fireworks, but they hadn't been bright enough to make that leap. I *may* have told them it was a prank. It was, sort of. Mostly, the theft was a way to make myself look good. *Grady saves the fireworks display*, would be the headline.

"Please tell me you're not setting those off on here."

"You are correct," I said. "I am not. You'll see. It's a grand gesture of a sort. One that'll be sure to get Maggie's panties in a twist." An unfortunate choice of words.

Maggie's panties.

The mental picture almost made me groan. A thong? A piece of lace? Simple cotton? For years, I'd done my best not to think about her. Deep under the surface, her hooks were secured. During my travels, I'd wake up soaked from a dream, those dark eyes, auburn hair, and the smattering of freckles across her nose the feature attraction. I'd sit on the edge of my bed, head in my hands and wish I'd dreamed of anyone but her. In some ways, the insane pull toward her was half of the reason I disliked her. My desire for her had overshadowed any loyalty to Trent. *Unforgivable*.

"Where'd the fireworks come from?" Kelvin gave me a skeptical look. An expression I was used to seeing.

"It was a goods and services exchange."

"You did something illegal, didn't you?"

"Me? No. Did I encourage other people to do illegal things? Possibly." Kelvin sighed.

"Petty theft," I clarified. Though, I wasn't sure the fireworks qualified for petty theft since these ones were probably expensive. I'd avoided an internet search so I could claim ignorance. That was a defense, wasn't it? "It'll be fine. The only people who could charge anyone would be Pete or Maggie, and they won't."

Kelvin laughed, but the sound didn't hold much humor. "By the end of this, Maggie might be quite happy to see you in jail."

My expression clouded at the mention of prison, and Kelvin reached out a hand to squeeze my shoulder.

"Sorry, man. That was shitty." Crossing his arms, Kelvin looked at me. "Why haven't you looped your brother into this, anyway?"

A loaded question. I'd called Trent the other night, but the conversation hadn't accomplished much. Maggie had gotten Trent his job in Utica when he got out of prison. No matter how I had tried to position my campaign for the mayor's job, Trent hadn't believed I was running for the right reasons. In fact, he'd told me even if I won, I'd never stay in Little Falls, so why bother? Those words had made me clench my jaw and hang up on Trent. What did he know?

"It's complicated," I said.

"Yeah," Kelvin agreed. "I guess. Most people around here didn't give him much leeway when he got out of jail. Maybe having him as part of the campaign isn't a great idea. He was lucky that mechanic in Utica took him on as an apprentice."

I checked my phone, more to avoid talking about Trent than because I wanted to know the time. It was later than I expected, and I nodded at Kelvin. "You driving into town or coming on the float?"

"What would I do on the float?" Kelvin raised his eyebrows.

"Talk. I sing. I don't talk. You can work the crowd anytime I need a little break."

Kelvin looked thoughtful and then gave a slow nod. "I could do that."

My cheeks were sore from grinning, and Kelvin continued his spiel for the crowd. There were few friends like Kelvin.

"When you have day-old donuts, do you keep them? No! Why? Because no one likes the taste of stale things. You don't keep that—you throw it out. Get something newer, fresher, better."

For a guy who had hated my choice of slogan, he was embracing the absurdity of it while the float glided through the streets, and the crowds cheered us on.

"How about another song? Who wants to hear your soon-to-be mayor play another tune?" Kelvin nodded at me as a burst of cheers erupted from the crowd.

Maggie's float had led the parade, and when they got to the end of the route, she was supposed to be there thanking everyone for participating and inviting them to the fireworks display tonight. I wondered how much of a panic my petty theft had caused her earlier in the day. As I sang another song from my hit record, my grin widened. I couldn't wait to see Maggie's frustrated face. There were only a few streets left and then the grand finale.

As the parade slowed near the end, I turned up the speakers on my float, hoping the song would carry all the way to her. There were days when playing felt tiresome, but today wasn't one of them. We glided past her like I'd instructed What's-his-face the summer intern to do. The song finished as we came to a stop, and I was sure if we'd practiced, we couldn't have timed it better.

I removed the microphone from its stand and jumped off the stage. "Ladies and Gentlemen of Little Falls," my voice boomed out, echoing all around, overtaking the noise from the crowd and the other floats. "I want this year's fireworks display to be better than any other year, so I'm donating to tonight's display. It's going to be the longest, biggest display yet. We're breaking bylaws tonight, people!"

Another burst of cheering soared all around us as I put down the microphone and picked up one of the boxes at my feet. I stepped off the back of the truck bed and stood in front of Maggie, relishing the pissed-off look she was trying so hard to hide. I held out the box.

Her eyes narrowed, and she took the box from my hands, her shoulders curling under the strain. When she looked down, her jaw clenched.

"So kind of you to already have the boxes stamped with *Property of Little Falls City Hall.*"

I chuckled. "Summer interns did that for me earlier. I didn't want these boxes to get lost. Can you imagine losing all these expensive fireworks? Pretty irresponsible. It would be a shame if the people didn't get a decent display for once." The women who handed out my buttons crowded around me, talking to each other and grinning. The buzz amongst them propped me up, made me bolder.

"Gosh, Grady. It's so good of you to buy more fireworks. The last few years the display hasn't been the greatest." Sabrina touched my bicep and fluttered her fake lashes. She had on more makeup than she needed, but there was still something pretty about her with her petite features, shoulder-length dark hair, and dark eyes. I couldn't deny her attractiveness, but the presentation seemed so empty and fake, as though the makeup was compensating for something she felt was missing. Had my high school self really been so swayed by the package? It made me a little sad for both of us.

"Oh." Maggie gave Sabrina a pointed look. "Will you be attending the fireworks display? I was under the impression you'd be home looking after your three children." The artificial sweetness in her voice almost puckered my lips.

"Of course not." Sabrina smiled. "They'll be with their dads. I'll be helping Grady."

"Seems you've already been quite busy doing that already," Maggie mumbled so low I was sure I was the only one who heard her.

I held back a laugh threatening to burst forth. The contrast between Sabrina's obliviousness and Maggie's laser focus amused me more than I expected. Maggie had always been sharp, witty, a verbal sparring partner like no other.

She turned her attention back to me. "You've assembled quite the team." She looked from me to all the women crowding around. They ran a spectrum of age and for that, I was quite proud.

"I know my demographic."

Maggie's eyes reminded me of dark chocolate, and she scanned my face. "Demographic. That's a big word. Did one of them teach it to you?" Her words had a bite, but her tone danced across them so lightly anyone casually listening might not catch it.

"Kelvin, actually." I let my gaze roam over Maggie in a way I hadn't since I'd returned. Sinking into this was dangerous. Better if I skimmed the surface of things. When we made eye contact, a jolt of electricity shot through me, a feeling I hadn't felt in a long time. Pinpricks darted across my skin. An awareness of her electrified me. I closed the distance between us a little more, our gazes locked.

"Interesting choice of slogan," Maggie murmured.

I grinned, but it faded when my attention strayed to her lips. People were talking in close proximity, but the bubble around us muted everything else. "Kelvin said it was in poor taste."

A hint of a smile tugged at Maggie's lips. "You seem to have a lot of volunteers willing to risk poor taste." Maggie's eyebrows arched, and she flicked her gaze pointedly to the women still hovering.

While Maggie might be a liar, and someone I didn't quite trust, I'd loved this aspect of her. Few women I'd met had made me hold back a smile or a laugh quite as often as she did. Her sense of humor had been one of the things that had surprised me when she'd started coming to Sunday dinners. At twenty-one, I'd known seventeen-year-old Maggie was pretty—anyone could have seen that—but the glossy façade had held a sharpness, slicing me open. She saw me, all of me, and it had been fucking terrifying and exhilarating.

"Grady." Sabrina cut into our moment with a tug on my arm. "Let's get out of here."

My eyes didn't leave Maggie's face when I said, "We need to unload the rest of those boxes."

"Kelvin already did." Sabrina's tone rang with annoyance.

At that, I half turned, reluctantly breaking the connection between Maggie and me. The loss was a bit like coming off a Tilt-A-Whirl or stepping onto a rocky boat only to discover I didn't have the sea legs I'd expected. Kelvin stood on the back of the float, and his focus shifted between Maggie and me, a frown creasing his brow.

"Enjoy the fireworks," I threw over my shoulder.

Maggie muttered something I didn't catch. I wanted to turn back, ask her to say it again, watch her lips move as each word left her mouth.

Instead, I hopped onto the float and said, "It's not what you think," in a low voice to Kelvin.

A laugh burst from Kelvin, and then his hand stretched across his face before he slapped me on the back. "If you know how it looks, then it's exactly what I think." He leaned close to my ear. "Maggie Sullivan is your fucking wet dream come to life. How did I miss the signs the first time around?"

As all the women in my crew scooted onto the float to sit, legs dangling over the edge for the return ride to the parade's starting point, I didn't deny Kelvin's claim. What had everyone else seen between Maggie and me?

Fireworks of a different sort.

Chapter Seven

Maggie

I caught sight of Grady through the large pharmacy windows as I filled prescriptions. I loved days like today when the sun shone on angles through the tree-lined street right into the pharmacy. Seeing Grady was like having clouds move across the sun.

I'd been watching him from afar for weeks. He'd been avoiding me after the Fourth of July fireworks debacle, I was sure of it. Maybe he'd realized he shouldn't have pulled that prank? Probably asking for too much maturity from him. For someone who didn't go to college, he knew all the frat-boy tricks. As I'd fumed, I'd considered calling Grady out publicly on his bullshit, but I would have seemed petty, and that wasn't my style.

Instead, I'd torn a strip off the two summer students for assisting Grady and committing theft. I'd warned them both that their interference in the election or in more criminal activities would result in their firing. Seeing Tristan driving Grady's float had sent my pulse skyrocketing and clicked in some missing pieces about the fireworks and a few other annoying things happening at city hall since Grady declared his candidacy. He'd known the scheduled conclusion of the fireworks display despite the details not being made public. Clearly, Grady already had at least two votes in town.

My irritation was compounded by the gaggle of women who followed him around, eager to do his bidding. Each time one of them passed me with a clipboard or a badge, I wanted to take them aside and talk some sense into them. Did they really think he *wanted* to be mayor?

The parade and his false show of Fourth of July spirit had propelled him to the forefront of the election. Everyone was talking about how Grady had come back to *save* the town. Save the town from what? From me? I almost gagged on the stench of bullshit. To top it off, there were signs everywhere encouraging people to get a taste of Grady. He should be walking around covered in slobber or pinned to the ground so people could lick him.

That thought stopped me in my tracks for a moment, a partially filled prescription in my hand.

My tongue.

His skin.

Oh God.

Goose bumps rose across my arms. I'd had boyfriends in college, quite a few of them, but none of them had consumed my thoughts the way Grady had. All of them had felt temporary. Maybe forbidden fruit did taste a little sweeter. Or it had. I was older now and much wiser. No need to crave a taste anymore.

Lately, I'd been clearing my browser history more than normal. People had uploaded videos of Grady at the parade, and I'd watched them a few times for research purposes, of course. Understanding the appeal of the competition was critical to success.

Inevitably, videos from *Center Stage* would be on the right, only one click away. I'd avoided watching them when he was on the show, and muted or closed any posts about him on social media. But being prepared was important, and part of that was researching my opponent, right? How could I understand why people loved him if I'd never watched any of his performances? So, I let myself dip a toe into his history. One video.

I shook my head as I filled another prescription. When it was done, I opened the bottom drawer of the cabinet and dropped it into its alphabetized bucket.

It was never one video, though, was it?

The whole situation was oddly fascinating. Long before anyone else knew about Grady's singing, I'd been privy to his secret. In his mother's garage one day when I'd gone looking for Trent, I'd heard him. At the doorway, out of sight, I'd listened to him strum, sing, write, strum, sing, write for so long. I'd never have been able to explain if I'd been caught. For someone like me, who was more analytical than creative, the process had been enthralling, like watching a painter craft a masterpiece. Except it had been my ears, his voice, and the thought of his fingers dancing across the guitar strings that had made my heart beat erratically.

Then he'd gotten famous by writing the song about Trent and me. The creative process hadn't seemed so spectacular after that. I'd spent many a drunken night during the end of my college days raging to Lila how I needed to call Grady and tell him the truth. Doing that would have broken the promise I'd made to Trent. And that wasn't the type of person I wanted to be. A promise made was a promise kept. Thankfully, once Grady got famous enough, there wasn't an easy way to reach him after I'd had five or six drinks too many.

When I'd woken up one morning to discover I'd posted a long ranting message on one of his fan pages, I'd been so disgusted I'd deleted the post and vowed to no longer drink. I'd broken that vow the other night after seeing Grady, and I feared I'd break it again under the strain of having him back.

The bell above the door jingled, signaling someone had entered the pharmacy. I glanced up from filling another prescription to see Tyler, the wind whipping in behind him, causing some of the pamphlets at the front of the store to flutter. My pharmacy wasn't huge, and the breeze whistled back to me as well. Focused on the rug at the door, Tyler ran a hand through his hair before looking up.

"We've got a problem," Tyler said.

"Just give me a sec." I set down the prescription I was working on, scribbling a reminder on a scrap of paper about where I'd been in my list of medications to fill.

When I looked up again, I noticed his designer jeans were soaked from the knees down. "If the water was any further up your pant leg, I'd say it was you with a problem. The adult diapers are over to the right."

"Very funny." Tyler didn't laugh. "Burst water main at Canal and Elizabeth. People think the old train station might flood. Water is everywhere. We've called a crew to work on it, but it's a mess."

"Shit. Burst?" I whipped off my white coat and reached for my phone. Without pausing, I dialed my father to come oversee the pharmacy so I could handle the water crisis.

"It gets worse."

I raised my eyebrows at Tyler as I waited for Dad to pick up. Tyler'd pulled a lollipop out of his pocket, his go-to in stressful situations.

"Grady is down there with Kelvin, ranting about the lack of spending on infrastructure and how the town is falling apart."

With a sigh, I rolled my eyes. "What would he know about any of those words?" The desire to paint Grady as incompetent or less intelligent was hard to resist.

"He didn't *say* infrastructure, but it was implied."

My father's smooth voice came through the phone, and before he could ask any questions, I said, "I need you at the pharmacy if you're not busy." My dad often looked after my business when I was called away by some town-wide crisis. "Bring your keys."

"I'll be there," Jim said.

"Thanks, Dad. You're the best." Although I knew lots of townspeople missed him as their doctor, I was glad he'd retired early. He was a godsend in moments like this and during my weekly mayoral duties at city hall.

Jim chuckled in my ear. "I love you, kiddo. Go rescue the town."

As soon as he hung up, I folded my white coat and left it on a chair behind the prescription desk. There were rubber boots in the back room from the last time a water main had burst. Not that long ago, but I couldn't pinpoint the exact date.

"When was the last time this happened?" I yanked on the second boot and grabbed my keys off the desk.

"Mid-May. But that was only a substantial leak. Pete handled that easily. Shame he's on vacation because this is worse. We've called the water management company. They've sent some people to assist us."

"Great." I opened the door and stepped out onto the tree-lined street in front of Tyler. I was going to miss Pete today. He kept me centered in a crisis like this with sound advice and quick action. "How did Grady catch wind of this?"

"He's soaked. He was there when it exploded."

"Oh." I flipped the lock into place and imagined it for a moment. That must have been quite the scene. A smile, one I tried to stifle, played on my lips. "And Kelvin?"

"I'm guessing Grady called him, but they might have been together. The only one who was drenched was Grady. Good thing it's a warm day." Tyler gave me a wry smile.

"Who's watching your store?"

"Sign on the door. I couldn't find anyone, and I knew you'd need help with Pete away."

Moments like these drove home how lucky I was to have my family. Each of them always pulled more than their own weight in a crisis. Tyler unwrapped the lollipop from his pocket and popped it into his mouth. There were two stages to the lollipop—out of the pocket was somewhat stressed, but in the mouth was worse. I wasn't going to like what I saw in a few minutes.

We hurried to the parking lot behind the main street pharmacy. Would this incident turn out to be another plus for Grady? The break in the water main wasn't a freak accident. The council had known there was a problem since May. Investing in the water infrastructure of the town was on the budget for next term if I got reelected, but I hadn't thought to put it in my campaign. If Grady was cunning enough, he could sweep in and steal this right off my platform.

Of course, he'd also have to understand paying for those infrastructure changes meant an increase in taxes—not exactly a selling point in any election and definitely not in a town where their property tax was already higher than the state average. Would Grady know any of that?

"You're too quiet," Tyler said as they slowed at the final corner before turning onto Elizabeth Street.

"Trying to figure out how to spin this. It's unfortunate Grady is there."

"No kidding. And soaking wet to boot."

Down the street, emergency vehicles and the water company's repair vans littered the road. A ton of people stood around with expressions ranging from annoyed to outright angry. I searched the crowd for Grady or Kelvin. Did he stay? A good politician would, but that description didn't fit Grady.

"I don't see him."

"When I left, he was ordering sandbags to see if he could protect the old train station from the majority of the flooding."

"Thank God it's empty at the moment." The old redbrick train station had housed a few things over the years like a restaurant, storage facility, and train museum. But none of those seemed to stick for more than a few years. Now, it was up for sale again. The Rolston family would be grateful for Grady's quick thinking.

As soon as the car was parked, I hopped out and followed fast on Tyler's heels. In no time at all, the water sloshed around my boots, and walking became a challenge. The water pushed against my legs, resisting any progress toward the train station. This was definitely worse than the last break. Up ahead, a crowd of people had formed a human chain, passing sandbags out of the bed of a utility truck.

When we got close enough and the crowd parted, my heart thumped painfully, the beat swirling up into my throat. There, at the end of the line, stacking bags at an astonishing speed, was a soaking wet Grady. His round neck white T-shirt clung to him and was the best example of a wet T-shirt contest I had ever seen. The muscles outlined against the shirt made my mouth go dry. As far as I knew, Grady didn't work out. Of course, Trent never had either. When I'd teased him about his ripped body, he'd laughed and said he'd at least gotten lucky with his physical genes. The brothers weren't built the same—even if they were both physically gifted. Grady was tall, lean, his muscles defined in the same way a runner's would be. Trent was built more like a wrestler—or a street fighter—God knew he'd done that more than once.

"Maggie," Tyler prompted, and I dragged my gaze away from Grady's fluid, flexing movements.

When I met Tyler's eyes, I felt like I was emerging from a daze. Out of my peripheral vision, Grady's continual movements enticed me, and only half of me could focus on Tyler.

"You going to help, Mayor Maggie?" Grady's voice boomed across the crowd, an obvious edge to his tone. "Or are you too good to get wet with me?"

My focus shifted to Grady immediately, but he wasn't looking at me as he continued to pile bags. Getting wet with him wasn't the problem.

Or maybe it was? My body liquefied at the memory.

"Got a spot for you right here at the end." He tipped his head to a widening space between him and Kelvin as the bags were passed along the chain.

I sloshed through the crowd. The childish urge to stomp my feet was met with the thick water. I'd gone from admiring his muscles and thinking about the past to silently fuming. The implication I wouldn't do whatever it took to help people in my town brought the liquid feeling in me to a boil. What the hell would Grady Castillo know about me or my town anyway?

Our shoulders brushed as I took my place, and I tried to ignore the fire the touch ignited across my skin. I didn't want to feel anything for him, certainly not attraction. When I received the first bag from Kelvin and flopped it into Grady's hands, his brown eyes met mine. We were locked together for the briefest moment, and a spark struck. His gaze slipped down to my lips before going back to my eyes. A memory lit, one I'd worked so hard to keep far, far down in my consciousness. Sometimes, I convinced myself the memory wasn't there at all.

Then Kelvin bumped my shoulder to pass me the next bag, and my focus shifted. As I took the bag and rotated my shoulders to give it to Grady, I avoided looking at him. His breath in my ear and across the side of my face was labored as he accepted the bag. My stomach dipped into my toes, and I closed my eyes to recenter. His breathing, hot against my ear, called me back to another time, another moment. So long ago, and yet right here beside him, the memory was visceral, so alive my body tingled. Why was my body betraying me like this?

As we worked side-by-side in silence, my thoughts were locked on repeat. *I'm in trouble. I'm in so much trouble.*

Chapter Eight
Grady

Each time I grazed Maggie's hands or her shoulder nudged mine, I cursed my stupid mouth for encouraging her to wade in next to me. When I'd caught sight of her in her preppy cardigan, skirt, and knee-high rubber boots, I hadn't been able to resist goading her into getting wet beside me. She'd looked too perfect, too made up, and I'd been too frustrated the water main had burst half an hour after I'd closed the deal to purchase the train station. Just my luck. *Let's buy a run-down, ill-used building and then get massive water damage. What a great fucking idea!*

Maggie stood poised to pass me another bag. Off in the distance, the water company stemmed the flood rushing out of the ground.

"You tiring out? Need to lift some weights instead of walking your beasts around town?"

I chuckled and accepted the sandbag from her. I heaved it a little higher than needed before placing it. Her gaze followed the flex of my biceps, and I realized she wasn't immune to at least some of my charms. "You don't need to worry about my stamina. I could go for days."

Maggie took another bag from Kelvin and rotated toward me. "A marathon man, are you? Sounds boring."

"A marathon? All that sweat, heavy breathing, quivering muscles? That sounds boring? Maggie May, delayed gratification is where it's at. You can't beat the feeling of sliding into the finish."

A wry smile passed across Maggie's face as she gave me another bag to stack and took another step further down the line to hold off the flow of water, which wasn't rising as quickly as before. We might be able to stop stacking the sandbags soon and hope for the best.

"Isn't it interesting most men slide into the finish before women?"

I tsked. "Sounds like a physiological problem. Or a chemistry problem. You're the expert on substances mixing, aren't you?" I took another bag from her and stacked it, my heart hammering. My tone had gone from teasing to pointed almost against my will.

Maggie frowned and turned to take another bag from Kelvin. A gust of cool air blew between us.

The taunt had been instinctual, but I'd been enjoying our banter. I could salvage the easiness between us, and I only hesitated a moment. "Isn't friction the key?" She glanced up at me, and I wanted to drown in her brown depths.

"Ahh." A hint of a smile passed across her face before she dropped another bag into my arms. "Rookie mistake. Friction isn't enough. You need combustion."

"Sounds explosive."

Maggie stifled a laugh as she turned back to me with another bag. "Done right? It's earth-shattering."

When our eyes connected, she placed another sandbag in my hands. Sparks jumped between us, threatening to start a fire. I wasn't sure I'd be able to put it out this time. Did I even want to? Her smile faded, and her gaze traveled to my lips. Instead of putting the bag down, I searched

Maggie's face, my own smile vanishing. How could it still be like this between us? Right now, I wanted to drop the sandbag, sweep her into my arms, and kiss her with all the pent-up feelings that had been simmering for years. She'd kiss me back. Her expression was naked with need.

But what good would kissing her do? She was still the same Maggie who'd stayed silent when Trent was arrested, the same one I'd never be able to trust.

"Maggie!" Tyler's voice pulled me out of my head and back to the moment. "Come here!"

Maggie's eyes widened and flicked back up to meet mine as though suddenly realizing we were surrounded by other people. Truthfully, I forgot too. Panic was evident on her face.

She backed out of the sandbag line, and Kelvin came closer, shooting me a knowing smile.

I took the bags from Kelvin while trying to keep an eye on Maggie and Tyler's heated conversation. When half the workers from the water company along with Maggie and Tyler disappeared, I knew there was trouble somewhere else.

"I wonder where the problem is now," I muttered as I stacked another bag.

"What?" Kelvin asked.

"Maggie and Tyler disappeared along with half the water company."

"I have a police scanner in my SUV if you want to know. It would probably make you look good to head over and help out with whatever else is happening. I can keep things going here. The water seems to have mostly stopped."

I stood taller and rolled my shoulders. The water was more ankle-deep instead of knee-deep. Glancing behind me, it was clear they'd managed to stop most of the water from reaching the base of the train station. A heavy rain rather than a flood. Wherever the water had rushed, it hadn't been into the train station. I hoped the runoff had gone straight into the river, which was only about two streets south of the station. Could the town be that lucky?

"Yeah, okay," I conceded, taking Kelvin's keys and passing him my own.

As I walked to Kelvin's vehicle, I made sure to thank everyone who'd been in the line or who'd helped the emergency workers. Many of them slapped me on the back and congratulated me on my quick action. Moments like these reminded me what I'd loved about Little Falls. I'd never experienced this feeling of community, of knowing every person you worked beside, of being part of a bigger picture when I'd traveled. Now, looking around the sea of people, all talking and helping each other, I wasn't sure why I'd wanted to leave so badly when I was younger.

Inside the SUV, I switched on the scanner. It only took a moment before I heard the intersection of the newest burst water main. At first, a feeling of dread settled across my chest. Unlike the train station incident, this one was right in the middle of town. While it was terrible for Maggie, it might not be bad for me. I shifted the car into drive and navigated along the familiar streets until the rushing water sloshed against the SUV's tires. I slowed and parked next to the curb. As I opened the door, water squished out of my clothes onto the seat. Unknowingly, Kelvin and I had been standing right beside the water main when it burst, dousing me in water and narrowly missing Kelvin. At least it hadn't been sewage. Small mercies.

As I ambled toward Maggie's pharmacy, I caught a glimpse of a moving white thing rising into the air, which gave me a moment of pause.

Come to think of it, the air seemed misty, like it did when you stood beside Niagara Falls. Frowning, I picked up my pace a little, and soon water was pouring onto me like rain. With a hand shielding my eyes from the spray of water, I rushed forward to see a swarm of people, including a now soaking wet Maggie, frantically trying to prevent the water from doing optimal damage everywhere. Even from where I stood, I knew their efforts were a lost cause. What was coming out of the ground here resembled the Jet d'Eau Fountain in Geneva more than a burst water main.

When I reached Maggie, I lowered my head as rain drenched us. "Jesus, Maggie. I can't believe you didn't fix this when you knew there was a problem."

Her eyes blazed black when she turned. "You think it's that simple? Where the hell does the money come from, Grady? What do you even know about the town's finances or the tax structure or even how a water main works?"

"I got the basic plumbing down, Mags."

"Well, good for you. One out of the however many things I listed is so incredibly impressive."

We were shouting over the roar of the water, but even if we hadn't needed to, we probably would have been.

"I'll call a truck for more sandbags." I stepped toward Kelvin's SUV.

"Someone already did!"

With a burst of annoyance, I brushed the water off my face, but it was fruitless. Maggie's auburn hair was plastered to the sides of her face, and I was sure we both looked like we were standing under a faucet. Other people were working around them. I knew I should help, but this did seem beyond my limited knowledge.

"We don't need your help, Grady."

Her words caused my jaw to clench, and I stormed closer, the geyser of water separating us. I pointed my finger up at the water shooting from the ground. "Clearly, you need help."

"Not yours. I don't know why you came back here, but you're not the town savior."

"I don't want to save the town. I want to save your goddamned pharmacy from flooding." The words spilled out of me, but I realized it was true when I saw Jim emerge from the glass storefront to approach Maggie from behind.

"I don't need you to save me either!" she yelled.

I shook my head and pushed my waterlogged hair off my forehead. Maggie moved away to speak to her father, and I let out a frustrated sigh.

"Grady!"

I took a deep breath, recognizing the high-pitched tone without having to look. With a half turn, I squinted at Sabrina through the water tumbling between them.

"Grady! I need your help. My nail salon is going to flood. Save me!"

Rotating on my heel, I waded toward her through the rushing water. As I went down the slope, I realized why Maggie didn't need my help. Her pharmacy sat on high ground. All the water was rushing downhill directly into other businesses on the main street. A truck with sandbags pulled up at the bottom of the hill just as I reached it. Water was already butting against Sabrina's salon door, but if we could stem the flow, the place might be salvageable.

Grabbing an armful of bags from the truck, I quickly surveyed the angle of the water and threw them down. I heaved more bags off the truck, interlocking them and hoping the rushing water didn't get any stronger.

"Thank you, Grady. You're like my knight in shining armor."

Instead of answering her, I put my head down and got to work. The water was rising at an alarming rate. Level with my ankles when Sabrina had called for help, the water now inched toward my knees.

"It's not working!" Sabrina cried.

Unlike the train station, the water wasn't being easily diverted elsewhere. This time, the flood had a mind of its own.

"Biscuits!" Someone up the hill screamed the name. "Grab Biscuits. Her leash broke. Grab her, please!"

I dropped the sandbag at the piercing wail of distress from an older woman at the top of the hill. Who the hell was Biscuits? In the rush of water, down the slope, a brown swirl of fur bobbed up and down, little paws struggling to keep afloat in the torrent. Abandoning the sandbags, a useless fight anyway, I tried to intersect with the dog as it came toward me. At the last minute, the water and the dog weaved away. I lunged for the frayed leash and missed. My foot slipped, and I struggled to right myself, arms whirling for balance, but another blast of water hit my knee, throwing me back. I sank into the wave and then tried to right myself, but the water was too deep and the momentum from behind too strong.

Where was the dog? In the distance, people were calling my name. Was that Maggie?

As I was propelled along by the current, I kept trying to get my feet under me, but it was no use. Every time my foot hit the ground, it was swept up again, the force greater than my ability to right myself or the ground slipperier than I expected. Where was the water taking me?

Toward the river, maybe. My heart was in my throat. Would I make it that far without being injured?

Debris floated around me, small pieces and larger chunks. In places, cars were partially submerged. I was a decent swimmer. Even still, I wasn't stupid enough to believe I couldn't drown. All it would take was one blow to the head from something heavy swept into the current.

Up ahead, the water slammed into a house, and pinned against it was the dog, Biscuits, struggling to keep its head clear. I swam sideways against the current, determined to pin my body to the house to grab the dog instead of riding the wave around. I didn't want to end up in the river—who knew what direction the water would take next? The dog was tiny, easy to cradle in my arms while I figured out a means of escape. I hoped my feet would find purchase on the ground and not slip, causing me to fall into the deepening water.

From the roof of the house, a young boy waved frantically and gestured to the drowning dog.

"I see it," I yelled and kept paddling, fighting the rush of the water to land in the path of the house. When my body hit the bricks, I let out an *oof*. My fingers dug into the white bricks, finding purchase, and I managed to get my feet under me. Although it felt like I was wading through waist-deep concrete, I got close enough to the dog to grab it by its bright-pink collar and hoisted it into my arms, out of the water. The dog trembled, and I scratched its head, murmuring words of reassurance. Somehow, we'd get out of this mess. The water swirled around us.

"Grady!" Tyler's voice carried across two houses to the right, both on higher ground, just outside the rushing water. Kelvin was with him with a long rope in his hand, and one of the reporters from the local paper behind him.

Had they followed me? How had they gotten there? Since I'd slipped, this was the first time I'd had a chance to take in the destruction. The water was getting deeper, but the water's path was narrower than I'd thought when I was in it. Still, the rope they had probably wouldn't reach from high ground to me.

"Did you get the dog?" The boy's voice floated down, caught by the wind.

I couldn't see the boy above me on the roof anymore. "Yeah, I got her. Are you in the house alone? Not sure it's safe to stay with all this water hitting it."

"I'm the babysitter."

I could hear the panic in the kid's voice. To the right were a set of stairs to the front door, and with the dog tucked against my chest, I fought the current to get a foot on the first stair not covered in water. Hoisting myself up, I carried the dog like a football and entered the house. Inside, a toddler or baby wailed. My heart clenched. They might be relatively safe in the house, but they might not. If Maggie and her crews couldn't stem the tide, the water would only keep rising.

I made my way through the house to the balcony. From there, I scanned the roofline. The little one's cries had halted at the sound of my footsteps, but I wasn't going near the child in the house until I had a plan. "Kid?"

Over the edge of the roof, the boy's brown head appeared. "The water is rising so fast. I—I tried to call Callie's parents and couldn't get an answer."

"Okay, okay." My mind ticked through all the options. Over the balcony edge, the water was now covering the steps, at the door to the house. Going back that way would be too dangerous to wrangle a dog and two kids. If we got swept away, we all might drown because I'd go down before I let anything happen to either of these kids. A memory was surfacing from when I took a disaster training course in China. On a lark, and with nothing better to do at the time, I'd loved the adrenaline rush of all the dangerous situations we'd been put in for a week. "Tyler, Kelvin!" I waited for them to find me from the shore. When they pinned me with their gazes, I said, "Get a ladder and get to the roof of the neighbor's house. A long ladder. A really long ladder." I didn't wait to see if they'd comply. I needed to calm the baby in the house and the babysitter. "Okay," I said, turning my attention to the kid on the roof. "How old are you? How old is the one you're babysitting?"

"Callie is a year old. I'm twelve."

"All right. Does Callie have one of those baby carrier things?"

"I don't know."

"Can you come down and check for me? I've got a plan to get us out of here, but it's not going to be easy."

The boy nodded and scrambled off the roof to the balcony and disappeared into the house. I ran a hand through my hair, the shaking dog still clutched like a football. Was my plan a good or foolish one? When the boy returned, he had a modified backpack clutched in his hand.

"Like this?"

I eyed it, trying to remember the ones I'd seen while traveling. In Vietnam, I'd strapped a woman's baby to me when the single mother had fallen behind during our group hike. The carrier had been easy enough to figure out. "Hold the dog." I passed the boy the shivering bundle and slid the pack on my shoulders, testing the feel of it. "We're going to Callie's room, and I need you to strap her into the backpack, okay?"

"Okay." The kid nodded and led us to Callie's room.

There in a crib, a chubby, tear-stained face almost stole my heart. When her dark-brown eyes met mine, I was reminded of another pair of eyes this dark, this soulful. Ones I'd probably gladly drown for, even if I'd never admit it out loud.

The boy dropped the dog in the crib and lifted Callie out. I went on my knees while the kid clipped her in and tightened the straps. Once he was done, I carefully removed the pack from my back and checked all the connections. For my plan, I had to be certain Callie was secure.

The house groaned, and the boy jumped. "What was that?"

"Nothing to worry about," I said, easing the backpack with Callie bundled tight onto my shoulders, and I grabbed the dog. "To the balcony." I wasn't sure the noises were nothing, but instead could be a sign that the house wasn't going to hold against the force of the water. We needed to get out of there.

On the balcony, I called to Kelvin and Tyler to get to the roof of the house across from us with the ladder. The kid scrambled onto the roof, and I passed him the pup before hoisting myself over the ledge onto the pitched surface. Luckily, my wet boots had no trouble gripping the shingles. I searched the roof for a good place to wedge the ladder, and when I'd found one, I signaled to Kelvin and Tyler to lower the ladder across. In the distance, sirens wailed.

"The firetrucks are trying to figure out a way to get here," Tyler called as he and Kelvin worked to close the gap between the houses. Luckily, the houses were of similar heights and closer together than most houses in Little Falls. The road was a court, a dead end, and staring out, it was clear the path had been consumed with the rapidly rising river from the broken water main.

"You be careful, Grady! You're going to be our next mayor." An older woman stuck her head out her second-story window, the screen gone.

I grimaced at the reminder and pressed the ladder into the roof, testing. It slipped. I righted the ladder and cursed under my breath, starting to sweat. The wail of sirens grew closer. Underneath us, the house shuddered.

"What was that?" The boy's voice shook with terror, and he clutched the dog to his chest.

"It's fine," I said, but when I glanced up, I could see the panic on Tyler and Kelvin's faces. Had the house actually shifted? I needed to get this ladder secured. Panic rose in my throat. We'd had all the necessary tools in the disaster training course, which in hindsight didn't make sense. Who has everything they need in a disaster? The ladder we used had spikes on it to secure it to the roof. I let out a frustrated noise.

The firetruck bounced along neighbors' lawns as it made its way toward us. How far did their ladders reach? Almost as soon as the truck came to a stop, the fire chief was out of the vehicle along with other firefighters, securing the truck. The ladder began to extend, and a firefighter headed toward them. I breathed a sigh of relief that I wouldn't have to rely on my shoddy across-the-roofs plan.

"You go first." I put the young boy in front of me. "Take the dog."

"I'll take the dog," the firefighter said, holding out her hands for the boy to drop the dog into them. "Hold onto both rails and come down the ladder backward. I'll be—"

The house groaned and jerked, almost tossing me to my knees. Callie let out a cry of distress.

"Down the ladder," the firefighter ordered before calling over to Tyler and Kelvin. "Evacuate that house—everyone who lives in it. If this one goes, it might take others." She radioed to her colleagues while she coached them onto the ladder with her.

As I left the roof and followed the boy and the firefighter down, the house groaned again. "What about the people in this house's path?" I called over my shoulder, careful to hold on tight, aware of the bundle on my back.

"We've got units evacuating everyone in the water's path," she replied as they continued to scale the ladder.

At the bottom, I turned Callie and the boy over to the firefighters and went to join Tyler, Kelvin, and the reporter on dry land.

"Who else needs help?" I asked, running a hand through my hair, adrenaline still pumping at full speed. "There must be other people who still need help."

"Lots of chaos in the downtown core," Kelvin admitted. "We can head there if you want. According to my scanner, the water is rushing this way, which is what's making it so vicious."

"All right," I said, heading for Tyler's truck in the distance. "Let's go see what we can do."

What was Maggie doing right now? Was she scrambling to stem the flow of water? Helping other members of the town? Or had she thrown her hands up in defeat?

The last one was unlikely. I knew her. She wouldn't let anyone get the best of her, if she could help it, and I resented the slither of worry that snaked down my spine. I knew how dangerous it was out there, which is why I needed to head back out, throw myself into the thick of things again. If anyone was in trouble, I'd do my best to help.

Chapter Nine
Maggie

I'd been staring at the newspaper Ruth had put on my desk with a fire in my belly, which flamed between disgust and desire. Hiran Paul, the editor of the Little Falls newspaper, had taken photos of the water disaster. Normally, I was in favor of informing the town of any and all events that stimulated interest in the news and in the town itself. However, the two photos he'd selected for the front page made me want to simultaneously blush and rage.

There, in the middle of the page, with the headline "Mayoral Race Heats Up," were two photos of me and Grady. Unfortunately, in the first photo the heat between us, even in the photo, was palpable. Our shoulders were touching, and the expression on both of our faces as we passed sandbags looked like *wanting* personified. And in the second photo, we were very clearly arguing outside my pharmacy as a geyser of water rose into the air between us. A bit on the nose, perhaps. What must people think?

At least Grady was fine and hadn't been swept to his death when he'd slipped in the flood.

The memory made my heart skip. I placed my hand over my chest. Worry had leapt into my throat when he'd gone down.

"Knock, knock." Lila poked her head in the office door without knocking. "Oh, good." She wandered to the desk and pointed at the newspaper. "I was afraid I was going to have to tell you about that."

I closed my eyes and sank into my chair. "Hiran is trying to make me look bad."

"No, he's trying to sell papers. That first photo? The two of you? Hawt! My God. I'm surprised all the water around you didn't evaporate with the way you two were looking at one another."

Given Lila was my best friend, I *could* admit we were exchanging sexual innuendos when the photo was taken, but it went against everything in me to admit the Grady pilot light still flickered. The only person who'd been close enough to hear our flirting was Kelvin. He'd spoken to the reporter about Grady's epic rescue of Matthew Long's son, Reese, and Callie Arbour, the baby he'd been babysitting on Saturday, and of course, the dog, Biscuits. The picture of the two of us locked in sexual tension was meant to stand on its own.

"If the paper had run the first photo only, then fine. But I look like a big ball of rage in the second one. What must people think?"

Lila pursed her lips and opened the paper, flipping to the next page. "So, I guess you didn't make it very far?"

My stomach dipped at the headline on the next page. It was a photo spread of Grady helping the various businesses on the main street with sandbags. In the very last one, Burt Maynard, the owner of the indoor playground for kids, had his arm slung around a drenched Grady, who was outfitted in a Superman costume that they must use as cosplay for adults when they were bored with their kids. The headline? "The Savior of Little Falls."

"You've got to be kidding me." I wasn't sure if I was referring to the butterflies in my stomach at how heroic Grady looked or at the headline itself.

Above the paper, Lila's fingers twirled her sunglasses. "I'm sure it could be worse."

I pressed my palms into the top of the desk and rose. "This is so infuriating." He'd saved Callie and Reese and Biscuits. An accomplishment, sure. But he hadn't saved the *town*.

"Yeah, it's not good for your campaign."

"I told him Little Falls didn't need a savior."

Lila stared at me, silent.

"I wanted to lose my mind when Sabrina Kim came running over crying *Save Me, Grady. Save me.* And then he flounced off after her." Of course, then I'd watched him lose his footing trying to rescue Biscuits and tumble down into the current. I didn't want to think about the panic that had flooded me, how I'd called every fire department in a thirty-mile radius to come assist us. An overreaction, surely, but no matter who had been caught up in the flood, I'd have done the same. Or at least, that's what I kept telling myself.

"Her nail salon was flooding," Lila reminded me.

"He's not supposed to do good things. He's supposed to be the screwup, the liar, the guy with stupid frat-boy tricks. He's not supposed to save babies and children and dogs."

"Ruth is a wise woman. She left that sitting there, didn't she? Didn't wait around to discuss it, didn't seek you out to talk it through..."

"This is unbelievable." I riffled through the pages. "No other pictures of me. I was running around putting out fires all day. Well, not fires because it was flooding, but you know what I mean. I'm sure no one even reads the paper anymore." All of this would be replicated online, shared over social media, its reach far wider than any paper product. There was a grainy video of Grady on the roof of Callie's house, looking tall and sure of himself while disaster raged around him. Two small children and a dog with him. Could his PR be any better?

"So wise, that Ruth." Lila retreated from my desk. "Clearly more seasoned in irate Maggie than me."

I refolded the paper, and when the creases wouldn't fall into line, I crumpled it up. When Grady's Superman photo somehow ended up on top, I groaned in frustration.

"Why? Why?" I gestured to the photo.

Lila slid a foot closer to the door. "He's very photogenic."

"You're not helping." I looked up from the mess of newsprint on my desk. "Where are you going?"

"Um, well." Lila stumbled, her hand on the doorknob.

"Am I interrupting?" Emily's strawberry-blond head appeared in the cracked open door.

"Nope. Nope. Not at all. I was leaving." Lila patted Emily on the shoulder. "Good luck, soldier."

Emily laughed.

My frown deepened.

As she approached my desk, Emily's eyes strayed to the paper. "You've seen it."

"Yes. All of it. Two photos on the front. Both of them make Grady look like some sort of sex god, and I look like an enraged lunatic. And then, you know, all the other stuff circulating because of his *daring* rescue." Although my tone was mocking, nothing was a lie or false. His genuine desire to help people, to do the right thing, shook me to the core.

"It's not quite that bad."

"It's that bad. You heard Lila use the *soldier* word, so you know it's bad."

Emily chuckled and slid into one of the chairs across from me. "You should probably sit down and do some deep breathing exercises."

"It won't help."

"It will. It works all the time with Amir."

"Your son is four."

"Exactly."

In a huff, I eased down into my chair and leaned back. It wasn't so much the photos. The bigger issue was how the photos made me feel, how seeing Grady racing off to Sabrina's rescue had made me feel, how seeing him being carried away made my heart squeeze so painfully in my chest that I almost couldn't breathe. After the third deep breath, I nodded at Emily.

A small smile spread across her face. "We need to chat, and you're not going to like it."

"This morning already feels like a dumpster fire. Let's add more fuel to it."

"I think you should call Trent and invite him to help Grady."

"No." I pressed my hands into the desk and rose again, my heart rate climbing once more. "No."

"The last few days have been golden for Grady. He could literally take a shit in the middle of Main Street right now and people would covet it. That's how golden he is. People will believe he's shitting gold bars."

The imagery was disgusting and priceless. "That's ridiculous."

"Tell me it's not true."

"You know I can't. I mean, I've heard the buzz around town. He's in a frigging Superman costume in the weekly paper."

"His kryptonite is his convict brother."

"*Don't* say that."

"A few people's kids went down in the bust with Trent. Voters have long memories."

"And some of those voters probably think I had something to do with what happened. Just because people don't say anything to my face doesn't mean they haven't thought it or talked about it."

"Anyone who knows you doesn't think anything of the sort, but everyone believes Grady is the town savior. We need to humanize him."

"I can't use Trent like that."

"So, you're saying you think Trent and Grady becoming closer is a bad thing?"

"Emily."

"I'm only asking." Emily held up her hands. "Strategy, Maggie. Do you want to win? 'Cause right now, you're losing."

"Elections favor the long game. Even if I was okay with using Trent, which I'm not, but if I was, it's too early to use him." My jaw felt tight with annoyance.

Calling in Trent was good strategy, but it made me a shitty friend. Trent and I had never been what people believed—even my family didn't know all the details of what happened between me, Trent, and Grady—but what had come out of our situation had made Trent and me loyal to each other in a way I had with few people. "If I ask Trent to come here, I'll tell him the truth about why I need him."

Emily looked at me for a long moment before bracing her hands on the arms of the chair. "What if he tells Grady? Wouldn't his loyalty lie with Grady?"

I eased into my chair. "I doubt it." I met Emily's eyes. "They've hardly spoken since Trent got out of jail."

"Why?"

"I don't know. I'm not sure Trent knows."

"What do you think?"

"The only thing that makes sense to me is Grady's ashamed of his brother."

Emily seemed to mull over my answer and pursed her lips. "Being honest with Trent is risky. But the two of you have always had a relationship none of us understood. So, as your campaign manager, I'll defer to you. But you need to come up with something to sway people back in your direction. Donate some money. Push through an initiative people have been begging to get. Start a GoFundMe for all the businesses and houses suffering from water damage and don't have enough insurance. Something. And yell it from the rooftops, okay?"

I didn't look at Emily but gave her a half-hearted thumbs-up. "Got it." With a sigh, I said, "I know the drill. We change the narrative."

"You bet." Emily held up her hands. "When people are focused over here"—she waggled her left hand—"you say, 'oh, look, shiny thing' and *bam*. New narrative."

"Sometimes I think you should be the one sitting here."

"No way." Emily rose and headed for the door. "I hate getting my hair wet. You look like a drowned rat in those photos."

I followed Emily to the door. "Gee, thanks."

"Hey, if your sister can't be honest with you, who can?" Emily grabbed the door handle and then turned back. "On that note." She took a deep breath. "You need to mute that sexual chemistry with Grady."

"What?" I reared back.

"It jumps off the page. Jumps out everywhere. People are talking." She pushed the door tight. "It's the sad truth of politics, of any job, and I know you know. Men can look at women like he looked at you in those photos and they're better off. Doesn't work that way for us."

Although I wasn't admitting it to Emily, I'd said something similar to Lila already.

"Shut it down."

"I know." And I did. But I also knew if Trent was Grady's kryptonite, then Grady was mine. Try as I might, the connection I felt to him was magnetic. I'd hoped time and distance would have weakened it. As we'd passed sandbags back and forth the other day, I'd been faced with the hard truth.

I might not like Grady, but the idea of sleeping with him wasn't nearly as repulsive as it should be. "I won't let anything get out of control."

Chapter Ten

Grady

My dogs wrestled in the middle of the train station, their leashes tangling and then releasing when I took a step in their direction. Joseph Goldtooth, the contractor I'd hired, was busy measuring the rooms. The station had been built up and torn down several times, depending on who bought it. Like many of the run-down buildings in Little Falls, I bought this for a song—or rather, the price of one, quite literally.

The old redbrick building was one of my favorite places in Little Falls. Every time I'd ridden my bike past or come here in any of its various incarnations, I'd longed to own it. Something about the history of the station made me feel solid, secure. Assuming Joseph Goldtooth was as good as Kelvin said, I was sure he could get this building to strike a balance that honored the past but projected toward the future. It was time I set down roots, whether I won this mayoral race or not.

Kelvin burst into the train station, cracking my thoughts. "Maggie's GoFundMe for the town hit another milestone."

"Maggie set up a GoFundMe?" My pulse jumped at her name crossing my lips. "Send me the link. How long has it been up?"

"A few hours ago. Clever what she did, though." Kelvin typed into his phone, and my pocket vibrated with the incoming message.

"What's that?" I asked, amused despite myself. No matter what else I believed about Maggie, she wasn't a quitter. I'd run around town during the flood helping anyone who asked. I'd been exhausted afterward, but I'd become reacquainted with so many people I hadn't seen in years, remembered names and events I'd thought long forgotten. Getting one over on Maggie had been good, but connecting with my community had been a pleasant reward.

"She took that photo of you in the Superman outfit and attached the GoFundMe to it somehow. Then she posted it all over your fan pages and sent it to major entertainment outlets. The fund has gone viral. Your famous friends are donating."

Every muscle in my body tensed in a mixture of panic and anger. Many of those famous people I'd never met in person. Online meetups, Face-time videos, phone calls, email exchanges, yes, but face-to-face? Nope.

"They've done what?"

"Donated." Kelvin pointed at his pocket. "Check your phone. I sent you the link. God, she's brilliant."

"She made it seem like I'd lost something in the flood?" Anger floated to the surface, overtaking my initial panic. Lies. Again. There were few things I was protective about, but my business reputation was one of them. I was never going back to doing odd jobs when I could do something I loved.

"Nah," Kelvin said, shaking his head. "That'd be too simple. Her post is this moving message about how important the town and its people are to her." Kelvin pointed to the corner of his eye. "I might have spawned a tear."

My mind strayed to an image of Maggie, her clothes plastered to her, highlighting all those curves. The look in her eyes before I'd turned to help Sabrina haunted me, even though I couldn't pinpoint *what* was there. I'd been stuck on the meaning behind her expression for days.

A text from my agent, Jack, appeared on my screen asking about *this GoFundMe and flooding business* for an official comment.

Running a hand through my hair, I swore under my breath. Fucking ridiculous. She was going to turn my life into a shitstorm and a PR nightmare. As distractions went, it *was* brilliant. Kelvin was right. The viral post probably made her look as inviting and nostalgic as her vanilla-scented perfume, but since the photo was of me and I was the one with all the famous friends, I'd be the one fielding all the calls for comment.

"I need to talk to her. Can you drop Zeus and Hite off at my place? I can't leave them in the truck in this heat."

"Uh." Kelvin eyed them. "Will they bite me?"

"Doesn't your new boyfriend have a dog?"

"Yeah, but it's like a puffy little thing that barks a lot. It's not"—he stared at the two dogs circling him—"these things."

"Fine," I said, impatience winning out. "I'll do it myself before I head over to Maggie's."

"Maybe walk them home, give yourself time to cool off. We can work with this!" Kelvin called as I headed out the door, my dogs trailing behind.

The pharmacy windows had taunted me for weeks. Each time I walked past, it took everything in me not to peer in, to hope for a glimpse of auburn hair, a swish of a white lab coat. Now, I stood outside the scope of those windows, taking some deep breaths. If there were other people in the pharmacy, I couldn't go in verbal guns blazing, or we'd end up with casualties and maybe another story in the paper. I didn't need more press.

One way or another, Maggie Sullivan was the most likely candidate to ruin my life. But I didn't want her to know that. I didn't want her to know any of it. A few people called out a 'hello' as I stepped from the shadows of Maggie's building to open the door. With a smile and a wave, I landed inside the pharmacy. When I glanced up, Maggie looked startled from behind the high counter at the back, her coal eyes wide.

We were the only people in the place.

"I see business is booming." I smirked.

"Not all of us need a harem following us around from place to place validating our existence."

"Is that what you think they do? You know what a harem is, right?" I wandered closer to where she stood, the two counters still separating us.

She flushed. "You're right. Your house isn't nearly big enough to keep them all." Almost under her breath, she continued, "I hear you sleep on the floor."

"Asking around about me, are you?"

"You're running for mayor. People talk." She raised her chin.

"People are talking. Mostly about a GoFundMe attached to my name." The reminder sent another shot of annoyance zipping through.

A sly smile spread across Maggie's face. "Hiran allowed me to use the original photo. I didn't figure the town savior would mind saving the town." Her lips turned down into a fake frown, and she tilted her head, a look of confusion clouding her face. "Unless—I'm sure I have this wrong—you don't *want* to help the town?"

"Cut the shit, Maggie. We're the only people in here."

"Fine. I wanted to help the people who lost out in the flood, so I did it the best way I knew how."

"By plastering my photo and some sentimental bullshit all over social media?"

"Is it working?" She raised her eyebrows and circled around the taller workspace at the back to the front counter. "I haven't checked in the last few minutes. You wouldn't happen to know the latest total, would you?"

Clearly, she knew it. I had no idea.

Maggie took out her phone and glanced up. "Also, I had no idea you knew Ariana Grande. What's she like?"

Anger and frustration swelled in my chest. Maggie leaned across the counter, phone clutched in one of her hands, with her teeth caught on her bottom lip. Desire tried to push out my anger, but I won't let *that* emotional response win today.

"I don't appreciate you messing with my career. She's a professional contact."

"To the tune of five thousand dollars. That's probably peanuts for her, if it makes you feel any better."

"Whether she can afford it isn't the point," I gritted out. "You should have asked me."

"A professional contact?" Maggie raised her eyebrows, curiosity lighting her gaze.

A critical mistake. I'd come to tell Maggie to stop using me to further her own agenda because it was so lame and transparent. If only rewinding time were possible, I'd reel those words back into my mouth.

"What sort of professional contact have you two had?"

I narrowed my eyes. "Why am I not surprised? I guess I've always known you were willing to stoop to any low to make yourself look good, to make sure you win."

Maggie rose to her full height, which was far shorter than me, visibly bristling. "You don't know me. You've never known me."

"So, this GoFundMe didn't have any ulterior motive? You posted my photo and that message just to get support for the town?"

Maggie crossed her arms. "We're in a race for mayor."

"You did it to get ahead."

"I did it to help the people in town who had water damage."

"And to win them to your side."

She stared at me but didn't say anything in return. I couldn't decide whether I wanted to turn this place upside down or toss her under my arm and carry her home. Being around her was so fucking confusing.

"Just like when you were seventeen, you'll do anything to protect your own interests."

"And just like when you were twenty-one, you're talking out of your ass. Newsflash." Maggie waved her hands around. "Your ass doesn't know shit."

We faced each other, and I wondered if there was literal steam coming out of my head. The bell above Maggie's door rang, but neither of us turned.

"Maggie?"

I stiffened at the sound of the familiar voice behind me.

"I need your help."

Without turning, I knew who I'd find. It had been six years since we'd seen each other face-to-face. Text messages. The occasional phone call. That'd been it. When I glanced over my shoulder, Trent was in the doorway, his focus trained on Maggie.

"Sorry." Trent's obvious affection for Maggie made me clench my fists. "I didn't mean to interrupt."

Maggie's attention ping-ponged between me and Trent until Trent tore his gaze from her to take me in. A deep frown replaced his open tenderness. His brown hair was close-cropped, and his tank top made it look like he'd been hitting the gym harder than normal. When we were younger, Trent had told people he didn't work out. I knew better.

The tattoos littering Trent's arms were new. For the first one, we'd used our uncle's homemade tattoo gun one night in high school after a few too many beers. Matching tattoos—brothers first—in crooked cursive. At one time, we'd kept each other's secrets. Now, we kept secrets from each other. Scanning his arms, I was sure Trent had covered over our high school folly. The crevice between us widened before me.

"Grady." Trent tipped his chin.

"It's been a while, brother. How ya been?" I rotated so I could see Trent and Maggie—one on either side of me. I was the monkey in the middle.

"I didn't realize you'd be here." Trent shoved his hands in his jean pockets, his brown gaze flicking to Maggie.

My chest tightened at the awkwardness between us. Somewhere along the line, I'd fucked up royally. I wished I didn't know when it had happened or why. For the longest time, I would have given anything to turn the clock back, to have been sober that night, to have made better, more loyal choices.

"Mom said you bought the train station."

At the slip in front of Maggie, I tensed. I didn't need her knowing anything more than necessary. Her focus shifted from Trent to me.

"The train station?" she asked.

"Gotta put down roots sometime." I shrugged as if the purchase wasn't the most important thing I'd ever done.

"We weren't enough to keep him here." Trent's voice was tinged with bitterness. "I doubt some old building will ground him any better."

I felt like the outsider in the room, the one who didn't belong. Maggie should be the one out of step, not me. That's how it used to be.

"Were you leaving?" Trent asked. "I need to talk to Maggie about something."

I hesitated for a beat before slipping past Trent toward the pharmacy door. "I'll see you around, Trent."

"Doubtful. I'm headed back to Utica after I talk to Maggie."

The clipped tone of his voice grated as I opened the pharmacy door. When I looked over my shoulder, Maggie was stepping around the desk to embrace Trent.

"It's good to see you, Mags," Trent said.

Worse than how Trent spoke to me was the full history apparent between him and Maggie. A dull ache spread across my chest at the realization little had changed. From the minute Maggie had shown up at the first Sunday dinner, a crack had zigzagged between us brothers, and now we were two tectonic plates, broken apart, never to re-form one landmass.

My focus lingered on Trent's back for another moment before I turned on my heel and walked away.

Chapter Eleven

Maggie

I pulled back from Trent and examined his face. His dark-brown eyes were different from Grady's, a shade lighter. They'd never sucked me in the same way, even though I'd tried once or twice to drown.

"You need my help?"

"More like I want to offer my help." A small smile played at the edges of his lips. "This used to be my town too."

I nodded in agreement, but my attention strayed from Trent to Grady's back as he wandered down the street in the direction of Sabrina's nail salon. A gaggle of women approached him with clipboards and *Taste the New* badges proudly displayed. I pursed my lips and tried to push down the annoyance threatening to rise.

"We've got the GoFundMe going already." I was only half following the conversation.

"Yeah." Trent turned and tracked my gaze. "Did I interrupt something between you and my brother? It seemed kinda tense."

"No." I stiffened. "Well, yes. It was tense. Grady was being Grady."

Trent scratched the back of his neck. "Anyway, I saw the GoFundMe, but I also drove around town. Place is a mess."

I forced myself to stay present with Trent. Before Grady had returned, I never had a problem focusing on a conversation. Lately, it felt like my attention was constantly divided. "I'm sure Grady is looking for a way to make a difference too." Trent gave me a blank look. "Since he's also running for mayor."

"Grady?"

"Go talk to him. I'm sure he'd welcome the help." Inside, I cringed. I told Emily I'd only suggest Trent work with Grady if I was honest with him about my reasoning. But seeing him in person and knowing he wanted to help the town, gently prodding him in Grady's direction didn't seem *too* wrong. Just a *little* wrong.

"No."

"Trent."

"I went to jail, and he turned his back on me. There's no fucking way I'm helping him."

"He's here now. Maybe you should bury the hatchet." At least this part was honest. Their damaged relationship was a sore spot for Trent. One of them needed to close the gap.

"The only place I want to bury it is in his back. I don't care that he's here, just like he hasn't cared at any point during the last six years since I got out of jail."

I crossed my arms and let my gaze drift to the windows and to Grady holding court down the street. I hated how tall he was, how broad his shoulders were, how the late-August breeze caught the tips of his hair, ruffling them artfully. But mostly, I hated how guilty I felt because Trent and Grady drifted apart. They'd been tight when I first started hanging around them with the banter between them sharp but affectionate.

"If I could go back, Trent—"

"Nah, Mags. We're not doing that. Last time you tried to play the what-if or if-only or what-the-fuck game, I told you to cut it out. What's done is done. None of it was ever your fault."

"Do you think we should have been more honest with people back then? Not that I wasn't grateful."

Trent laughed. "You got that persistence thing going for you. Not doing it. Here's the bridge." He lifted his hand in the air. "And here's the torrent of water underneath." His other hand ran in a back-and-forth motion. "You didn't want to be honest with them, and I wasn't even honest with you. Right? There's no point in going down this river."

I sighed. Trent was right. Looking back didn't do us any good. We'd both made questionable choices, and it had led us here. Our relationship had been forged in a firestorm of lies.

"We're not the same people." My reasons for getting involved with Trent had been so flawed.

"Exactly," Trent said. "Grady needs to get over himself. You can't do that for him, and I sure as hell can't. The truth doesn't matter. Whatever pickle is up his ass, he needs to shit it out on his own."

"You're so articulate." I laughed.

"Shut up." Trent grinned. "I didn't live for books and culture like you."

"I'm sure your mom tried." Outside the pharmacy from across the street, Grady cast another glance my way, and my heart thudded in response. Sabrina waved in the distance, drawing his gaze away, and my pulse rose into my throat.

Both of the men were rough around the edges, but Grady had spent enough time away from this place that he and Trent didn't resemble each other so much anymore. Where one lacked books and culture, I suspected the other had eaten them like candy while he traveled the world.

"My mom was too busy scraping two pennies together to check what Grady and I were up to. Food on the table, roof over our heads. Dad was the reader. He died, and I stopped trying so much. I guess I don't need to tell you that. But Grady clung to his memory, had a book in his hand a lot of the time."

I remembered. One of the things Grady and I bonded over was books. Perhaps bonded was the wrong word. A guy like Grady reading literary fiction and book club discussion books? Impossible. So, I'd grilled him casually at the dinner table over the book I saw him reading before we sat down. He answered all my questions, and then when Trent and his mother were lost in conversation that bored me, Grady winked at me, amusement dancing across his face.

That had been the start of our book club for two. Each week, I would go to the library to discover what book Grady had signed out. Then, I'd read it too. Did he still go to the library, or had leaving Little Falls given him the escape he'd so badly needed?

"Maggie?"

Trent's voice yanked me out of my head, and I flushed. I needed to get a handle on my obsessive thoughts about his brother. Wasn't doing me any good. Emily was right. I needed to find a way to detach from Grady and those memories. They were like a faucet which hadn't been shut tight, each drip designed to drive me crazy.

"Sorry. I was thinking about the campaign." I tucked a few strands of hair behind my ear and avoided his gaze while I tried to collect myself. "What were you saying?"

"Can I help you?" he asked.

"Um." I floundered to come up with a reason he couldn't help me and had to help Grady instead.

His gaze bored into me. "Are you okay? You're acting weird today."

"Yes, right. Sorry. There's been a lot going on here. Um…"

The bell above the pharmacy door sounded, drawing my attention toward it. Lila strolled in, pulling her sunglasses off her face and dangling them in her fingers.

"Oh," Lila said, seeing Trent. "Hey, Trent. I came to congratulate Maggie on her brilliant social media campaign for the town."

Lila's grin was so wide I couldn't help smiling in response. "Liked that, did you?"

"So much. Have you seen Grady yet?" Lila leaned against my counter. "I would *love* to watch those fireworks."

Trent narrowed his eyes. "Is that what I interrupted?"

"You were here?" Lila took out her lip gloss and pressed it to her lips. "Did the heat of their gazes melt you?"

Trent laughed. "You gotta be kidding me. The heat of their gazes?"

"It's nothing." I glared at Lila.

"If you didn't come for the sexual tension show, what are you doing here?" Lila ignored me and sized up Trent. "Not that I'm ever sorry to see you."

"Sexual tension show?" Trent frowned and turned toward me. "What the hell? You and Grady?"

"No. Nope. Not even a little bit." I stared at Lila, avoiding his intense gaze. "He hates me anyway. Besides, we're running against each other for mayor. Any tension is… hate and competition."

Lila coughed into her hand, and I swore I heard the word "Liar."

Trent sighed. "All I care about is figuring out a way to help the town. You know? Maybe win some people around who think I'm still the black sheep."

"What's that?" Lila perked up. "You need help?"

"Trent asked to help me help Little Falls." I stared at Lila meaningfully, hoping she remembered the conversation we'd had over coffee the other week. As much as I loved Trent, he was a liability.

"Hmm. Right." Lila twirled her glasses. "I'm always a fan of a good redemption arc. I'm sure we could find something for you."

I bit my tongue so hard I worried it would bleed.

"I don't want to donate money," Trent said. "I don't have much anyway. But I got a lot of sweat equity. I can build stuff, or I don't know."

Lila hummed. "There's been a lot of damage to Little Falls. A couple of the houses literally floated away. The GoFundMe is great, but will it be enough?"

"What are you talking about, Lila?" I asked, frustration eating at me.

"Another fundraiser. A bit of…" She grinned at Trent. "Sweat equity. And, it'll be great for community building as well as getting Trent back into the town dynamic."

"Sweat equity? So, we're going to build something, or…?"

"A Magic Mike show."

"What?" Trent looked between me and Lila. "A magic show?"

I stifled a grin. We hadn't talked about this, but it would definitely cause a stir. "Male strippers."

"You want me to strip?" Trent eyed Lila.

A wicked grin broke out across Lila's face. "I'd even pay money."

"Naked?"

I shrugged, and Lila pretended to think. "Definitely down to your boxers or briefs. Right now, I'm imagining the classic boxer briefs, but I'm open to surprises." She gave Trent a theatrical wink.

Trent chuckled, and his eyes trailed over Lila. "You're not so quiet anymore."

"I'm going to take that as a compliment." Lila slid her sunglasses to the top of her head. "You'll raise money, I guarantee it."

"No one is going to pay enough money to build a house just to see me strip."

I watched the exchange between the two of them with amusement. Lila was great at coming up with outrageous plans. Most of the time, she knew how to pull them off too.

"Leave the recruiting to us." Lila met my gaze over Trent's shoulder. "All you have to do is say yes."

"Do you think this is a good idea, Maggie?"

"I have absolute faith in Lila. I have no idea what this will look like, other than you in your underwear, but I am sure we can pull something together that will bring you back into the town's good graces."

"We're heading into the fall. People can only pick so many apples before they start looking for the pumpkin spice."

"I don't know what that means exactly, but I'm guessing I'm the spice?" Trent walked backward to the door. "Mags, you'll call me with the details? Let me know what else I can do other than get naked?"

"We'll work it out," I agreed.

"Lila," Trent said. "It's been interesting."

As soon as he'd ducked out the door, Lila turned. "Do you think I'm too smart for him?"

"Oh, Lord. Lila. He's not dumb. Far from it. Please tell me you're joking."

"Something about the haircut and the tattoos and all those muscles." She twirled her lip gloss around her fingers. "Seeing him naked will probably help me decide for sure if I'm interested."

I rolled my eyes. "Have you always had a thing for him?"

Lila laughed. "No. He used to scare me. That's why I was always so quiet around him. But my loins"—she circled her groin with her hand—"were feeling his look today. My ovaries went into overdrive."

With a laugh, I moved around the counter toward my workspace. "I love you. But I also hate you for adding another thing to my plate. A Magic Mike show?"

"Actually, I was thinking we could combine it with a concert. Stripping and music go together like wine and cheese. Maybe you could sweet-talk Grady? Bat those chocolate-brown eyes at him a little?"

"No. I'm not asking him for anything. For one, I'm on a Grady detox. And for two, Trent wouldn't be happy with me getting him involved."

"Fine. I'll ask him. I can plead ignorance to Trent, and I'll get a front row seat to the Maggie-Grady show. *And* if Trent wants to take out his frustration on someone, I'll volunteer as tribute."

"I think your ovaries are exploding, and it's impacting your brain."

"Could be." Lila slid her sunglasses over her eyes. "Either way, you and I have agreed to plan a strip show and concert to help the town see Trent in a new light." She rubbed her hands together. "Now, I get to recruit. First stop, Tyler. Your brother needs a reason to start working out. He's getting a little flabby."

"Oh my God. Lila!"

"Your job is to pick a date—sometime in October would be good. That would give us four to six weeks to plan and advertise. And—added bonus—it should be fresh enough in people's minds come election day."

"Then no Grady, Lila. I'm serious. If we're using it to prop up my campaign, no Grady."

Lila strolled toward the front door. "Fine. But you're missing out. I think he'd look good in his underwear too." She peered at me over the top of her sunglasses as her butt connected with the pharmacy door. "You know you've thought about it."

When the door clicked closed and silence filled the pharmacy, my thoughts zeroed in on Grady and his underwear. A flash of him, sprawled out in his bed, me crawling across his torso, rose up unbidden. Try as I might, I couldn't shove the memory back down. My heart raced, and pinpricks of feeling burst across my skin.

Staring out the large pharmacy windows, I worried Lila wasn't the only one with ovaries in overdrive.

Chapter Twelve
Grady

I settled into the opening chords of "The Phantom of the Opera." The tune often brought me out of a writing funk and sometimes delayed my desire to throw something in frustration. Not that there was much to throw. My keyboard, some books, and this very heavy mattress. Maybe I should try living like a grown-up. After all, I finally owned a house.

My phone buzzed, and I glanced at the caller ID. Agent Jack. Picking it up, I hit the green circle before I could talk myself out of this conversation. If it was another job, I wouldn't turn it down. Money was my muse now, and Jack never failed to feed it, which was something I was starting to lose sight of.

"What do you have?" I asked by way of introduction.

"Mia Malone is looking for contributors for her next album."

"Mia Malone." Her name was at the forefront of everyone's lips. "Her last album went platinum, right?"

"It did. And it's still chugging right along. She might make multiplatinum."

"She's got a country-pop blend to most of her music."

"You bet. It gets picked up by both genres, which is what makes it so lucrative. Think you can write it?"

I picked up the pen beside my notebook and tapped the page in a rhythm. That was what moved me now, the challenge. "Does she have a timeline? Or start writing and if she likes something, we'll go from there?"

"You don't have anything ready that might fit the bill?"

"No. You know me. I don't start until you dangle the money. Seems to work well enough."

There was a deep silence across the phone before Jack spoke. "You writing for yourself yet? I know a few labels who would love to put out another album for you."

This was the part of the conversation I hated. Without fail, Jack circled back to my inability to write with myself in mind. Of course, my agent didn't understand what was happening. All he knew was that I hadn't written a single song meant for me since my first album's release. When I thought about my writing process too long, it sent me into a creative panic. For whatever reason, the personal well had run dry. I needed direction—a genre, sometimes even a topic—and I could get up and running. But creating new material on my own without an incentive? Didn't happen anymore.

"Someday." I'd stopped being sure of that a few years ago. It was still my go-to line with Jack.

"You'd tell me if something was wrong, right? The plan is to get back in the game as a singer and a songwriter, yeah?"

I chuckled and settled deeper into my lawn chair. "Jack, are you getting paid? Do you make money off these songwriting deals?"

"That's not the point."

"Yeah, it is. The rest of it doesn't fucking matter. You get paid, I get paid. We both get to keep doing what we love."

"This is the part you love?"

"Yeah." For the most part, that was true. I loved the creative spark, the flurry of mental activity, puzzling out a melody or chorus. I never admitted to anyone how I missed feeling a rush from something in my own life. My muse—the one who didn't live in my bank account—had abandoned me. Quite often, I longed for her return.

"You're amassing a long list of song credits."

While I traveled, I'd taken every songwriting gig Jack had thrown my way. Once I figured out that money and some direction were the keys to my new process, I latched onto them like an addict. I wrote in jungles, on rickety buses, in tented camps while hyenas called out around, at the tops of mountains, and once while trying to recover from food poisoning.

"What are you getting at?"

"Your old label is wondering if you might want to consider taking on a music producer role for some of their up-and-coming talent. You've written a string of hit songs. It's incredible, actually."

I nodded even though Jack couldn't see me. What to do with the train station had been on my mind, and becoming a producer would be an incredible next career step. Perhaps this was a goal for renovating that space. "Would they let me do it here?"

"There's a studio in Little Falls?"

"If I made one, could I do it here?"

"It's not too far from New York City. I'll make some calls. You have the space?"

"Yeah. That's not a problem." The familiar itch to get up and walk rose under my skin. Every time doing something truly permanent in this town came up, I needed to move. Truthfully, I wasn't sure I could force my roots deep enough to ground me here. There was a chance I'd never be truly happy here. Right now, I was as happy here as I'd been anywhere.

"Listen, I gotta go. Call me back when you know more. I'm definitely interested. But I'm also pretty happy writing songs."

"Noted," Jack said.

I hovered my finger over the red button to disconnect.

"Hey, Grady." Jack's voice echoed in the almost-empty room. "Are you actually running for mayor?"

I put the phone back to my ear and chuckled. "Yes and no." When Jack sighed, I continued, "At first it was a 'no,' but I think it might be a 'yes.' I could do the job."

"But do you want the job?"

With a frown, I threw my pen at the wall. "I guess we'll see. I gotta go." The itch to move, to escape was back. I'd walk the dogs on the edge of the town as though I was daring myself to leave, to duck out into the darkness, discover another place.

Grabbing the dogs' leashes, I hooked them up and shut my front door. This time, I locked it. Before I'd gotten my keyboard delivered, I hadn't been worried about anything being stolen. But that thing was worth good money.

It was a warm night for late August, and I relished the fading sun against my skin. I turned my face to catch the warmth as I passed another abandoned building. I wished there was an easy solution to the town's empty storefronts. If there had been an easy way to fix it, Maggie would have done it. Admitting that was uncomfortable, but it was true. Ahead, Jim and a little boy were exiting one of the plaza spaces.

Jim waved, and his free hand fell to the top of the boy's head, ruffling his hair. The movement made my chest ache in remembrance of my dad.

The things that caused the ache to rush to the front were surprising. The smallest memory could cause the biggest chasm to open. Something about Jim Sullivan always managed to do it.

"Grady," Jim said. As I approached, I tightened my hold on Zeus and Hite so they didn't scare the kid. "This is Emily's little guy, Amir. We were at the indoor playground." Jim gestured behind them.

I crouched and extended my free hand to Amir while my dogs sniffed Jim and the boy. "Nice to meet you." Amir took my hand and grinned.

"My Aunt Maggie says you're the devil."

A laugh burst out of me, and I glanced up at Jim who was shaking his head.

Jim grimaced but didn't deny the child's claim.

"I heard her and Mom talking."

"It's okay," I said, rising. "Your Aunt Maggie and I are competing to be mayor."

"Why would you want to be mayor?" Amir cocked his head. "Is that a good job?"

At a loss, I spared Jim a glance. The question was simple, but I didn't know how to answer it. To spite Maggie didn't seem like the best response to give either of them.

"I saw that social media thing—you know—the money for the flooding victims." Jim let me off one hook and thrust me onto another.

"Right, yeah, that was Maggie."

"Still, I thought it was good of you to let her use your photo. Seemed like a lot of your friends stepped up."

With my free hand, I massaged my cheek. "Your daughter is resourceful."

"She does well when she's challenged, always has." Jim wrapped his arm around Amir's slight shoulders and brought him in a little closer. "I'm assuming you'll be part of this concert thing she and Lila are organizing for October?"

"Concert?" I frowned.

"Lila is recruiting. She's already got Tyler at the gym working out for some reason. I haven't quite figured out why he needs to work out. I thought Lila told me it was a magic show?"

A concert and a magic show? Jim had to have missed some vital piece of information. Unless they were organizing a variety show? I was drawing a blank about where something like that would even take place. "What's this all about?"

"Oh." Jim's expression turned uneasy. "I assumed you'd know about it. I don't know much about what's happening. Trent's involved, and I guess I assumed…"

"Right." I rocked back on my heels and pretended I'd suddenly remembered. Obviously, he didn't know Trent and I weren't as tight as we once were. "Yeah. With everything else, I haven't had a chance to get much information on the event yet."

"You were all over the place the day of the flood. A lot of people were really grateful. It's nice that Trent's looking for a way to give back to the community."

I grinned, trying to maintain a façade. Inside, pieces stirred in anger while others cringed at how far Trent and I had drifted. I hated that Trent chose Maggie. When I'd been out of the country, I'd known Trent went to Maggie for help. Since I'd never been close enough to do much, it hadn't stirred these feelings of resentment. But I was back, and Trent was still choosing her. Made me feel like shit. Guilt ate at me for a new reason. Could I fix it? Did I deserve to have Trent back?

"Are you planning to stick around Little Falls whether or not you win the election?"

I frowned and dug my hand into my dogs' fur, lost in thought. I'd gone out for the walk because the itch to leave had taken hold. In all these years, I'd never figured out what I was running from or to, I was just running. Auburn hair and brown eyes danced across my consciousness. I shoved the image down. "Maybe. Yeah."

"I'm sure the town would appreciate having you back."

The dogs whined, and I tightened my hand on their leashes. I crouched to Amir's level. "You tell your Aunt Maggie the devil says hello."

Amir grinned. "Okay. She'll like that."

I chuckled as I rose and offered Jim my hand. "It was nice running into you."

"And you."

Something new that had cropped up was the way that Jim spoke to me now, like he couldn't decide how to treat me. I hadn't noticed the shift at first. Jim had never been cool before I left Little Falls, but our last few exchanges had a layer of frost, a new guardedness. Had Maggie told her dad what my album was about? What had happened between us all? She'd have spun the truth to make herself look better, maybe to make me appear petty. None of us had been good.

I stared at the cloudless sky. What were Maggie, Lila, and Trent planning?

As we parted ways, I found myself turning in the direction of Maggie's street. I rubbed my bicep where the *brothers first* tattoo blazed across my skin. I'd let the disconnect go on long enough. It was time I started acting like that was true. Instead of existing on the fringes of people's lives, I needed to start setting things right.

Chapter Thirteen

Maggie

When the doorbell rang, I glanced at the clock. After nine. Frowning, I crossed the kitchen to the door and opened it without checking the peephole.

Shit.

"Grady." A strained smile rose to my lips, and my heart galloped into my throat. Why did he have to be so freaking attractive?

His gaze trailed over me in a leisurely way while his two dogs strained on their leashes.

Self-conscious, I touched a hand to my hair piled on top of my head in a messy bun. I took off my makeup when I closed the pharmacy at eight, and I was dressed in sweats. If I was naked, I couldn't have been more embarrassed.

"Can I come in?"

"You want to come in here?" I hoped my body blocked the view inside my open-plan house. Not that it was messy, but having Grady here, in my personal space, was unnerving. How had he gotten my address?

"Pretty sure that's what that phrase means."

I eyed his dogs. "I have a cat."

"They like cats." Grady's brown eyes were tinged with humor. "Mostly to eat."

"You're not coming in here." I started to close the door, but Grady snuck his foot into the opening.

"I don't want to be that guy, but—"

"You *love* being that guy."

"I heard you're helping to organize a concert with my brother."

I opened the door wider and braced my shoulder on the frame, still not inviting him in. Both dogs and Grady inside my small bungalow would be too much. "And you care because?"

"Come on. Trent is my brother. Of course, I care. And concerts are my thing."

"I'm not sure Trent would agree." I tucked a strand of hair that had fallen out of my bun behind my ear. "He doesn't want you involved, or he would have asked you." Not to mention he'd flat out told me I couldn't include Grady.

"What do you, Trent, or even Lila, know about organizing a concert?"

"It's not *simply* a concert."

Grady frowned. "I heard something about a magic show. I'm not going to claim I can help there. But I know concerts."

A burst of laughter escaped before I could hold it in. Grady's gaze slid to my lips and then back up to my eyes. My heart stuttered.

"Why is that funny?" he asked.

"Who told you it was a magic show?"

"I can't reveal my sources."

"Good night, Grady." I slid the door closed.

"Your dad. Okay? It was your dad."

Another laugh tumbled out before I could stop it. "He told you it was a magic show? Oh my god. That's hilarious."

Grady's frown deepened. "It's not a magic show?"

On impulse, I swung the door wide and waved Grady in. My whole body was lit with amusement. I was going to replay this conversation later and then make Lila call my dad to explain the only magic would be inside the men's underpants. Or the tighty-whiteys Lila thought all the volunteers should wear. I wasn't sure about that idea.

"If your dogs so much as look at my cat sideways, you're all getting kicked out the door."

He chuckled. "I was joking."

"You make jokes?"

"Apparently ones I don't even know I'm making. What's the deal with the magic show or not magic show or whatever the hell is going on?"

I grabbed a bowl from one of the cupboards and filled it with water. I set it down in front of the two dogs, and they drank eagerly. When Grady caught my gaze, there was a new softness in his face which sent shivers across my body. Goose bumps rose along my arms.

"You cold?" The back of his hand skimmed my upper arm.

"No," I admitted. "I'm not cold." Our gazes met, and the air crackled. This feeling between us was something I loved and hated. How was it possible to feel unhinged and penned-in by one person?

The leashes hit the tile floor with a soft thud. I waited for his arm to circle my waist, for him to tug me flush against him, for his lips to descend, and the taste of wintergreen to invade my mouth. He'd loved those mints.

Instead, he pulled out a chair at my kitchen table and sank into it. A thread of disappointment laced around my heart, and I tried to brush it aside. I rounded the island to turn down the TV and attempted to get a handle on my erratic feelings.

Calm down. Calm down. You don't want him to kiss you. You don't even like him. It would ruin everything—again.

"Are you going to tell me?" Grady called.

"Trent doesn't want you involved." I came back and pressed my side into the island, hoping I looked confident and in control.

"I want to help."

"You don't know anything about it. How can you say that?"

"All right. I came back home to reconnect with my family. That means Trent too."

I pursed my lips. "Exactly how much effort have you put into that so far? I haven't heard of any trips to Utica to see him. It's a thirty-minute drive."

With a sigh, he ran a hand through his hair. He leaned forward to rest his forearms on his knees. "I've made mistakes." He glanced up, and his eyes were haunted. "We made mistakes."

I swallowed, and another memory of Grady lying on his bed, my lips trailing across his stomach surfaced. The desire to close my eyes and live in that moment stirred. What happened had been a mistake, but it hadn't been as dire as Grady believed. I wished I could tell him the truth, even if some of it was deeply embarrassing. The folly of youth.

"I don't want to talk about that," I said.

"Course not. We pretend like it didn't happen."

I needed a distraction. Opening a cupboard, I took down a glass and filled it with water from the tap. "The magic show is a Magic Mike show—male strippers. We're calling it Small Town Saviors. Lila is recruiting. Should I tell her you're volunteering?" I promised Trent I wouldn't rehash the past. None of it mattered anymore. Grady had to figure out how to move forward without dragging all of us back. I should take that advice.

Rising, Grady wandered to the island and leaned against it, close enough for me to catch the scent of his sweat and cologne, which brought back more memories than I'd ever admit. The smell of him, some mix of pheromones, made my stomach clench. I met his gaze.

"Talk to me, Maggie."

"We're not wading through the past right now." Could I convince Trent to tell his mother and Grady the truth? I wasn't sure he would agree to be honest with his mom. God, I couldn't even decide. What was the right thing to do?

"Then let me help."

"Why? Why do you want to horn in on this?"

"I miss my brother."

"Easy. Call him and go for a beer."

He pressed his palms into the granite top and his gaze seared me with his intensity. "You think he'd go?"

I searched his face. Sincerity was written all over him, but this was the first indication I'd had that he regretted the distance between them. "What happened? How did it get this bad?"

"You know what happened."

My heart thumped. Deep down, I'd worried I'd had something to do with him drawing away from his brother. But to this extent? Didn't make sense. "That can't be the only reason."

He held my gaze for a moment, his jaw tightening before his focus slid away.

With only a small hesitation, I trailed my fingers from his shoulder down to his hand. I'd missed him, this connection between us was thrilling and baffling. He'd been my secret shame for years, the one I'd never really had but who had gotten away, nonetheless. Now, he was back, but most of the time I was sure he disliked me. If he blamed me for the rift between him and Trent, it made sense for him to hate me. I'd hate anyone who drove a wedge between me and one of my siblings.

His fingers found a tendril of my hair. He looped it around his finger, and I tried to catch his gaze. The air around us hummed.

"I'll strip for you if that'll get me on the planning committee."

Heat spread across my body at the pitch of his voice. His tone was meant for dark rooms and sweaty bodies. I angled toward him, begging for something I'd never say aloud. He met my gaze. "You want to get on the committee that badly?"

"I want something that badly, yeah."

My breath caught in my throat at the husky shift in his voice. I wanted to close my eyes and replay his words over and over. God, I was pathetic. "This is the best way to get it?"

He released the tendril. "I want you to help me get my brother back. After all, you're part of the reason we're not close anymore."

The gate was lowering between them. I wondered if I could slip one more question in before the crack sealed shut. "Will you tell me the other reason?"

As though I hadn't spoken, he turned his back and headed for the door, snapping his fingers at the dogs. They trotted obediently to him. I'd forgotten they were in the house.

"When's the first meeting?"

"We've already had a meeting." I followed him to the door but left enough space, so I wasn't tempted to reach for him. He probably hated me. Better to keep my distance. I needed to keep focused on the election. This sexual attraction would fade, burn out, go away if I ignored it.

He scooped up the dogs' leashes and met my gaze. "The next one?"

"Trent is going to be angry."

"Let him be angry. We gotta start somewhere. And he has a right to be angry. I've been a shitty brother."

I wanted to dig, to uncover what else lay buried in the past. "Why the sudden change?"

"It's not sudden." He ran his hand across the back of his neck. "Since I got here, I didn't know where to start." He shrugged. "Seeing him at the pharmacy the other day, it drove home how far I'd let it go."

The urge to apologize was overwhelming. We'd made stupid choices back then. Maybe it was time we all stopped paying for them.

"Next Monday in the mayor's office. We're meeting next Monday."

Grady gripped the dogs' leashes and opened the door. "A concert and male strippers."

"Yes."

Over his shoulder, Grady grinned. "Your dad is in for a hell of a surprise."

Another laugh rose up before I could stifle it. "His face will be priceless. I think I might let him in on the secret before then."

His gaze was wistful before he pulled the door closed. "Probably a good idea. Most of the time, secrets just fuck things up."

The smile faded from my face as he shut the door tight behind him. Had that comment been directed at me? Probably. I'd once told Grady that Trent and I weren't what we appeared to be. We kept the lie going out of habit or necessity, maybe both. I yanked the elastic out of my hair and then redid my bun.

Did the truth really set people free, or did it only make things worse?

Chapter Fourteen

I sipped my coffee and admired Maggie across the conference table. She was a magnet. Wanting her was wrong. So, so wrong. It would be better if she was repellent to me, but every glance she cast my way only drew me closer. For so long, I'd hated her, convinced myself it was true. Whether it was the passage of time or being around her again, our close quarters were making me second-guess the hatred I'd clung to.

Had my feelings for her ever been hatred or something much more complicated? The corners of her lips tipped up in a partial smile, and I wondered what Emily had said to amuse her.

I wish I was the one making her smile.

The thought hit me square in the chest. Whatever shift was happening was occurring at an alarming rate. But I was coming around to the fact that maybe, just maybe, I'd been lying to myself all along.

Kelvin, Emily, Tyler, and Lila were already there. We were waiting for Trent. I could tell by the tension across Maggie's shoulders she was anticipating a fight. If I let myself get wound up before Trent appeared, I'd say things to divide us more.

Lila flicked through her phone and stopped on something. "Okay, I know Trent isn't here yet, which is a shame." She grinned at Maggie, and Maggie rolled her eyes. "But I have the list of people I've roped into getting naked."

Tyler sighed and ran a hand through his hair. He'd lost weight compared to the last time I saw him. Lila's fitness regime was working. I took another sip of my coffee and eyed Kelvin.

"You on that list, buddy?"

"I am," Kelvin confirmed. "Lila agreed to let me wear my snake briefs."

I held up a hand. "I really don't need the details." I swirled the coffee in my cup and then couldn't help myself. "Snake briefs?"

Kelvin chuckled. "A gift from an ex. He thought it was funny. My current boyfriend isn't as keen."

"Grady," Lila said.

Lila and Maggie were on the other side of the table, expectant expressions on their faces. A hint of mischief lit Maggie's brown eyes.

"What can I do for you ladies?"

Maggie smirked, and Lila raised her eyebrows. "Maggie tells me you're willing to do whatever it takes to make this a success."

I squirmed in my chair. Sounded like a challenge, but I sure as hell wasn't going to back down. Most of the time, losing wasn't an option. "You bet. What do you need?"

"Someone to teach the men with two left feet how to move sexy on stage." Lila swayed her hips. "She thought you'd be the best person."

My throat closed, and I nearly choked on my coffee. "What?"

Lila rotated her phone toward a clip of me dancing on *Center Stage*, which made heat rise to my cheeks. One of many examples of why I was glad I could write songs for other people. Some of the shit the show had made me do was still fucking embarrassing.

"I didn't come up with that myself."

"But you learned it, right? Got any friends who could pop down and choreograph a strip show?" Lila pressed.

I pinched the bridge of my nose and grimaced. "Leave it with me."

Kelvin's elbow dug into my side as Emily, Maggie, and Lila conferred over some master plan in the middle of the table. Tyler was absorbed in his phone, a frown creasing his brow.

"You know people?" Kelvin whispered.

"I know lots of people. Someone willing to come here to choreograph a strip show for free? Probably not. Not exactly a resume builder."

"I've taken hip-hop lessons, if you get desperate. I might be able to teach people a thing or two."

Before I could respond, the door to the conference room squeaked open, and I tensed.

"Sorry, I'm late, Mags. I went to your office first."

Trent hadn't spotted me yet, and I braced myself while his gaze traveled around the room. Our eyes locked, and then his focus flipped to Maggie.

"Are you kidding me?" Trent glared at Maggie. "Can we talk in the hall?"

Maggie weaved around everyone, and as she passed me, I rose.

"I'll handle this," Maggie whispered.

"Not fucking likely," I muttered to her back as I trailed her out the door. I wasn't leaving her to bear the brunt of Trent's anger when I'd talked her into letting me help with the event.

"Are you fucking with me?" Trent glared at Maggie, ignoring me. "I asked for one thing."

"Probably two," I said. "Help from her and to cut me out. Math was never your strong suit. But that's two things."

"Grady, don't be a dick," Maggie warned.

Was I being a dick? Trent and I had spoken to each other that way for as long as I could remember. Saying anything else would have felt false. "Truth hurts." But the lies were so much worse.

"Fuck you. You can't come back to town, make no effort—again—and expect me to shrug my shoulders and move on."

"I'm offering my help."

"We don't want it."

"Maggie does."

"Actually—" Maggie held up a hand.

"Yeah, right. Maggie came to you? Asked *you* to help? Bullshit. You caught wind of this and thought it would be a good way to score some points for the election. Everything is always about you. Grady first." Trent threw up his hands. "I don't know why you want to be mayor. Makes zero sense. At least Maggie gives a shit about other people."

I straightened under Trent's verbal assault. Six years and I'd never considered staying away was creating this firestorm in him. Was Trent wrong? Probably not. I wasn't even sure why I wanted to be mayor anymore. But I was terrible at backing down from a challenge. It wasn't surprising Trent thought I was a shitty person; I already believed it about myself.

"Trent." Her hand was on his forearm. "He's trying. Would you rather he didn't?"

Seeing the physical contact, the closeness between her and Trent, made my chest ache. Jealous. I was jealous. So fucking jealous that it felt like it might eat a hole right through me. But I wasn't sure if it was him or her. Both. Probably both. I rolled my shoulders to ease the tension. When I looked up, Trent was staring, and I met his gaze, defiant.

"I'm trying to be better," I said. "I want to be better."

Trent eyed Maggie. "It's up to you. You think we need him? Fine. I don't give a shit."

Her gaze sought mine. "To have the best chance at raising a lot of money, we need him."

Warmth flooded me at her words and the way her brown eyes scanned my face. She said she'd help me reconnect with Trent, and she was already doing more than I would have expected given the way I'd treated her.

"I'm going to talk to everyone else," Trent said, brushing past Maggie into the conference room.

"Thank you," I said before Maggie disappeared behind Trent.

"Don't let him down, okay?" Her hand rested on the door.

I scratched the back of my head and resisted the urge to touch her, to reestablish the connection which had crackled between us at her house the other night. *Addictive.* I'd felt it with a few women, in other places, other times but never with the intensity I did with Maggie. Nothing had ever felt the same as it did with Maggie.

The relationship she had with Trent was confounding. They were so close, even now. One way or another, she had lied to me back then, might even be lying now. That realization kept sticking like slime coating all our interactions. I wanted the truth, but I wasn't sure I'd ever get it.

Regardless, if I was trying to get my brother back, I couldn't make the same mistakes. Taunting her the other night had been a mistake. Whatever was resurrecting between us couldn't take hold. *Brothers first.*

"I'll find a choreographer. Some people owe me favors. Maybe I can get some guest appearances." I'd been saving those favors for a rainy day. The situation between Trent and me qualified as a downpour.

Her gaze slid away, and she slipped into the conference room. I followed her and was surprised to see Lila and Trent chuckling over something on her phone.

"We've got a venue," Emily said as soon as we were settled in our chairs.

"Where?" Maggie picked up her phone and then set it back down.

"Stanley Theater in Utica. The capacity is almost three thousand, which we think is enough." Emily looked between all of us. "October eighteenth. It's a Friday."

"Seven weeks," Maggie said. "What do you think, Grady? Lila?"

"I can plan anything in seven weeks." Lila grinned.

"The Stanley is pretty fancy for stripping." Though, it might be easier for me to convince some people to help with a venue like that. I'd been worried it would be outside. October in New York State was a weather gamble.

"We'll be classy strippers," Trent said.

"I gotta go, Maggie." Tyler gestured over his shoulder with his thumb. "Another order of campaign signs arrived at the house. I'll deliver those over the next couple of days. Where's the list?"

When Maggie's gaze shifted to mine and then away, I felt a twinge of unease. Did I still want to be in competition with her? Hating her had been easier. A lot more straightforward. This new middle ground was confusing. How did I exist in this space with her?

"It's on my desk," Maggie said.

"Okay. Good work everyone." Tyler backed out the door. "Lila, I'm taking tomorrow off from the gym. No need to pick me up."

"No, no, no. Tyler! There are seven weeks until showtime. Now is not the time to slack off." Lila circled the table and followed him into the hall.

"I'll email everyone with their to-do lists. We'll meet in a couple weeks." Maggie rose from her chair and then looked at me. "Once you've got some people lined up, we should probably touch base, okay?"

I nodded and shoved my hands into my pockets. Her phrasing sent my thoughts spiraling out of control. There were all kinds of places I'd like to touch, bases I'd like to round. Maybe if I gave into one of the women trying to coax me into bed, I wouldn't feel this tension with Maggie.

Lila popped her head into the conference room door as everyone was filing out. "Grady, choreography. I need that as soon as you can get it. Some of these guys are going to need a lot of practice. Their auditions weren't great."

"Auditions?" I frowned, my mind somewhere else.

"Don't worry. I won't make you strip for me. You're a shoo-in." She gave an exaggerated wink before leaving with her arm tucked into the crook of Emily's.

When Trent walked past, he muttered, "Don't fuck this up."

Exiting on my brother's heels, I looked back at Maggie, who was gathering her papers. "Wouldn't dream of it."

Chapter Fifteen
Maggie

I drained my second coffee and took my empty cup to the sink. I was still in my robe, but I couldn't get motivated without caffeine, and two cups were the sweet spot. Ginger, my cat, weaved around my feet, meowing for her breakfast. Reaching down, I ran a hand along her back and right up her fluffy tail.

"Hungry?" I grabbed a can of food out of the cupboard.

A brisk knock sounded on the door. Who was here at this ungodly hour? Seven in the morning wasn't exactly a normal time to have a visitor. Drawing the ends of my robe a little tighter, I checked the peephole.

"Lila?" I opened the door, surprise coloring my voice. "Why are you here so early?"

She slipped past me and then plugged her nose. "God, I hate the smell of cat food. Is there a worse smell?"

I laughed. "There are lots of worse smells. Seriously, why so early?" I ran a knife around the open tin of food and plopped the mush into a bowl, setting it on the ground for Ginger.

"Tyler hasn't called you yet?" Lila leaned against the island and then sprang off it, grabbing a cup from the cupboard. "Coffee! You're one of the only people I know who makes a pot in the morning. Right now, I love you for it."

"Why would Tyler be calling me this early? You still haven't told me why you're here."

"We were at the gym this morning, and he told me what was going on."

With a sigh, I eyed Lila. I loved her, and I was well-versed in these half conversations, but whether it was too early, or Lila was being particularly cryptic, I wasn't following. "Just tell me."

"Someone," she paused, waggling her eyebrows before heaping spoonfuls of sugar into her mug, "is a thief."

"Okay, Lila. I need to get ready to go to the pharmacy for my Saturday regulars. When you have more information, call me, or stop in there, or maybe just keep the information to yourself. That sounds like a problem for the police, not me." I headed around the island for the hallway that led to the bedrooms.

"The thief is Sabrina Kim, and she's stealing your campaign signs." She put a piece of bread in the toaster and pushed down the handle.

"What?" I retied my robe and wandered over to Lila. "Sabrina Kim is stealing my campaign signs?"

"Yep." Lila sipped her coffee and sighed with pleasure. "In the middle of the night. God knows who is watching her kids. I know women shouldn't judge other women, and that's like your mantra or whatever, but man, that woman is a fucking mess."

I pursed my lips to keep from agreeing. Of all the women in town, Sabrina and I had the most contentious relationship. I'd never been able to put my finger on why. Years ago, I had hated Sabrina for the way she drifted so easily in and out of Grady's bed. But my dislike of her had lasted long after he was gone. Seeing Sabrina in a crowd was enough to raise my hackles. My mother would say Sabrina and I were chalk and cheese. We couldn't be more different.

"What's she doing with them?" Visions of Sabrina selling them on some black market campaign website to make enough money to feed her kids popped into my head.

"According to Tyler? Putting them in Grady's back shed."

My eyes felt like they bulged out of my head at the revelation. Fumbling for a chair, I sank into it. *Grady and Sabrina.* My stomach rolled, and coffee sloshed around, souring. If they were back on, I'd need a sick day to lie in bed and contemplate my life choices.

"You okay?" Lila bit into her toast.

"Processing."

"Even if he's sleeping with her, it probably doesn't mean anything."

"It probably means she's pregnant." I slapped a hand over my mouth and turned wide eyes to my best friend.

Lila laughed and then choked on her toast. With a sip of her coffee, she grinned. "Ah, I love it when Catty-Maggie comes out to play. Such a rare sighting."

"I shouldn't have said that."

"Whatever. You know you don't need to play the politician in front of me." She tipped her mug and took a long drink. "Besides, I think Grady's the only man Sabrina has slept with and not gotten pregnant. He's probably shooting blanks."

I groaned. "Please, don't. Okay? I can't."

Lila frowned and leaned forward to peer closer. "Oh, shit. You *like* Grady. It's not just some scorching sexual chemistry. You have *feelings.*"

With a shake of my head, I went to the sink and rinsed out my coffee cup before pouring another cup. The last thing I needed was more caffeine. Adrenaline was already pumping. "No, that's not it."

"Yes, that's it." She let out a whoosh of air. "How did I miss this?"

Her gaze was like hot coals as I stirred my coffee.

"Have you made out with him yet?"

Heat rose to my cheeks, and I wished Lila wasn't peering at me quite so closely.

"Oh my God. You have! When?"

"It's not what you think."

Silence draped around us. Expectation practically vibrated off Lila while she waited for me to cave, to explain, but I planned to hold strong. This was the piece I hadn't told her about the night Trent was arrested. After months of Grady and I dancing around each other, he'd come home drunk to find me in Trent's room. Like so many other times, I'd gone to the Castillo house knowing Trent was out. It hadn't been him I'd wanted to see. When Grady had seen me sprawled across Trent's bed, he'd flirted from the doorway and then invited me to look through his bookshelf.

In his room, I'd moved the conversation from books to his songwriting. When I'd taunted him, he'd given me a wry look and dug his guitar out of his closet, settling on the bed, patting the spot beside him. I'd sat, watching him strum away while he walked me through how he came up with lyrics and melodies. Intoxicating. Being there, with him, seeing him do it. A secret unfolding right in front of me. When I'd glanced up, his look had been raw with hunger, and without thinking I'd stretched up and pressed my lips to his. *Trent and I aren't what you think.* Those words had hung between us for a beat before sending us spiraling out of control. His guitar sliding to the floor, me falling into his arms.

"You're really not going to tell me?" She huffed.

My phone rang in the living room, and I left Lila to answer it. One of my loyal supporters from Grady's street was so irate, I could barely understand her. I half listened as Mrs. Hernandez complained about the two campaign signs which had gone missing, and how Tyler needed to get her another one, but he wasn't answering his phone. That meant she'd called Tyler and me at seven thirty in the morning. Some people had no boundaries.

After I'd appeased Mrs. Hernandez and hung up, I turned to Lila. "Do you think he knows what Sabrina is doing?"

She shrugged. "You know Grady better than I do." She smirked.

"No point in guessing when I can just ask him in person." I headed down the hall toward my bedroom.

"Do you want me to come?" Lila called.

"No!" I didn't need her to witness the sinking of my stomach if he knew what Sabrina was doing and didn't have a problem with her taking the signs. We'd been starting to thaw. This next conversation might lead to another cold snap, possibly even frostbite.

I slammed the obnoxious brass knocker on Grady's door and then rang the doorbell right away. Patience was a virtue I usually possessed. Sabrina's car was in the driveway, and it made me want to tuck my tail between my legs and leave. Cowardliness wasn't my style anymore, and the realization Grady could make me feel that way, that Grady's actions mattered, fanned the flames of my rage.

The only thing I cared about was getting my signs back. Whether he was sleeping with Sabrina Kim or not was none of my concern. The coffee in my stomach swirled.

The door swung back, and he rubbed his eyes with the heels of his hands. "Maggie? Is someone dead? Why are you here so early?"

"I'm feeling a bit murderous, but no one is dead yet."

"Grady?" Sabrina's high-pitched voice sounded from behind him. "Come back to bed. It's too early."

"I know you don't have a job, but doesn't she have one?" I hissed. "Or, I don't know, three small kids she needs to get to school?"

He cocked his head and narrowed his eyes. "It's Saturday. Why are you here?"

"Some of my campaign signs have gone missing."

"I'm sorry to hear that. But you should probably be knocking obnoxiously on Tyler's door. He's the one who orders those, right?" He stepped back from the door to ease it closed.

"Someone has been stealing them." I shoved my heeled foot in the entryway, cringing at the thought of it getting caught in the door. The two dogs poked their heads into the gap, helping my cause.

"Grady!" Sabrina whined from inside the house. "Tell them to go away."

He leaned his shoulder against the doorframe, and the movement made my heart squeeze in my chest. Such a familiar pose, and it never failed to make my insides flutter. At one time, seeing him like this had churned my insides to butter. I gritted my teeth, and the beat of sexual attraction throbbed between us, unwanted, at least by me.

Hate. That was all I felt.

"All right, I'll bite, Maggie May. Who's been stealing from you?" There was a tenderness in his gaze I tried to ignore, as though he found me more amusing than infuriating. One of his hands strayed to stroke the dog beside him. Clearly, he had Sabrina Kim in his bed, and that told me all I needed to know.

"You know the thief quite intimately."

He chuckled and rolled off the door to stretch his arms along the top of the frame. "Doesn't exactly narrow it down."

"Gross."

Amusement played across his features. "Quit playing games and spill it."

"It's Sabrina. Your neighbor's cameras caught her carting my campaign signs into *your* shed every night this week." I was particularly queasy at the thought of Sabrina spending every night in bed with Grady. I shouldn't care. I didn't want to care.

Confusion marred his face, and he glanced over his shoulder. "Sabrina?" He frowned.

"I need to talk to her." I tried to step into the house.

He shook his head and barred the door. "You're not coming in here, Maggie. I'll talk to her."

"Fine. I'm going to your back shed, which I see is locked. I want my signs back."

"I'll be out in a minute." He swung the door closed.

I stood on the doorstep, tempted to listen in, to see if he congratulated Sabrina or kicked her out. Staying would mean I cared enough to listen, and I didn't. Not at all. Anger, which had been my companion all morning, propelled me to the back shed where I paced and tapped my foot until I saw Sabrina beside the driver's side of her car. We stared each other down, time stretching between us, elastic and tension-filled before Sabrina slid into the driver's seat and backed out of the driveway.

It was official. I hated her.

He ambled down the side of the house once Sabrina was gone, his head down while rooting through a set of keys. "I've never locked or unlocked this goddamned thing." He tried two or three keys while I looked on.

"You should have asked Sabrina which one before she left."

With an annoyed glance, Grady slid one last key into the lock, and it flipped open. "She says she doesn't know anything about it." He eased open the double doors, and signs of all sizes poured out, landing at his feet. "Oh, for fuck's sake."

"Right," I said, drawing out the word. "Nothing about it. That means this is all you, correct?"

He ran a frustrated hand through his hair. "No, I didn't know this was happening."

"That's a lot of signs. Sabrina must be losing weight or out of breath or something carting all those around." I surveyed the pile. In spite of myself, I was impressed with Sabrina's commitment to the task. With a sigh, I realized I was going to need to redistribute these to whoever had them taken, assuming they'd even noticed.

"I'll talk to her." He picked up a sign from the ground and propped it against the door.

"Don't bother. I'll call Mike and let him know what's been happening."

"There's no need to get the police chief involved. Your signs are here. I'll help you take them to your car."

"This is espionage. Stealing campaign signs is a felony, especially when you're sleeping with a candidate."

He stared at me for a moment, frustration pouring out of him. He wanted to say something and was holding back. I wondered if I pushed him just a little further if he'd come out with it. Perhaps then I wouldn't be the only one irrationally angry.

"You're not getting Sabrina arrested. She's got three kids."

"I'm sure she takes really great care of them while she's servicing you." Inside, I cringed as the words left my mouth. This wasn't like me. Why was I saying these things?

His jaw tightened. "What Sabrina does or doesn't do with her kids is no concern of mine."

"It will be when baby number four is on the way." I needed to put a lid on my temper. I sounded like a jealous, out-of-control fool. The neighbors were probably watching this exchange on their cameras while eating popcorn.

"You're not giving me much credit." He grabbed a bunch of signs from the ground and propped them under his arm.

"Oh, please. If you're sleeping with her, you don't deserve *any* credit. You're following the wrong head." I snatched a sign off the ground and stalked toward my vehicle at the curb. It was a small SUV. There was no way all the signs Sabrina accumulated would fit in the back.

"Tell me how you really feel." Grady threw his armload into the back. "You jealous, Maggie? Is that what this is? There's no way you're this pissed off about a bunch of campaign signs."

I tossed my sign into the back. "Did you see how many signs were in your shed? It's not one or two, it's probably somewhere between fifty and a hundred. She did it all on her own, and you didn't notice?"

"I was busy admiring other things." His gaze raked over me.

Another burst of anger and annoyance surged through me. I slammed the back of my SUV closed and stalked to the driver's side. "I'll send Tyler to get the rest. Tell Sabrina to expect a visit from Mike. I'll suggest he check your bed before looking elsewhere."

He let out a whistle and then chuckled. "Maggie, come on."

I was done listening to Grady, and I peeled away from the curb, desperate for some distance. He hadn't denied my comment—not once. His reply merely made it seem like I was being irrational. My blood hummed with rage and an overwhelming desire to either rip Grady's clothes off or beat him to a pulp. He was one of the few people who could inspire such drastic feelings. When I was younger, I'd found that magnetism exhilarating. Being around Grady made me feel alive in a way no one else did. Now, I wasn't sure I wanted that feeling. Far, far too volatile and out of control.

I *was* being irrational, and I hated him for noticing and for being the cause of it. Had anyone else stolen my signs, I would have given them a stern talking-to and threatened legal action, but I wouldn't have done it.

Outside the police station, I put my SUV in park and stared at the steering wheel. Remembering Emily's advice about deep breathing, I sucked in a breath and let it out slowly.

This wasn't right. Turning Sabrina into Mike, even if she only got a slap on the wrist, wasn't just. Whether she was a good mother or not, those kids didn't deserve to have her arrested for this. A foolish, dumb prank. Grady inspired foolish behavior. I knew that better than most.

It was already 9:30 a.m. I was half an hour late to open the pharmacy, and I was lucky none of my customers had called me yet to complain. Putting the car in reverse, I steered toward my storefront and tried to clear Grady from my mind. Tyler would get the signs. I could forget about the whole thing.

If only it was that simple.

Chapter Sixteen

Grady

The one emotion I couldn't stomach was guilt. I spent years running from it, dodging it, playing it off, wishing it would disappear in a puff of smoke. Watching Maggie peel away from the curb of my house, guilt latched onto my gut and wouldn't let go. I went into the house and flicked on the coffee maker, trying to figure out how to calm my unease.

The guilt wasn't about the signs; I could care less whether Sabrina had taken them. Was it misguided? Yeah. But that was the story of her life. I'd contributed to her series of bad choices last night when I'd caved and let her stay over. We hadn't had sex, but I'm not sure I was clear about where I stood.

I was going to have to tell her last night wasn't a prelude, it was the grand finale. When she showed up here, I almost fell back into long-dead habits. Hanging out with her was easy; we had a rhythm, even after all these years. But after the third beer, I'd realized sliding back into a relationship with her wouldn't be progress, and she wouldn't solve the ache in my chest every time I looked at Maggie.

Christ, that fucking ache.

It dogged me, made me want to do things I knew I shouldn't. Desiring her increased my guilt. I was one wrong move away from fucking everything up. If I kissed Maggie, I knew I'd be a goner. There'd be no going back. I'd gladly ride to hell latched to her, savoring all the feelings she inspired. The thought of her was a kind of addiction, worse than any drug I'd ever tried. Being with her would corrupt me, make me throw everything and everyone else aside.

Coupled with that knowledge was the way Maggie had looked at me at the shed. Disgust. Disappointment. Not that I didn't deserve those. I'd let Sabrina in during a fit of weakness, and then we'd drank enough that she couldn't drive home. For a minute, any warm body was better than lying in bed thinking about the one I couldn't have.

The last two weeks, while I sought people for the Small Town Saviors show, Maggie had been right there at the forefront of my mind. Explaining that to her was impossible. She might feel the same ache I did, but it wasn't enough to make her tell me the truth, to bury the past. We'd been around each other enough I was beginning to believe the truth would never surface. Coated over, layer upon layer, and if we couldn't uncover the past, we had no chance of anything now.

Of course, I'd have to tell Trent the truth if she confessed her part. So many things we'd all left unsaid. These suspended connections were my punishment. I'd been a shitty brother, and I was doomed to the fringes of Trent's life, and by extension, hers too.

I chugged my coffee and set the cup beside the sink. Maybe I'd go see Trent today. I'd promised Mom I'd try to repair the rift between us, that I wouldn't let it continue. So far, I'd done little to fulfill my promise. She wasn't the kind to peer over my shoulder. She'd always had more faith in me and Trent than we'd probably deserved.

Grabbing my keys from the kitchen counter, I pointed to the dog beds so Hite and Zeus knew they weren't invited. I had the address on my phone, courtesy of Mom. All I needed was gas and a bit of time, and I could start to set things right.

At the gas station, I filled my truck and looked around at the shops which had changed hands or sprung up since I'd last lived here. In some ways, the town was stagnant, and in others, the changes were quite striking. Big-box stores. More houses. Run-down buildings. At least this gas station hadn't changed. Ed Krakow had owned it for years, but I'd heard Ed had sold it recently. The end of an era.

Opening the convenience store door, my pulse skyrocketed at the sight of the man tending cash. Dan Ramouli. I stared at him for a long time while Dan served the only other customer in the store. Why would he come back to Little Falls? He'd left in a blaze of betrayal. I nodded to the other customer as he left but didn't move any closer to the counter.

"What are you doing here?" I asked.

"Grady Castillo. I heard you were back in town. Small-town hero coming home. Such a heart-warmer." His gaze bored into me. "I bought this place off Ed the other week. How you doing? It's been a while." Dan leaned across the counter, a smug smile turning up the corners of his lips.

Not long enough. "I'm surprised Ed would sell it to you. I didn't think you'd come back here."

"This is my home, you know. Besides, Trent lives in Utica. What does he care if I'm here?"

"I care that you're here."

"It's all water under the bridge. I never told Trent what you did. You should thank me."

"What *I* did? All I did was let you into my house to 'get something for Trent.' Then suddenly Trent is arrested, and you're a key witness in his trial? The only 'proof' they had of Trent's operation came from you and from whatever you stole that night."

After the morning I'd had, and the realization I'd probably never be with Maggie in any real way, my anger was lit. There was a good chance if this escalated, I might resort to violence. I wasn't like Trent. Words, not fists, were my weapons. The coiled tension in me needed a release, and I wasn't sure words would be enough this time.

I'd never confessed to Trent how Dan had gotten the evidence. By the time I'd put the sequence of events together, it had been too late to do anything. Probably from the minute Dan set foot in our house it had been too late. Letting him into Trent's room ate at me. Each piece of 'recovered' evidence had driven into me like spikes to a stake. I'd let my brother down in so many ways.

"I got caught. I made a deal. Trent was a bigger fish. Anyone in my place would have done the same. Six years in prison, man. I wasn't doing that."

"You had no problem nailing Trent's coffin shut."

"So fucking melodramatic. He's not dead. He did a bit of time. Lots of people got a record." Dan shuffled some gum on the counter. "I heard he landed on his feet. Mayor Maggie loved him enough to hook him up." Dan smirked. "Always felt a bit of envy for Trent being able to bang her while she was still in high school. So fucking uptight, but I bet she was a tiger in the—"

My hand, unattached to my brain, connected with Dan's face. A satisfying *crack* echoed through the store, and Dan's fingers flew to his nose, where blood started to leak out.

Mentioning Maggie had tipped the scales. People couldn't talk about her like that, especially not Dan. I shook out my hand, flexing it. Now I remembered why I didn't do that.

Dan chuckled, grabbing some tissues from under the counter. "You feel better? We square now?"

"We'll never be square. And if I ever hear you talking about Maggie Sullivan like that again, I'll start pushing so many corporate bylaws down your throat, it'll feel like you're gagging on them." In that moment, I was grateful for the 'mayor school' Kelvin had been making me attend during lunch hours at his office. I wasn't sure I had the specifics right, but the phrasing sounded good.

I was tempted to leave without paying for my gas. But Dan had proven himself a snake once. There was no point in giving someone like him leverage. I threw forty dollars on the counter and left the station without a backward glance.

Too wound up to go to Utica, I found myself on Kelvin's doorstep. The outside of the gray brick two-story was immaculate with flower beds, and his hanging baskets were still going strong despite the cooling September weather.

"What's up, man?" Kelvin asked when he answered the door.

"Came for a beer."

He chuckled and stepped back to let me into his house. We did a lot of our planning in Kelvin's office or at the train station.

Unlike my place, Kelvin's house looked like he'd had it professionally decorated. Everything was neutral tones, uncomfortable-looking furniture, and wide-open spaces. I liked the fact my old run-down place had lots of walls.

"Sorry to drop in without calling." I scanned the room, looking for a good place to sit.

"What's going on? You seem wound up." Kelvin waved me into the kitchen.

The white kitchen was blinding, every surface shiny and probably disinfected a dozen times this morning alone. I slid onto a stool and accepted the beer Kelvin offered, even though it wasn't quite noon.

"It's been a hell of a morning." I tipped the beer and chugged it dry.

He chuckled. "Give me the highlights."

"Maggie showed up and lost her mind over Sabrina stealing her campaign signs and putting them in my shed."

A choking sound drew my attention as Kelvin tried to keep his beer in his mouth. "You gotta be kidding me. Did you know?"

"Of course I didn't fucking know."

"Did you ask Sabrina about it yet?"

I shifted on the stool and avoided meeting Kelvin's gaze. "She was there when Maggie showed up."

"What time was this?" He furrowed his brow.

"Too early."

"Jesus, Grady. Please tell me you're not fucking Sabrina Kim."

I held up a finger in Kelvin's direction. "I am not fucking Sabrina Kim."

"You know stealing someone's campaign signs is a felony."

With a wry smile, I said, "I do know that. Guess who told me?"

Kelvin laughed. "Maggie. If I wasn't gay, and in a relationship, you'd have a run for your money landing her. She's fucking brilliant."

Warmth settled across my chest at Kelvin's words. The memory of the look on Maggie's face as we'd stood toe-to-toe outside my house pushed out the warmth, leaving a chill in its place. "She's not too happy with me."

Shaking his head, Kelvin took another mouthful of beer and gave me a thoughtful look. "You two need to bang, get it out of your system."

The temptation to admit we had already been there and done that sprung up, but as far as I knew, she'd never told anyone. Maybe Lila, but I doubted it. The words had never left my lips. "That wouldn't work." The last time she'd slithered along me, I'd turned myself in knots avoiding her until she'd fled to Florida. I'd let my anger build a wall between us. My emotional fortress had probably saved at least some of my sanity. Had I been right to be angry with her? Maybe not. The woman I was starting to know didn't seem like the type to do the things I'd accused her of. But I still didn't know for sure.

Stoking the ember that glowed between us wouldn't snuff it out. It would ignite a blaze which would probably consume me whole.

"Screwing Sabrina isn't going to make you forget about Maggie. You know that, right?"

"Yeah, my dick got that memo from my head sometime last night. Not to worry."

"So, you came here 'cause she's pissed at you, and you don't know how to fix it?" Kelvin shook his head. "Look how far we've come, son." He clapped me on the shoulder.

I slid my empty beer along the granite counter and scrubbed my face with my hands. Was I upset she was angry? All my thoughts were muddled, history and present lives mingling too much.

"I need some advice."

"Go after her," Kelvin said.

I sighed. "Beyond Maggie, I need to get Trent back. Going after her isn't going to bring me closer to my brother."

"Oh." Kelvin took a few thoughtful sips of his beer. "In theory, if they were going to start something up, they already would have."

"Brothers first."

"Good brothers want each other to be happy. Would you be happy with her?"

"Who knows? I've only ever been miserable thinking about her."

He let out a bark of laughter. "If you're not sure how Trent will react, maybe ask him?"

"I thought you'd give me good advice," I muttered. Talking to Trent about Maggie was more likely to cause an aneurysm in one of us instead of a truce. From the minute she'd started coming to the house, Trent had been protective of her. Before Maggie, Trent had gone for girls who wore crop tops and cutoff jeans. Her sweater sets and knee-length skirts had amused me until she'd shown up Sunday after Sunday. The first time she'd tried to call me illiterate, our verbal sparring had commenced. I'd never ever tired of listening to her speak. Pretty, smart, and Trent's was an absolutely lethal combo for my mental health.

"You and Trent are already pretty far apart. Asking about her can't possibly push you further away, right? They're not together. Last I heard, she was dating some banker in Utica."

A pit formed in my stomach. She was in a relationship with someone? Here I was contemplating all the reasons I couldn't sleep with her and she was sleeping with someone else. The soul-sucking reality of another thing standing in the way made my head pound. I cleared my throat. "Is that still happening?"

"Nah. I heard she kicked him to the curb just before Lila's birthday celebration. She never keeps them around for long." He took a deep breath. "You know your brother better than me. Maybe you're right to wait until you've mended some fences before talking to him about her."

"I'll think about it." I grabbed my empty beer bottle and tipped it from side to side. Lately, thinking had been both a blessing and a curse. Songs bubbled up. I couldn't quite grasp any of the words or the melody yet. Maybe if the song would come, I could pour some of these feelings into the lyrics, get some peace. At the back of my mind, her name and image were seared. She was a burn which blazed hot below the surface of everything I did.

"Why don't we plan some of that concert? You got some RSVPs from a few of your industry buddies, right?"

I nodded and sat a little straighter in my chair. "Yeah."

"I'll grab my laptop. Be right back."

A distraction was exactly what I needed. Forget Trent and Maggie for a while and get lost in something I could do.

Confronting Trent, confessing my sins, asking for his forgiveness might be the only way to knock down the walls between us. But I wasn't ready. The sledgehammer of certainty hadn't settled into my gut yet.

Chapter Seventeen

Maggie

We were four weeks into planning the concert and strip show, and Lila and I needed to get the promotional materials pumping out to fill the venue. The lineup was good enough, thanks to Grady, so selling tickets wouldn't be an issue.

Lila had offered to meet with him today to get all the details, so I wouldn't have to face him, but I declined.

After my confrontation with Grady, the fumes of my anger had carried me through to the end of the workday. I'd grabbed a bottle of wine and showed up at Lila's house where we'd spent the evening commiserating.

I didn't want Grady to know the Sabrina debacle had driven a stake through my heart. Going to this meeting with him, alone, was the only way to prove to him and to myself that I could control my feelings. This roller-coaster ride was coming to an end; I was throwing on the brakes.

In the doorway of the conference room, he cleared his throat. I looked up from the papers spread out in front of me, startled out of my thoughts. He was dressed in worn jeans and a T-shirt, and I could imagine the buttery slide of the gray material under my fingers if I were to run my hands down his chest.

No butter. No sliding. No fingers. I didn't want that. I didn't want him.

He'd been in the doorway for thirty seconds, and I was already fighting the urge to climb aboard the coaster to ride it one more time.

Why couldn't he be repulsive? Or be one of those people who I could admit was attractive without wanting to explore the package under his clothes? That's what I needed—objective indifference. Grady was attractive, with his messy brown hair, dark-brown eyes, and tan skin, but I wasn't attracted to him. Well-sculpted muscles were a great asset for a man to have. Objectively speaking, it meant he took care of his body. I could admire that without admiring him. There. Easy.

"Are you ready for me?"

My heart dropped into my feet at his words. "Oh, uh—" I stumbled around, shuffling the papers, not seeing anything. Heat climbed into my face. This was a disaster. I was a disaster. "Sorry, I'm—"

He came around the conference table, his shoulder brushing mine, and helped me sort the papers. They'd been in order, but in my fluster, I'd messed them up. So stupid.

"You okay?" Grady checked page numbers and headers without looking at me.

My hands stilled on the table. "I'm sorry I overreacted about Sabrina." Those words hadn't been what I'd planned to say to him. I'd intended to ignore the whole thing, pretend it hadn't happened.

"Thanks for leaving Mike out of it." He ran a hand through his hair.

When I snuck a glance at him, he tucked a stray strand of my hair behind my ear, tenderness in his gaze. The touch was so intimate, so unexpected, it caused warmth to pool in places it shouldn't. He'd done something similar to me before, but it was his lack of hesitation which surprised me, as though he had a right to touch me. My body hummed in anticipation.

"I feel like I should explain what was going on—"

I shook my head and grabbed more papers. "No. You don't owe me any explanation. We're rivals for the mayoral race, and we're working together to help the town, to help Trent. That's it." My heart thumped in my chest, betraying how much I wished he'd explain. Did it mean he hadn't slept with her? Why was she there so early if that was the case? The objectivity I'd been clinging to before he stepped in the door was beating against the windows, threatening to fly out of the room. More than anything, I wanted Sabrina to be a misunderstanding.

He tried to catch my gaze, but I sidestepped him and turned on the projector to go through my PowerPoint presentation. As soon as he realized what I was doing, he lowered himself into a chair and started chuckling.

"You're going to present to me?" He crossed his arms over his toned middle, and I averted my gaze.

"It seemed like the easiest way to get you up to speed on what the night will look like."

"Whatever you think. I'm your captive audience."

I clicked through the slides, explaining what everyone else had been able to accomplish in the last four weeks. The material was dry, and I was fairly certain he didn't care, but it created some distance between us, which made me more comfortable.

At the end, he clapped. "That's great. Really great, Maggie. You've thought of everything—even better than some of the concert organizers I've worked with professionally."

Pride spread through me at his words. I couldn't hold back my grin as I tucked my hair behind my ears. "Really? That means a lot, actually. It's been a huge project to undertake, and sometimes I've wondered why I agreed to do this for Trent..."

He held up his finger. "There's just one thing."

I raised my eyebrows. What had I forgotten?

"I feel like some parts of the night might need a demonstration for me to appreciate the full impact." He stared at me expectantly, a small smirk on his face.

I frowned and then his implication clicked. "I'm not stripping for you."

"It would really liven up your presentation. Give it some authenticity."

"The only person I'm giving it to is you."

Our eyes connected, and my breath caught. Why was it always like this with him? My pulse quickened, and a flush rose to my cheeks.

He wanted me to strip for him. His desire should horrify me, but it didn't, not even close. What would he do if I did it?

"I'd watch the whole thing again, if you wanted to go for a different tactic. A small sample of what I could expect on the night as if you were one of the male performers." His voice rumbled through the room, husky with undisguised need.

A knock on the door made us both start.

Ruth poked her head in. "Sorry to interrupt. Here's the rest of the paperwork you were after, Maggie."

"Oh, right." I crossed to the door, fighting gratitude and exasperation at the interruption. Nothing would have happened between us in the conference room. He'd slept with Sabrina Kim, hadn't he? Clearly, any warm body would do. I didn't want him or his drama. "Thanks."

He rose from his seat and wandered around the table to stand near me. The scent of his cologne and the distinctive smell of wintergreen wafted closer, circling around, testing my resolve. We were in a conference room at city hall for God's sake. I needed to pull myself together.

"So." I took the opposite side, far from him. "Tell me about these people you have coming." I'd gotten the basics from Kelvin. Some of the names had been significant, while others were unknown. Lila and I needed to know how to market his musical connections and their talents.

He reached into his back pocket, his T-shirt stretching across his chest, the bottom riding up, so a glimpse of skin made my pulse skyrocket. I should have let Lila do this meeting. Why hadn't I just swallowed my pride and let Lila do this? Whether he knew it or not, my insides were acting like a bloody fool every time he moved.

From his pocket, a folded piece of paper emerged. He smoothed it out and tossed it across the table. "I made some notes."

I scanned the list of ten or twelve names. At the bottom, there was a new name added. "Mia Malone?" I glanced up, and Grady shifted uncomfortably.

"Part of a contract I signed with her. Subcontract asked her to perform something at a benefit of my choosing."

"She's huge right now."

He nodded but didn't elaborate.

"What kind of contract would you be signing with Mia Malone?" I raised my eyebrows and set the paper on the table.

His gaze connected with mine across the space between us, drawing me in despite my desire to stay distant. There was a moment of hesitation before he confessed, "I'm one of the songwriters on her next album."

"Oh," I whispered. "So, that's why you don't make money off your voice anymore. Do you do that a lot? Write songs for people?" The memory of sitting beside Grady on his bed, lost in the thrall of his creative process, rose up, filling the space between us. I could watch him do that every day of my life and never tire of the experience.

"I seem to be good at it." He gave me a small grin. "Pays the bills." He shrugged. "My old label asked me to consider producing a few up-and-comers."

"Where would you do that?" The thought of him leaving caused my stomach to twist in knots. No one believed he'd stay. It shouldn't be a surprise. That knowledge didn't stop the ache from coming.

"We're just talking about it. Nothing firm yet. It's a great opportunity for me. Something I've always been interested in. A step up. We'll see." He came around the table and took the list. With a hint of pride, he pointed to a few other well-known names. "Written songs for all of them."

I stared into his warm, brown eyes and felt myself slipping. He was being uncharacteristically open. I couldn't remember the last time I'd felt like we were on even footing, not in danger of bursting into an argument. A match to a can of gas. Instead, we felt like still, deep water, the kind you didn't just dip a toe into but rather the sort made for drowning.

"Even while you did all that traveling?" I remembered hearing about the places he'd visited. I hadn't been able to stay away from the Castillo family. I'd visited Penny, their mother, whenever I'd come back from college. After Trent got out and I returned to Little Falls, Penny was so used to my company we met for coffee once a week. I didn't think Grady knew. Trent did, but he wasn't worried. He knew I'd keep his secrets.

"Technology is an amazing thing." His lips quirked up into an almost smile.

"You don't write for yourself? Just other people?"

He took a deep breath and rubbed the back of his neck. "Would you believe I can't?"

"You can't write for yourself?"

With a shake of his head, he grimaced. "Forget I said that. I shouldn't have said that." A chuckle escaped, and he rolled his shoulders. "I *don't* write for myself anymore."

I ran a hand down his arm, and I almost sighed at the solid feel of him under my fingertips. "I used to love listening to you write."

His thumb grazed my cheek. "I only know about one time."

Heat swept through my body at the memory. There had been a first that night, but listening to him hadn't been it. I shook my head, lost in the thrall of being this close, his calloused hands on me.

"How do you think I knew you were doing it? I'd stand outside the garage door, outside your bedroom door. Sometimes I came to the house, hoping you'd be so lost in your own world you wouldn't know I was around."

Surprise lit his eyes. "I had no idea."

I'd wondered if he'd sensed me lurking around a corner, just out of sight. His ignorance made me happy and sad at the same time. I'd been so deeply, so keenly aware of him. The idea he hadn't been as attuned made me wish I'd have revealed myself. Would it have changed the outcome? He was four years older than me, and back then, that was a lot. Older, wiser, far more experienced. Had I been able to overcome those things, the agreement between me and Trent would have sealed our fates anyway.

"I wish I'd known," he said, reading my thoughts.

"Do you?" I whispered, my gaze straying to his lips. I wanted to forget about everything else and sink into the depths of this desire.

He cupped my cheek, and I leaned into his hand. "No, I'm glad I didn't know. You were with Trent. I already feel shitty enough about what happened."

The truth bubbled up my throat. I could confess, tell him what had really been going on. Embarrassing, but maybe that was better than this. The cost would be Trent's trust, perhaps even our friendship.

And for what?

Sabrina's voice calling him back to bed the other morning sprang up between us. He was toying with me, and I was letting him. Playing games.

Don't be foolish.

Scanning his face one last time, I stepped back and picked up his sheet of scrawled notes. "I'll grab my laptop, and we can chat about these people and what they do."

"Are you ever going to tell me the truth, Maggie?"

Silence stretched between us while I considered ignoring his question. "I don't know why it matters anymore." I averted my eyes. "It was a long time ago. We aren't the same people." Taking a deep breath, I met his gaze.

"I betrayed my brother, and you act like what happened wasn't a big deal. You said you'd help me get him back." He sliced a frustrated hand through the air. "So, yeah, it matters. If the truth means I didn't do what I think I did, then it matters. A hell of a lot."

I searched his face, indecision warring in me. Perhaps I could tell him a little, enough to make him understand. I swallowed. "We had an agreement. We weren't dating, not really. People thought we were. We let people believe that for a few reasons. But we were never dating."

He shook his head. "I don't believe it."

"That's not the whole truth, but I can't give you more. I can't betray his trust."

"I saw you two—you kissed, you held hands. That's not—it wasn't fake."

My palms were clammy. "When you decide to lie about something, you have to commit to the lie. It was important your mom thought we were dating." I gave him a helpless look. "I can't. God, Grady. He'd be so angry with me. I can't say any more. If you want the rest, you ask him."

"When we slept together—"

"I didn't cheat on him. Not in the conventional sense, anyway."

"But I didn't know that..." He searched my face, his brown eyes assessing. "If we hadn't gotten the call he'd been arrested, would you have told me everything?"

"Everything has never been mine to tell. Back then, I needed him, and he needed me."

"Why?"

I gathered the papers and put his handwritten notes on top. "I'll get Lila to connect with you about the rest of this list."

"Tell me why, Maggie."

Tears sprang to my eyes, but I kept my head down and continued tidying up. "If that was what was holding you back from being a real brother, you can rest assured he wouldn't have cared."

"Maggie." His voice was pleading.

I swept away the tears trickling down my cheeks. "Lila will call you." I opened the conference room door and retreated down the hall to my office.

As I set the stack of papers on my desk, my hands shook. I stared at them, wondering if I'd done the right thing.

Would that satisfy him, or would that small confession only make things worse?

Chapter Eighteen

The streetlights shining through my big living room windows illuminated the cracked ceiling. I'd been staring at it for hours. I couldn't sleep. *You have to commit to the lie.* Her words played in a loop. What agreement had she and Trent had? The only thing that made sense meant she'd been involved in Trent's drug trade after all. Which version of her was the right one? I dragged my hands down my face, frustration eating away at any peace of mind.

When I'd first heard why Trent was arrested and the intricate nature of his operation, I'd been sure Maggie was the mastermind. The anger had been a gift. Hating her had propelled me far away from her in the immediate aftermath. Being with her had been the best and worst thing I'd ever done.

Eventually, once I'd found a way out of Little Falls, I'd let my fury and my guilty conscience drive me. At first, the rage had merely driven me to win *Center Stage*, then the guilt drove me out of LA to places I'd never thought about before. My emotions had steered me back here, only to realize fury might not have been what I'd felt toward Maggie. Certainly wasn't how I felt now.

Frustrated. That's how I felt. Really fucking frustrated. She had given enough information to pique my interest. A giant puzzle, and at the end of it laid my absolution. Flinging back the cover, I rose and stretched. My hand trailed around the back of my neck as I grabbed my keys from the table by the front door. It was two in the morning. This was a terrible idea, but I needed answers. If I waited until daylight, I'd lose my nerve.

I pounded on the door and laid on the doorbell of the ground-floor apartment. A drunk guy had let me in the secure entrance, so now I was making an ass of myself in the dimly lit hallway. People probably worked tomorrow. At some point, Trent would either answer the door or the police would drag me away. As a kid, Trent had been a deep sleeper.

I was half expecting the police at any moment.

"What the actual fuck?" Trent yanked open his door.

I squeezed around him into the apartment, not waiting for an invitation. "What was going on between you and Maggie that year you were together? You know, when you were doing your third try at senior year?"

Trent barked out a laugh and slammed the door. "It wasn't my third, it was my second, and you're here at stupid o'clock in the morning asking about Maggie? You'd better not be trying to get into her pants, or I swear to God, I'll beat you to a bloody pulp."

Shit.

Subtlety had never been my strongest quality. I couldn't tell Trent I'd already been in her pants, and I was looking to ease my guilt. In frustration, I scrubbed my face and sighed.

"She told me the two of you had an arrangement in high school. You weren't dating."

"So, you *are* trying to get in her pants. I heard you were back with Sabrina Kim. Talk about reliving your high school years. Doesn't she have like ten kids or something?"

"Three, but nothing's going on there."

"Doesn't matter. Maggie's too good for you. You stay away from her." Trent pointed an accusing finger. "All the mayor bullshit had to have something to do with her. I knew it. You think I didn't see the way you used to look at her?"

I ran a hand along my chin and shifted my feet. I wasn't sure *I* knew the way I used to look at her. We'd been like magnets at the dinner table, around the house, monopolizing each other's attention. Had Maggie looked at me the same way I'd looked at her? I was older now, more experienced, and I didn't simply have a vague sense of the attraction between us anymore. Being around her was like having all my senses on red alert. She wasn't just a want, she felt like someone I *needed*.

"I'm trying to figure out the truth."

"What truth have you got for *me*? Huh? You come here in the middle of the night expecting me to lay myself bare. That's not fucking happening. I would have told you anything after I got arrested. You should have asked."

After a brief hesitation, I sank into the couch. The apartment was small, with everything sectioned off the way I liked. Entryway, living room, kitchen, hallway. No open-concept bullshit. "I didn't know how to ask you."

"What the hell does that mean? You open your mouth and words come out."

I put my elbows on my knees. "I let you down. I should have known what you were doing. I should have asked where you were getting all your money. Bagging groceries wasn't it. Deep down, I knew that. If Dad had still been alive—"

"Don't go there." Trent held up his hand. "Dad died, and it was you and me, Grady. You and me against the world." He yanked up the sleeve of his shirt and pointed to the spot we'd put our matching tattoo. "Brothers first." Trent swallowed. "And then I fucked up, and you left me. You fucking left me."

"That's not what happened." Trent had it all wrong—they'd all screwed up. This mess didn't fall on anyone's head alone.

"Unless you've got some alternate set of events I know nothing about, that's exactly what happened. I got caught with my hand in the cookie jar, and I lost my brother. So, don't come in here asking about Maggie. You can't have her. You don't fucking deserve her."

I stood, anxious, angry, hands on my hips. "I'm looking for the truth."

Trent scoffed and leaned against the wall across from the couch. "The truth is you leave when things get tough. Prove me wrong, and then I'll tell you whatever you wanna know."

Frustration spilled out of me. "I'm doing this fundraiser. I'm running for mayor. Neither of those things has been easy. I'm here, now, talking to you." Without knowing what had been going on between them, I was stuck.

"Nah, that's not tough. Tough is some life-altering shit. It's the kind of thing that happens and no one's the same. You weather one of those without tucking your tail between your legs and scurrying off, and I'll believe you've changed." His voice had grown rough, and he cleared his throat. "You earn the truth. You've got no right to demand it, not anymore."

For the first time in my life, I'd been beaten by my brother's words instead of his fists. Why hadn't I seen how badly I was fucking things up by staying away? "I thought you were better off without me."

"I've gotten used to being without you. Jury's out on whether I've been better off." He walked over to his door and opened it, making a grand gesture with his hand. "I've got work in the morning. Get the fuck out. And next time, have the guts to come during daylight hours."

I wanted to say more, to find a way to get the information from Trent. Tomorrow afternoon would have been better, after I'd considered his words, come up with something that would win him over. Instead, I'd come in a fit of frustration and was leaving worse off than when I'd arrived. She wouldn't tell me the truth, and Trent had given me a timeline which could take years to complete. Sometimes I was astounded at my level of incompetence in basic human relationships.

"Thanks for letting me in, Trent."

"You're my brother. I'll always let you in. But I might not let you stay." He threw the door closed behind me, and the lock snapped into place.

As goodbyes went, it wasn't the worst one I'd ever heard.

Chapter Nineteen
Maggie

I was ready to be amused when I entered the two-story brick building where all the men were gathered. Lila said Grady and his choreographer were at the studio working with a bunch of the performers. Although I'd avoided him after our meeting turned awkward, I was feeling strong enough to face him tonight. He hadn't sought me out during the last week, so I guessed the avoidance was mutual. Or maybe he was too busy with Sabrina to worry about what I'd been doing.

That thought soured my stomach. At least the campaign signs weren't disappearing anymore.

The studio itself was closed off from onlookers, but the owner had given me a key to slip into the room to check the choreographer's progress. Lila had been hoarding the list of *dancers* and wasn't letting me peruse the lineup. A buzz had been building around town. Events like this were built for small communities. People in Little Falls excelled at supporting each other. Their sense of comradery was one of the things I loved best.

I opened the door of the last studio and slipped inside. The men were all facing the incredibly fit woman at the front of the room with fire-engine red hair who was contorting her body in ways I never imagined possible. People danced like this?

"When you're done stretching, we'll get started," the choreographer said, twisting her body into another unbelievable shape.

A wave of embarrassment hit me. They were stretching, not dancing. I'd never been particularly athletic. Thank God I hadn't said anything out loud.

"We're going to take it from the top. Remember, I'm teaching you moves, but you can mix and match them any way you want based on the music you've selected for your performance."

She had a melodic voice which rang through the wide-open studio. Her red hair was in a pixie cut, and even from the back of the room, I could tell she was pretty. Somehow, Grady had convinced her to work with the men she didn't know every day for a week straight. A local bed-and-breakfast place was putting her up for free.

I leaned against the wall and crossed my arms. Grady was in the front row, and he glanced over his shoulder at someone behind him who I couldn't quite see. The choreographer did some fancy footwork at a quick pace and then slowed it down. It was fascinating to watch, and I wished I was more coordinated.

Once the choreographer had done the sequence a few times, she went over to her phone and announced they'd be putting the moves they'd learned that week to music. The men could practice whatever they wanted, and she and a few others would circulate to make corrections. A hip-hop song blasted through the speakers, and I grinned at the mishmash of activity from the men. Almost everyone was doing something different, from the hospital doctors and nurses, to the mechanics, to the restaurant owners, to the teachers—every facet of life in Little Falls seemed to be represented somewhere.

Grady turned around to help the person who kept stealing his attention, but I couldn't see through the throng of other dancers and onlookers.

I moved farther down the wall, loath for anyone to spot me or to interrupt the group. A familiar head of dark hair with a slight graying at the temples came into view. *Sweet Jesus.* My heart contracted. Why was my father learning how to dance? I shifted forward and then rocked back when I saw Grady demonstrating the footwork they'd been taught. Dad watched, brow furrowed and then attempted to do it. Rather than laughing at him, Grady nodded his head and then showed him again. Unlike my father, Grady oozed confidence. The smoothness to his movements made my mouth go dry.

Behind me, Emily slipped into the studio, Amir attached to her side.

"Pretty great, right?" she whispered as Amir raced over to Grady and his grandfather.

"I'm actually a little horrified. He's not going to strip, is he?"

Emily laughed. "He's in the group number. So, yes and no. Mom thinks this is a great idea. I didn't want to ask why. Knowing her, she would have given me far too much information." Her smile was wry. "Grady has been tutoring him on the steps all week."

When I turned to focus on Dad, my gaze connected with Grady's. He gave me a sheepish grin that was reminiscent of the boy I'd known. Instinct nudged me to cross the room, slip under Grady's arm, and squeeze him tight. For once, my desire to be close to him wasn't fueled by lust, but rather genuine affection. In his free time, he'd been teaching Dad how to dance. My heart was going to burst out of my chest.

Amir stole Grady's attention, and the familiar surge of longing flooded me as he crouched down to my nephew's level to talk.

"I love it when men do that," Emily said as though reading my mind.

"Do what?" My ovaries were going to spontaneously combust at any moment. I pressed a hand to my pelvis.

"Get down to his level, talk to him like he matters. Dad does it, of course. When I see other men do it, though, it gets me right in the feels."

I knew Emily wasn't angling for an apology or condolences. Her husband, Omar, had died four years ago. Amir would never remember him. When Emily had a few too many drinks, that line of thinking was enough to elicit tears. My sister hadn't so much as looked at another man since he died. She'd told me that falling in love was a risky business, and you had to be absolutely certain the highs would be worth the inevitable lows or else the emotional bankruptcy wasn't worth it.

Looking at Grady, I wondered how much I'd already invested. He had Amir in his arms and was twirling him around the room while Dad continued to practice his footwork.

"He's good with kids." Emily's focus was locked on her son.

"He'd better be. Sabrina has three of them."

"That still going on?"

"I don't know, and I don't care." Emily probably knew I was lying. After all, I couldn't seem to look away from him as he balanced Amir on his feet and helped him copy the footwork. The choreographer approached him and put her hand on his forearm, laughing at the silliness between them. My palms broke into a sweat when he grinned back at her, at the familiarity between them.

"You're turning a little green." Emily circled her own face without looking away from her son.

I glared at her. "No, I'm not. There is no envy or jealousy. I could care less what Grady Castillo does." As an afterthought, I added, "Or *who* he does."

Emily laughed. "I know I told you to stay away from him, or at least cut out the sexual tension, but you've been terrible at both. Maybe you need to tell him how you feel?"

"Absolutely not." I flipped my key ring around my finger repeatedly before dragging my gaze from him to look at Emily. "We'd be a terrible idea." Almost against my will, my focus went back to him. "He's attractive, sure. Doesn't mean *I'm* attracted to him."

Emily burst into laughter, drawing more attention toward us at the back of the room.

I gave a little wave to the twenty or so men in the room and called out, "Great job, everyone! You look amazing."

"You're such a liar. Please tell me you don't actually believe yourself."

"Do you want me to hook up with him in the middle of our campaign for mayor?" I arched my eyebrows in challenge. I knew Emily. Much like me, Emily liked to win.

Emily searched my face and sighed. "The campaign manager in me thinks it's a terrible idea. So much room for error in every direction." She ran her hand from the top of my head and along my back in a motherly gesture. "But more than that, I want you to be happy. I always wondered what held you back. You drifted from guy to guy, test-driving them and discarding them like they weren't quite good enough. For the longest time, I thought Trent was the reason. Never made sense to me, but he was the best I could come up with." She nodded toward Grady. "Trent wasn't the reason. He never was. It was him, wasn't it? None of the guys were *him*."

I shook my head, panic welling up. "That's—that's—" I wanted to say 'ridiculous,' but the word kept getting stuck in my throat.

"True," Emily finished in a whisper as Amir barreled into her legs. Dad and Grady trailed behind him, too close for us to continue our conversation, even if I had been able to formulate a reply.

When our gazes met, Grady's expression was filled with concern. "Maggie?" He scanned me, his brow furrowing. "Are you sick? You've gone really pale."

Emily gave me a sideways glance but didn't say anything.

Was Emily right? Her words played on a loop. If Emily was right. *Oh, God. If Emily was right...* Which meant—*No, nope.* That was not how I felt. I didn't. Impossible. That feeling, the one Emily was implying, couldn't be sprung on someone like a surprise. I'd have known if I'd felt that way. Right? Panic swelled. Right?

"Maggie May?"

I glanced up and realized people were streaming out of the room around them.

"See you tomorrow night, Grady." The choreographer grazed his arm on the way past.

"Thanks again for your help, Amy," he called after her.

My teeth clenched in annoyance. Why did she keep touching him? "I need a drink," I muttered.

A slow smile spread across his face. "The one thing I have at my house in abundance is cold beer. You're welcome to a few of them if you want."

There was a chance I was going to need more than a few to bury the realization threatening to burst out. I intended to ignore what Emily had just put in front of me for as long as I possibly could. Feeling anything other than hate for Grady wasn't helpful. Objective lust. That's all I could feel. Maybe I'd sleep with him and maybe I wouldn't, but that was the furthest we'd ever go.

"Do you still have your mattress in the middle of the living room?"

"Nope."

I narrowed my eyes. "Kelvin moved it for you?"

He chuckled. "No, your dad came over this week and gave me a hand. For some reason, he thought the living room was a silly place to be sleeping. Helped me put together the frame too. It's like a real bed now."

With a nod, I raised my index finger. "One drink."

I was pretty sure it wouldn't be one drink. Like so many other things where he was concerned, once I started, I couldn't seem to stop.

Chapter Twenty
Grady

It was strange having her in my house. She trailed her hand along books piled on the shelves, flicking open a few of them and flipping through the pages. A beer hung from her other hand, her fingers clasping the neck, occasionally shooting me amused glances when she found a book she knew. I leaned my shoulder against the doorway. There was nothing better than watching her mind at work.

"So many books on these shelves." Her chocolate-brown eyes were lit with a teasing light as she raised her beer to her lips. "If these were organized and you were anyone else, I'd say you were a man after my heart."

I wasn't sure what I was after, but I wasn't ruling out her heart. Perhaps I'd organize those shelves and see what happened.

She picked up one of the well-worn books and turned it. "Remember this one?" Her light laugh filled the room. "*A Thousand Splendid Suns.* I was convinced you hadn't read this."

With a grin, I pushed off the doorframe and took the book from her hand. This was the first one she'd grilled me about reading. I'd carted this paperback on all my travels, one of the few books I'd reread. "My book club reading days. Or rather," I said with a wry grin, "weeks. I was always racing to get a goddamned book done before you came on Sunday."

"Really?" Her eyes lit with surprise, and a grin tugged at the edges of her lips.

"Sometimes I'd wait until Thursday to pick a book, hoping you wouldn't have time to read it before Sunday."

A real laugh escaped her, and she eyed me as she sipped her beer. "Wanna know a secret?"

I placed the book back in the pile. "You never read any of them?"

She shoved my shoulder and shook her head. "No, the librarian used to call me as soon as you'd left and let me know what you'd picked up. The Thursday reads were fine. It was when you took out more than one book that screwed me over."

I grinned. "I wish I'd been clever enough to do it on purpose more often."

"I am glad you were not." She took a sip of her beer, picked up another book and read the back cover before replacing it. "Those weeks, I'd get so caught up in reading, Trent would complain I wasn't giving him enough help."

The moment the slip registered, her face fell. She turned and her shoulders tensed, as though she was waiting for me to jump all over her admission. The words *help with what* floated between us, but I let them pass. I was enjoying her company, and a full-court press would send her fleeing. There was an ease developing between us that we'd never had before.

Besides, the longer I had mulled over Trent's words about earning the truth, the more I'd wondered if he was right. I'd never given her the benefit of the doubt—never gave her the chance to explain. That night sent me spiraling. Not once had I asked Trent about her, about the drug trafficking, about how he had probably lied to them all. I'd been too busy blaming myself for not seeing the signs, for sleeping with Maggie, for letting Dan into the house. Every betrayal was mine to bear, intentional or not. Assigning some of the blame to her had seemed fair, then. She'd cheated Trent in more ways than one, hadn't she?

I was pretty sure now that I'd gotten it all wrong.

Maggie ran her hands along a few more books, avoiding eye contact.

"Our book club for two is a highlight for me." I leaned against the wall beside the closest bookcase.

From across the room, her lips quirked up into a smile. "Me too. I never knew what you were thinking about me. But I loved talking to you about books. You felt so much older—four years. A lifetime." Nostalgia tinged her expression. "I won't say wiser."

"I'll accept that." I drank my beer and relished the sight of her in this house, talking like we were friends instead of rivals. I'd thought about her a lot, too much, more than I could ever have expressed in words.

"And you approached things so differently," she said. "I was analytical, and you were straight from the gut, from the heart. You loved a book or hated it, and you had reasons why you felt that way."

"I'd never had anyone to talk to about books before." The light from the floor lamp cast a glow over the room, softening everything. Books had been a connection to my dad. Mom and Trent hadn't shared it, and my friends had been into dating, drinking, drugs, sports, but not reading.

"No?" Maggie glanced over her shoulder. "Sabrina isn't much of a reader?"

The warm feeling in my chest cooled. "She wasn't, no."

"But she is now?"

I shook my head. "Maggie, I—"

"I need another drink." She breezed past me and out the door before I had a chance to stop her.

I followed her to the kitchen. She paused in the middle of the room and then spied the beer cases by the back door. Slotting the bottle into an empty space, she grabbed another cold one from my new fridge. I liked the way she moved around my house with so much self-assurance. It was also possible she was already a bit drunk.

"You a lightweight?" I got myself another beer.

"What do you mean?" Maggie flicked the cap off her bottle and then tossed it in the trash.

"Not much of a drinker?"

She laughed and rolled the bottle in her hands. "I haven't drunk more than a glass of wine since..." She looked at the ceiling and squinted. "You wrote that asshole song about me and Trent."

Yeah, she was definitely a bit drunk. Granted, the beer was European, so it was probably stronger than she was used to drinking.

"Was that the night you wrote your little diatribe on my fan page?" I'd never thought too much about Maggie's message. Hadn't made a whole lot of sense, which I remembered thinking was odd. Before I could reply, the post had disappeared, and then when I'd tried searching for her username, there had been no results. Later on, I'd figured out she'd blocked me.

Color rose to her cheeks. "In fact, it was. I deleted the post as soon as I sobered up. So stupid. Why would you give a shit what I thought?" She let out a derisive laugh. "Trent was really pissed off at you, you know."

I did. One of a thousand fractures in our relationship. Felt like a lifetime ago, remembering how badly I'd wanted to punish her. For what? I couldn't even be sure anymore. I'd been ridiculous. Juvenile. Idiotic.

The idea I might have caused her pain made my insides twist. Hurting Trent hadn't occurred, either. Everything just felt so fucked-up. "I was an asshole."

With a grin, she raised her bottle. "I'll drink to that." She spun around the room in a slow circle. "I can't believe you live like this."

"I'm not here much." Most of my time was spent at the train station overseeing the renovations Joseph Goldtooth was completing.

"I want to disinfect, paint, and decorate this place. Being here might make me break out in hives."

"You sound like Kelvin." I tried to see the room through her eyes. Gray walls that should probably be white. Cupboards made of thin wood. The linoleum floor had some tears in places. The house didn't smell, though. Or at least, I didn't think it did.

As though she suddenly realized something, she narrowed her eyes. "Where are your beasts?"

"With Emily. Amir was here this week with your dad, and they bonded. He wanted to have a sleepover with them." I shrugged and picked at the label of my beer, focused on the task. "I dropped them off on my way to the studio."

When I glanced up, our gazes locked, and the room popped to life. Her hand was pressed against her pelvis. Was she holding her breath? We scanned each other's faces, and I resisted the urge to slide my beer onto the counter and sweep her into my arms to cart her upstairs. Trent had told me to stay away. I needed to fix my relationship with him before I tried to figure out if this feeling between us was more than rampant lust. My chances with Trent were numbered. Another screwup on my part and I might never get us back to where we'd once been.

"Do you want to see where the magic happens?"

"If that's an invitation to your bed, you're giving yourself a lot of credit."

I grinned. The temptation to tell her the credit was well-deserved rested on my tongue. She was drunk, but I wasn't sure she was drunk enough to joke about my sexual conquests. None of them mattered much with her standing so close, with this electrical current humming between us. Maggie's name ran through my veins like oxygen.

I held out my hand, and she slipped her free one into mine, glancing up under her lashes. Would she object if I led her upstairs? God, I was playing with fire by having her here.

She followed me down the hall into the front room where there were chairs of various shapes and sizes. Jim had also insisted on getting someplace for Amir to sit while we'd practiced for the concert. For anyone else, I might have balked at the suggestion that what I had wasn't good enough. But it was hard to say no to Maggie's dad.

Releasing her hand, I pulled the bench seat over to the keyboard and slid onto one side. I patted the seat beside me and glanced at her over my shoulder. Her focus shifted from me to the keyboard, to the bench, indecision written all over her.

"Just a sec." She disappeared down the hall. When she returned, she had another beer.

"You finish the last one?"

"Liquid courage."

At first, I thought it was a joke and almost laughed. But when she avoided eye contact, I realized she was serious. "What do you need courage for?" She slid onto the bench beside me, and our shoulders grazed.

"Being around you." She set her beer on the far side and placed her fingers on the keyboard. "Teach me, Mozart."

I leaned toward her, my lips grazing her temple. Her eyes fluttered closed at the contact.

"You don't use a guitar anymore?" Her eyes were still closed, and I wondered what she was thinking. I wanted to kiss her again—for real.

"Sometimes. Most of the time, this is better for composing. It can do a lot. Far more than any guitar." I didn't want to talk about songwriting; I wanted to talk about how the scent of vanilla surrounded me, even in my dreams.

She picked up her beer and chugged half of it.

Liquid courage, indeed.

"You're not going to throw up on me, are you? Or on the keyboard? It's actually quite expensive."

The bottle dangled from her fingers. "If I promise to make it to your bathroom, will you hold my hair back?"

"Holding your hair back is the gold standard, isn't it?" My hands itched to thread through the loose locks, test out the texture, draw her lips closer.

She nodded.

"Then I'd do it, even if you were sick all over my keyboard."

Her forehead fell against my shoulder, and I kissed the crown of her head. The air around us was dense with barely suppressed desire.

She sighed. "I always thought you *could* be sweet."

I put my arm around her, drawing her tight to my side. "But I never was?" Having her this close was a bad idea. The places my mind kept straying would snap the uneasy truce between Trent and me.

"No, you never were." She glanced up under her lashes. "I always thought it was kinda unfair you didn't believe me about me and Trent."

I scanned her face, searching for whatever she was leaving unsaid. "Why's that?"

"Trent slept with lots of girls before we were together. Probably while we were together too. I never asked. No one could find out. That's all I told him. I didn't want people to think I was a fool."

How could my brother choose another woman, any woman, over Maggie? The idea caused my stomach to twist in knots. I examined her claim, trying to figure out why the arrangement would have suited either of them. Why would she have agreed to let him sleep with other women? Why would Trent want to be with anyone but her? I hated the jealous surge zipping through at the thought of them together, at the notion that Trent would betray her.

"Didn't it seem weird to you?" she asked.

I frowned, not following her drunken logic.

She stretched up toward my ear and whispered, "Oh, Maggie, you're so fucking *tight*. You feel so *fucking* good."

My dick twitched at her words, the tone of her voice. That voice was designed for seduction. My heart raced, and my fingers tugged at the front of my pants which had grown painfully snug. The memory of being inside her was visceral. I'd relived it far too many times without her voice whispering those words in my ear. To go back to that moment, I didn't need to close my eyes because it had always lived too close to the surface. Now the two versions would be melded together, that voice, that memory, forever.

"Do you know how many times I've gotten off thinking about you saying those words in my ear when you slipped into me the first time?" she asked.

My mouth went dry. She wasn't going to be the only one getting off to the memory. "Maggie—"

"I thought you'd be able to tell, but you couldn't, could you?" Her voice was hushed in the room.

Like a key being fit into a lock, her meaning clicked. Up to then, I hadn't considered where this conversation was going. I searched her face in careful disbelief, trying to make sure I was reading her right. "You and Trent weren't..."

"We weren't together, not like that."

"So, I was..."

She slid off the bench, putting some distance between us. I rotated to follow her, wanted to reach for her. I couldn't decide if I was grateful or disappointed at her physical absence. Was I processing this right? I *hadn't* realized. How had I missed that truth? Of course, I'd been drunk. My brother was no virgin, and I'd believed they were dating for real. It never occurred to me for even a minute that they weren't sleeping together. The thought of them together had often made my stomach queasy with jealousy.

Tipping back the rest of her beer, she flopped into the beanbag chair near the windows on the other side of the room.

"Christ, Maggie. I'm sorry. I didn't know." The call about my brother's arrest had come right after, and everything had been blown to hell. "I don't remember exactly how I treated you—"

"After?" She laughed but it had no humor. "Pretty shitty. I mean, I didn't *blame* you. I didn't know what I was doing, so I thought it probably hadn't been very good for you."

I sucked in a sharp breath. "That's pretty fucking far from the truth." Our night had haunted me, been the source of many sleepless nights, and my inability to let go hadn't been because being with her wasn't good. The opposite. I'd *never* felt so much for someone in a moment like that before, and I'd been caught by surprise.

She ignored me and continued, "Then, you were so mad at me about Trent. I didn't know what he'd been doing any more than anyone else. Not a clue. Sometimes I look back and think, *God, Maggie, you were so dumb.*"

"None of us were at our finest." I'd led her to believe our night meant nothing. So callous. I wished I'd been a better man for her and for Trent. There was still time to be better. I just needed to figure out how.

"Got that right." She eyed me from her seat, contemplating something. "Can I watch you write a song?"

I stared at her for a beat, unsure. "We're done talking about the other thing?" I couldn't bring myself to say it.

"About how you stole my virginity? Yeah, I'm over it. Also, I'm drunk. There's not a snowball's chance in hell I would have said *any* of this otherwise. Can we play the game where we pretend this conversation didn't happen? It seems to be one of our favorites."

"I'm getting kinda tired of that one."

"Shame." Maggie pursed her lips.

"You going to be sick?"

"Nope, just thinking about what a bad idea this was."

I took in her furrowed brow, and the way her eyes kept shifting as she analyzed whatever was bouncing around her head. Overthinking what she'd said would end up driving a wedge between us. Whether or not it was smart, I didn't want distance between us, not anymore. I wanted to figure out a way to make amends.

"Watching me write a song would make you happy?"

Surprise registered on her face. "Can you? Does it work like that? Can you switch it on? I know it used to, or it seemed like it used to, work like that. But you said you don't write for yourself much anymore."

Her babbling was adorable. I smiled and wished she was close enough to touch. Already, I missed the connection, the intimacy that shrouded us as soon as we got close. Utterly astonishing how quickly my emotions were spiraling out of control.

Trent. I *had* to remember our deal.

Turning back to the keyboard, I played the opening notes of a song which had been dancing at the edges of my consciousness for the last week.

"That's pretty," she said.

"Bit of a ballad."

"A love song."

"Something like that." I played for a while, feeling it out and writing down notes when I thought I'd found something that worked.

"What's the secret?" she asked.

I glanced over my shoulder. She was flopped in the beanbag, her head tilted toward the ceiling. I loved the sight of her in this house, so relaxed and at ease...even if it had taken several beers to get her there. "To what?"

"Writing a good song."

I turned back to the keyboard and played the opening notes from a few of the songs I'd written recently. "For me, the music comes first. Different people write different ways. That's my way. If I can get the music to be something which wells up in people, makes it easy for them to get swept away, it'll sell." I chuckled. "Even if the lyrics make no sense."

"That's when you write for other people?"

"Yeah."

"What about your songs? The ones for you."

I paused my fingers on the keys, and I rolled my shoulders. This bench wasn't particularly comfortable for songwriting. It was meant for collaborating, for having someone sitting next to me, not across the room. "Beyond the music, at least if I'm writing for myself, it's the feeling behind the lyrics. When an emotion needs to come out. When the overflowing happens *in me*."

"Does that happen a lot?"

I kept my back to her when I admitted, "Almost never." Not anymore.

There was a heavy silence, and I was tempted to look at her. I wasn't sure if I'd like what I'd see on her face.

"It must make you sad," she whispered.

"Sometimes," I agreed. I played a few random notes which served no purpose other than to break the melancholy mood between us. "But I'm well paid either way."

If I kept busy enough, I didn't have time to think about what I was missing. Everything she'd said played in my mind while I continued to work out the melody. How did Trent and Maggie not hate me? I'd gotten so many things wrong for so long.

Lost in the rhythm of writing, it took me a while to realize she wasn't participating in the process. Frowning, I turned to see her passed out in the beanbag chair, curled up on her side. Her auburn hair partially covered her pale face. That familiar ache spread across my chest at the sight of her looking so peaceful and vulnerable. We hadn't talked about where she'd sleep, but after the amount she and I drank, there was no way she could easily get home.

I dropped my pencil and wandered over to crouch beside her. Would she rather I woke her? A better option was carrying her up to my bed. It was king-sized. We could sleep there comfortably without any danger of touching. I didn't want her to wake up tomorrow and think I took advantage of her. The changes taking place between us needed to be protected.

Unable to resist, I scooped her into my arms. She murmured something, her head resting on my shoulder. In my bedroom, I slid her under the covers. For a moment, I watched her, wishing it was okay to stay, but I couldn't risk her hating me again in the morning. With a sigh, I headed for the bedroom door.

"Grady?"

I halted and turned to lean against the frame. "What's up Maggie May?"

"Stay with me?"

Never had I been drawn to another person like I was with her. "You sure?"

"You owe me cuddles." She cracked open one eye.

Drunk Maggie's ability to cut to the truth made me chuckle. Circling the bed, I slid under the covers beside her. She rolled over to face me and then scooted closer to rest her head on my shoulder.

"Is this okay?" she whispered.

I extended my arm around her, tucking her tight to my side. Her leg came across mine, and our hands laced on my stomach. "More than okay."

Within minutes, her even breathing floated across my neck. As I listened to her, I stared at the ceiling, wondering which one of us would be let down first.

Chapter Twenty-One

Maggie

I stretched my arms over my head, feeling warm and relaxed. There was a dull ache behind my eyes, but I couldn't remember the last time I'd gotten such a restful night of sleep. The covers on my chest felt heavier than normal. With a frown, I opened my eyes to an unfamiliar ceiling.

I wasn't at home.

The night came flooding back.

Oh, no. No, no, no.

A wave of embarrassment swept over me, and I glanced to the side, praying the bed was empty. There, next to me, was Grady, still sleeping. He looked so peaceful and vulnerable my hand itched to stroke his face, run my thumb along the stubble. Maybe he'd be happy to realize I was still here instead of resigned at having to deal with me? Had I really passed out in his bed?

"Like what you see?" he mumbled before opening his eyes.

"I should go." I rolled away from him.

His hand latched onto my waist and dragged me back. "What if I want you to stay?"

I covered my face with one hand. "Not sure why you would. I made a total ass of myself last night."

"I've been making an ass of myself for years. It's nice you're finally catching up."

A soft laugh escaped. I appreciated he was trying to make this easier. "If only I'd known alcohol was the key factor in winning that race."

He chuckled, the sound warming my heart. "Oh, I think you've known for a while."

True. I had. Alcohol hadn't been my friend in a very long time. Last night, the devilish liquid had loosened my lips to an almost unbearable level. I closed my eyes and groaned.

"Aspirin?"

"Nope. A brain transplant would be more helpful."

"It wasn't that bad. There's nothing wrong with your brain."

"Okay, a memory transplant. We agreed to pretend last night didn't happen, right?"

"Uh," he said, tugging me closer to his chest. "Those words never left *my* lips."

"What time is it?" I tried to remember what day it was. Yesterday had been Wednesday, a little over two weeks until the concert. So that meant today was Thursday. My eyes snapped open again. "Seriously, what time is it?" I sat up, looking around the room. Of course, there wasn't a clock. Where had I put my phone?

He rolled away and grabbed his phone off the bedside table. "Ten."

"Ten in the morning?"

"You were still drunk at ten last night."

"Oh my God. I have to go. I should have opened the pharmacy two hours ago." I scooted off the bed, tucking my hair behind my ears and scanning the floor for my phone. "I'm never late. I'm so late. I've lost my phone!"

"It's downstairs on the table by the door."

My shoulders loosened at the realization that at least he knew where I'd dropped all my things. Turning on my heel, I dashed down the stairs. I stepped into my heels, grabbed my keys, purse, and phone from the small table and hurried out the door. My phone was lit up with missed calls and texts from clients and Dad.

As soon as I was in my SUV, I closed my eyes and made the call I was dreading. "Dad?"

"Maggie! We've been so worried. Are you okay? Tyler went out looking for you."

Heat flooded my cheeks. "I overslept." I drove away from Grady's house and headed toward my own place. I needed to change clothes before I showed up to work.

"Are you feeling okay? I came to the pharmacy to open up while Tyler and your mother tried to track you down."

Would Tyler know I'd spent the night at Grady's place? He hadn't knocked on his door, but my vehicle was in his driveway. How many other people would have noticed my SUV there all night? I tried to quiet the panic threatening to carve out a hole in my chest. So embarrassing. Grady would get backslaps and high fives. People would think he'd charmed me right out of my underwear.

Not long ago, Sabrina's car was the one in his driveway.

Foolish. I was a fool. We were locked in a mayoral race. What had I been thinking?

"I'm fine, Dad. I just overslept. I'll be there as soon as I'm dressed. Thank you for opening for me." I took a deep breath. "I'm sorry I worried you all."

"Glad you're okay. I'll see you when you get here. Love you, kiddo."

I had blushed at least a thousand times as I'd taken over the store from Dad. He hadn't asked too many questions when it became obvious the answers were going to be personal and embarrassing.

After lunch, the bell rang, drawing me away from my latest prescription refill. Sabrina stood in the doorway with a fuchsia skirt barely covering her ass and heels which looked better suited to a catwalk instead of a sidewalk. She tugged on the hem of her skirt before teetering over to the low counter.

Didn't Sabrina and I have an unspoken agreement that we didn't interact? Sabrina didn't use my pharmacy, probably going to one of the big-box stores on the outskirts of town, and I didn't get my nails done at Sabrina's shop, preferring one of the more upscale spas. Curious, and more than a little annoying, to have her here.

She passed me a prescription in silence. I didn't look at the paper but took in Sabrina's tiny smirk.

"When do you need this?" I asked. "Are you coming back later to get it?" Best case scenario, Sabrina would leave and perhaps come back on a day when Dad was here. Some game was being played, and I didn't understand the rules.

"The doctor said the sooner I take it, the more effective it'll be." She shrugged. "Whatever that means."

Reluctantly, I glanced down at the prescription. The Plan B pill. The emergency contraceptive was meant to prevent pregnancy after unprotected sex. My stomach rolled, but I hoped my expression remained neutral. Unprotected sex with who?

"Of course. Just a moment." I circled around the low counter to the taller one, turning my back on Sabrina. My hands shook as I doled out the prescription and printed off the information sheet. Stepping back down to the lower counter, I set the bag between us.

"Have you used this medication before?"

She shook her head. "I've always been with men who wanted kids." The hint of a smile played on her lips. "That's why I've got three."

I wanted to say, *Always, Sabrina? You're telling me you've only slept with three men?* Like so many things about Sabrina, her comment made no sense. But I refused to ask. Whether the guy was Grady or not, I didn't need to know. Gossip wasn't part of my job.

"Right, well." I turned the information sheet toward Sabrina and took her through all the important pieces. Each time I glanced at her, Sabrina wasn't looking at the sheet, she was studying me. "Do you have any questions?"

"No, no questions. I still might get pregnant, I guess. But at least I'll have tried. It's weird Grady doesn't want kids. He seemed to like them before. He's great with my other three."

My throat closed. He was great with Amir too. So much so I'd thought my ovaries might have been overproducing at the sight of him with my nephew. Apparently, I wasn't the only one. "Is there anything else I can help you with?" I rang up the charge and took Sabrina's money.

"No." She looked over my head and then around the store. "It's so great he's back. Isn't it? Feels like old times. Me and him, together. You know, we never could stay away from each other." She met my gaze. "If he hadn't gone on *Center Stage*, I bet we'd be married by now."

Each claim she spoke was like sharp knives in my side, forcing me to see what I'd let myself forget last night. "Do you think?" I floated around the counter, putting away products that didn't need to be put away.

"Oh yeah. He told me he'd never really gotten over me. Isn't that sweet?" Her tone was tinged with syrupy sweetness.

Something in her voice didn't feel truthful. My heart beat erratically at the thought of him saying those words to her. Despite the roller coaster of emotions inside, I'd learned a long time ago that letting people like Sabrina walk all over me wasn't good for my emotional well-being.

Meeting her gaze, I said, "That's wonderful Grady said that to you. I hope those words weren't in exchange for stealing my campaign signs." I tried to imitate Sabrina's overly sweet smile. "I didn't press charges, but I'm still considering my options. Video evidence and some eyewitnesses have been so helpful. It's amazing how many people have cameras at their houses now, isn't it?" I waited for a beat to let my words sink in. "Taking those signs was a felony. And since you took so many, the crime would be considered a state felony and you'd spend some time in jail." Sabrina's face went bright red and then deathly pale. "I want you to think about that next time you decide to sashay in here to talk to me about Grady."

Sabrina gaped. "You wouldn't put a mother in prison."

"Sometimes," I said in a conspiratorial whisper. "I think your kids might be better off with their dads. Don't you?"

With a gasp, Sabrina rocked back on her heel and stomped toward the door.

"Good luck with your Plan B. Next time, remember not to be silly and get him to wrap his willy."

Sabrina glared over her shoulder before pushing open the pharmacy door with torrential force. Good thing no one was walking on the sidewalk in either direction.

As soon as the door clicked closed, I went behind the tall desk and sank into a chair. *Grady and Sabrina. Sabrina and Grady.* Their names spun around my head in a haze. He'd been my first, and I'd admitted that to him last night. Regret ate at me. He hadn't known, had no clue. Back then, I'd been another conquest. He'd probably laughed about me with his buddies. Some lovesick high school girl.

At the time, the extreme emotional distance he put between us from that night onward, had hurt. I'd been convinced that how I felt about him, the way he made me feel, how important it had been that he was my first, outweighed his indifference. The choice had been mine, and I refused to regret it.

Maybe I would have been okay if he'd stuck with indifference, but his attitude toward me had morphed into hate. A hate so specific, so all-consuming, I'd inspired multiple songs on his first album. I'd recognized parts of me, dissected, even if no one else had.

Now, I'd been a fool for him again. Back with Sabrina? The proof had stood right in front of me, and I'd heard it with my own ears. *Come back to bed. It's too early.* The words had been seared into my brain that morning.

So, what had last night been about? My brain was muddled.

The last few times we'd been around each other, he'd been kind and open. The burst of hate and the surge of lust had been replaced with other, more complicated feelings. I genuinely liked him. How did I reconcile the Grady I'd come to know with the one who'd have unprotected sex with Sabrina and then suggest she take Plan B? I ran my hands down my face in frustration. Both versions of him couldn't exist, could they?

Maybe he'd decided if he couldn't win the mayoral race, he'd make a fool of me instead. Emily's words of caution played in my head. Any affair would make him look like a sex god and me like some weak, simpering woman who couldn't resist him. Especially true if people believed he was also involved with Sabrina.

I wasn't going to let him make a fool out of me. Walls would go back up between us, and

I wouldn't let him tear them down this time.

Chapter Twenty-Two
Grady

Maggie had been avoiding me. At first, I'd figured she was embarrassed, and she'd get over it. Maybe she was busy between the pharmacy and her mayor duties? Watching her talk to some of the setup crew from across the stage, I realized I'd been fooling myself. She hadn't looked at me once since I'd arrived. I'd crossed her line of sight several times since I'd started helping Trent organize the back of the stage, and you'd think I was invisible.

"Quit fucking slacking," Trent muttered as he moved another prop into a box labeled with someone's name back behind the stage. "And stop looking at her like that."

"Looking at who? Like what?" I grabbed a stool and moved it to a far corner. Almost every man who'd agreed to strip wanted a prop of some sort or a costume, sometimes both. Locating and organizing each item into labeled boxes had been left to me and Trent. Costumes we couldn't find were being pieced together by Tyler from his secondhand shop and his creative brain. With only one week to go, we needed to figure out what we still needed to track down.

"Maggie. Like she kicked your puppy." Trent flipped a drumstick around his hand repeatedly and then dropped it into another box.

The analogy was pretty apt. I would probably feel bewildered and angry if she did that too. "She's avoiding me."

"I swear to God," Trent said, anger tinging his voice. He threw a fake microphone into a box, and it bounced back out. "If you try anything—"

"Did you have feelings for her?" I asked in a burst of annoyance. "At least answer me that. This ex-boyfriend overly protective vibe doesn't seem too legit from what she's told me." I crossed my arms and glared at Trent.

A hint of red bloomed on Trent's cheeks. "You don't know anything."

"Then fucking tell me!" Even if Maggie believed she and Trent had been nothing, it didn't mean my brother believed it.

"There are lots of women in Little Falls who'd be happy to look after you. Leave her be."

"It's not that simple." I *couldn't* do what Trent wanted. She was in my blood. Going a day without seeing her was torture. A week had passed since she'd slept in my bed. I walked past the pharmacy with the dogs daily, sometimes more than once, so I could look in the window, catch a glimpse of a white coat, auburn hair. I invented reasons to go into city hall in case she might be out of her office wandering around. All week, I'd been obsessed with the lingering smell on the pillow next to mine.

At some point, I might have been able to stop these feelings, but I was past the point of no return. There was no longer anything rational about how much I wanted Maggie Sullivan.

"Yeah, it is that simple. You turn to one of those clipboard women who follow you around town organizing all your campaign things, and you offer to screw them. Probably ninety percent of them would go for it. Those are good odds." Trent frowned. "You don't pay them, right? I don't know how this political shit works. But I know you can get in trouble for fucking your employees. Maybe go to Utica instead and play some songs. Being that close to someone famous is like a panty remover, isn't it?"

I gritted my teeth. Nothing Trent had said was wrong, exactly. Didn't make me feel like a very good person. The guy Trent described wasn't someone I wanted to be. I scooped up a clipboard from the pile of props between them. "Forget I asked."

When I looked up, Trent was examining me, eyes narrowed. "Fuck me. You actually give a shit." His jaw tensed. "Of all the women, why her?"

I decided it was probably time I told the truth, or at least some of it. "It's been her for a while. I can't help it. I tried. Believe me, I tried."

Trent stared at me in silence for a beat, maybe gauging my sincerity. "I'm not saying shit until I get a chance to talk to Maggie." He ran the palm of his hand over his shorn head. "I'm not convinced you deserve to know."

"I let you down. I let Maggie down. I'm not going to do it again."

"The song that got you all famous and rich really hurt her. I always felt like there was something I was missing. Why would someone like Maggie care if you got all the facts wrong?"

I couldn't meet Trent's gaze. With a flick of my wrist, I flipped the clipboard in my hands. Over my shoulder, I glimpsed Maggie, and that familiar ache rose to the surface.

"Unless there was something going on between you two I didn't know about," Trent said.

I focused on the pile of things between us. "We'd better get back to it."

Trent's hands landed on my chest, propelling me backward. "You fucking asshole." He pushed me again, and I stumbled, but I didn't fight back. If Trent hit me, I deserved the blow.

Maggie's heels clicked along the wooden surface of the stage as Trent pushed me a third time.

"Tell me the truth. Be honest with *me*, Grady."

"Trent!" Maggie stretched between us, arms out, as we eyed each other. "What are you doing?" she hissed.

Normally, Maggie stepping between me and Trent would have been amusing. Did she think she could stop us if we decided to go at it? I didn't want her to get hurt, and I didn't want her around if I admitted we'd slept together. She didn't deserve Trent's wrath or any embarrassment in front of the crew setting up. Trent glared at me, and I glared right back, willing him to look away first.

"I don't know what's going on here, but the show is next week. I need both of you healthy and not in various shades of black and blue." She looked between us. "Do you want to tell me what's going on?"

"No." My gaze bored into my brother. Trent's protective instinct where Maggie was concerned had better extend to this moment too. I'd take a swing at him if he accused her of anything in front of other people.

"No," Trent agreed. "Grady needs another job. I've got this one covered." He stalked across the stage to the pile of items on the floor.

With a sigh, I started to walk away. She snagged my forearm and then released it as though the contact scalded her.

"Wait," she said.

My heart rate wasn't quite back to normal from my almost-confrontation with Trent, and her touch caused another spike. Maybe I should have told Trent everything, gotten it over with. Deep down, I knew now wasn't the right time, especially if we were going to exchange more than words.

"What was that all about?"

I peered at her, trying to read her motives. "Have you been avoiding me?"

She waved a dismissive hand. "Forget it. Whatever is going on between you and him is none of my business."

One of the stagehands wandered past and grinned at her, pausing beside us. "We're still on for tomorrow night?"

She returned his smile, but it looked forced, as though she was gathering enthusiasm from down in her toes. "Looking forward to it."

"I'll have to think about what I can come up with to top our first date." He winked and then continued past us.

Being punched in the kidney would have been better than hearing their exchange. "A date?"

"People do that." She avoided eye contact. "They don't just screw each other and walk away, leaving the other person to clean up the mess."

"Oh." My gut twisted. "So, you're screwing him too. Good to know." I cocked my head. "Probably more information than I needed, but the visual is crystal clear." I circled the side of my head with my index finger. "I have a great imagination where you're concerned. And some highlight reels to back that up."

She shoved me. Hard. Or tried to. The look on her face told me she'd put all her weight behind it. But unlike Trent, she didn't have much luck in making me move.

I leaned down, so my mouth almost touched her ear. "If you wanted to put your hands on me, I can think of better places for them."

"You're gross. You repulse me," her voice cracked.

"Come on, Maggie. At least say something you believe."

Meeting my gaze, she hissed, "I *hate* you."

My stomach clenched at her words, but the tears brimming in her eyes evaporated any desire to fight. She stormed past me and down the stairs of the stage before I could collect myself.

When I turned to follow her, Trent called, "Leave her the fuck alone, Grady."

But Trent didn't stop me. Good enough. I wasn't letting her flee from me, crying.

I'd made her cry. I'd made her fucking cry.

Rushing around the building, I searched the places being used for the concert. As a last resort, I put my ear to the door of the women's bathroom. If she wasn't in there, she'd gone home.

Propping it open with my foot, there was a line of stalls, sinks, and a counter in a dark gray. From the furthest stall, I heard a distinct sniff. "Maggie?"

"It's the women's bathroom."

Grabbing the Cleaning in Progress sign from the back of the door, I stuck it on the front and let the door fall shut behind me.

Quickly, I scanned the other stalls for feet. We were alone. "I'm sorry, Maggie May. I was being an asshole, and I'm just... I'm sorry."

"Go away. Just go away."

Outside her locked stall, I leaned my shoulder against it. "Come out and talk to me."

She sniffed, and her voice was thick when she said, "I have nothing to say to you."

"You hate me, and you're not going to talk to me?" A cold sweat broke out across my chest. How had we gone from her sleeping in my bed to this much anger when we hadn't even spoken this week?

She'd gone on a fucking date.

I was in the twilight zone—the only logical explanation. What the hell had I done?

"Hate sums it up." Her voice was garbled. Was she still crying? The toilet paper holder rumbled, and the sound of her blowing her nose echoed throughout the bathroom.

I almost fell into the stall when the lock snapped back, and she opened the door.

She tapped underneath her eyes with her fingertips as she strolled past me. Looking in the mirror, she pumped soap into her hands. As she washed them, I stood behind her, unsure in the face of her calm indifference.

"Why were you crying?" Our gazes met in the mirror.

"Because you were being an asshole. For some reason, there's a tiny part of me that thought I might care for half a second. Turns out," she said with a shrug, "I don't."

When she turned to leave, I stepped in front of her. "I'm sorry."

She didn't look up and instead tried to step again.

I stepped with her. "I'm sorry." The tightness in my chest was like a vice, reminding me how much I cared, how sorry I was. Whatever I'd done wrong, I wanted to put it right. I'd apologize a thousand times, a million times, as many times as it took to get her to look at me the way she had in my bed when she'd asked me to stay.

Her brown eyes scanned my face. "I don't forgive you." Her voice was thick with unshed tears.

Putting my hands under her armpits, I lifted her onto the counter and smoothed back her hair. Her gray skirt rode up her thighs. "I'm sorry." I leaned forward and kissed her forehead. The apology wasn't just for whatever I'd done this time—it was for everything I'd done in the past too.

She sighed, her eyes closed. "I don't forgive you," she whispered.

Cupping her face in my hands, I kissed her temple and murmured in her ear. "I'm sorry." I was sorry for so many things. I wasn't even sure I needed the truth anymore. If whatever had happened would rip us apart, I didn't want to know any of it.

A tear slipped down her cheek, and I scooped it up with my thumb.

"I don't want to feel this way anymore," Maggie choked out.

"Me neither," I admitted, kissing her cheek.

"Being around you hurts."

"I don't want to hurt you." I found her earlobe with my lips, nibbling.

She sucked in a sharp breath, her hands sliding along my shoulders. Silence lapsed between us as I feathered kisses across her skin, reveling in the softness, letting me worship her.

"Did you sleep with Sabrina?"

Her words broke the bubble of longing encircling us. For a moment, I didn't move, processing her words. Frowning, I rocked back on my heel, examining her face. She was serious. "No. Not since I've been back."

"Why was she at your house?"

Grimacing, I hesitated and laced my fingers with Maggie's, my thumb caressing the back of her hand. "I made a poor choice and let her spend the night."

"But you didn't sleep with her."

I shook my head, meeting her gaze. "I slept beside her. We didn't have sex."

"Like with me."

"Not even close. I *wanted* you there. I *let* her stay. Might not seem like a big difference, but it is."

She searched my face, and I held her gaze each time our eyes made contact. "She came to my pharmacy for emergency contraceptive." She pinched the bridge of her nose. "I shouldn't have said that. What is wrong with me?"

"Emergency contraceptive?" With my fingers, I tucked stray strands of Maggie's hair behind her ear. God, I wanted to kiss her. The kind of kiss which only led in one direction.

"That was unprofessional, I shouldn't have—"

"Probably for the best. She doesn't need more kids." Her lips were a soft coral color. What would they taste like? Strawberry lip balm the last time.

She smacked me in the chest, forcing my gaze from her lips to her eyes. "She implied the pill was because of *you*, and I shouldn't even be telling you this because it's wrong, and I don't know what's gotten into me..."

My eyes widened, realization dawning. I framed Maggie's face with my hands. "*That's* why you're so upset?"

"She said you'd never gotten over her. You said that to her."

"Over *her*?" I scoffed. "I never said that. I wouldn't have. It's not true. I was over her probably even when I was with her in high school. Makes me sound like a shitty person. But that's the truth."

"So, you and her..."

"Aren't together. We're nothing. After she took your signs and lied to me, I talked to her and then stopped taking her calls. I haven't spoken to her in weeks." I drew her closer, and she went willingly, wrapping her arms around me. "Feel better?"

She nodded against my chest, and when she sniffed, I tipped her chin up. "You're crying. You're not feeling better."

"I am." Her voice was thick with unshed tears.

"Why the waterworks?" I passed her a tissue from the box on the counter and studied her.

"I hate that I care."

"About me?"

"About any of this. I thought you were making a fool out of me." Her voice hitched on the word fool, and she dabbed at her eyes.

"Hey." I kissed her forehead. "Hey."

More tears streaked down her face.

"The only thing I want to make you is happy. That's it. Nothing else matters to me anymore."

When she looked up, the last of my resolve crumbled and fell away. I couldn't remember why being with her was a bad idea, why I'd ever wanted to be anywhere else. Her tear-stained cheeks tugged at the strings of my heart, strumming a song only she could play. Her fingertips grazed my cheek as though she was testing out the contact. Under her lashes, her dark eyes flicked to my lips, and it was all the invitation I needed. Lowering my head, my lips grazed hers, tentative at first, teasing. Would she kiss me back or slap me for trying?

But when I angled my head to deepen the kiss, she sighed into my mouth, and her fingers tangled into my hair, pulling me closer, deeper. I spanned her back with my arms, using my palm to draw her pelvis tight against mine. Then I slid my hand up her thigh, my fingertips just under the edge of her skirt.

Her back arched, and the kiss between us became more insistent, less controlled. Nothing else mattered but the feel of her pressed against me, her breasts skimming my chest, her fingers twisting in my hair, her tongue slipping in and out of my mouth in sync with my own.

I groaned and yanked her forward a little more, needing her to feel how much I wanted this, wanted her. I ached with wanting.

"Grady," she gasped, breaking the kiss.

I found the hollow of her neck, grazed my teeth against her earlobe and discovered the most sensitive spots, the ones that made her wiggle against me. I could do this all day, touch her, kiss her, taste her. Exploring her was like arriving in a new country, and I wanted to light up all the paths, explore each one, map her body with my hands, then my tongue.

The door creaked. But I ignored the sound. Whoever it was would go away. We were busy. There was a sign on the door.

"I fucking knew you wouldn't listen to me," Trent said.

My pulse stuttered to a stop, and I broke off the kiss. I rested my head against hers for a beat, collecting myself, before turning to face Trent.

Fists clenched, Trent was inside the bathroom door, glaring at me, not acknowledging Maggie at all.

Brothers first.

Chapter Twenty-Three

Maggie

I gathered my sweater tighter. Grady angled himself so I could barely make out Trent's form around his shoulders. I closed my eyes, trying to gather my wits. Why had I let him kiss me? Not just kiss but devour me. If Trent hadn't come in, how far would we have gone? My body was throbbing, primed for him, desperate for more contact. Half of me wanted to drag him into the stall, pretend Trent wasn't there at all. Why had Trent come in here? Did no one care that it was the ladies' room?

"I fucking told you to leave her alone," Trent said.

At that, I hopped down from the counter and straightened my skirt. I wasn't a kid anymore. Beside Grady, I put my hand on the small of his back. Unlike last time, we didn't need to bear this tryst alone, in isolation.

"I know why you're saying that to him, but whether I'm with him or not is my choice." I kept my voice even, reasoned. None of us needed this situation to escalate. I'd already been afraid they'd come to blows on the stage earlier. The tension in the room was palpable. When they were younger, they'd be laughing and joking one minute, hurling insults and wrestling the next. Good-natured, if a little violent. That wasn't the vibe in the room now.

"He didn't see you." Trent flicked his hand in Grady's direction and eyed his brother with disgust.

His meaning was clear, but I was glad he didn't spell it out in front of his brother. I hoped Grady never knew all the tears I'd cried over his stupid song, how I'd sat across from Trent when I'd visited him in jail and refused to tell him why his brother's opinion mattered so much. "We can't go back. We all did dumb things, sometimes for the right reasons, sometimes for the wrong ones. You can't deny it."

Trent looked away, pushing his hands deep into the pockets of his jeans. "I never wanted you to get hurt."

"And I didn't want you to go to jail." I sighed. "Choices don't always lead to the consequences we expect."

"I'm still in the fucking dark," Grady muttered, slipping his arm around my waist and securing me to his side.

I met Trent's gaze for a beat, and he shook his head, almost imperceptible. With a sigh, I eased away from Grady. "I need to talk to Trent."

Grady's eyes were filled with indecision. Was he as worried as I was? This truce between us, this new understanding, was fragile, a thin glass that might crack or smash at any moment.

"Are you sure?" he asked.

"Yeah," I said.

"We should talk about this later."

Trent shifted his feet by the door and let out a loud sigh. A small smile played at the edges of my mouth, and then I nodded. Grady's hand trailed along my waist before he walked past Trent to the door.

"I asked for one thing," Trent muttered.

"It was the one thing I couldn't give you." He opened the door and left.

"What was that all about?" I asked.

"My brother's been trying to get in your pants for weeks. Maybe he already has, what do I know? He's never going to stay, Maggie. Some offer will come along from somewhere, and he won't be able to turn it down. He's not the guy who stays when things get tough. I don't want you hurt again."

"I'm not a seventeen-year-old girl anymore."

"You've had a thing for him since then?" He frowned and leaned his hand against the bathroom wall.

"Is that so hard to believe?"

He looked thoughtful for a moment. "Nah, I guess it's not. You two were always following each other around the house talking about books, and other shit I couldn't be bothered with. Is that why you were so upset about his song?"

"Mostly, sort of. Grady and I—we—*connected* before you got arrested."

"Is that some sort of Urban Dictionary thing? Did Gwyneth Paltrow use that phrase on her stupid-ass website in relation to some guy she hooked up with?" He raised his eyebrows and made air quotes. "Connected? The kind of connected I walked in on?"

I flushed, and he shook his head. "I want to tell him the truth."

Time stretched between us. "If he made a move on you when he thought you were my girlfriend, he doesn't deserve to know shit."

"I wasn't your girlfriend. We were more like best friends. I shouldn't have to explain this to you."

"And that's why I'm not mad at *you*. *He* didn't know."

"You're going to argue principles with me after the lies we were living?"

He stared at me and crossed his arms.

"Why are you really so mad at him? You didn't even know about us." A huff of frustration spewed out. I was tired of keeping my feelings bottled up. I wanted Grady to know everything, to clear the air. Even while arguing with Trent, my lips tingled from the memory of his kiss.

He wouldn't meet my gaze. "After our dad died, it was just me and Grady. Mom worked too much trying to keep us all together under one roof. You know that. It's why I didn't want her to know. She'd blame herself." He pressed the heels of his hands into his forehead and sighed. "Me and Grady caused shit, stirred up trouble, got into everything together. And then, I don't know, even before I got arrested, we'd drifted. I didn't tell him about the meth. He didn't tell me about the music."

"You're mad at him because the two of you aren't close?" I said the words slowly, trying to figure out if I was putting the situation together correctly.

"I guess? I don't fucking know. But I'm angry. I'm really fucking angry at him."

"He let you down."

"In ways I didn't even know or understand."

I ran my hand up Trent's arm and cupped his cheek. "He's here and he wants to make things right. He's not the same guy he was. He's figuring himself out."

"That's not what it looked like when I walked in here."

"You worry about you, and I'll worry about me. Unless there's something you're not telling me, something you've never told me, the only relationship you need to worry about is yours with Grady. You don't need to take care of me. I grew up."

He chuckled and took my hand between his. His gaze searched my face. I hoped I was showing him whatever he needed to see.

"I'll tell him."

"When?" I crossed my arms. Would Grady blame me for what had happened with Trent? Probably not. But a part of me still blamed myself. What I'd said to Trent was true. Choices had consequences. Sometimes those were unexpected. I hoped telling Grady didn't blow up in our faces.

"Tonight. I'll tell him tonight." He gave me a half smile. "That'll make you happy?"

A small laugh escaped. "Who knows? But I think it's time we found out."

Chapter Twenty-Four

Grady

I rubbed my eyes with the heels of my hands and then flipped the pencil around, using the eraser to rub out the final six notes. Placing my fingers on the keyboard, I played the last third of the song another time, trying to figure out exactly how I wanted it to close.

Hopeful.

I wanted the song to sound hopeful, but I kept ending on notes which were desperate. With a snap of my wrist, I threw the pencil across the room, and I squeezed the sides of my head in frustration. What was wrong?

I couldn't concentrate. Every time I tried to get the ending notes right, my mind veered to Trent and Maggie. What had they talked about after I'd left? Would Trent ever speak to me again? I hadn't been able to keep my promise to him. My feelings for Maggie were too big, too hard to control. I should never have agreed to stay away from her.

Hite and Zeus whined and stirred off their beds in the front hallway. My phone rested beside me, and I checked the time. Just before midnight. Wasn't too late for a walk, but I wasn't sure getting out would clear my head. Talking to either Maggie or Trent might help, but it also might tip the scales in a direction I didn't like. I wanted to make things right with Trent. I wanted to be with Maggie. Could I do both? Was either of them possible?

A sharp knock sounded on the door, and the dogs circled in excitement. They rarely barked when I was home, but I'd heard from the neighbors that wasn't the case when I was away. Pushing back the ergonomic chair I used when I was digging into a song, I crossed to the front door with a frown. With one eye pressed to the peephole and the dogs on either side, I couldn't decide if I was relieved or surprised.

I opened the door. "Trent. It's late."

"I had to have a few drinks before I showed up. Then I had to fucking walk from the restaurant downtown. I don't want to be here, but I promised her I'd come."

"Come in." I ushered him into the living room with the assortment of mismatched chairs.

Trent stood in the entryway of the room and looked around, his gaze finally landing on me. "What a fucking dump. Has Maggie been here? She hasn't dropped off some paint and scrub brushes? A matching couch and chair?"

A smile threatened at how accurately he knew her. "That sounds about right. But no, she hasn't done any of that yet."

We stood across from each other with our hands in our pockets. The awkwardness was overwhelming. How had we grown this far apart? There'd been a time when Trent would have shown up with a six-pack and a heap of stories about women he knew, things he'd done, notches he'd made on his bedpost. We would have laughed and joked around. Equal in our debauchery.

Before Maggie.

Part of the reason we had drifted apart was because of how I had felt about her. At first my desire for her had been bearable, but by the time we kissed, by the time Trent was arrested, I'd been bordering on an obsession. Having Trent talk about her, hearing about her as a conquest, had been something I couldn't handle. How could I have admitted my fixation with Maggie to Trent? As far as I'd known, she was Trent's girlfriend.

"Are we doing this or what?" Trent gestured to the chairs.

"I'll start." I didn't bother to sit while Trent sank into the recliner in the corner. "I know I got things wrong about you and Maggie even if I don't know exactly how wrong." I scratched the back of my head. "But I think I owe you an explanation for my distance, for being a shitty fucking brother the last six years."

"Ten years."

I took a deep breath. "Ten years."

"All right, I'm listening." He eased back into the recliner, skepticism burning bright.

Summoning my courage, I said, "I'm the one who let Dan into the house. I'm the reason he got so much evidence on you."

"No, you're not." Trent didn't miss a beat.

"I am. I put the sequence of events together. Too late, sure. But the timeline matches when he came to the house and I was there. I was in the middle of writing a song in the garage, and I didn't pay attention to what he was doing."

"Dickhead Dan had been in and out of our house all week. I'd told him where the spare key was one time when we were drunk. Maybe you let him in, and maybe he got some of the notebooks and other shit that night that he hadn't gotten before. But he would have gotten it either way. I was too confident. Left too much in my room not locked up."

I sank into the beanbag chair and stared at Trent. "I ran into Dan the other day at the gas station and he—he made it seem like I was at fault."

Trent shrugged. "Like I said, maybe he did get some of it that night. But he was there a lot after he got flipped by the cops trying to cover his ass and bury mine. I asked around. Lots of people talking once it had been six years and I was out of jail. Nothing for people to lose anymore. Dan was a snake, and I didn't see it. How could you?"

"Christ, Trent. I've blamed myself for years."

"You shoulda talked to me, shoulda asked me." He sat forward and put his forearms on his knees. "But here's the thing. Even if that *is* what happened, what happened to me still wouldn't be your fault. Did you know I was cooking meth? That I'd built myself a little empire? Did you let him in knowing he was going to nail me in court?"

I shook my head and dragged a hand down my face. "Not a fucking clue. In hindsight, I should have known something was up."

"You sound like Maggie." Trent smirked and scanned my face. A few beats passed between us. "She the other reason we're not tight anymore?"

Easing deeper into my chair, I drew one foot across my knee and gave a curt nod without looking at Trent. "I think so, yeah."

"Were you fucking her when she was supposedly my girlfriend?"

Trent's gaze was on me like hot coals. "The night you got arrested." I shifted uncomfortably in my chair. "I could give you all kinds of excuses—I was drunk; she told me you two weren't really together; I'd been half in love with her for months. But none of them make what happened better, and I know that."

"I've been trying to wrap my head around this one." He made a whirling motion beside his temple with his index finger. "I knew you liked her. It was clear as fucking day to me from the way you looked at her and teased her. I'm not sure she saw it, not really. But I did. And I could have told you what was going on between her and me, let you two work out whatever was brewing." Trent ran a hand along the top of his head and didn't meet my gaze. "I've been doing a lot of thinking about this the last few weeks 'cause I've been so angry with you. Just"—he made a filling-up gesture near his chest—"so mad."

"I let you down."

"Yeah, you did." He hesitated. "Being with Maggie was the only time in *my* life where I had something you wanted. You know? Mom was all happy I'd finally brought home a good girl, and you were impressed too. I could see it. The first time you and Maggie went off about some book you'd read, I was proud she was my girlfriend, and you found her interesting."

He swallowed, not sure what to say. He had found her interesting, fascinating, and that fixation had doomed them.

"I guess if I'm honest, me not telling you was as much of a problem as you not telling me. You get what I'm saying?"

"Why *didn't* you tell me?" I didn't know what I would have done with the information. Would it have made me bolder sooner? Or would I have stayed away at all costs? What I'd felt for her had consumed me, and at twenty-one, I probably wouldn't have had the sense to keep my distance.

"You were the smart one. Even now, you make fun of me for being a high school senior for two years."

A wave of shame washed over me. My teasing had bothered Trent? It *had* taken him two years. I figured it was because Trent didn't apply himself. Who wouldn't give their brother a hassle when the only thing holding them back was laziness and a lack of drive?

"The one thing Mom was always on me about was getting my diploma. And I couldn't get it, not without help. I thought I wasn't smart enough."

"I don't know why you'd think that," I said. "I *never* thought that."

Trent shrugged. Silence coated the room for a moment. "I couldn't read."

With a frown, I rocked forward in my chair. "Fuck off." I reached back into my memories, trying to recall when I'd seen Trent read something, anything when we'd been younger. "Doesn't make any sense." He must have read something, right? People couldn't get along in life without being able to read.

"Couldn't read past a grade two level as a senior in high school. The guidance counselor caught on toward the start of my second attempt at graduating."

He couldn't read? The revelation was stunning. "How does Maggie fit in?" Had she done his schoolwork for him? Maggie as a cheater didn't sit right. I knew her now, really knew her. She wouldn't have done Trent's work for him.

"I was pissed about the guidance counselor telling me I'd probably never get all my credits or pass my exams if I couldn't read properly. I went to a party and got really fucking drunk. She was there, end of her junior year, getting bullied by this group of junior fuckwits. They'd been making her life miserable for a while, I guess. She hadn't told anyone. Tried to handle the abuse on her own, and it was getting a lot worse. She's one of the best people I know, but it took her a long time to stand up for herself."

"You stepped in and helped her?" I rubbed the center of my chest. People had been hurting Maggie? A few short months ago, I'd been so hell-bent on making her pay for all of my wrong perceptions. Ludicrous. Pay for what? Being a good person? It was a miracle she was still talking to me at all.

He laughed. "Not quite. She stormed out of the party, and I followed her out and gave her a cigarette."

"She smoked it?"

With an unsteady chuckle, Trent nodded. "She did. And we talked. The drinking loosened my lips. Soon enough, I was handing her a crazy scheme. As her pretend boyfriend, she could win all those other shits around." He grinned. "Or I'd do it for her." He rammed his fist into his other hand. "I never thought she'd agree to be my real girlfriend. A girl like her? So fucking smart? Her and Emily—smartest girls in that school." He raised his eyebrows at me.

I wasn't sure what to say. Was I surprised when Trent brought Maggie home? Yeah. But eventually, she and Trent had seemed so comfortable together I'd never questioned their connection.

"In exchange for my social skills, all she had to do was teach me how to read." He flung out his hands. "And the rest is history. The first time Maggie came over, we were going to tell you and Mom the truth, or at least how she was helping me with school stuff. But Mom was so excited Maggie was smart and pretty and funny. A girl like her was *mine*. I convinced Maggie to keep the secret from everyone."

"She helped you learn how to read." I didn't know how I'd missed that Trent's reading was so far behind. We'd been very different—still were—so I always figured Trent didn't like reading, not that he couldn't.

"I wouldn't have graduated without her. She taught me how to read, and she helped me with any other subject when I got in trouble." He sighed and ran a hand along the top of his head. "Including chemistry."

"You gotta be fucking kidding me. Your meth business?"

"She didn't *know* she was helping me. I got the other guys working with me to write out the problems we were having like it was some kinda riddle or math problem the teacher gave me or something like that. Then I'd ask her about those things like the question was an assignment or I'd overheard someone else talking about the problem. She's so fucking smart she'd come up with some answer off the top of her head. Every time I dug myself into a hole that year, she got me out."

I digested Trent's revelations in silence. She'd unknowingly helped Trent with his meth operation; she'd knowingly taught him how to read. "She couldn't get you out of your biggest hole."

"Her mom was my lawyer for a while. I don't know if you remember. But then the cops were sniffing around Maggie, trying to drag her into the mess, and her mom backed out. Couldn't blame her. God, I was so fucking worried I'd put her in danger."

None of this sounded familiar. Our mother had gone into debt because of a lawyer change. But I'd never thought much about the reason. When I'd gotten famous, I'd given her enough money to pay off all her debts. Had I been so far gone, so far up my own ass I hadn't realized any of the intricacies of Trent's case?

"Maggie has been nothing but good to me," Trent continued. "So, when she asked me to come tonight and tell you the truth, I came." He gave me a hard stare. "But we're not square yet, you and me. I don't know how to feel about what went down between you and her. And I don't know how we get back to a good place."

"I would have helped you to read," I said, my voice thick. "If you'd asked, I would have helped you."

"Yeah, sure. But you would have teased me. That's just how it was with us. And then Mom would have found out. I didn't want her to know. After Dad died, she worked so hard to keep the house and us together. She would have thought she let me down. And I didn't want her stressing I wouldn't get that damn piece of paper." Trent gave a frustrated sigh. "I knew I had a problem, and I never asked her for help. That's on me."

"How did you—I don't understand how you even got to senior year?"

He grinned. "Every girl I was ever with *except* for Maggie did my homework for me, did my assignments for me, got me through school."

"And Maggie?" Jealousy stirred again, even though I knew the emotion was irrational. Any mention of her with someone else made me uneasy, even when it was fake.

"Made me do all my own fucking work. Often while she was trying to read some book so she could make you look bad at Sunday dinner." He laughed and then grinned.

We stared at each other across the room for a few minutes. I wasn't sure what to do with everything Trent was revealing. I'd gotten the situation so wrong, and my attitude had cost all of us so much. But our misunderstanding had also led me to take a chance on my music career, to find the courage to go after something else I loved. I didn't regret that part, but I sure as hell regretted the rest.

"I should have told you," Trent said. "Looking back, it's clear who Maggie should have been with."

"We were young, and I was stupid. So fucking stupid. But I definitely had some pretty strong feelings for her. And then, I don't know, it seemed impossible you'd built the whole meth thing alone."

"'Cause she was so smart."

"And you'd never been particularly motivated to do *anything* before."

Trent barked out a laugh. "Yeah, I guess. You were out hustling for odd jobs and trying to get Mom extra money, and most of the time I got fired from whatever job I was working." He stared at me for a moment. "I know I'm not supposed to say this, but I liked running the business. Made me feel smart which made me work harder. Obviously, that didn't turn out so good for me."

"How are you doing now?" I eased out of my chair and crossed to the large windows.

"All right. They diagnosed me with severe dyslexia in prison. Bright side, I guess, so I get why I have trouble with reading. I have my apartment. I have the apprenticeship Maggie got me." He grimaced. "And I wanna figure out how you and I get square with each other." He rubbed his thighs. "Some text messages, random phone calls when you've had a few drinks, and like six letters while I was in prison doesn't cut it."

The fact he could count all those things, and I didn't think it was far off, was proof we'd let things go too far. "I want that, too, but I—" I struggled to find the right words.

"Still got it bad for Maggie?" Trent gave me a wry smile.

I looked up at the ceiling and then met Trent's gaze. "Basically, yeah."

"Like she told me, she's not a kid anymore. If she wants to take a chance on you, that's up to her. I never had a right to say shit about what she wanted. I just hate the idea of her getting hurt. I think we've both done enough of that."

I sighed and rubbed my hands down my face. "I've been such a fucking idiot. I don't know how either of you could be around me when I came home. So sure of myself, and I didn't know anything."

"You're my brother. I've been mad at you for years. But you're still my brother. Having you home has been… good. I think it'll be even better once we put all this shit behind us." Trent eyed me. "Why has Maggie put up with you? 'Cause she's got more goodness in her than you and me combined." He let out a huff of annoyance. "Or else she's got it just as bad for you. And if that's the case, God help you both."

The thought that Maggie might feel anything close to the vise wrapped around my heart was oddly comforting. "I've really been missing out." I looked down at my feet. "You grew up smarter than me about people."

Trent grinned. "I was people smart, and you were book smart." His smile faded a little. "And the mandatory counseling in prison helped me sort out some of my other issues. It was helpful."

"Prison?"

"Nah, you fuckwit. Counseling. Want me to spell it out for you?"

The reply was on the tip of my tongue, but I swallowed it.

"You gotta say it. I set you up."

A hint of a grin threatened. "*Can* you spell it?"

His phone beeped, and Trent tugged it out of his pocket. "I could spell it, but I won't bore you. I gotta go."

"You can't drive."

"Thank you, Captain Obvious. Lila and Emily are coming to pick me up." His fingers flew across his phone in response to whoever had messaged him. He glanced up. "Lila says Maggie's still up. They went to see her after we all had a late dinner while I came here. You know, if you care." His lips twisted trying to hold back his smile.

"At two a.m. on a weeknight? Has she been drinking again?" I frowned at my phone. I wasn't sure what I expected to find. Was Maggie waiting for me?

There was a knock on the door, and Trent waved me off when I moved to answer it. The dogs circled him. "It's Lila. I got it. Listen. Don't fuck things up with Maggie, okay?"

"I won't," I said, following Trent. I was going to try really hard not to.

When Trent opened the door, he grinned at Lila, and Emily waved from the driver's seat of the car. As soon as she reversed out of the driveway, I let the dogs out in the backyard and grabbed my coat. I hoped I wouldn't be returning to my own place tonight.

Chapter Twenty-Five

Maggie

I paced from the living room to the kitchen and back again. Ginger wound herself between my feet every time I stood still long enough for her to try to claim my attention. Lila and Emily had left almost an hour ago. Grady's house was across town, but it wouldn't have taken long for him to come over after Trent left—*if* he was coming.

I checked the clock. Tomorrow was another workday. Staying awake until two-thirty on the chance he might appear was ridiculous. With a sigh, I flipped the lock on the front door and turned out the porch light. As I turned away, a knock sounded.

Grady?

Heart pounding, I checked the peephole and then tried to center myself. My blood seemed to have rushed out of my vital organs, and I felt like I was going to faint. One way or another, things would change when I opened the door.

Either he wouldn't be able to forgive me for the lies, or we'd move past what happened to something else. The *something else* catapulted my pulse. I wanted him, even if the wanting made me uneasy. He was a gamble, a wild card.

I smoothed my T-shirt and skirt and took a deep breath. When I swung back the door, our gazes connected. My stomach fluttered.

"I am so fucking sorry," he said, his tone anguished. "I was so completely and utterly wrong."

The sincerity in his gaze mixed with his words was enough for the last film of my protective shell to disintegrate. All rational thought vanished, and I launched myself at him, throwing my arms around his neck. He stumbled back, chuckling as our lips connected. I wound my legs around his waist, and he carried me into the house, our lips in constant contact. One of his hands cupped my ass while his other hand buried into my loose hair, keeping it off my face as our kiss deepened. With impressive balance, he kicked the door closed.

My stomach kept dropping and recovering as though I was riding big roller-coaster hills. Maybe I was finally safe to want these things, to feel these things.

He set me on the kitchen counter and wrapped his arms around my back. Our tongues slid over each other, dueling and retreating. I'd spar like this forever. Kissing, kissing, more kissing. Nothing would ever be enough. Years, lifetimes, that's what I needed to come close to getting my fill.

His hand slid up my inner thigh, and a shiver raced through, goose bumps rising. I snuck my hands under his shirt, gliding up his back, taking his T-shirt with me. He helped me get it over his head, his lips only leaving mine long enough for the shirt to fly through the air and land with a soft thud by the fridge. I loved the firmness of his muscles flexing under my hands as we kissed. How had I resisted this long? From now on, I'd touch him at every opportunity, for any reason.

He tugged me closer to the edge of the counter, my skirt riding up. He slid it farther up my thighs, and I shivered, awareness humming. He groaned into my mouth when his fingers skimmed my most sensitive place. By now he'd know how much I wanted this, how eager I'd been for this to happen. I squirmed, keen for his hand to explore, to feel his calloused fingers rubbing against the building ache.

Lifting me off the counter, his hands spanned my ass as he walked us toward the hallway, my legs around his waist, clinging on.

"Left," I said, guiding him to my room between kisses.

He tossed me onto the bed, and the plush white duvet enveloped me. I laughed until he followed me down, his lips back, each part he touched catching fire, burning down all my defenses. I never wanted this feeling to end. Happiness and desire were the most potent combination. His hands traced my rib cage while his lips trailed along my neck. In one quick movement, he had my shirt over my head.

When I landed back on the pillow, he searched my expression for a beat. "All signs point to a 'yes.' But I wanna be sure. I need to be sure. I don't ever want to do anything to hurt you again."

"That's a pretty high bar," I whispered, tracing his face with my fingertips. There'd always been something in his eyes which had drawn me in. The light in them felt like it shone just for me. Beyond the brown eyes, he was my idea of perfect. Would I really get to keep him for more than one night?

A half smile touched his lips. "It's good to have a goal." A crease formed between his eyebrows. "I don't want you to regret this. Ever. And I'm so fucking sorry that might have been what happened last time."

I lifted my hips to meet him, and I drew his mouth toward mine. "I want you. I want this. No regrets. I promise." I'd spent all night after I parted with Trent thinking about the ways this night could go once Grady knew the truth. Having him pressed up against me, as tight as two bodies could be, had been the best-case scenario. I wanted him maybe even more than I'd wanted him thirteen years ago.

"I was hoping you'd say that," he said against my lips. "Considering you're not wearing any underwear."

I laughed. "Did you like that?" I ran my hands to the edge of his jeans, my fingers tracing the waistband, dancing along his abs. "I wasn't sure if I'd need to win you over."

He sucked in a sharp breath before burying his head in my neck. "Consider me won. This is quite possibly the best *apology accepted* I've ever received."

"I'll keep that in mind," I breathed as I arched against him. I unsnapped the button on his jeans, pulled down the zipper, and pushed them off his hips. It had been far too long since he'd been as close as I wanted.

He drew back from me enough to let his jeans fall to the floor before crawling across the bed. I loved the mix of tenderness and desire I saw on his face just before our lips met. When I rose up to deepen the kiss, he unsnapped my bra, drawing it down my arms before tossing it aside. His hand massaged my breast, and then his thumb teased my taut nipple.

I ran my hands through his brown hair and then along his biceps. Nothing about this felt quite real yet, but the longer I touched him, the more he was coming into focus, embedding in my consciousness.

He kissed his way down my body, stopping to worship each breast, swirling his tongue across each mound before grazing the nipple with his teeth. Each time he did it, a shock wave surged through me.

After Grady, every other guy had paled in comparison. My sister had been right—I'd test-driven a few makes and models of men, longing for whatever I'd felt with Grady. I'd never found the same level of attraction, of desperation, as if it was impossible to be close enough.

If being with Grady was what drowning felt like, I never wanted to breathe again.

My body was reaching full volume, and I wasn't sure I'd last to the main event. I was tuned, one plucked string away from crying out, begging him to take me. He slid my skirt down, and it landed on the wood floor with a soft thump. With my legs spread, his fingers slid along my folds, and I clutched onto his shoulders. God, why did this feel so good? When his fingers eased inside, we sighed into each other's mouths. Desire surged through me.

"Fuck, Maggie," he groaned, his fingers sliding in and out of me while his thumb massaged my clit. Bending his head, his teeth grazed my nipple. Fireworks went off behind my eyelids, and it was impossible to focus on anything but the sensations he was creating. My hands tangled in his hair, and my breathing was so labored I felt like I was running a marathon.

Reaching between us, I slipped my hand into his boxer briefs and gripped his shaft, stroking over the tip and back to the base. I wanted him to need this release as much as I did. He sucked in a sharp breath, and when he breathed out, hot beside my ear, I moaned.

"Please, Grady." I wiggled and panted, not even sure what I needed. How long could I go without losing myself completely? Each stroke of his fingers, each circle of his thumb drove me closer to the edge. "I want you. I want to feel you inside me."

His lips returned to mine, and he settled between my legs. Deepening the kiss, his hips rocked against me, his underwear the only barrier between us. When he slid along, I gripped his ass.

"Please." I kept him tight. The friction was delicious, maddening.

When he moved back, I tried to grab for him. He chuckled and reached over the bed for his pants, extracting a foil wrapper.

"Gotta look after you." He planted a quick kiss on my lips.

"Can I?" I nodded to the wrapper and rose on my knees.

His gaze connected with mine, and he handed the condom over.

I pushed down his boxers and stroked the length of him while our tongues tangled. I ripped open the package and rolled the condom on, savoring the long, hard feel of him under my fingers. Lightly, I pushed on his chest, and he fell back, pulling me with him, our lips connecting as I straddled him.

His hands were on my hips, guiding me, until his tip was poised at my entrance. My hands were splayed on his chest as I eased over him. Mentally, I traced his face, one which had haunted my dreams for years, one I never thought I'd see filled with desire for me again. He'd always been the one, or at least the idea of him had held me back, stopped me from giving myself to anyone else. Scary and thrilling in equal measure.

His eyes were so dark with desire they almost looked black. He drew me to him, so our foreheads touched. I rocked back, loving the connection, the skin-to-skin contact.

"God, you feel so *fucking* good," he whispered, his voice strained.

I'd dreamed about doing this, gotten off at the memory of him saying those words. No one else had inspired the emotion threatening to burst forth. I was close to coming apart, but whatever was swelling in my chest was so much bigger, scarier, and all-consuming than an orgasm. Instead of examining the feeling, I ground down on him, and he steadied my hips, helping me to get the resistance I needed.

"Say it again," I whispered before kissing him.

"You feel so *fucking* good," his voice was raspy with need as he arched his back, plunging in deeper, securing me tighter.

It didn't take long for us to get into a rhythm, and each movement took us both closer to the edge.

"Oh God. Grady." I braced against his chest, so close my arms quivered.

One of his hands drew me to him, our tongues intertwining as I ground down on him one last time before toppling over the edge. His name was a moan on my lips. His arms circled my back, keeping me pressed tightly to him while he maintained the rhythm, seeking his own release.

"Fuck, Maggie. I'm coming." As he let out a long groan of satisfaction, I kissed him, swallowing his cries of pleasure while he pulsed inside me.

I yawned into his neck as I snuggled into his side. The words which had threatened to burst out of me while we'd been locked together were circling. I needed to talk about something else before they snuck out. "So, you and Trent are okay?"

"We're working on okay." He smoothed down my hair. "I made a lot of mistakes."

"We all did."

"I'm not sure you did." He kissed the top of my head.

"Uh, how about how I inadvertently made Trent's drug operation bigger and better?" My role in his drug empire and his subsequent arrest had bothered me for a long time. Would Trent have gotten far enough to interest the police without me?

"It's that bigger, better brain of yours."

I pinched his nipple, and he laughed, stilling my hand. The sound warmed my heart. Grady had felt like a lost cause, someone who would never bother to discover the truth, content to think the worst. He was starting to prove me wrong.

"Honestly, if I think about what he did, it'll piss me off. You could have gotten arrested because of him," Grady said, an edge to his voice.

"There were lots of people in town who did get arrested." I sometimes saw a few of them who'd come back to town after they'd been released from jail. Or I'd run into their parents at functions. I'd never asked any of them to vote for me for mayor. My involvement hadn't been intentional, but I *had* been involved.

Since I'd become mayor, I'd been trying my best to find sustainable employment for the residents of Little Falls. Maybe if Trent and his friends had better choices in high school, they wouldn't have turned to making and selling drugs.

"Yeah, I remember," Grady said, his tone quiet. "That whole thing is part of the reason I bailed from the town when I could. First my dad died when I was a kid, then my brother operates a meth ring. People don't get over that shit."

I traced patterns on his chest and considered his words. "Should they?"

"Trent couldn't read. The system failed him. I—" Grady's voice cracked, and he cleared his throat. "I failed him."

"I didn't fare much better. I taught him to read, but I also helped him build a meth empire." I took a deep breath. After years of analyzing the situation, I didn't have an easy answer to the guilt—mine or his. My solution had been to repay the community I'd let down through ignorance. Trent had served his time, and now he was trying to help rebuild the town through this fundraiser.

Grady squeezed me tighter and sighed into my hair. "He made his choices." He kissed my temple. "And I made mine. None of them were good. I don't know how we're here right now after the way I treated you."

I didn't want the heaviness of the past weighing down our whole night. We'd found our way to this moment. For years, I'd wished for a moment like this with him—no secrets, no more anger. "I find you irresistible," I said in a teasing tone. "It must be a pheromone thing."

That wasn't exactly a joke. There had to be something chemical in the connection, a reason we were so drawn to each other. My first time with him had resulted in my first orgasm. Imagine my surprise when I figured out orgasms didn't happen every time or with every guy.

Eventually, I'd discovered the thought of Grady could get the job done whether I was with a partner or I was solo.

Inevitably, once the orgasm passed, shame would settle in its place. Why did it need to be him, his image, when he'd treated me so unjustly? My desire for him wasn't normal.

"You like the way I smell?"

"Basically, yeah. There are worse things."

He laughed, the sound rumbling through his chest to my ear. I draped across him more fully, staking my claim. Part of me still couldn't believe we were together like this. I'd wanted him—at one time more than I'd wanted anything else in the world—but I hadn't allowed myself to dwell on desire once he turned on me. Wishing he'd come to believe me had been on the same level as reversing time to see the first moon landing in person. Impossible.

"And the smell is linked to what?" he asked.

"Genetics."

"Meaning?" He ran his hand up and down my arm which was laid across his chest. "We'd have exceptional children?"

My breath caught in my throat. "Something like that."

"Hmm…" he murmured, kissing the top of my head. "Wanna play a game with me?"

Relaxing at the change in subject, I grinned. "Hide the sausage again?"

"Oh, I'm sure we'll be hiding that again. Maybe in a few different places."

A laugh escaped at his implication, and I hit his chest. He rolled us so he stared down at me. The depth of tenderness in his face surprised me.

How had I gotten lucky enough to have this moment? My insides unfurled and bloomed, reaching for the sunlight in his gaze.

"That's not the game I want to play right now." His lips brushed mine. I wrapped my arms around his neck and yanked him closer.

"All right, player," I said when we broke apart. "How do we play?"

"It's called This or That. I give you two scenarios, and you tell me your preference."

"How do you win?"

He laughed and braced himself on his forearms above me. "There's no winning. It's a getting-to-know-you game. I used to play it all the time when I was traveling."

I rolled my eyes. "Oh, please, play it with me too."

With his fingers, he pushed a few strands of my hair back and shook his head. "So many assumptions in your response."

When I made a grumbling noise, he kissed both of my cheeks before brushing his lips across mine again. "I played it on buses, trains, airplanes, in bars... not in beds. Feel better?"

I framed his face, and I stared into his deep brown eyes. "I don't *ever* want to feel like just some girl again." The pain I'd felt when I was younger wasn't something I could relive. No one had known about what had happened, my feelings, the way he'd treated me with such indifference. I wouldn't be that girl again. Above all else, I needed to be important this time.

His expression softened, and he nuzzled the hollow of my neck. "You were *never* just some girl," his rough voice whispered in my ear.

My stomach fluttered, back on the roller coaster at the crest of a hill. "I wish I'd known." My heart ached for the seventeen-year-old girl who'd cried herself to sleep over Grady, who'd thought maybe she'd gotten the connection between them all wrong. I'd pushed all those memories down, buried them as deep as the experience itself, told myself nothing with him had been as good as I remembered. Instead, I poisoned my thoughts until any reminder of him made me angry, not sad.

"I swear to you I'll never make you feel that way again."

His clear gaze said he meant it, and I wanted to believe him. At the back of my mind, Trent's words about Grady getting an offer he couldn't refuse, a better offer, played. The reminder wasn't loud enough to make me regret what just happened, but I couldn't let the words welling up inside out. Last time I'd laid myself bare, I'd been burned. Once was a mistake, twice was foolishness. And this time there'd be more witnesses to any foolish mistakes.

"This or That," I whispered. "I'm going to win."

He placed a quick kiss on my lips. I loved that he couldn't stop doing it, that it seemed instinctual. How many times had I wished for this when I was a kid?

He rolled to his side, and he cradled his head with his palm. "Always so competitive."

"Give it to me," I said with a wicked grin.

"Oh, I'll give it to you. But first we play." He kissed my shoulder. "Big house or nice car?"

"House." I narrowed my eyes. "Please tell me you're not a car guy in this scenario?"

"I think I might be a 'neither.' You've seen my house and truck, right?"

I laughed and leaned over for another kiss. "Okay, again."

"Cat or dog?"

With a grimace, I admitted, "Dog."

"Poor Ginger." He shook his head in mock horror. "Are you serious?"

"I work long hours at the pharmacy. I couldn't handle a dog." I shrugged. "I'd never get rid of Ginger, but I would love a dog." I flopped back onto the pillow.

"How about two?"

"I don't know how to answer that question." I grinned. "Would I have to pick which of your beasts I like better?" Tapping my lips with my finger, I pretended to think.

"Let's not get carried away." His lips twitched. The amusement left his face, and he propped himself onto his elbow before leaning down to kiss me.

"One more," I murmured against his lips. "And then I propose we race to a different kind of finish."

He kissed me deeply, his hand running up my side, and I turned to face him, putting us chest to chest. When he drew back, he said, "Travel the world or live in Little Falls forever?"

I frowned and hesitated. "Is there a fence in this scenario? Kinda both?"

He traced my face with his finger. "You gotta choose."

I searched for the right answer in his posture. The truth was neither, and it was both. "Travel the world. You?"

A hint of a smile touched his face. "I'd travel the world with you. Or I'd stay in Little Falls with you."

With my index finger, I poked him in the ribs. "I had to choose. You have to choose." I held my breath while he seemed to think, our gazes locked.

"I choose you. Wherever you are, that's where I want to be."

A fizzy sensation ran through my veins at the sincerity in his expression. My words, three of them, were stuck in the back of my throat. I shoved them deeper, trying to pretend they didn't exist, afraid that they did. Saying anything close to what I thought I might feel was reckless. After how badly things ended last time, it was hard to fully trust him, trust us.

I wiped my negative thoughts from my head. I had lots of time later to stew about things I couldn't predict or change. Grady Castillo was in my bed, and I didn't want to waste a moment. Last time, I didn't know it would be years and so many hurt feelings before I got this again.

I slid my hand into his hair and tugged him closer. "The next time you say that," I whispered in his ear, "I want you inside me."

He drew my leg over his and kissed my neck. "As far as requests go, that one might be my favorite."

This time, we went slower, discovering each other all over again, in ways we hadn't ever done before. Later, when I came apart in his arms, I was sure I'd never loved anyone more.

Chapter Twenty-Six

Grady

I left Maggie's house when she headed to the pharmacy for the day. I couldn't remember the last time I'd been so at peace, so sure I was on the right path. As soon as I got home, I went straight to my keyboard. Creativity rushed out of me like a burst water main. By the time the clock struck noon, I'd written three songs, and I was loath to leave the house.

I was supposed to meet Kelvin for lunch in half an hour. Tearing myself from the songwriting process would take a monumental effort. Years had gone by without this blast of creative power, and I'd forgotten how addictive it was. When the words and melody flowed like this, a song wasn't a puzzle or challenge to be solved; instead the rush was impossible to stop. I had to get the song out. Writing wasn't a choice.

Kelvin texted me when I was fifteen minutes late. Probably a record in patience for him. Clearing the message from my screen, I opened the dental office door. The glaring whiteness made me pause for a moment to let my eyes adjust. Kelvin liked the simplicity and cleanliness of the all-white space. I found the shade boring and too cold.

On Thursdays, Kelvin ordered in lunch while we went over various town procedures and bylaws, so I didn't look like a complete idiot in the election debates. Maggie hadn't so much as hinted at a debate, but Kelvin was sure we'd have one.

After last night, I wasn't sure I wanted to do any of this mayor malarkey. I wanted to sink into Maggie again and again and forget the rest of the world existed.

All the other employees were already gone for lunch. Kelvin ran a tight ship, and they were rarely behind schedule.

"You lock the front door?" He shuffled some papers behind his desk.

"You bet." I sank into the chair opposite Kelvin. There was a sandwich on the glossy white surface, and I unwrapped it to take a large bite. I'd been so busy writing I'd forgotten to eat.

"Rumor has it Maggie Sullivan's SUV was parked overnight at your house last week. I wasn't going to say anything, but someone called me this morning to say they'd seen your truck parked at her place last night… and this morning."

I stopped chewing and eyed Kelvin across the desk. "So?" The whole town could mind their own damn business. Any gossip about me, I could handle, but the idea of people talking about her raised my hackles. This was the part of small towns I hated. Everyone thought everyone's business was their own.

"Wondered if there was anything you wanted to tell your campaign manager?"

I wiped my mouth with a napkin and then took a long swig from the reusable water bottle Kelvin kept for me. "It's none of my campaign manager's business. But if my *friend* wants to ask, I *might* tell him."

"I think I could probably guess." With his hand, Kelvin made a circling gesture around me. "There's some interesting energy coming off you today. Keyed up, but also weirdly relaxed. You finally forgive yourself for having the hots for your brother's girl and tell her how you feel?"

Taking another bite of my sandwich, I contemplated Kelvin's words. He might not have gotten what happened right, but he'd gotten pretty damn close. "I had it all wrong about her, about her and Trent. About a lot of things."

Kelvin's lips twitched. "You don't say."

"Yeah, yeah. You told me right from the get-go I was being a dick for no reason."

"Can we agree I should run your life? Would have saved you a few months of wasted effort in the wrong place."

"No," I said, holding up a finger, "no, we cannot agree on that. You got this mayor campaign to run. Which, honestly, I'm thinking I should just abandon."

"Seems about right." He grabbed his own sandwich and unwrapped it. "You tell Maggie yet?"

A flush heated my cheeks. "Uh," I said. "Not yet. I've been mulling it over."

"Since when? This morning?"

"I spent all morning writing. No time for thinking about this mayor gig." I flipped a coin across the back of my fingers, my sandwich done. My mind was divided in three: Maggie, a half-written song, and this conversation. "The last week or so, I guess I've been unsure of what I'm doing. I didn't go into the election for the right reasons."

Kelvin chewed and appeared to be considering something. I swigged my water and waited. What wisdom would Kelvin impart? Our friendship worked because we didn't think alike in the slightest. It was good for getting a new perspective—at least it was good when I was ready for that conversation.

"What do you think Maggie will say when you admit that?"

I was mid-drink when the implication hit, and my water slid down the wrong spot. I coughed, almost choking on the realization. "She'll think I'm an asshole."

"You've caused her a lot of extra time, effort, and money to then throw up your hands and say, *you win*."

I couldn't help the smirk that rose to my lips. She'd won a few times last night, and she hadn't complained.

"The mayor job might not matter to you, but I *guarantee* it matters to her," Kelvin said, dousing my memories.

Whether or not Maggie realized it, I'd run for mayor to fuck with her, and that made me the shittiest person alive. "You think I should see the election through to the end."

"You want to back off some campaign things, fine. But backing out? If I was her, I'd be pissed. It's a hollow victory for her after the grief you've caused."

Kelvin was right. She liked to win. So did I. But I'd never really wanted to win the mayor race. Maggie should hate me, but I was so fucking glad she didn't.

Now, I had a bigger and better prize in mind than being mayor of Little Falls.

"Maybe I can float removing myself past her and see how she reacts," I suggested.

"Be prepared for cannon fire to sink that ship." He replied to a text on his phone and then sighed. "Trent okay with you and Maggie getting together?"

"As long as I don't fuck things up, I think 'okay' is the right word there."

"So, you're sticking around here no matter what?"

"That's the plan." I nodded. "Write some songs, walk my dogs, organize fundraisers. A jack of all trades if you will."

"That'll be enough for you?"

The lure of the producer gigs my agent had dangled rose to the surface. The way I felt about songwriting today, I couldn't imagine writing ever getting old. But I knew that the well could dry up or I might long for something different. Becoming a producer was the right career step for someone like me, who embraced variety.

The only constant in my life since leaving Little Falls almost eleven years ago had been change. I'd never stopped moving. In the last twenty-four hours, Maggie and I had worked out our differences, and I hadn't had a chance to really dig into Kelvin's question. Would being in Little Falls be enough for me? I'd meant what I'd said to her. Wherever she was, that's where I wanted to be.

"I don't know," I admitted. "But I want to try."

Last night, after she'd fallen asleep draped across me, I'd wondered if I'd been running from my feelings for her the whole time. Perhaps I'd spent the last twelve years restless *for her*, not for places or experiences. Her absence had made me roam. All along what I'd been seeking had been in Little Falls; I just hadn't known how to get her back, get this feeling back. Honestly, I'd never even considered it a possibility.

"Well," Kelvin said, tossing his bunched-up sandwich wrapper toward the garbage can and missing. "Until you get whatever this is worked out with her, I say we keep the campaign running in a low-key mode. Status quo."

"Yeah, okay. You got some shit for me to take home to read?"

Kelvin pointed to a stack on the edge of the desk. "You still going to do that? Low-key means we're kinda giving up without giving up."

With a shrug, I rose and grabbed the stapled stack from the corner of the desk. "I figure one way or another, I'm going to end up involved in mayor business. Maybe I can actually be helpful to Maggie going forward instead of the thorn in her side."

"You're growing up, man. Right before my eyes. Course, I always knew if anyone could make a guy strive for their potential, it was Maggie." Kelvin walked me to the front door.

The truth of his statement struck me. Maggie's influence had been tremendous for both me and Trent. She'd taught Trent to read and had inadvertently given him the confidence to build a business. An illegal one, sure, but it had been something Trent had felt proud of. Now, she was inspiring me to write again. She was the key to this flood of creativity. If I managed to string together enough songs, this album would be the opposite of my first one. Where the first had been a diatribe against her, this one would be a love letter.

God, I'd been such a fool.

As I walked toward her pharmacy, I was determined to deliver a coffee and gauge how she was feeling about last night. There was no doubt in my mind about how I felt.

My phone vibrated, yanking me back to the present. My agent. For once, I didn't want to avoid his call. I hoped Jack would ask the dreaded question. Maybe I'd tell him I'd started writing for myself again. The dam had broken. Not that Jack knew there'd been a dam.

"Jack," I said. "Got work for me?"

"I do." His self-conscious laugh traveled through the phone line. "Not sure how you're going to feel about it. The label wants you to come to LA for a producing gig. It'll be a trial of sorts. You prove yourself here, you'll get more work, more opportunities."

I stopped walking. The leaves on the trees had turned from green to shades of gold, red, and brown, and were falling around me. October was a pretty time of year to be in Little Falls, which was one of the things I'd missed on my travels. There was nothing quite like the fall colors. I'd pulled this seasonal vibe into a song this morning—the reddish-brown leaves reminded me of Maggie's hair. "When do they want an answer?"

"As soon as possible. Don't they always. You can take a week or so, if you want. I can hold them off that long. You'd probably need to be in LA for six months to a year, start to finish. You do well, maybe another stretch after."

"Six months to a year," I repeated as the wind whipped past, stirring the leaves at my feet. My gut reaction was to say 'yes.' I hadn't been back to LA since my *Center Stage* days, and it'd be fun to explore the city again. For once in my life, I couldn't think only of myself. "I'll need the whole week. I gotta talk this through with a few people."

"Putting down roots already?" There was surprise in his voice. "This about the mayor thing?"

"Something like that." I ran my free hand through my hair and walked toward Maggie's pharmacy. Before I said anything to her, I needed to know where I stood on this opportunity. Today didn't feel like a good day for life-changing decisions.

If Maggie was as tired as I was, she'd appreciate a coffee and not the added complication. We were sorting out our differences, and whether I wanted this job wasn't a discussion we needed to have today. Maybe not for a few days. We needed time before I sprung this on her. The job complicated everything, but I couldn't deny that I wanted it.

"Look, Grady. I'm not trying to pressure you, but I want you to understand exactly what this offer means. You'll have a lot more freedom and control down the road. More money, obviously. Your old label is the only one asking. If you turn this down, I can't guarantee you'll get this opportunity again anytime soon, maybe never."

"Nothing in New York?" At least there, I'd be a few hours from Little Falls by car rather than across the country by plane.

"I asked. I knew you'd prefer it there. That's not what they're offering. Not right now."

I sighed and looked up at the clear blue sky. The wind came up the street in a whoosh, rustling the leaves and reminding me that winter was coming. I hadn't missed the deluge of New York snow. The changing weather also meant the election was coming to a close. At the start of November, the town would be headed to the polls. This offer would give me a better reason to withdraw.

"I'll let you know as soon as I get my head wrapped around exactly what this means," I said.

"No more than a week."

After I ended the call, I leaned against the wall outside Kathy's Café where I normally bought coffee. I was torn about whether to mention the offer to Maggie. If I didn't take the job, it wouldn't matter, anyway. Unless I decided I wanted to go, I didn't need to tell her about the opportunity. What we had last night felt fragile, and I'd do anything to keep from breaking it.

I grabbed two coffees and wandered to her storefront. Inside, the pharmacy was bustling. I balanced the coffees on top of each other and opened the door. She looked up from the customer in front of her and grinned.

Relief rushed through me. No regrets. I hadn't realized I'd been a little on edge after talking to Kelvin. She'd been in such a hurry this morning

I hadn't been able to assess her feelings, and my two conversations had thrown me off a bit.

I waded through the customers shopping and waiting for their prescriptions to reach her at the counter. I slid the steaming hot coffee across.

The memory of the night before seemed to play between us, thickening the air with things we wouldn't say here. I couldn't wait to get her alone. Just my luck, her place was busy today. I'd passed by lots of times when there had been hardly anyone around. As I'd written this morning, various scenarios had sprung to mind. Setting her on the high counter at the back, pushing up her skirt, and giving her a reminder of how good it was between us had been high on my list of priorities for today. I'd have to save that one for another day.

She picked up the coffee and smelled it, smiling across the top. "My favorite hazelnut. I could get used to this."

I returned her smile, loving the ease between us. "Me too."

All thoughts of going to LA vanished from my head.

Chapter Twenty-Seven

Maggie

Sundays were my favorite. It was the only day of the week when the pharmacy was closed, and I didn't work a twelve-to-fourteen-hour day. Rolling onto my side, I plucked a berry from the bowl balanced on Grady's taut stomach. His arm was behind his head, and he was chewing, contemplating something, grabbing berries from the bowl at regular intervals.

He'd made me pancakes and brought them to bed. Waking up with him and not having to rush out of the house was an added bonus. Next Saturday was the Small Town Saviors extravaganza, and I had to meet Lila later to go over what still needed to be done. Despite all the extra work, I felt good about how much money we were projected to raise.

"What are you thinking about?" I ran my hand through his hair, toying with the ends, twisting them between my fingers.

He grinned but didn't look at me. "You. Always you. You in this bed. You on the kitchen counter. You on the floor. You on a table. Want me to keep going?"

I laughed and kissed his cheek. He wrapped one arm around me, popped the last berry into his mouth, and slid the bowl onto the nightstand. Having him here made me giddy. Champagne in my veins.

All these intense emotions scared the shit out of me.

When I let myself dwell on the fear, it doused all joy, so I covered my anxiety, shoved it down, pretended the fear wasn't there. Everything bubbling up made me realize how much I'd kept other men at arm's length. Emily had been right in that regard. Grady got under my skin, burrowed deep, and nestled next to my heart, stopping anyone else from getting too close.

Grady rolled us so he was propped above. He scanned my face and seemed to debate something.

"Out with it," I said with a grin.

"I get why Trent wanted your help, but I'm not too clear on what you got out of the deal. A bunch of lies. Almost dragged into a court case. I guess it just hasn't quite added up."

Uneasiness settled over me at his questions. I should have expected it. I squirmed under him and pushed his shoulder, so he shifted to the side. He propped his head on his hand while he looked down at me. I could feel his eyes on me, but I couldn't return the contact.

"You were so loyal to him, even when it might have been better to walk away."

"What did Trent tell you?" Trent guarded my heart and secrets in the same way he guarded his own.

Grady narrowed his eyes and brushed a strand of hair out of my face. "Why does that matter?"

"No point in repeating things you already know." I glanced at him before looking at the ceiling. "What'd he tell you?"

He stroked my cheek with his thumb. "Maggie May, you're being evasive. I'm an open book, and you're still shut tight."

Was he an open book? I hadn't pushed him on anything he'd said or done the last few days. As far as I knew, he'd spent time at his house writing. I didn't know who he was writing for since he'd told me he couldn't write for himself anymore.

"Are you an open book, Grady? There's nothing going on I should know about?" Our first night together he'd been open and honest, but the next day there'd been a crack, a fracture. He'd brought me the coffee at the pharmacy and then when he'd stayed over that night, a piece of him had seemed like it had been somewhere else, already drifting away.

He collapsed onto his back. "I want to know about your side of the deal with Trent. After, you can ask me whatever you want, and I'll answer."

"Not exactly a comforting response."

"I don't know what you want to know." He rolled again to face me. "You're avoiding my question. I want to know why."

"None of it is particularly flattering."

"You think I give a shit about what's flattering after the way I behaved? Nothing you say will change how I perceive you. You're smart and funny and when you're in a room, you're the only woman I see. If you were in my head, it would probably freak you the fuck out how much I think about you."

My stomach swooped, back on the roller coaster. Sometimes, the things he said made me think my fears were unjustified. Nothing spoken had passed between us the first time. We'd been closed off from each other, cautious, protecting ourselves from whatever had been building between us. Neither of us had understood what to do with how we felt.

After him, I'd spent a lot of time inching into emotional water with men, but I'd never gotten too deep. How did I know the deep end was safe this time, especially with Grady, the one who'd made me afraid in the first place?

"I don't want something to come up ten years from now, and I look like an ass for not asking these questions," he said. "I don't want secrets."

Ten years from now. My thoughts stuttered. That was a long time. Was he really looking so far into the future? Any other guy who'd brought up the future in such a concrete way, I'd become distant immediately. I could never seem to cope with long term. But my feelings for him had lingered for so long, and they'd exploded in the last few days. When I took a beat to examine how the claim made me feel, I realized his timeline didn't scare me. What scared me was that I might not get those years.

I swallowed down my fear. "There were two reasons I agreed to help Trent. Well, three. But you probably won't like the third one."

"Okay," he said carefully, "consider me prepared."

"The first reason is probably the one Trent told you. I'd been having some problems with other juniors in my class. They were being awful to me. I hadn't told anyone the things they'd been doing. Stupid, I know. Someone would have helped me, but I just... I couldn't seem to ask. Maybe because I'd always been so self-sufficient, and asking for help was a weakness I couldn't tolerate. Trent was two years older, and let's be honest, kinda intimidating. He said he could get them off my back." I tried to gauge whether I guessed right about what Trent told him based on Grady's expression. Trent and I protected each other, always had.

"Did he?"

"He did. I never asked how, but as soon as Trent made our involvement clear, they disappeared."

He raised his eyebrows.

"Not literally." I laughed. "He's not some mafia boss. I still saw them around, but from a distance. They never did anything to hurt me again."

"And the second reason?"

Taking a deep breath, I let it out slowly. "I've always been a bit competitive."

"You don't say."

I shoved his shoulder, and he kissed my temple.

"I wanted, more than anything, to get voted in as student body president for my senior year. But I had an image problem. I guess. I don't know. I thought I was likable enough. But I'd overheard some things." I twisted the covers in my fingers. "Trent taught me how to network. How to make people think I cared about them even if I didn't know them that well. At every party we attended before senior year, he introduced me to people I didn't normally talk to, had already coached me on things they were interested in." Heat crept into my face. Who needed to be taught how to interact with people? Trent had been a natural, never at a loss for something to say to someone. Even now, he made friends naturally, effortlessly, but because of him, I did too.

"That's a useful skill. I don't know why you're embarrassed. I wish he'd taught me how to do it before I went to LA. I was so fucking awkward all the time."

Trent's tips had saved me at more than one party in college, and once I'd come back to Little Falls, those skills had won me the mayor's job. But I'd hated needing his help to find authentic ways to connect with people. My father and mother had always been good at it, and even Emily and Tyler didn't seem to struggle. Reading books appealed to me more than reading people, and I'd had to force myself out of my shell.

"I detest the speaking part of performing," Grady says, giving me a gentle nudge. "It's why I had Kelvin on the mic during the Fourth of July. I hate having to entertain a crowd. A falseness to the performance, like I'm being someone I'm not."

"Always?" I turned on my side to face him. I loved looking at him, and I wondered how he'd changed in those ten years he talked about.

"So far. I haven't been 'me' on stage. I'm trying to win the crowd over. Buy my album. Pick me. I fucking hate pimping myself." He gave me the side-eye and took a deep breath. "And the other reason you didn't mind helping Trent?"

I gave him a sheepish smile. "He was nice to look at and fun to be around."

He winced and collapsed onto his pillow. I followed him, curling up against his side. He wrapped his arm around me. "But you and he were never together?"

I hesitated. I'd been hoping he wouldn't ask. How would he take this? But honesty was important. If the ten-year thing proved true, I didn't want him to find out by accident from Lila or Trent or anyone else. "Not like you and I were, no."

"Maggie," his voice was tight with tension.

"Before I even met you, before the first Sunday dinner, Trent and I sort of made out once. But it didn't go very far before I realized as much as I liked him, I didn't like him like that, and I was worried we'd ruin our arrangement if I let our friendship go in that direction." I rushed through the words. With a nervous laugh, I could see that I'd always felt the way about Trent I'd desperately wanted to feel about Grady. Trent was attractive, yes, but not to me. "Being with him didn't feel right." I ran my hand along his cheek and jaw, trying to ease the tension. Inching up, I feathered kisses along his jawline.

"That all?"

"You do realize I haven't been celibate since we were together, right?"

"Yep."

"Grady," I purred in his ear, biting his earlobe. "You wanted to know."

"And now I'm going to file it away in a part of my brain which never gets used." He flipped us over and settled between my legs. He kissed my neck. "I organized my bookshelves yesterday," he whispered in my ear. "Alphabetical."

"Oh." I wiggled against him, feeling him harden, and I let out a fake moan. "Oh, Grady. I love when you talk organization to me."

He chuckled. "You *pretending* to get turned on should *not* turn me on."

I wrapped my hand around his neck and drew him toward my lips. "If you tell me you're cleaning and painting today, I might have a sponta-neous orgasm."

With a groan, he slid against me. "Fuck, Maggie."

"Exactly." I drew my fingers across his back and then dug my nails into his ass. "Get on it. Or rather, in it."

"Patience, Maggie May. I hear it's a virtue."

"Glad to hear you only see it as a vicious rumor too."

He laughed against my ear, and the sound warmed my heart. How was it possible to feel this happy and content with him when I'd felt so much anxiety and angst about him for years? But every part of me—my heart, my mind, and my body—were so sure of him now that it created a different sort of anxiety.

His hand was on my inner thigh, smooth caresses that made me forget my train of thought. He was on the spot that made my body begin to ache with longing.

"I love watching you get turned on, yanked out of your head and into this moment," he said, and he wrapped his fingers around my thigh as he shifted to press his hard length against my core.

He rocked back and forth, the movement subtle but oh-so right as he kissed me. And I locked my ankles around him, keeping the connection tight. His palm cradled my head, and each movement built more and more urgency in me.

"Oh God," I murmured as he found the sensitive spot behind my ear, his tongue flicking over my earlobe and sucking.

"I'm going to make you come like this," he said, as I couldn't help digging my nails into his ass. "And then I'm going to make you come again when I take you from behind."

"Yes," I gasped, almost desperate for what he promised. "Faster."

"I'm not rushing this one," he said. "Not when I get to watch the expression on your face as you get closer and closer to coming undone." He gazed down at me with barely restrained passion. "Sometimes all I can think about are the soft sounds of pleasure you make, the way you can't catch your breath just before you come, how tightly you squeeze when you finally let go. If I could find some way to spend the rest of my life in this bed with you, that's what I'd do."

"You'd be a professional fucker," I said, barely able to get the words out, my brain so focused on the movement of his body over mine.

A grin split his face. "Can you decree that a job as mayor?" The smile left his face as he stared down at me, his gaze shifting across my face, as though he's reading how quickly I approach the edge. "An official job," he murmurs. "Maggie Sullivan's professional fucker."

"Yes," I said, clutching onto him, and then he slid into me, quick and smooth, and I gasped at the sudden fullness.

"I need to feel you," he said, his thumb on my clit, circling as he thrust long and deep.

It was exactly what I needed, too, and I could feel myself tightening and cresting. "Grady," I cried out as I felt the orgasm pulsing through me.

"Oh, fuck, Maggie," he said against my ear. "You're so tight. So wet. I don't know how much longer I can hold it together."

"Don't hold it," I said.

"Can I come on your stomach?"

I nodded, and he pulled out, pumping his large hand along his shaft as he spilled himself across my pale stomach, a guttural groan escaping.

When he was done, he leaned forward and kissed me before heading to the bathroom. There, I heard the shower turn on, and then he came back, scooped me into his arms and carried me there.

"Change of plans," he said. "Round two can happen in the shower instead."

"You're going to get me all clean?" I asked, clinging onto his neck as he bridal carried me.

"I do like you dirty," he said, glancing down at my stomach. "But I like you wet even more."

In the shower, he set me down, the hot water the exact temperature I liked it. It wasn't the first shower we'd taken together, but I still loved the feel of his hands on me, lathering soap across my body, taking care to get every inch of me slippery and clean.

"Do you want your hair washed?" he asked, reaching for the shampoo.

"Yeah," I said, turning my back to him.

His long fingers in my hair were magical. There was something about the soothing rhythm of someone else's hands working through the tangles, massaging my scalp, that sent tingles shooting down each of my limbs. If this were the only foreplay he ever did, I'd consider it a win, but he was surprisingly kind and considerate in and out of bed.

When he turned me to rinse my hair, he kissed me to distraction as he worked the shampoo out with his gentle fingers. Then he kissed down my body until his mouth was on my inner thighs, seeking entrance, asking for permission. I widened my stance, my hands digging into his hair as his tongue found my sensitive core.

Each lick and circle with the flat of his tongue made me long for more. The hot water beat on my back, a pleasant massage before cascading down my body.

"I love how you taste," he said, and then he slid two fingers inside me, pumping in time with the movement of his tongue, and I clung onto him, barely able to keep standing.

"Tell me when you're close, Maggie May," he said, sucking on my clit. "I want to be inside you when you come."

Between the swirling and sucking and his fingers pumping, I could barely think straight. "Please," I said. It was all I could manage.

In one swift movement, he lifted me up and pressed me against the wall of the shower. My ankles locked around him as he slid into me, his mouth on mine, his thumb finishing what his tongue started.

"Oh God," I said, my hands digging into the nape of his neck.

"Yes," he said, thrusting deeper and harder. "Yes."

And then I was tumbling over the edge again, crying out from the intensity of my second release. Keeping me tight against the wall, he followed right behind me.

"Drink?" Grady asked when I came out of the bathroom. "I gotta let the dogs out, but I can get you something when I'm downstairs."

"Sure, thanks," I said, drying my hair a little more with my towel before sliding back under the covers.

Once he disappeared out the bedroom door, I checked my phone and thought about ordering in some lunch. I worked such long hours I didn't have a lot of fresh food in the house. He'd been lucky to find any breakfast ingredients.

Something in the bed vibrated. I threw back the covers, searching for Grady's phone. At the bottom of the bed, I found it, and without meaning to, I read the sender. It was a message from Agent Jack.

The name made me laugh. Grady sounded like he was involved in the FBI or CIA giving Jack that contact name. As I went to set the phone on the bedside table, the words *job* and LA jumped out from the text preview.

A twinge of guilt stabbed my heart when I read as much of the message as I could see. His phone was password protected or else I might have tried to read the whole thing. A producing job in LA? That was a promotion, wasn't it? A better job, more opportunities.

Why hadn't he said something?

A cold sweat broke out under my armpits and across my palms. He hadn't told me, which felt very deliberate. It wasn't like there hadn't been time for him to say something. The text suggested that this offer wasn't new.

His footsteps coming down the hall startled me, and I almost dropped his phone trying to get it on the nightstand before he got back.

Entering the room, he gave me a half smile before passing me a glass of water. "You okay?"

My insides were a jumbled mass of confusion. What had I just read? Jumping all over him was a bad idea. Maybe he'd tell me.

Even if he ended up leaving, it'd be okay. I'd be okay.

My stomach dipped. After the morning we'd had, the text felt disorienting, like maybe I'd imagined how close Grady and I were getting, how much he wanted to be here.

I didn't want him to leave. Asking him to stay would be selfish. Trent warned me that he'd never stay, and it looked like that prophecy was coming true. Grady had never been meant for Little Falls.

What about the mayoral race? What if he won? Would he stay or leave no matter what?

My mind spun with questions I didn't want to ask. Truthfully, I wasn't sure I could handle the answers to those questions.

"Yeah." I focused on the ice in the glass. "Everything is fine."

Chapter Twenty-Eight

Maggie

We were going through the last spreadsheet at the kitchen table in Lila's house when Lila flipped the laptop screen shut, turned and stared at me.

"Something is wrong."

"Nothing is wrong."

"For the last two or three days, you've been unbearable. On cloud nine. Grady. Grady. Grady. Today? You haven't said his name once, and a few times, you would've been right to mention him since he did so much work for the concert and strip show."

I picked up my coffee and took a sip, waving off Lila with fake nonchalance. Since I'd seen his text message, I'd been whirling, lost in a haze of negative thoughts. "I'm taking a deep breath and getting some perspective."

"What does that mean?" Lila arched her eyebrows and threw another teaspoon of sugar into her mug.

"It means Grady and I have been having fun the last few days, but it doesn't mean whatever this is will last."

"Whoa, whoa, whoa. Are you kidding me?" She held up her hand and shook her head. "The two of you have been a jumble of knots, sexual tension, and misunderstandings for months, and now you've banged a few times and you're *over* him? That might happen to other people, but I don't believe that's happening *to you*."

I picked up my spoon and stirred my coffee, even though I was drinking it black today. That wasn't what I was saying, but how did I tell Lila the truth without admitting I'd read his text message? When he checked his phone later and frowned, his expression only confirmed that Jack's message hadn't been a surprise. Then, he hadn't brought up the offer over lunch or at any other point before he left my house, which only confirmed he didn't want me involved.

Lila grabbed my spoon, heaped it full of sugar and dumped it in my cup, stirring furiously.

"Hey!" I snatched the spoon back. "What was that for?"

"Black coffee? That's the drink of depressed people."

"No, it's not."

Lila shrugged. "Maybe it's serial killers. You take sugar in your coffee. Always. And when you're feeling really good, it's hazelnut from Kathy's Café."

I hadn't been able to stir up the enthusiasm for drinking coffee at all. This one was almost cold. Maybe Lila had a point.

"Just tell me. You only hesitate when you think you've done something to make *you* look bad. Hello? I don't care. You're my bestie. You could be plotting to destroy the world, and I'd ask how to help."

"You think you know me that well?" I sipped my coffee and had to admit it was better with sugar. Perhaps telling Lila what I'd read would make the news easier to digest.

Lila stared expectantly and then picked up her coffee and took a sip. Her gaze never left my face.

"When Grady was in the kitchen today, I saw a text on his phone."

"As long as the text wasn't from Sabrina about the Plan B pill, nothing can be that bad." She gestured to my slumped position in the chair.

"He's been offered a producing job in LA and hasn't told me."

"Oh." Her face fell. "I think I might almost prefer him banging Sabrina."

I winced. "I would not. Gross. No. Just, no. But I don't know why he hasn't told me about the job."

"Did you ask him?"

"Obviously not. Then I'd have to admit I looked at his phone. I'd also have to admit I care whether he stays or goes."

Lila frowned and chugged the last of her coffee before taking the cup to the sink. "You *do* care."

My extreme caring was the biggest problem in this scenario. If I didn't have all these stupid feelings, I could enjoy the sex and let him leave, off on another adventure. The temporary relationship would be a blip in our respective lives.

I cared far, far too much. The thought of him leaving made me physically ill, and that intensity was after three days of sleeping with him. How would I feel if we managed to last any longer? I rubbed my face and took another drink before following Lila to the sink. "Trent warned me Grady would probably leave."

"He's still running for mayor."

"Do you honestly think he cares? I'm pretty sure he ran because he knew it would piss me off." I'd come to that conclusion after hours of obsessive Grady thoughts.

"That's a fair point," she agreed. "But Maggie, the way he looks at you."

His expression was probably filled with lust—so was mine. Not a surprise. The two of us couldn't get enough of each other. Even this afternoon when I'd been frustrated and hurt he hadn't told me about the producing job, I'd let him take me from behind, making me come again that morning. The minute he touched me, a fire lit and blazed so bright and hot my brain shut off.

"Someday, when I grow up, I want a man to look at me like that," Lila said.

"It's not hard. Unlimited sex. That's your ticket."

Lila ran her hand down my arm. "He hurt you last time. I was there. I saw it. I didn't understand how much or why until you finally told me most of the truth. Once you gave me the last piece, that he was the first guy you slept with, your emotions and reactions made a lot more sense." She searched my face, tenderness in her gaze. A rare moment of seriousness from her. "The two of you aren't the same people. You're not teenagers. The lies have been flushed out. And if you think the way he looks at you has more to do with lust than love, you're fucking blind."

"It's not like he's told me he loves me or anything." I crossed my arms and stared at my feet.

"Have *you* told him?"

The words were there and instead of saying them, I held them back. If he didn't feel the same way about me, I didn't want to embarrass myself. That old hurt was still there, under the surface, coloring our interactions. I didn't know how to get past what had happened last time. Truthfully, I hadn't known I needed to get over our past until I'd seen his message this morning.

Maybe time was what I needed, a sense he would stay the course, not abandon me again. Now with the threat of him leaving looming over me,

I wasn't sure I'd be able to tell him how I felt. Keeping the job offer from me was a sign he didn't see a future with me and was just biding his time. That's what I'd done with every *just for now* guy in the past. They were on a need-to-know basis, and looking back, I realized I told them enough to know my life, but not enough to know me.

"Being honest with him is scary. But if you risk nothing, you get nothing in return."

"I risked last time. What'd I get in return? Twelve, almost thirteen years of heartache and that fucking song on the radio." There was bitterness on my tongue, which surprised me. Had I always felt this way? For so long, I'd blamed myself, but now that we'd talked about our past, I couldn't understand where I'd gone wrong other than trusting Grady would see me for who I was, that he'd recognize I wasn't the kind of person who'd betray Trent in any context. I wouldn't have let him go to jail if I'd known how to stop it, and I certainly wouldn't have fucked his brother behind his back. Well, I did do that, but not the way Grady thought.

The text message this morning had caused all these old hurts I'd buried to rise to the surface. He'd crushed my heart last time with his indifference, and I wasn't sure I could offer my reconstructed heart. What if he did it again?

Letting him go was a piercing arrow to my heart, but I could survive that. Telling him my feelings and having him reject me wouldn't be so easy to stitch up. Whether he decided to leave or not wasn't something I could control.

I told him I'd travel the world, but that was a lie. A calculated one because I wanted whatever was blooming between us to survive. But the truth was that Little Falls was where I'd made my home. Maybe we'd been a bad idea from the start. A poor fit. Without honesty, we were nothing, and we had built our entire relationship on a foundation of lies.

"Until he either tells me he loves me or tells me about the job offer, we're temporary," I said. "I can't go all in with him when it feels like he's not all in with me." When Lila opened her mouth to protest, I held up my hand. "I need time to get my head wrapped around everything. Process what's happened. I don't want more advice. Let's finish this spreadsheet so I can get home."

Lila was quiet for a beat. "All right, if that's what you want." She opened the laptop, and the two of us peered at the last spreadsheet in silence.

Chapter Twenty-Nine
Grady

I had spent Monday writing and tracking down the last of the props and costumes for the following weekend. I hadn't had much of a chance to clear my head and get some perspective. Now it was Tuesday afternoon, and I strolled through the center of town with my dogs in an effort to sort out my feelings.

Jack would expect a response from me by Friday, and I wasn't sure what answer to give. Maggie had been distant Sunday and Monday. Not physically, at least. We'd been all over each other. Emotionally, she'd thrown up a barrier, thin but impenetrable. While I definitely had her body, I wasn't anywhere close to winning her heart.

Where had I gone wrong? A couple of times, I'd considered asking her, but I didn't want to scare her away. The conversations I'd had with Emily during prep for the Small Town Saviors show made me think Maggie would get spooked by too much too soon. Emily told me none of the men Maggie dated had measured up. I hadn't had the guts to ask her what bar they'd missed. I could tell I wasn't clearing it either, at least not yet.

Without thinking, I steered toward her pharmacy. She was working a shorter day to take care of some business around winter parking in the town. The current system wasn't working, and we'd talked about the options last night in bed. Being on the same team, working together to solve a problem instead of creating them for each other had been nice. I loved the way her mind worked.

Up ahead, Jim cleaned the pharmacy windows. A grin formed at the sight. If I could figure out how to win Maggie's heart, I'd get the additional prize of her family.

"Hard at work?" I tightened my grip on the dogs as I approached. They'd taken a shine to Jim and were straining on their leashes.

Jim rocked back on his heels to admire his cleaning job and then returned my grin. "Maggie is never short of ideas to keep her employee busy." His brown eyes twinkled with amusement. "I hear you've been keeping each other busy lately."

There were so many ways I could take Jim's comment, but I doubted Maggie's dad meant for my mind to land on a sexual innuendo. I scrubbed a hand across my face and tried to conceal where my mind went. "We have been spending some time together, yeah."

Jim examined me while the rag and spray bottle swung in one hand. "You seem happy. She's happy. Nice to see. I wasn't sure where this whole election thing was going."

While I'd walked, I'd been tempted to remove my election signs from people's front lawns. I'd dismissed most of my campaign helpers yesterday, telling them the rest was in voters' hands. Maggie had teased me for two days straight about my gaggle of mothers and daughters who trailed me around town to do my bidding. Her gentle teasing was an indication she didn't approve. Despite the way I'd run my campaign, Kelvin was probably right. Maggie wouldn't appreciate winning on a concession instead of a true victory. She'd worked hard for her position, and she deserved to win it fairly.

"Life doesn't always go the way you expect it to." Jim squinted at the pharmacy glass and then sprayed and wiped a dull spot.

"No, it definitely does not." I dug my fingers into the fur at Hite's neck. The dog pressed against my knees, eager for more. "Hindsight makes me wish I'd... I don't know. Done things differently, I guess."

"Those big moments in life take you by surprise. I've had a few of those myself." His smile was strained. "The last thing I say to my kids, every time, is I love them."

I'd never been able to remember the last words I'd said to my father. Nothing of significance, nothing to note the gravity of speaking for the last time. As a doctor, Jim would have witnessed loved ones lamenting the things they hadn't said, or perhaps what they had said as a parting remark. Like me, Jim had lost his father at a young age. Jim clung to his connections, and I wondered if my loss had caused me to be too wary of letting people in. "I like that. Might have to steal it someday."

"So, do you have a plan? If you don't win the mayoral race, what do you intend to do with yourself? Maggie said you write songs for other singers? Nothing for yourself?"

A smile threatened, and I swallowed it down. I liked that she talked about me to her parents. "I'm actually contemplating what direction I want to take. It's been years since I've spent so much time in one place."

"Getting restless?"

Was I? That was the big question. As I thought about Jim's question, I waved and called out a 'hello' to a few people who passed in cars. For the last few days, I hadn't had any desire to wander. Looking back, the urge hadn't been there for a few weeks—not since things began to thaw between me and Maggie. "No, I don't think I am. But an opportunity came up, and I'm not sure if I should seize it or let it pass."

"What's your heart telling you?" He set the spray bottle down, threw the rag over top, and crouched to pet Hite and Zeus.

"All kinds of things lately." I ran a hand through my hair and sighed. My heart was telling me to stay, but my head was worried she'd find me lacking like the other men she'd cast aside, and I'd miss this producing opportunity.

When I was younger, her and Trent's fictional relationship had been enough to send me spiraling. Now, after having had her so completely, I wasn't sure I could stay in Little Falls if we weren't together. I could keep in touch with Trent, my mother, and Kelvin if I went to LA, better than I'd done before. She was my reason to stay, and after only a few days together, we didn't exactly feel stable with her so distant.

But I wanted her, more than I'd ever wanted anything in my life. "Both options feel like a gamble."

Jim's fingers were embedded in the dogs' fur when he looked up. "Any time I had one of those crossroads, something happened to let me know which way was best. You'll get a sign."

I wasn't a religious man, and this sounded like divine intervention. People made their own luck through the choices they made. I had too much respect for Jim to question his beliefs, and so I made a joke instead. "It better be neon and flashing. I'm slow sometimes."

He chuckled and stood up. "I doubt you're that slow. Maggie says you're a brilliant songwriter. She played a few of the ones you'd written for other people today in the pharmacy when we were switching off. You have a way with words."

Heat rose to my cheeks, and I ran the back of my cool hand over them. Maggie and Jim had been listening to songs I'd written? She called me brilliant? A surge of pride lit me up. "She said that?"

Jim grinned. "She glows when she talks about you. It's incredible. I wasn't sure I'd ever see that in her. She can be closed off, resistant to forming that connection. My greatest wish for my kids is for them to find what I have with Joanna. Emily had it and lost it. Nearly broke my heart to see her struggling after Omar died. Tyler was close once, but he's still searching. But I think Maggie's found that connection with you." He waved a dismissive hand. "She'd probably string me up for saying that." He paused and seemed to be holding back another grin. "Especially for saying it *to* you. She'd be mortified."

He'd never know how much I needed to hear Maggie's perspective from someone close. The barrier she'd placed between us had made me wonder if I was alone in these feelings. "I feel the same way about her." The words left before I could consider holding them back. "She's the best woman I know."

"That's the secret." Jim nodded. "When you feel you've gotten the better end of the relationship deal, you never need to look for more."

She was exactly what I wanted. I'd been a fool for far too long. "Do you ever wish you could tell your younger self it would turn out okay? That the shitty feelings wouldn't last forever?"

Jim pursed his lips and shook his head. "I used to feel that way. I don't think I do anymore. You learn by getting through those bad times. That's true as an individual but in a relationship too. If you didn't have to put in the hard work, do you really grow? What do you learn?" He eyed me for a moment and shoved his hands in his pockets. He took a deep breath. "Those songs you wrote hurt Maggie. Hurt her deeply. Nothing she ever told me, but any time any news about you came up or any song you'd written started to play, she tuned out, switched off."

Shame hit me in the chest as though Jim had thrown a punch. I'd hurt Maggie, and the realization, once again, made my chest ache painfully. For the rest of my life, I would do everything I could to make that up to her, to never cause her pain again. When I'd written that album, I'd been so confused and hurt I hadn't been able to see past it. She'd consumed my thoughts and not in the good way she did now.

"I'm deeply sorry I hurt her. I just—" I searched for the words. "There's no good reason or excuse. I intend to spend the rest of my life making it up to her. I'm sorry I let you down too." My voice felt thick with emotion. I'd hoped Jim hadn't connected the hit album with Maggie when I'd first come back to town, but I'd wondered. His opinion had been in the back of my mind when I'd written the songs, and it was the only reason I backed off in some of my lyrics, using veiled language instead of outright attacking her. What I'd written had been bad enough. I couldn't even imagine the damage I would have done if Jim hadn't also been on my mind back then.

Jim sighed. "I try to stay out of my kids' lives unless they ask for my help. It's hard to see your kids hurting and to know there's nothing you can do. So, when you came back to town, when you and Maggie were circling each other, I was worried. Seemed to me you had a lot of growing up to do."

"What happened before was all my fault." My voice was rough. "I assumed a lot of things. I should never have done what I did."

Jim looked down the street over my shoulder, lost in thought. "The two of you seem to be working your differences out. Here's my advice, for what it's worth. Communication is vital. So is perseverance. Sometimes talking a problem out is painful or excruciatingly hard. One of you has to put yourselves out there, embrace the discomfort. Otherwise, the relationship slips away."

"That's what you and your wife do?" I hadn't had the privilege of seeing a marriage up close since my father died when I was twelve.

He rocked back on his heels and shoved his hands in his pockets. "Most of the time. Sometimes it takes a while for one of us to get our head out of our ass, but we get there eventually. Neither of us has ever dug our heels in so long we couldn't fix what we broke. At some point, you gotta meet the difficulties head-on and fight for what you want. The relationship comes before whether or not you were right in what you said or did or whatever has happened. You put each other first."

You put each other first. The words reverberated in my soul. I could do that. For the rest of my life, I was confident I could find a way to put her first. "That's good advice."

"You need to know each other, understand each other. Maggie always likes time to come around to whatever she's mulling over. But she gets there. Once she's made a decision, she tends to stick to it." Behind him, the bells of the pharmacy jingled as someone walked in. "I need to go look after things before my daughter strings me up."

"You all set for Saturday?"

Jim's hand was on the door, one foot already inside. "I'm not as smooth as you yet. But I have most of the moves."

"Well, if you want a bit more practice tomorrow, I'll be home in the afternoon, and we can go over the group routine again."

Another smile stretched across his face. Jim looked in the pharmacy to check on the customer and then nodded. "I'd like that. I don't mind looking like a fool for a good cause, but not being a fool is always prefer-able." He hesitated. "And I meant what I said earlier. I'm glad you and

Maggie are so happy together, and you're working out whatever caused the rift between you before."

My heart swelled in my chest as the door to the pharmacy clicked closed. Through the window, Jim greeted the customer and rang up their purchases. Talking to him had made me steadier, as though the tightrope I'd been walking might be all in my head.

At home, I filled the dog's water dish for the second time. Once I'd left the pharmacy, I'd gone for a longer walk than normal, trying to decide about the job and whether the right thing was to discuss the opportunity with Maggie. I wouldn't leave her, but I wanted the job. There was no doubt in my mind I'd enjoy it, be good at it. Producing would open doors in my career and lead to a steadier, better income. The only cons were the location and timeframe. Managing long-distance with Maggie was the biggest con of all.

I was halfway through a song an established artist had commissioned me to write when my phone rang. Frowning, I grabbed it off the coffee table in the middle of the room. *Lila.* I sent it to voicemail. In a few minutes, I'd call her back. I was close to nailing down the chorus and didn't want to break my flow. Concert business could wait.

As soon as I was back in the zone, my phone buzzed again. Annoyance shot through me, and I grabbed the phone, prepared to send Lila to voicemail again. She tended to be persistent. But it wasn't Lila.

Trent.

Trent called me now, but never in the middle of a workday. He was usually too busy to even answer a text message, and his lunch break was long gone.

"What's up?" I twirled my pencil across my fingers.

There was a lengthy silence, and I checked my phone to see whether the call had dropped or maybe Trent had pocket dialed.

"Hello?" I said again.

"Sorry," Trent's voice was thick, and he cleared his throat. "Lila called me." His voice cracked.

My heart dropped out of my chest and into my feet. A sweat broke out across my back. "Jesus, Trent. You're scaring me. Is Maggie okay?" I should have answered Lila's call. If I'd wasted precious time sending the call to voicemail, I didn't think I could forgive myself. A car accident? Something worse? The tightness in my chest was unbearable.

"It's her dad. He collapsed in the pharmacy." The words were garbled, hard to understand.

Maggie was okay. Thank God, she was okay. Relief flooded in, and I released the breath I'd been holding. But Jim, Jim was not okay.

"Collapsed? At the pharmacy?" I'd been there an hour ago. I'd just seen him. "Is he at the hospital?" I tucked my phone between my ear and neck, grabbing my keys and coat. Whatever was going on, I needed to be there for Maggie.

"Yeah," Trent said. "But, Grady..."

"What is it?" I locked my house and jogged to the truck. With a yank on the driver's door, my thoughts flickered between Maggie and Jim. An hour ago, we'd been chatting. Jim had looked fine, and he was in good health. Fit. Strong. We were dancing together tomorrow. He'd be fine. A blip.

"He didn't make it." Through the phone, Trent sniffed, and his voice broke. "He died. Jim's dead."

With my hand on the steering wheel, I stared at the back shed, my heart fracturing into a million pieces. "What?" The word left before I could think it through. *Shock*. I remembered this weightlessness, as though time and space had somehow shifted and no longer made sense. Jim was dead? "What?"

"I'll meet you at the hospital, okay? I'm on my way now." Trent sniffed, and for the first time, I realized I was on speaker phone in a car, the traffic noises audible.

Numbness rose like a fog. On autopilot, I started my truck and sat there, staring into the distance.

"Grady?"

"Yeah?"

"She's gonna need you, man. I know what you're feeling right now." He took a deep breath, and his voice was thick with tears. "But you and I gotta get out of our own fucking heads. 'Cause we know." He exhaled sharply. "We fucking *know*."

A chill settled in my bones. Throwing the vehicle into reverse, I backed out of the driveway and pointed the truck toward the hospital. When my father died, I shrank into myself, refusing help from anyone except that lone conversation with Jim. Having the security only a parent could provide ripped out of your life was catastrophic. People often described grief as a hole, but I considered it a weight, one that had buckled my knees, almost crushing. A person dragged the weight of grief around, eventually learning to carry it, but they were never the same again. If I had a choice, Maggie wouldn't bear the load alone.

Chapter Thirty

Maggie

My knees buckled when Grady strode through the emergency room doors. Relief hit so hard darkness tinged the edges of my vision, threatening to drag me under. He swooped me into his arms and kept me from sliding to the ground. His lips skimmed the top of my head, and I sighed. How had he known I needed him?

My thoughts were so muddled. The minute I'd answered Joseph Goldtooth's frantic phone call about finding Dad on the floor, all logic or reason had fled. On autopilot, I'd met the ambulance at the hospital, but I hadn't been able to see my father. Instead, Dad's closest colleague, David Rigilotto, had entered the waiting room with tears in his eyes, and I'd known, before he said a word. Dad's condition was grave. Not once had I considered what had happened would be *this* bad.

"How are you here?" I clutched his shirt, my words garbled, trying to keep in my sob.

"Lila and Trent called. It's awful. It's so fucking awful." He squeezed me tighter.

Inexplicably, Lila had been the first one I'd called when David delivered the news. My mother or Tyler or Emily would have been the logical choices, but I couldn't bear to say the words aloud. David had offered, but I hadn't known how to organize my thoughts.

This all had to be a mistake. A dozen times, I'd opened my mouth to tell David he had to be wrong. Dad couldn't be dead. I'd seen him a few hours ago, and he'd been fine. We'd listened to Grady's music together, marveling at his talent, at how funny life could be, how the bad things didn't always stay bad.

I'd stared at David who reminded me of Dad in age, height, and that doctorly way he carried himself. My mouth had kept opening and closing, a fish suffocating, and no words had come out.

My father. My dad. Daddy.

The numbness spun, attaching like the stickiest web. I'd called Lila, and with panic in her voice, Lila had said she'd call everyone else. A testament to our friendship, she'd known everyone else included Grady, and Trent was the best person to get him here.

The next person to arrive was Lila, and she looked how I felt, as though she'd spent hours ugly crying. I hadn't shed a tear. Without a word, Lila turned our two-person hug into a three-person one by embracing me and Grady. We'd stood like that for a long time before my mother arrived, who'd been out of town shopping, then Emily, then Tyler, and finally Trent. Each time I saw the reality of Dad's death hit a family member, a piece of my heart ripped. I clung to Grady, letting his strength seep into me. He took all my pain and confusion, and he absorbed it, never telling me to be strong or trying to make the awfulness less awful.

I listened at the hospital while my mother made arrangements with one of the local funeral homes over the phone. We had to go to the funeral parlor tomorrow to form a plan. For the first time, I was a reluctant organizer. No matter how I turned my father's death around, it made no sense. While Mom talked about the things that needed to be done, I tuned out, tried to pretend it wasn't happening. A part of me admired

Mom's bravery, her composure, and I hated her for it too. Organizing was Mom's way to cope in a crisis—the lawyer in her liked order and structure. I was usually like that too. This time, I wanted to avoid, avoid, avoid. But there was nowhere to hide.

I left my car in the hospital parking lot, and Grady drove us in his truck to my parents' sweeping brick two-story house. Except my childhood home wasn't my parents' house anymore. From now on, it would be my mother's house. All these little injustices hit one after another.

We sat on the couches in the warm, wood-infused open-concept living room, and everywhere I looked I saw my father. He was on the walls in photos from our childhood right up until a few weeks ago when we'd had fall family photos done. His gym bag was by the door. His messy doctor scrawl was across the whiteboard my parents used to communicate with each other. When I glanced at the recliner, I could imagine him sitting there, the outline of his body, a grin on his face.

He was writ large in the house.

Time would erase his presence.

I couldn't bear for him to be gone. I didn't know how to bear his absence, the erosion of his presence in this house, in our life.

Beside me, Grady squeezed my knee as though sensing my shifting mood. The night passed in a blur of conversations happening around me as my siblings and Mom came to terms with Dad's death. A brain aneurysm. He never stood a chance.

When it got so late everyone seemed to fuse to the couches, Mom suggested we sleep there. I couldn't stomach the thought of waking up and knowing Dad would never be in the house again.

Instead, I turned to Grady with pleading eyes, and he used his dogs as an excuse to get us out of there.

In the truck, we rode in silence for a while before he smoothed my hair, drawing my attention. "I know how hard this is. Cry. Don't cry. But you gotta let yourself feel his absence, Maggie." He pressed the heel of his hand to his chest. "You gotta let yourself live in the awfulness for a while, or the awfulness goes on for too long."

Tears flooded my eyes, and I blinked them away. A few stray tears trickled down my cheeks. "How do people survive this? How do people lose a parent and keep going as if part of their world hasn't come to an end?"

He glanced at me as he pulled into his driveway. Half turning in his seat, he wiped my tears with his thumbs and cradled my face. "I don't think any of us survive it unscathed. We carry the wound for the rest of our lives. But the more time that passes, the less the weight feels like it's going to crush you. Grief won't crush you, Maggie. Okay? I won't let it crush you."

I stared into his deep brown eyes. "I'm sorry. I'm so sorry."

He shook his head, and his brow creased. His thumbs brushed away the tears that kept falling. "Sorry about what?"

"That I never knew, that I never understood how awful it must have been for you, all these years, without your dad."

He swallowed and our foreheads touched. "Your dad was there the night my dad died."

Just the mention of him made my heart constrict. "He was?"

"He was the doctor on call, and he sat with me while I waited for my turn to say goodbye. I loved your dad from that moment on. He saved me from myself more than once." There were tears in his eyes now. "Don't ever be sorry you didn't know, Maggie May," his voice was gruff. "I wish you still didn't know."

My throat closed up, a sob threatening to burst forth. I tried to swallow the grief, think of something else. But each time my gaze met Grady's, I saw the two men I loved most in the world sitting side-by-side in the same hospital waiting room I'd been in today, one young, one old, having no idea how their lives would intersect in the years to come.

"He loved us so hard." A half sob escaped me. Tears filled my eyes and blurred my view of Grady. "He knew what it was like to lose a dad."

"He did." His voice was thick with tears, and the moonlight caught the glint of moisture on his cheeks before he could wipe them away.

The silence stretched between us, filled with all the things we could say to each other. But I couldn't handle any confessions, wasn't sure I had the language to express the grief welling up, swirling around my chest, hardening into something solid and substantial, and far too heavy to accept.

"Can we go in? I don't want to talk anymore. I don't want to think anymore." I rubbed my face, exhaustion settling like a cloak.

"Yeah." He climbed out and came around to slide his arm around me as we walked to the house. "Whatever you need." He pressed a kiss to my temple, and I leaned into his side, wrapping my arms around his middle.

While he let out his dogs, I got undressed and slipped under the covers, trying to keep my mind from straying to thoughts of Dad. Each time my brain touched on him, my stomach rolled, and my chest tightened with the weight resting on top of it.

When Grady slid into bed behind me, he tugged me flush against his chest, fitting us together like two puzzle pieces. I wanted him to tell me everything would be okay. But I was sure that would be a lie, one he'd never tell. How could anything ever be okay again?

As I drifted to sleep, he kissed my neck and secured me more firmly. For the first time in hours, the thought which had plagued me for days resurfaced. My eyes popped open.

Grady planned to leave.

His breathing evened out, and I stared into the darkness, wondering how to prevent Grady from ripping what was left of my heart into a thousand pieces.

The next day tore through the fabric of my heart as I helped to pick out a coffin, chose a date for the funeral, decided which of Dad's many suits best exemplified him, selected family photos for the digital tribute, and gave Emily and Tyler input for the eulogy. People had been everywhere paying their respects, giving condolences, and delivering food. Each act of kindness had threatened to suck my polite mask right off my face.

Every step was excruciating, exhausting, and at the back of my mind had been the realization that I couldn't rely on Grady. If he was considering LA without talking to me, keeping that secret told me all I needed to know. He'd clearly had time before now to talk to me about it, and he'd chosen not to.

Rather than dwell on the awfulness of my father, I'd spent most of the day wrapped in thoughts of Grady and his imminent abandonment. Separately, the two events would've been overwhelming, but together I couldn't process either one. Emotional overload had hit me hard.

By the time I got home at nine that night, I couldn't call Grady. I didn't have anything left to give him. A bit of distance was the best idea. I could ease out of whatever was happening, and maybe that would lessen the hurt—whenever I could feel something, anything, again.

He probably felt bad for me right now. He knew what it was like to lose a parent. I didn't want him to stay in Little Falls out of a sense of obligation. When he texted to see if I was home, I couldn't even open his message.

At ten, I was brushing my teeth for bed when my doorbell rang. Ginger skittered across the floor, startled by the sound. I usually laughed at Ginger's foolish behavior, but there was no room for humor tonight. I laid my hand against the front door. Grady was the only person who'd come this late at night, but I was too afraid to look.

My vehicle was in the driveway. Maybe he'd think I was asleep if I didn't answer?

"Come on, Maggie. I can feel you on the other side of the door. I know you're there. Let me in."

I jumped back, startled. "You can *feel* me?" A frown settled between my brows as I opened the door.

"I've developed a Maggie sense. Well, I think that sense developed a long time ago. I'm just finally listening to whatever causes it." He stepped past me into the house, carrying a take-out bag.

The smell of Thai food wafted in with him. There wasn't a Thai restaurant in Little Falls. People drove to Utica. Grady had driven to Utica. "What's that?"

"Thai from the restaurant you raved about the other night when we were talking about food and travel." He unpacked the bag onto the kitchen table.

As the dishes came out, I read the labels in silence. He'd bought every dish I'd listed as a favorite. There was enough food to feed a small army.

I would be eating it for weeks. I rubbed my face, my resolve wavering. Why did he have to be trying so hard at the wrong things? I couldn't even articulate exactly what I needed, but it wasn't this. It wasn't any of this.

"I figured," he said, moving around my kitchen with ease, "you probably had a shitty day and likely didn't eat much. Maybe you don't want this either, I don't know. Worth a try. We can freeze some of it." He put the two plates and cutlery on the table and glanced at me. "Are you—are you hungry?"

"How did you know I was home?"

"Emily." He examined me from across the small table, neither of us sitting down. "I texted her when you didn't respond. She said you were probably in the shower or something, and you'd all had a long day."

I hadn't told anyone I planned to let things end with Grady. Given what else was going on, they'd probably try to talk me out of my decision. But if he intended to leave, I might as well rip off this Band-Aid while the other wound was still bleeding. At the moment, I felt so unlike myself that I couldn't imagine feeling worse. It couldn't get any worse.

"Did you want to talk? Or just eat? Or go to bed? If you're tired, I can put this in the fridge for tomorrow."

"I can't do this anymore."

He took a step toward me and tried to draw me into a hug. I sidestepped him and went to the cupboard to take out a glass. My hand shook while I filled it at the tap.

"It's not easy—"

"I don't mean about my dad," I said, closing my eyes, but I kept my back to him. "I mean us. I just—I don't have the emotional energy to do this right now. I'm tapped out."

"I'm not asking for anything from you. I know how hard it is to lose your dad. I want to help. I don't want to make things harder."

With a sigh, I straightened my shoulders and turned to face him. "LA is pretty far away to be helpful."

He reared back and drew a hand down his face, but not before I saw the surprise in his eyes. "What are you talking about?"

"I saw the text message from your agent the other day. I know about the LA job offer." Ginger had reappeared and was weaving herself between my legs. I scooped her up, burying my face in the cat's fluffy fur so I didn't have to see the indecision flash across Grady's face. Obviously, he'd never meant for me to find out. Another rip frayed the edges of my heart. "I think you should go to LA. Take the job. It's a great opportunity for you. There's nothing keeping you here except a half-assed race for mayor." I took a deep breath. "You never wanted any of this, anyway. It just kinda happened."

"*Any* of this?" His jaw clenched. "What's that mean?"

"The mayor job. You ran to piss me off. It worked. Job well-done. And, I don't know, whatever's been happening with us. We were never serious. I get that. No need to spell it out now."

"Did *I* say that?" He stepped toward me. "Where the hell is this coming from, Maggie? How did you come to the conclusion I don't want to be with you?" His brown eyes blazed with hurt and anger.

I looked away. I didn't want to see those things in his eyes. Instead, I clung to the surprise and indecision I'd read on his face a minute ago. "Were you going to take the job in LA?"

He rubbed his cheeks and sighed. "I don't know. I haven't had enough time to think about it. I'm sorry I didn't say anything to you."

"Little Falls will never be enough for you." What I wanted to say was *I* would never be enough, but I held the words close to my heart.

"I never said that. Don't do that. Don't put words in my mouth." He reached for me.

I stepped to the side. If he touched me, I'd go up in flames. Let him and this feeling consume me, and my heart would be burned to a crisp when he left. "I don't want to do this anymore. Go to LA. Take the job. It's okay. I'm telling you it's okay. You don't owe me anything."

He shook his head, and his frustration was palpable in the room. "I don't want to fight with you right now. You've got a lot going on."

"We're not fighting."

"Trust me. We could be fighting right now." Grady stole my calming move by drawing his index and thumb down the center of his chest. In any other circumstance, the motion would have made me smile. The action softened my resolve the tiniest bit to see another reminder he'd been paying attention to.

His gaze bored into me. "I'm deep breathing the shit out of my inner monologue to keep from saying all kinds of crap that'll probably piss you off. I don't want to fight."

"What would we even fight about? You want to go. I'm telling you to go."

"Come with me."

"What?"

"Come to LA with me."

I dragged my hair into a ponytail and twisted it into a fist before letting it fall. "I can't do that." Even if I could, having him ask after I'd outed him didn't show he wanted me along but rather he was attempting to salvage something between us. I had a business, and I was the mayor of the goddamn town. I couldn't pick up and leave on a whim. I wasn't him.

"Why not?" He shifted closer, and the scent of wintergreen enveloped me.

"Grady, you're being ridiculous. I'm not mad, okay? I'm just done. You don't need to try to make me feel better. We had fun for a little while, but something better came along, and you want that. I get it."

"I haven't accepted the job." He huffed out a breath. "You're really fucking frustrating right now." He shoved his hands in his pockets and took a deep, steadying breath. "But there's a lot going on, and this job offer is another thing to add to the pile. That's part of the reason I didn't tell you." He ran a hand through his hair. "I was wrong. I should have told you. I should have told you right away, clearly. I didn't want you to get hurt by something I wasn't even sure I wanted."

"Tell me you don't have any urge to leave." I'd heard the way he talked about his travels, how much he loved being on the road, and deep down, he must know I'd hold him back. "Tell me, and be honest, that the idea of leaving doesn't appeal to you at all."

"I know what I want. Are you telling me you don't want to be with me? And are you saying this because your dad died or because that's really how you feel?"

He couldn't even answer my question. Of course he wanted to leave. Isn't that what Trent had told me? And it's not like I hadn't experienced it firsthand already.

"I think you should go," I whispered. "I need you to go." Numbness was sweeping over again, saving me.

"Maggie," he pleaded. "We need to talk about this."

"You're going to leave. I never expected you to stay. I'm trying to make it easier on both of us. I can't do more hard things right now. Please, just go."

His gaze was hot on me for a few moments, and silence sat between them. "I'll go," he murmured. "It's been a long couple of days for you. I get it. I don't want to make things worse. But I don't agree with whatever version of us you've got in your head."

"The real version is in my head, finally. I might have said I'd travel the world, but the truth is that Little Falls has my heart. This is where I belong. I'm never going to leave, and you're never going to stay."

He hung his head, and his hands went white from pressing into the granite countertop. He sighed and pushed away from the island. When his fingers brushed my jaw, the contact startled me, but then he pressed his lips to my temple, and I leaned toward him like a tree bent by the wind. I wanted to bend and bend and bend and never have to worry about standing upright alone again. But I didn't know how to trust that he'd be there to hold me up.

In my ear, Grady whispered, "You're my heart. You're where I belong. I'm not giving up on you. But I'll give you the space you want."

Then he grabbed his coat and walked out the door. I followed him, torn between throwing open the door and begging him to come back and flicking the lock in place, guarding my tattered heart. I didn't know what to believe, and I didn't have the mental energy to figure it out. With a decisiveness I didn't feel, I rotated the deadbolt. The familiar weight of loss stretched across my chest as the lock tumbled into place.

Chapter Thirty-One

The last two nights, I'd dreamed of her. They'd been so vivid, I'd woken up convinced she was somewhere in the house: the kitchen, the bathroom, outside with the dogs, anywhere but gone. After each dream, I'd lain in bed, staring into the darkness. Would this be my life now? Would she ever come around? Or would I stare into the darkness for years, like I had the first time? Except back then, hate had been the emotional fuel. I'd been restless and energized by my negative feelings, spurred on to new places and adventures, desperate to get her out of my system.

Now, the will to live was being sucked out. I had no desire to do anything but sleep, dream of her, fix what I'd broken. Love was a starving vampire.

My alarm buzzed beside me, and I rolled over to snooze my phone. The dogs stirred at the bottom of the stairs, their nails clipping against the wood floor. I had to go see Tyler to pick up the last of the costumes for tomorrow night. Trent, Lila, and I had convinced the Sullivans to turn over all the organizational things for the concert, and we'd made it clear no one expected them to show up on Saturday night. The funeral was Sunday. I remembered what a mess I'd been the night before my dad's funeral. All my pent-up anger at the injustice of losing my dad so suddenly had begged for an outlet, and I'd done stupid, reckless things.

Yesterday, I'd given Maggie some space, sort of. I'd ordered more food and had it delivered to her house at dinner. I'd given Pete, her right-hand man from the mayor's office, her favorite flowers and asked him to make sure she got them. Crowding her was a bad idea, but I had to do something to show her I cared, that even if some part of her wanted me gone, I wasn't going quietly. She was hurting because of her father, because of me. I'd fucked up at the worst possible time, again.

After I'd showered and fed the dogs, I headed to my truck. In the cab, I closed my eyes, hands on the steering wheel. Just out of reach was the memory of Maggie sitting beside me the other night, and if I concentrated hard enough, she filled the space again. I should have said 'no' to the LA job. Or told her right away, gauged if she'd be able to do long-distance. 'Cause if she was out, so was I. I didn't want any life without her.

On autopilot, I ended up at Tyler's shop. Far too early for it to be open yet. I'd meant to go grocery shopping before coming here. From the parking lot, a crack of light shone out of the back room. When I tried the door, I found it unlocked.

"Hello?" I called into the stillness. Clothes racks lined almost every conceivable space, and the counter with the cash register sat over to his left. "Tyler?"

"Come on back." Tyler's voice drifted from the cracked door at the back.

I eased the door open. Tyler stood behind one of the worktables, pieces of a colorful costume all around him, a cloth tape measure over his shoulder, a needle with thread dangling in his hand.

"I'm running a bit behind. I can't sleep, so I don't know how far I'm behind, but I am. Sorry, man. Take a seat. This is the last one."

"I'm early." I scraped one of the chairs across the concrete floor and plopped into it. Sketches lined the back wall, and a rack of costumes was off to the side, ready to take to the theater.

"Not sure the time matters. I can't focus." He sighed and rubbed his face. "Can't sleep. Can't focus."

"How is everyone else doing?" Her name hung in the room unsaid.

"Emily is doing okay. She doesn't have much choice because of Amir, same with my mom. They're both trying to be strong for him. My dad was—" Tyler's voice hitched, and he rubbed his eyes with his fingers. "He was a good grandpa."

"And you?" The pain of losing a parent was such a wall of grief. The week after my dad died, Trent and I had run wild. Looking back, we hadn't made our mom's life easy, our poor choices piled on top of her grief.

"I'm a fucking disaster pretending I'm doing okay. I can't wrap my head around him being gone, and then when I do, the realization is crushing." He shook his head.

"And Maggie?" I'd hoped Tyler would bring her up without prompting. No luck. My gut clenched, waiting for him to respond, to give me something. A breadcrumb.

"She asked me not to talk about her with, uh, anyone." Tyler picked up two pieces of fabric and used pins to connect them.

He was a shitty liar. She'd probably mentioned me by name. "Right."

"She'll come around." Tyler glanced at me before focusing on the cloth in front of him again.

"Will she?" I didn't want to get my hopes up, but I was clinging to any shred of light in the darkness.

"I don't think she wants to cut you out. She just doesn't know how to let you in. Probably feels risky for her." Tyler sighed and grabbed more fabric, piecing it together. "We're all reeling, emotionally fragile."

"I get the reeling. I just wish she'd let me be there."

"You taking the LA job?" Tyler was focused on sewing pieces together.

"She told you about that?"

"Had to give us some reason why you two weren't going to work out. That was it." Tyler stuck some pins between his lips while he brought two pieces of cloth together, a distinct pattern forming on the table.

"I'm supposed to tell my agent today what I'm doing."

"What are you going to do?" Tyler mumbled around the pins.

"What would you do?"

He dropped the pins into his hand. "Nah, you can't ask me that. I'm not you."

"If I turn the job down, and I don't get her back, I'll regret it."

"And the other side of that coin?"

"If I take the job and move to LA, I'll probably never get another chance with Maggie."

"So, twenty years from now, which one will be the bigger regret?" Tyler gave me a meaningful look. "Nothing worse than regret."

The answer was obvious. I'd spent thirteen years pining for Maggie in one way or another. "Do you think if I went to see her, she'd let me in?"

The pins were bobbing in Tyler's mouth again. "Not a chance." He slotted the last one into place in the fabric. "I'm not trying to sway your decision, but the two of you were just starting to get past what happened when you were kids. The timing of the job, of Dad... It's just shitty, man."

With a frustrated grunt, I hauled myself out of the chair. "I'll come back later to get the costumes. Just give me a call when they're done."

"Will do. Shouldn't be too much longer. Are you sure you, Trent, Lila, and Kelvin can handle tomorrow night?"

"Yeah, don't worry about us. Most of the hard work is done now." While that was true, the organization portion of the concert and strip show was going to be chaotic. Kelvin had reassigned everyone's jobs, but when I'd looked at how many places I'd need to be at once, I'd had a mini-heart attack.

One way or another, we'd figure everything out tomorrow night. I wasn't putting pressure on any of the Sullivan family to show up and definitely not to help out given the funeral was on Sunday. "I'll see you on Sunday."

Tyler pressed his fingers into his eyes and nodded. "See you Sunday."

I had searched the parking lot for Trent's car and then followed a resident into the apartment building. At Trent's door, I knocked briskly before I lost my nerve.

When the door swung back, Trent's brows lifted in surprise. "What are you doing here? Shouldn't you be glued to your keyboard or guitar expelling your feelings into a song?"

I grimaced. "Doesn't quite work like that. I have to be inspired or motivated."

"Ah, so, what happened with your first album? Inspiration or motivation?" Trent leaned into the door, not inviting me in.

Hadn't we been making progress? That was an attack, one I would ignore. "Can I come in?"

Trent stepped back and opened the door wider. "Yeah, I guess. Maggie called me fucking crying the other night, so you're on my shit list."

"You talked to her?"

"For like two minutes. She called to apologize that she wasn't going to see the Small Town Saviors show through to the end. Like I care about that right now."

"Oh, so she didn't—"

"Mention she'd broken things off with you? Yeah, she did. Didn't say why, but Emily and Lila filled me in." He popped open a beer and took a long drink. "I told you not to hurt her."

"I was trying not to."

"By moving to LA?"

"I'm not taking the job. Why does everyone act like there wasn't another option? I already called my agent and left him a message."

"So, you broke her heart over nothing?"

Only my brother could make me feel worse than I already did. I rubbed my face. Since Trent wasn't going to offer me a beer, I'd help myself. From the fridge, I took out a bottle, popped the top, and chugged half of it. "Will you go over and talk to her for me? See how she's doing?"

"If you're asking me to go plead your case, that'd be a 'no.'"

"I'm not." I held up my hands. "I swear. I'm not. Everyone says she's not doing well, and she won't let me anywhere near her to help. I've tried texting her, calling. I sent her flowers yesterday. Had lunch delivered. Silence." I examined my beer, the sheer magnitude of how completely she'd cut me off sitting on my shoulders. "She'll let you in. I know she will. I don't want her to be so alone. Don't even mention my name when you're there."

"So, you don't want me going over there for you?" Trent eyed me, his skepticism clear.

"I want to know she's okay and that she's got support. If that makes my request about me, then sure, Trent. It's all about me."

"If Maggie wasn't here, would you be going to LA?"

I met Trent's gaze. How honest should I be? Jim's words about communication and difficult conversations rose up. I wasn't hiding from anyone anymore. "Yeah, I probably would have taken the job."

"So, Mom and I, we aren't worth staying for?"

I pinched my lips with my fingers. "Last time I left, I was weighed down by guilt. I'd let Dan into the house, I'd coveted Maggie to the point where I'd been disloyal to you. I didn't know how to deal with the things I'd done. I realize now that I should have talked to you, that I should have talked to her. Fear of the unknown held me back. My avoidance of this town had nothing to do with anything you'd done. You're my brother, and I love you. I'll always love you, root for you. I am beyond sorry I ever made you feel anything other than those things. Whether I stay in Little Falls or I end up halfway around the world again, I'm going to do better by you and by Mom. We aren't going to keep drifting apart. I'm tethered to you." I pushed up the sleeve on his shirt to reveal our tattoo, partially covered by a medieval lock and key, but still visible. "You're not getting rid of me."

"I'll go see Maggie," Trent said, his voice gruff. "I'm trying to let the past go between us."

"We all are," I said. "Just gonna take a while. We've got time. I'm not making the same mistakes again."

"Yeah?" Trent gave me a wry grin. "You got some different ones lined up?"

I smiled. "Probably. I take one foot out of my mouth just to jam the other one in."

"If you need some salt and pepper for taste, just let me know."

"Nah, it's feet, man. You gotta use hot sauce on those to disguise the stench." We both laughed, and Trent held out his hand to shake. "We're brothers. We're gonna hug it out." We embraced, and I held him tight, patting him on the back.

Chapter Thirty-Two
Maggie

Ginger purred on my chest, her little paws kneading my shirt. Was there anything more perfect than a contented cat? The purring and the kneading motion were soothing.

When the door vibrated with someone's fist after the doorbell had gone off three times, I knew I should get up, but I just couldn't summon the energy.

Beside me, my phone started up a familiar chorus. Great, now Trent was trying to check up on me. I sent him to voicemail.

Another *boom, boom, boom* sounded on my door, followed by the repeated ring of my doorbell.

"Maggie! Get your ass to the door. You're starting to worry me. If you don't answer this door, I'm going to think something has happened to you, and I'll break the damn thing down."

Dropping Ginger to the ground, I heaved myself off the couch and ambled to the door, defeated. Opening it, I leaned against the edge of the frame. "Don't break my door." I hadn't showered or left the house in almost two days. The pharmacy was being run by a semiretired pharmacist friend who'd heard about my dad's death. The offer to take over the store for a week had been a weight off my shoulders, but the absence of something to do with my time was letting me sink into grief in a way that wasn't healthy, but that I couldn't seem to prevent.

"Don't ignore me. It's rude," Trent said.

"If you're here to plead Grady's case—"

"We were friends before my brother ever got involved." His pissed off expression would be intimidating if I didn't know him so well. "I'm here because people are worried about you."

Should I be happy or sad Grady hadn't sent him? Not that I had a choice. Sadness was all I was capable of feeling right now. "As you can see, I'm fine."

"You're not fine." He huffed out a breath. "Let me in, Mags. You gotta let someone in."

Of all the people in my life who could have come banging on my door, Trent was the easiest to deal with. He wouldn't ask me to reconsider breaking off my relationship with Grady or try to say I'd get over the loss of Dad. I stepped back from the entryway, leaving the door open for Trent to follow.

Once we were in the living room, I resumed my sprawl on the couch, and Trent took one of the recliners to the right. When the silence became too much, I said, "Is everything all set for tomorrow night?"

"You don't need to be worrying about that." Trent waved me off.

"What should I worry about? My dead father? My boyfriend who kept his impending move across the country from me?"

"Maggie."

"What? It's a legitimate question. Maybe I should think about the election for mayor and how I could be beaten by someone who doesn't even want the job. How's that for something to worry about?"

"I didn't come here to talk about Grady. I told you that."

"Well, maybe *I* want to talk about him. You told me this would happen. That he'd leave. Would never stay."

Trent grimaced. "Maybe I shouldn't have said that."

"Why not? Looks like it's coming true. He had a job offer on the other side of the country, and he didn't even mention it."

"Maybe he had a good reason."

"Are you really defending him? Really?"

Trent flushed and ran a hand across the top of his hair. The arms of his T-shirt bulged when he crossed them. "He's my brother. I'm not going to *not* defend him."

Resentment flared before I pushed it aside. I'd be the same way with my siblings. Whatever flaws they had, I could point them out, tease them, be annoyed by them, but God forbid anyone else say a word against them. "Are you two getting along better?"

Trent shrugged. "We got a ways to go. You're not seriously worried you won't win the election?"

I brushed my tangled hair out of my face and sighed. "A little worried—super low on my list of concerns. But I—I originally ran for mayor as a way to, I don't know, make amends to everyone for what you and I did."

Trent shook his head, his jaw tight. "Not what you and I did. What *I* did."

"I never got in trouble, but I was part of the process. I gave you advice that let the business grow, gave you more confidence, lured in more people's sons and daughters."

"We all made our choices. Those kids, every single one, knew exactly what they were getting into. *You* didn't know."

"Maybe. Didn't make it any easier to see all those people hurting."

He huffed out a breath. "That's what Saturday's about. Trying to make amends or start to, I guess. I want this town to remember me for something other than a drug ring and a long jail sentence."

"They will. Just takes time."

Ginger wound herself around Trent's legs, begging for attention. He stroked her long tail, and she banged her head into his leg in approval, pressing her face against his jeans. She'd loved Grady too. Something about the Castillo men made anything of the female persuasion want to rub themselves all over them.

"He didn't mean to hurt you," Trent said, his tone gentle.

"Didn't he?" I pressed my fingers into my forehead. Ginger wandered past my dangling hand, arching her back, eager to be touched. "Historically, Grady has been very good at hurting me." And the possibility that might be true this time has haunted me. Deep down, I'm not sure if I really believe he'd hurt me on purpose again, but picking apart my feelings was more emotional labor than I was capable of.

"I know. Trust me, I know. But I also believe he's trying to be better."

"Why not tell me? If I was a factor in any decision, why not tell me?"

"I don't know." He took a deep breath. "He's crazy about you."

For the last few days, I'd let myself live in the numbness. It felt like the only way to survive. Block out what happened to my dad. Block out any feelings for Grady. All I could manage to do was exist.

"My heart feels really broken right now, Trent." I could barely keep the tears in check. "Like... Unmendable. I don't know what to do about Grady because I am terrified, absolutely terrified that he'll discard me, treat me like I don't matter, just like he did last time. Maybe not on purpose—like taking a job and not considering my feelings—but his behavior last time wrecked me in ways I'm only starting to understand. And I can't fall apart more than I already am. I can't. I won't survive."

"He's not gonna do that, Mags."

"You don't get it. Can't possibly understand. We slept together and he ghosted me. Cut me off completely. Looked past me, around me, *through* me whenever we shared the same space. And I think I've spent the last however many years avoiding any relationship that might do that to me again. It seems particularly foolish to walk back into one with the person who did the damage in the first place."

"He wants to make things right. I believe that."

"How do you know, though? We were together, like, together-together, and he didn't tell me about LA. If I was him, if I was in his shoes, I'd only keep news like that a secret if I didn't want the other person to be a factor. If I was only worried about doing what was best for me."

"I get that. Grady's a fucking idiot because I'm positive that's *not* what he intended when he didn't tell you."

"I just… I don't have the emotional bandwidth to sort out what's real and what's not real. I don't know how to do that right now when I feel this lost."

"But you love him?"

"I don't know." But I did. I knew I did. Admitting that felt like another slice across my emotions, and I was barely keeping a lid on what was bubbling under the surface. "I can't go there right now."

"I think the two of you have been in love with each other for years."

"Sometimes love isn't enough."

Trent moved from his chair to lift my legs and sat on the couch, setting my legs on his lap. He grabbed the remote off the armrest, and he flicked on the streaming service I paid for, searching through all my recommendations. Ginger jumped onto my legs and stretched along Trent's chest, kneading his shirt, practically begging for attention.

"Your taste in TV is shit," he said, scrolling with one hand while stroking Ginger with the other.

"You're not going to try to talk me around?" I asked, my voice small.

"I tried," he said with a shrug. "I told Grady I wouldn't even try, but I think you need him right now, even if you don't want to need him, even if you don't quite trust him. Sometimes," he said, trying to catch my gaze, "the only way you know if you can trust someone is to give them that trust and just hope they keep earning it."

"I don't know when I'll feel ready to do that," I admitted.

"What you need right now is comfort and certainty," Trent said with conviction. "*Mean Girls* it is."

"That's going to give me comfort and certainty?"

"You know the outcome. That's certainty. And Rachel McAdams is still hot, even after all these years. That's comfort."

"Comfort for who?" I asked, but I could feel the hint of a smile rising for the first time in days.

Trent didn't respond, he just patted my legs and pressed Play. I turned onto my side, trying not to let the numbness envelop me quite so completely this time.

Chapter Thirty-Three
Grady

Saturday night the concert hall buzzed. The heavy red curtains were drawn, and it was thirty minutes to showtime. The ornate gold-and-red décor of the Stanley was too regal for tonight's performances even if Trent insisted on calling the strip show classy. How many classy strip bars had Trent frequented over the years to be so sure the two places had even a passing resemblance?

With the clock ticking, I rushed around with a clipboard, trying to get a handle on who was performing and when. Emily had been slated to manage everything backstage, but with the Sullivans staying home, the four of us who were left had taken on multiple jobs. Part of me was grateful for the chaotic rush because the madness gave me less time to think about Maggie.

I'd sent Trent to talk to her since she was refusing to have anything to do with me. When I'd asked Trent later, he'd said Maggie "wasn't in a good place," "wasn't herself," and "needed time to sort out her shit," which hadn't exactly been comforting. What would more time do? Probably give her too many reasons to avoid me, convince herself we'd never work. We were supposed to be together. Years of being apart hadn't smothered my feelings. I had no doubts, and Maggie telling me to go to

LA had turned my certainty from cement to concrete. I'd do whatever I had to do to get her back.

From the other side of the stage, Joseph Goldtooth, who had been moved to props to compensate for their missing members, held up a pair of handcuffs. "Which box?"

"That one." I pointed with more confidence than I felt to a cardboard box labeled with a performer's name. We had sorted all those boxes. I didn't know why Joseph was moving things around, but I didn't have time to micromanage. There was no way tonight would go smoothly when our seven-person team had become four. Panic beat its wings against my chest. What if the event was a colossal flop?

We'd sold out. Maybe because I'd secured famous singers like Mia Malone, maybe because so many of the men in the town had stepped up—and out—for the cause. But if this fell apart, it would be on a grand scale, and it might burn some of my professional bridges to boot.

When Jason, a local groundskeeper and the third nervous man, hovered to say he was having doubts about performing, my head threatened to pop off and whirl around the stage. I was on the verge of letting loose with some not-so-carefully chosen words when a manicured hand snatched the clipboard from my grasp.

"Let me handle it," Emily said, smiling. Without missing a beat, she looped her arm around Jason's shoulders and talked about his hard work and the good cause. The performance was only a few minutes of his life, but the money they were raising might rebuild a resident's house or fix a local business. When Jason walked away, he was nodding his head, a smile on his face. She had a gift I did not possess.

"Thank fucking God," I muttered before assessing her appearance. In many ways, she was like Maggie. There wasn't a strawberry-blond hair out of place despite the circumstances. "Are you sure you're up for this?"

She nodded but didn't make eye contact. "I couldn't stay at home. The—the funeral is tomorrow. It's just all... you know."

My frustration dissolved as I assessed her. "Yeah, I know."

"Tyler came too."

Maggie's name was on my lips, and I couldn't decide if I'd be relieved to see her, or if it would cause more stress.

"Maggie's not coming. I'm sorry. None of us are doing well, but I think she's doing worse." She glanced down at her sheets and then at me. "She said you two were taking a break."

"That's what she called it? She told me to move to LA."

"Can you blame her? You didn't tell her about the job. Sends a clear signal."

I sucked in a deep breath and tried to keep the annoyance from spilling out. "I wasn't trying to send *any* signal which is why I didn't tell her. I didn't think I wanted the job, and by the time I decided I might, the timing was terrible."

She flicked through the pages on the clipboard without reading them. "Have you told her how you feel?"

Of course I had. Hadn't I? We'd talked about so many things in the days leading up to Jim's death. But I hadn't said the words, probably the most important ones I felt, not really. Circled them, definitely. I'd been having trouble reading Maggie. What did she feel? Still, the other night, I'd told her she had my heart. How much clearer could I be?

"Unless you've told her you love her," Trent said, approaching from the side, "and we all know you do, then she doesn't know how you feel, man. Maggie overthinks things. Even if she thought you might feel that way, her brain will talk her out of believing it, especially if you haven't said the words."

I raised my eyebrows at Trent. "Not those exact words, no. But I thought I'd been pretty clear."

Emily gestured toward Trent. "Pretty clear is not clear. And that is my sister in a nutshell. Sometimes she thinks too much about the wrong things."

"It's not like I've abandoned her." I surveyed them all. Had I read her and the situation wrong yet again? I flicked my wrist at Trent. "You told me she needed space to sort her head out."

"Yeah, well. You fucked up, man." He shrugged and ran his hand over the top of his hair. "Right now, she needs comfort and certainty." He hesitated for a beat. "And I might have told her weeks ago you'd never stay in Little Falls. That you'd leave no matter what."

"You did what?" I raised my voice, and people turned to stare at us.

Keeping my distance was excruciating when I knew what it was like to drown in grief. I'd fucked up by not telling her about the job offer. I understood that. Somehow, instead of protecting her, I'd made her think I didn't care enough. Nothing could be further from the truth. And I'd never make that mistake again. I'd tell her everything, forever.

At the back of my mind, my chat with Jim played. He'd said Maggie glowed when she talked about me. *Glowed*. That was a beacon to stay the course, to believe maybe there was hope. The way she'd leaned into me before I'd left her house, as though she was one stiff breeze away from toppling over, had convinced me that I could salvage our relationship. Eventually, with enough time, Maggie would come around. Giving up wasn't an option.

"I was still mad at you," Trent said. "I didn't know she meant that much to you. I was afraid you were killing time, and she'd get hurt. I wasn't wrong. You *did* hurt her."

I only half heard him, my mind consumed with ways to fix what had broken between me and Maggie. Comfort and security. I could give her those, I think.

I needed to lay myself bare, embrace enough discomfort for her to realize *she* was the most important factor in any decision. LA meant nothing if she wasn't there, or here in Little Falls with me in spirit or on weekends, or whenever I could convince her to fly to LA to snatch fragments of time. I wanted her, and I would take her in any capacity she'd allow.

Time was precious. Like my father, Jim had died with no warning. The last two days since she'd asked me to leave, I'd done a lot of thinking. I was done hiding my feelings and decisions. Instead of spending my life guarding my heart, I intended to live the rest of this life with my heart open.

"Add me to the bottom of the schedule for tonight." I glanced at Emily and ran a hand along the back of my neck. Impulsiveness hadn't always been my friend.

"What's going on?" Lila approached their group from behind Trent. "We have fifteen minutes to showtime. Isn't this when we panic because we've forgotten something? Has anyone looked at the crowd? It's insane. Kelvin is downstairs with his boyfriend running through dance moves with every panicked would-be stripper."

"Grady's going to close out the show." Emily flipped her pencil around and wrote my name at the bottom of the list.

"What?" Lila frowned. "But Maggie said you didn't enjoy performing in front of big crowds anymore."

"That's when I'm trying to be somebody I'm not. I'm just gonna be me tonight." I looked down at my feet before staring hard at Lila. Just the thought of what I was going to do made me squirm with discomfort. "Do you think Maggie loves me?"

A soft laugh escaped her. "I *know* she does. She's been half in love with you since she was seventeen." A wry smile touched her lips before she met my gaze. "Nobody else measured up."

A crease formed between my eyes as I looked at Emily. The phrasing clicked something into place which had been nagging me. "*I'm* the measure? She was measuring other men to *me*?" I needed to stop being such a fucking coward and ask the hard questions. Emily had said something similar a week ago, and I'd thought she meant I wasn't measuring up either, not that I was the standard. I'd been so sure I wasn't capable of meeting whatever invisible checklist Maggie had.

Emily's mouth twisted into an almost smile. "Yep."

"Jesus Christ. I'm such a fucking idiot."

They all made various gestures of agreement.

"All right," I said, my gaze shifting between them. "I'm going for it. Tonight, I'm laying it out there. No more misunderstandings."

"Thank fucking God," Trent said with a grin. "I was starting to think I needed to run a Communication 101 seminar for you two lemmings."

"Fuck off." I smiled to take the edge off the words. "Communication 101 with you as the professor?" I scoffed. "What textbook would you use?"

Trent pointed to the side of his head. "My superior brain."

"Useless." We grinned at each other. Our old comradery wasn't always there, but when it appeared, I embraced the moment.

"So," Emily said, running her finger down her list. "You'll be on right after the group number. We'll have to get Tyler to do an announcement at some point about the special performance or no one will know. It's not in the program."

The mention of the group performance brought forth a flood of memories. I'd spent hours helping Jim nail the footwork for that number. We should have been dancing together. My throat closed at the memory, and I was reminded again of what the Sullivans were enduring right now, what Maggie was trying to endure alone.

"Where's Tyler?" Emily looked around, blinking rapidly, a sheen across her eyes.

Had her mind gone to her father too?

"Helping Mia Malone," Lila said with a flick of her hand. "Some sort of wardrobe malfunction."

Grateful for the distraction, I cleared my throat. "Should I help?" I turned in the direction of the dressing rooms.

"No," Lila said. "She needed something sewed. Tyler found a sewing kit and is doing the mending in her dressing room."

"Oh, yeah," I agreed. "I guess he'd be the best one to help." If anyone could rectify a wardrobe malfunction with a standard emergency sewing kit, Tyler would be the guy. His creativity and ingenuity were truly amazing. All the costumes he'd cobbled together for tonight's performances were like pieces of art.

Without the costume distraction, my previous idea returned, and I considered the wisdom of what I was about to propose. If Maggie couldn't talk to me directly, I'd talk to her. "You guys think you can live stream the show and convince Maggie to watch?" I looked between Emily, Lila, and Trent. There would be people in the audience who'd post the concert to YouTube, but I didn't want to take a chance she might not see it, might not know.

"I already told you she loves you, which is against best friend code. But she's hurting. I think being with you makes the hurt less." Lila took a deep breath. "If what you're planning to do will embarrass her—"

"It might," I said, running a hand along my chin and down my throat. "Not in a hurtful way, I promise. I need her to hear me, really hear me. Maybe having my words recorded will help them sink in. She can play them back as much as she needs." Comfort and certainty in a video. Maggie needed time to sit with a decision or a dilemma, to let it process. Putting my feelings out there so publicly might give her the distance but also the repetition she needed to see I was offering her my heart. That if we both hadn't been a little on the back foot, letting our past cloud the present, she'd already know she had it.

Truthfully, I'd give her anything she asked for.

Lila, Emily, and Trent exchanged glances.

"I'll go over to Maggie's toward the end of the show, if everyone can run this without me for the last hour or so," Lila said.

"We'll be fine." Tyler stepped into the circle. I wondered how long he'd been listening.

"Oh, hey." Emily smiled. "You get Ms. Malone all fixed up?"

Tyler gave a sheepish grin. "Something like that. She's... uh... interesting."

Mia was into the spectacle aspect of her performances. Probably a phase, but I'd heard from lots of industry people she could be a bit much—demanding, childish, crazy clauses in her riders, blunt bordering on rude. I'd never had a problem with her or the things she'd wanted for her album. I liked straightforward, direct people, and Mia, for someone who was only twenty, was good at cutting to the chase. Her mother was a slightly different story, and I sometimes wondered if Laura was the root of the ugly rumors.

"If Lila is going there, I need someone to film." I glanced around.

"Filming," Kelvin said, clapping me on the shoulder. "I love to direct people."

Kelvin had reappeared from the basement with his boyfriend in tow. They must have managed to calm the mass of nervous men before the curtains parted. "Think you can handle the pressure?"

"Of course." He scanned the group, and he must have read their eagerness and uncertainty. "Wait. What am I filming?"

"Grady will fill you two in," Emily said while she checked her watch. "The rest of us have things to get done before the curtain disappears in five minutes."

"Five minutes?" Lila squeaked. "Ahh. Panic! This is what panic feels like." Her heels clacked across the floor as she strutted away with Emily. Tyler, Kelvin, and his boyfriend followed, chatting as they made their way to their places.

Standing in front of the heavy curtain, Trent turned to me.

"I don't need to hear I fucked up again," I said, holding up my hand. My own version of panic was seeping into my gut. If I did this and she still rejected me, the performance would live on the internet forever. Not exactly an appealing thought. I really valued my privacy. Songwriting, rather than singing, had a lot of perks.

"Nah, I wasn't going to say that. I mean, you did, but I don't need to say it again."

I gave him the side-eye and scratched the stubble emerging on my cheek.

"I'm proud of you," Trent said. "Yeah, the rest of us did a lot. But you brought big names here tonight for the town, people who drew the sold-out crowd." He stared at his feet and shoved his hands in his jean pockets. "And when Jim died, you didn't buckle. I thought you might. You carry Dad's death differently than me, and it's been pretty clear during the Small Town Saviors practices that Maggie's dad meant a lot to you. I didn't know how far you'd be set back."

I swallowed the lump in my throat and then cleared it, hoping my voice didn't portray how much Trent's words meant. "I'm trying. I'm really fucking trying."

"It shows. She's no fool. She'll see it too." He drew me into a hug before wandering to the side of the stage to talk to the first group of performers.

With a sigh, I followed his lead and grabbed the box of props to dish out to the dancers, a group of four men dressed as coal miners.

The show would open with a bang, and if I was lucky, it would finish with one too.

Two songs later, things were ticking along, and Trent was up for his solo performance. From the sidelines, I saw Emily straightening Trent's bow tie on the other side of the stage, and then she snapped one of his suspenders. Lila and Emily had decided to make Trent a straitlaced nerd. The image was the opposite of the rough, tattooed bad boy most of the town believed him to be. Trent took his spot in the middle of the stage with a clipboard in his hand. He glanced over at Emily and flashed her something on the clipboard. Whatever was there made Emily burst into laughter. My brother had never been short on charm.

The curtains rolled back, and Trent pushed his glass-less frames up his nose and pretended to read through the clipboard. When the opening beat of "SexyBack" by Justin Timberlake hit, Trent dropped the clipboard and looked around as though he wasn't sure who the song was talking about. Then, with a shrug, he peeled off a suspender, and the crowd went wild. The body rolls and the hip-hop dance moves followed in quick succession.

Kelvin had mentioned that Trent had gotten extra lessons from Amy, the dance coordinator I brought on board. I'd assumed that was a euphemism for Trent charming Amy into bed, but he'd definitely learned a thing or two.

On the other side of the stage, Emily and Lila stood in the wings, admiring their handiwork. Seeing them look so proud and happy was a nice change from how they'd both appeared the last couple of days. Would Maggie have stood beside them? Had the same pleased look on her face?

Trent was winning over the crowd with each hip thrust, each piece of discarded clothing. When Trent ripped off his tearaway pants, the sound of the crowd was deafening. I grinned. Were the citizens of Little Falls ready to welcome Trent back into the fold? Or were they just so rabid for a naked, ripped body they'd take anyone as long as he danced well and looked good? I hoped there were people in the crowd who scanned the organizing committee on their programs for the night and recognized Trent's name as a founding member.

"What do you think?" Kelvin asked.

"Feeling pretty proud of my little brother right about now."

"I hope you aren't the only one." Kelvin stared out at the crowd. "You nervous? Do you still get nervous?"

Nerves should've been fluttering in the pit of my stomach. The signs of an impending performance were almost always the same. Fluttering stomach, cold sweat down my back, a sinking feeling I'd fuck something up. But when I considered Kelvin's question, I realized something. "I'm not nervous, actually. Doing this feels right."

On stage, Trent was down to some tight, white boxer briefs. Had he gotten a spray tan? I rubbed my face at the thought.

As the song came to a close, Trent tossed his glasses across the stage and turned his back to the crowd. With his fingers in the waistband of his boxers at the back, he looked over his shoulder at the crowd.

Please let him remember we agreed there'd be no total nudity.

The final words of the song rang out and the lights cut out just as it appeared Trent was going to lose his last piece of clothing.

Thank God.

I breathed a sigh of relief while the crowd went wild with cries for an encore, and the curtains closed.

Joseph Goldtooth rushed around the stage gathering Trent's discarded items.

"What'd you think?" Trent asked, ambling over to us.

"Those lessons paid off," Kelvin said, grinning.

"She was an excellent teacher." His answering grin told me he hadn't been wrong about what the lessons had entailed.

"You definitely worked the crowd."

"I got a little nervous." Trent admitted, his smile fading. "I recognized a couple people right at the front. But then when they started cheering, I don't know, I just went for it."

"Definitely memorable." I clapped him on the shoulder. Other than Kelvin and the guys in the group routine, Trent was probably the only other solo performer I knew who could dance with some rhythm.

"I hope so." Trent accepted his discarded clothes from Joseph Goldtooth as the next performer took center stage. "It'd be nice to be known for something else, something positive."

I kept my gaze focused on the heavy red curtain and took a deep, steadying breath. Most of the buzz behind the stage had quieted down. The final huge group number had passed. Mia Malone had come and gone. A few of my other musical friends had left in limos, and now it was just me, a stage, and a guitar.

Unlike when I played in the open mic night months ago, I was wishing to see Maggie's face for an entirely different reason.

"Where do you want the camera?" Kelvin scrolled through some of his apps to find the one he and Lila had agreed would be best for recording and live streaming.

"Maggie needs to know I'm doing this for her. So, the tighter you can frame me, the better. I want her to feel like she's in the room with me."

He tapped some buttons on his phone and tested the volume. "It's been a good night," Kelvin said as Tyler continued his spiel out in front of the curtain. "I hope Lila can get her to watch."

The guitar was slung across my back, and there was a stool a few feet in front, which I might use after I'd spent time wooing the audience, which was really Maggie. I couldn't care less what anyone in the crowd thought when this was over.

I closed my eyes and sent a little prayer out into the universe, hoping it landed with Maggie's dad. Jim would want us to be happy, and he'd want Maggie to feel comforted and secure.

"Even if she can't watch tonight, I'm counting on all those people out there with their phones and cameras and curiosity to compel her to hear me out."

Jim's advice was at the forefront of my mind. I was meeting the hard things head-on and fighting for what I wanted.

Maggie.

I wanted Maggie, and I needed her to know exactly what I should have told her weeks ago.

From the other side of the curtain, Tyler said, "And now, to close out the show, a special performance from Grady Castillo. It's a real treat, ladies and gentlemen. What you're seeing tonight, you've never seen before, and you'll never see this exact performance again."

I sucked in a deep breath and looked at Kelvin. "Don't fuck up."

He laughed. "Same, man. Same." Then, Kelvin took a few steps back and raised his phone to me as the curtains parted.

Chapter Thirty-Four
Maggie

I lay in bed, staring at the ceiling, thinking about getting a second cat. Ginger was curled around my arm, purring. I really wanted a dog, perhaps two. Preferably following a tall, brown-haired, brown-eyed man back into my house, back into my life.

Each time my brain headed in that direction, I wished to slice out every memory of Grady and examine it, figure out why he had such a tremendous influence on me. The connection didn't make sense. Why did I care so much?

If I wasn't thinking about cats or about Grady and his dogs, my thoughts drifted to Dad. Those memories weren't ones I was ready to pluck out, to put under the microscope. No matter how much I tried to skirt around the realization that he was gone, it kept coming back like a vicious right hook, knocking me to the ground.

There'd been glimmers of a real, healthy relationship with Grady in the few days we'd been together. But then he'd kept the job from me. When someone was in a relationship they cared about, they didn't keep the big life moments from each other. From watching my parents, I knew couples navigated those moments together, and doing it separately was asking for trouble. The last piece of advice my father had given me had been about relationships.

Loving someone with all your heart means you aren't rivals, you're teammates. You cheer each other on.

Had Grady told me about the job, I might have cheered even as my heart broke. For him, the opportunity was amazing. I would never want to be a factor holding him back.

I'd wanted to feel important enough to be part of the discussion. Instead, I'd felt easy to leave behind yet again.

The doorbell pealed through the house, and Ginger skittered away as though the melody was a gunshot. I sighed and threw back the covers, my feet hitting the floor of my bedroom. Almost everyone I knew was at the Small Town Saviors show in Utica. I'd shunned social media in case I'd glimpsed something, and guilt had seeped in far enough to propel me there. I wasn't ready to face any of it.

With one eye pressed to the peephole, I frowned. "Lila?"

As soon as I opened the door, Lila grabbed my arm and led me to the couches in the living room.

Panic rose, and tears sprang to my eyes at the determined way she was acting. I sank into the plush leather beside Lila. "Did something happen? You're supposed to be at the Small Town Saviors show."

"Oh, Maggie. No. I'm sorry. I should have said something when I got here. It's just…" She pressed the home button on her phone. "I'm running out of time. Traffic was shit. I need you to watch something."

I frowned, taking Lila's phone from her hand. "Is it bad?"

"No, it's not." Lila punched in her security code.

My breath caught in my throat at the sight of Grady striding toward a microphone perched in the middle of the stage. With a sharp shake of my head, I tried to give the phone back to Lila. "I can't—I don't want—"

"If I thought this was a bad idea, I wouldn't be here. Okay? I'm not going to set off a bomb in your life. I'm trying to help you pick up some of the pieces." She rose and smoothed down her dress. "I'll make tea. You watch."

My stomach dropped as though I'd crested a hill on a roller coaster. His worn jeans were familiar. A few days ago, they laid on my bedroom floor. His navy shirt hinted at the muscles beneath, and my fingers clenched Lila's phone, remembering the feel of each ridge.

Why couldn't I stay numb?

When he approached the microphone, he angled himself to keep one of his hands on his guitar, which threatened to swing from behind his back. His lips were so close to the microphone I suppressed a groan of remembrance at how soft they'd been against my skin.

This must be how addicts feel. One glimpse of him wasn't enough. I wanted him, could maybe convince myself he was a need. Even if Lila dropped a pot of scalding water all over herself and the floor, I wasn't going to be able to look away. There he was, and he was everything.

He talked about the night and thanked people for attending. He gave credit to Trent for coming up with the idea of a community event to help repair our damaged town. My heart slowed at the deep timbre of his voice, such a comforting sound, even at this distance.

If I closed my eyes, I could pretend he was speaking to me, just me. He'd left me a voicemail a few days ago. I'd played it on repeat the day after I broke it off with him until I'd hit delete by accident, and I'd cried buckets of tears.

"But none of that is why I asked to close out the show tonight." He gazed into the camera, searing my soul. "I hope you're out there listening."

Warmth spread through me in a rush. Was he talking to me?

"Lila?" I called. The kettle whistled in the kitchen, but Lila didn't respond.

"A few years ago, I wrote an album." The crowd went wild, almost drowning out his chuckle into the mic. The mention of those songs made my stomach roll. "Yeah, yeah, you might have heard of it." He scratched the back of his neck.

My heart pierced at the realization he was nervous. Why was he doing this? He hated working a crowd.

"A long time ago, I knew an incredibly smart, incredibly gorgeous red-headed girl. She stole my heart. Ripped it right outta my chest." He grabbed his shirt and pulled his hand away, raising his fist into the air. "And I was so mad, I wrote a bunch of shitty songs about her. What I didn't realize at the time was I'd also fractured her heart. And I'd give anything to undo that damage." He looked at his feet and then into the camera again. My heart thundered in response. "You see, she's brave and strong and loyal and beautiful and about a million other things, and I was *lucky* it was her who snagged my heart so long ago. I couldn't imagine a worthier person."

"Lila?" I called, my voice tinged with panic. What was Grady doing?

He stared into the camera. "You protected my heart, even when I didn't deserve it, and I haven't been able to do the same for you. I want to, though. I want to spend hours, days, weeks, years tending to your heart."

The camera caught someone from the crowd yelling, "You can tend to my heart, Grady!"

He glanced up and squinted into the lights. "Only one heart I'm interested in, sorry." He grinned to take the sting from his words. Even as my heart beat erratically in my chest, I wondered why he hated wooing a crowd. He was good at it.

The guitar he'd been holding behind his back swung to his front. Glancing down, he strummed a few chords. Warmth spread to my core, and the glow of all the lingering love I'd been repressing the last few days spilled out.

He fiddled with a few things on his guitar as he strummed and continued to speak, "The other night, you asked me to write a song. So, I did. I wrote this for you, Maggie May." Gazing directly into the camera, he said, "If there's a choice to be made, I choose you. Wherever you are, that's where I want to be. With you. Always. I'll *always* choose you. I love you so fucking much."

My heart swooped down to my feet and then soared. Had he said that? Had he really declared his love in front of all those people?

Grady loved me.

Until this moment, I hadn't been sure I understood what I needed to hear to give me the confidence to trust Grady again like Trent suggested.

As the melody began, I recognized it. He'd been humming it in the days leading up to my dad's death. With a small smile, he leaned into the microphone and sang. The song looped around me. Each word was a thread, weaving itself into the fabric of my heart, finding my tattered edges and mending them.

Before this moment, I'd tried to convince myself that my forever person didn't have to be him. And perhaps I could have let him go. But the more he sang, the more I realized I might be able to live without him, but I didn't want to, not if he loved me like this, not when I loved him exactly the same way.

Each time he stepped toward the mic and belted out another line, my heart squeezed. All my anger and pain, both the old and the new, was being wrung out.

When the song ended, he threw up a hand and waved to the crowd and the applause was deafening. He leaned into the mic one last time and yelled, "Vote Maggie Sullivan for mayor of Little Falls. She loves this town. Loves you people. There's no better candidate."

My chest swelled, overflowing with so many emotions I didn't know how to identify them. The video cut out, and I glanced up. Lila was beside the island, tears in her eyes.

"Did you see it?" I asked, still in disbelief. "Did you see him?"

"Yeah," she whispered. "I grabbed your iPad. How are you feeling?" She wiped her tears and sniffed.

I stared at Lila's phone. "Overwhelmed. Shocked. Relieved. I—I thought maybe it was just me."

"You didn't think he loved you?"

"He kept the job from me. I couldn't see how it meant he felt anything close to how I felt. I wouldn't have done that to him." I shook my head, my voice growing thick with unshed tears. "I wanted to matter enough for him to tell me, for him to share those big decisions with me." I stared at Lila's phone, lost in a haze. After a minute, I peered at Lila, hopeful. "Can I watch it again? How do I watch it again?"

Instead of using her phone, Lila took my TV remote and scrolled through the applications until she got to the one they'd used, and she clicked on Kelvin's profile. "It's here." She took her phone from my outstretched hand. "I'm going to go. I need to help with cleanup."

My mind circled what he'd done as I accepted the remote from Lila. "Do you think he'll come here when you're finished?"

She shook her head. "No, he said he didn't want to push you into responding if you wanted the distance. He just wanted you to know how he felt."

I wiped at the few tears that rolled down my cheeks. Part of me wanted to hop in Lila's car and drive to the concert, fall into Grady's arms, pretend nothing else mattered. But I needed to absorb it all, analyze it, make sure I really knew in my heart everything he'd said. If I was going to risk my fragile emotions, I needed to be absolutely sure I could give him my trust again.

"Hey," Lila said from the door. "Switch off your brain for once, okay? Let your heart lead you. He'll protect it this time. I have faith." She shut the door behind her.

Holding my breath, I clicked on the button to stream it again. For a long time, I watched Grady's performance on repeat and little by little, pieces of my heart stitched together. By the time I rose from my seat in the living room, I knew I was ready.

Chapter Thirty-Five

Grady

I climbed into bed and refused to let disappointment drag me under. She hadn't come. It was unlikely she'd appear tomorrow either, since it was Jim's funeral.

Almost three hours ago, the concert had ended. We'd cleaned up, I'd signed autographs, and Lila had returned. She'd assured me that Maggie had seen my declaration and song, and she'd been rewatching it as Lila left. She hadn't given any indication of how Maggie had taken my performance and declaration.

She processed things deeply, which is something I'd come to realize since I'd allowed myself to get to know Maggie to the fullest. Decisions were never made on the spur of the moment, but they were always decisive. I was the opposite—quick, impulsive decisions I sometimes regretted. In my heart, I'd hoped we'd learn to balance each other. That was only possible if she gave me another chance.

Whatever happened between us now, I'd put everything I had into that performance. It might have been just for her, but the video was trending across social media. Jack had called within half an hour of the live stream to see if I had enough material for a whole album. I did. More than enough.

The writing had been a torrent, ripping through until Maggie broke off our relationship. Then, my creativity slowed to a trickle. So much of my brain had become consumed with supporting her from afar, and there hadn't been room for much else.

I tugged the blankets higher and rubbed my face. Hite and Zeus were on the bed on either side. Normally, I didn't let them upstairs. My bed was a king-size, but with the two dogs, it felt more like a single, and a tight one at that. I buried my hands in their fur, and they stretched and yawned, pressing the covers tight against my legs. The chances of getting a good night of sleep were slim, anyway. When I wasn't thinking about Maggie, my mind drifted to Jim.

Emily had confided her son, Amir, was struggling to understand his grandpa's death. They'd been close, with Jim acting as a second parent more than a grandparent. I couldn't imagine trying to explain death over and over to a young child who'd already lost his father. I knew from experience Amir might not remember all the memories made with his grandfather, but the feeling he'd gotten from the relationship would linger. It was a blessing, which sometimes felt like a curse, especially in those first few grief-filled days and weeks. You longed for the connection you'd never have again.

The doorbell pierced my dream. Without realizing it, I'd drifted to sleep. For a moment I wasn't sure the sound was real. Hite and Zeus stirred, jumping off the bed and trotting down the stairs. I didn't dare hope Maggie might be at the door so late at night. The funeral was tomorrow. It was just as likely to be a drunk Trent on my doorstep, looking to reminisce about our father, which he'd already done once this week. Where my memories of our dad sometimes felt too vivid, my brother mourned the lack of detail in his recollections. To me, Dad was a tangible person and to Trent, he was a shadow who loomed over our lives, never quite enough.

At the front door, I took a deep breath before opening it. On the other side, Maggie clutched her hands together, her cheeks stained with tears. I scanned her face, not sure what to make of her appearance. A lump was in my throat, making it impossible to speak.

"I thought," she said, her words garbled, "you were looking for a way to let me go."

"Come here." I drew her into my chest, cradling her close. "Never, Maggie May. I meant every word of that song. I love you. I'm not going anywhere. I promise."

Her hands circled my waist, and she sobbed into my chest. I smoothed her hair and kissed the top of her head. Crouching down, I lifted her into my arms and carried her up the stairs.

"My shoes," she said. "And my coat."

"Can go on my floor for one night. Or I'll put them on a chair if the floor will stress you out." I kissed her temple as she looped her arms around my neck and pressed her face into the hollow. "Maybe I'll hide them so you can't run away in the morning." I was teasing, mostly.

She looked up and framed my face with her hands. I stared into her tear-filled coffee eyes. With her in my arms, on the threshold of being in my bed once again, my heart had never felt so full, so complete. There was nothing better than this feeling, than being with her.

"I love you," she whispered, drawing my lips to hers.

Hearing those words was better than anything that had come before. I'd hoped she might return my feelings, or at least come to return them in time. Knowing she was there, that I'd won her heart made my chest expand. Nothing in my life compared to those words from her, not the places I'd seen, the things I'd won, not any other person I'd met. I hoped someday, when I was nearing the end of my life, this moment would be the one replaying.

"You love me?" My voice was hoarse with emotion. "You don't have to—"

She put her finger to my lips. "I want to. I've wanted to say it for a while. I think I've loved you for a long time, but every day you've been back here, my love has gotten stronger. More."

I laid her on the bed and stretched out beside her, my head resting against my palm. She traced the edge of my face, and I grinned. "You and me."

A smile lit her up, and I saw the glow Jim had talked about. "You and me. Weird, right? Were we ever really rivals?"

I smoothed the strands of her hair which had gone astray. "We just got confused about what we were fighting for."

Her smile faded. "Thanks for telling people to vote for me."

"*I'm* voting for you." I splayed my free hand against my chest. "We both know you're the best candidate."

"Are you going to drop out?"

"Not unless you want me to. Otherwise, I'll see it through. A lot of people put time and effort into helping me." I owed it to Kelvin at the very least. When no one else had been willing to go against Maggie, Kelvin had agreed even when he'd thought I was making a mistake, entering the race for the wrong reasons.

"Ah, yes. Your harem of women." Her lips twisted in amusement. She scanned my face, the amusement replaced with something softer. "You wrote me a song."

I kissed her. She looped her arms around my neck and tugged me tight. When I drew back, my forehead touched hers. "I wrote you a whole album. Maybe two."

"Really?"

"Yeah, it's been—being with you has turned the tap back on. The music is there again, racing out of me onto the sheets. I guess we'll see if it's any good."

"I liked tonight's song even before I heard all of it." Her fingers toyed with the tips of my hair. "You've been whistling it."

"For a couple weeks, yeah."

She twisted locks of my hair, lost in thought. "Kelvin's video of you has over a million views already. I think I'm only a thousand or so of those."

"You watched it that many times?"

"Mostly the part where you said you loved me *so fucking much*." She brushed my cheek with her thumb. "The words filled my heart. You looked like you meant them."

"Every word." My voice was gruff. "I've never felt this way about anyone but you."

"Kinda scares me a little." Her worried gaze met mine.

"That I love you this much?"

"No." She shook her head and offered a fleeting smile. "That I love *you* that much. My dad just died, and with the way I feel, I just don't know if I could take losing someone else."

I looked down at her, knowing the struggle. I was sure I'd been going through the same thing in my mind for years. Letting people in meant exposing yourself to risk. When you knew how deep the pain could run, how vicious the wound, protecting yourself became more important than anything.

But I'd never regretted how much I'd loved my dad, only that I hadn't gotten more time with him. Deep down, I hadn't regretted letting Maggie get close either, just the result. I was gunning for a different outcome this time.

"If you could give up the pain, would you give up the memories?" I kissed her forehead and gave her space to think.

"No." Her voice was thick with tears. "No."

I searched her face. "Then let's make some really great memories, so any pain is worth it."

Tears slipped down her cheeks, and I scooped them up with my thumbs. "I don't know how you went from the guy who caused me problems to the one solving them."

"I pulled my head outta my ass. It was warm there but kinda lonely."

She laughed through her tears and pushed my shoulder. "You're still gross." With two fingers, she swept away the last of the moisture on her cheeks. "I'm sorry I've been so distant."

"Your dad died. You get a pass. Maybe a few of them." I laid back and drew her into my side. She curled around, her head on my shoulder, her hand over my heart. "Can I come to the funeral with you tomorrow?"

Her lips skimmed my chest. "Yes." She took a deep breath that gave me pause.

"If you don't tell me what's still eating you, Trent will give us Communication 101 lessons."

"What textbook?" Maggie murmured. The movement of her lips across my skin caused a shiver to run through me.

"His brain."

Maggie giggled and shifted closer, stretching one leg across me. I let the silence seep over us while I waited for her to find the words. "Do you want the LA job?"

I rubbed her back in slow circles and considered tiptoeing around the topic. But I remembered Jim's words about communication and facing the hard conversations head-on. I remembered what I vowed about my relationship with Maggie from now on. "I do. I want the job."

"What would that mean for you and me? I get that you love me, and I love you. But we both love our jobs. And I love this town."

"Long-distance?" I held my breath.

"For how long?"

"Six months to a year." I rubbed my forehead and then jumped into the hard bit. "Possibly longer. Possibly until I have enough clout to use the studio I built here or get offered opportunities in New York."

Maggie drew figure eights on my chest. "Six months to a year."

"Possibly longer." I didn't want to hide the reality. In six months, if the role looked like it would be more than a year, I didn't want her to think I wasn't committed to her.

"What does that look like to you? How would we do that?"

"Honestly? I don't know. A lot of time on fucking airplanes, I think." Nothing about the distance appealed to me. But if Maggie wouldn't leave Little Falls for more than a vacation, I would take what I could get. "Long weekends, vacation time, meeting in the middle for a few hours, whatever we have to do to make it work."

"You'd do all that?"

"If you say you won't, I'm turning down the job."

"I don't want you to say no because of me."

I tipped her face up so our gazes locked. "If there's a choice, I choose you. I mean that with all my heart."

Tears pooled in her eyes. "When do you have to tell him?"

"I already turned it down, but Jack said I could still change my mind until Monday. He wasn't going to tell anyone until Monday." The timing couldn't be worse. Jim's funeral was tomorrow, and then I had to call Jack on Monday to tell him to move forward with negotiations or bow out. When I'd called Jack on Friday to turn down the job, Jack had extended the deadline to Monday so I could "have the weekend to be completely sure." I'd been prepared to turn down the job, and I'd do it again on Monday if she didn't think we could make long-distance work.

"Take the job."

"Maggie." I let frustration leak into my voice. I didn't want to go back down a road of miscommunication or one of us trying to do what was best for the other instead of what was best for us both.

"We'll figure it out together, okay? My brain doesn't want to do it right now. Feels too hard. But if you say yes to the producing job, I'm not going to bail on you, on us." She crawled along me until we were face-to-face. "Say 'yes.'"

A slow grin spread across my face. Was it possible I'd get Maggie and the job? What else could we agree on? "You wanna say 'yes' too?" I rolled us so I had her pinned to the bed, and I settled between her legs. "Join my team?"

She framed my face with her hands. "You mean, *my* team, right?"

I brushed my lips against hers. "Our team. I'll be part of your mayoral team when you win, and you can be part of my songwriting team. My muse is the most important aspect." I watched her face as she processed my comment.

"Our teams, then," she whispered. "I love you, Grady."

When the words circled around us for the second time, I wondered if I'd ever get tired of hearing them.

Months ago, when I'd returned to Little Falls, I'd done so many things wrong. Made so many mistakes. But they'd led us here, somehow. Looking down at her, I tried to solidify this moment, make it one I'd never forget. I'd gotten lucky.

"Where do you see us in five years?" she asked.

"More together and more in love than we are right now."

A smile spread across her face. "You think that's possible? To have more?"

No matter what the future held, if I had her in my arms, I knew I'd be doing just fine. "I will never stop trying to be the man you deserve."

Her face softened, and she stroked my cheek. "Aww, Grady. You already are." She drew me down, and our lips brushed together. "But I think you're right. This is only the beginning."

I couldn't be more grateful. With that thought in my head, I sought her lips again, deepening the kiss, and I proceeded to show her how great new beginnings could be.

Epilogue
Grady

Maggie looked radiant, absolutely glowing when she grinned at me from across the banquet hall on election night.

The result could have only gone two different ways, and although the victory was narrower than *I* liked to see, Maggie had beaten me fair and square.

In the weeks after the Small Town Savior show, the town had been rife with gossip about me, about Maggie, and even about Trent again. Old wounds had been reopened all around, but it had let a lot of the air clear in a way that I'm not sure it would have otherwise.

Whenever I caught wind of something incorrect about Maggie or Trent or even me, I set the record straight firmly and quickly. If Maggie and I intended to make our home here permanently and eventually raise a family here, I wasn't having any lingering doubts about her role in Trent's drug ring, about my brother's sense of remorse, about my love for both of them.

With my Small Town Savior performance going hugely viral, I'd been doing a lot of radio, television, YouTube, and social media lives with other creators, news people, and others in the industry. At every turn there, I shouldered the blame, without hesitation, for my portrayal of Maggie and Trent in my songs, for the folly of youth, and how I intended to work my ass off to make up my idiocy to Maggie and Trent for as long as they'd have me.

Tyler appeared at my shoulder, a victory beer in his hand. I'd had a special batch of beer and wine made up with customized labels for Mayor Maggie.

"Dad would be really proud," Tyler said, his voice thick with emotion.

"I suspect he was always proud of all of you," I said, not taking my eyes off Maggie. One of the joys of having her was that I didn't have to hide how much I wanted her, cherished her.

"It's made me think a lot about fatherhood," Tyler admitted, taking a long draught of his beer.

"I keep thinking about Amir," I said, shifting my focus to Emily's little guy who was running through the crowd of town supporters, streamers flying from his outstretched hands. "Two father figures gone."

"Trent's been taking him to the mechanic shop, I hear," Tyler said with a small smile. "And I've been trying to teach him how to sew."

"Any luck?"

"None," Tyler said. "But I hear he's learned the names and uses of some tools with Trent. Omar was always good with his hands."

"I never met him."

"He was a good guy. Firefighter. I hope Emily can find someone else who lights her up like you and Maggie are for each other."

I let out a little laugh. "We're lit up, are we?"

"Like the motherfucking sun," Tyler said, following my gaze back to Maggie, who was chatting with some of her regulars from the pharmacy.

It amazed me, sometimes, all the little things I knew about Maggie now. Her regular customers. The temperature she liked to sleep in. That putting my dishes in the sink instead of the dishwasher would make her huff out an annoyed breath at the sight. That she had slippers scattered around her house, and now mine, because her feet were always cold.

I watched as Maggie excused herself from the people she was talking to and made eye contact with me, a silent indication she was headed back to me, headed home to the crook under my arm. There was nothing I liked better than the weight and feel of her against me.

She didn't make it far before she was halted by someone else, congratulating her, or maybe asking a pharmacy-related question—we could never be sure which would win when we were stopped on the street.

"You leave for LA in two days?" Tyler asked.

"Yeah," I confirmed. "Which reminds me that I should be glued to my lady for the next forty-eight hours."

"Too much information, buddy."

I laughed. "Not literally," I said. "I mean, unless she'll let me." I gave him a half smile and left him to saunter over to Maggie.

As soon as I reached her, I looped my arm around her shoulders and kissed her on the temple. The older ladies she was speaking to went all soft in the eyes as they looked at us.

"You two make such a handsome couple," Margot Langly said.

"It's all her," I said. "I'm the scruffy one she took pity on."

Maggie gave me a gentle elbow to the ribs, and the ladies laughed before excusing themselves to track down Emily about a real estate deal they'd heard was coming on the market. As much as I wanted it not to be true, most of the real estate in Little Falls was a steal of a deal. I was hoping the recording studio at the train station might help to drive some famous traffic through here, increase tourism a little at least. Maggie had some other ideas to try to bring in more industries or encourage small businesses in the heart of town that she was going to try to implement in the next year.

"These are cute, by the way," Maggie said, turning one of the wine bottles on the closest table, custom label facing out, toward us.

"I love that photo of you," I admit. I took it the week after her dad's funeral, when we were still tentative, as though we were worried something might blow us apart again.

In the photo she's surrounded by the fall colors in her parents' backyard, and when she'd looked at me, there'd been so much love and affection in her expression, I'd snapped the pic without thinking. Then I'd realized that it was the perfect representation of how Maggie feels about Little Falls too—this place fills her up.

"Another four-year term," I said, giving her a squeeze. "I never had any doubt."

Maggie laughed. "Um, I think you had a lot of doubts. But I'm a champion, and I overcame them."

"You did rise to the top," I agree. "I feel like I should have to wear the court jester costume as punishment for my initial lack of faith."

"Costumes are allowed," Maggie agreed, "later at home."

"You want me all to yourself, do you?"

"Always," she said, rising on her toes to give me a quick kiss.

When she went to pull away, I slid my hand into her hair and deepened our kiss, not giving a damn about the crowd around us.

A loud wolf whistle broke my concentration before I could sink too far into the sensations that usually led to me blocking everything else out.

"Get a room," Trent yelled from across the hall.

"Gladly," I murmured against Maggie's lips before glancing up. "You offering to pay?"

"Oh, please," Trent hollered back. "That video of you groveling for Maggie's forgiveness has more than paid for a hotel room."

He was right. But I was trying to funnel as much of those funds as I could into things I knew would make Maggie happy—like renovations on my dilapidated house, so she felt more comfortable being there, or putting up a memorial bench for Jim Sullivan outside Maggie's pharmacy in the town center, complete with a plaque that accurately conveyed everything he'd meant to so many, or making sure she was well stocked with morning coffee while I was still here to hand deliver it to her at work—whichever work she was at.

"Do you think that means we can leave the party?" Maggie whispered to me. "I only get you for two more days."

"Ladies and gentlemen," I called out in a booming voice, "the mayor of Little Falls will now be taking her leave. Thank you so much for supporting her run for mayor. The best candidate was the victor." I gazed down at her. "But honestly, it feels like I'm the real winner. I'm so fucking proud to call you mine."

And without waiting for her reply, I scooped her into my arms, and I carried her out of the banquet hall and straight into the rest of our lives together.

Not done with Maggie and Grady yet? Grab some bonus content here: https://BookHip.com/PTMSPPG

Want to read Tyler and Mia's story? *Mending Hearts* is next. Grab it here: https://mybook.to/MendingHearts2024

What else have I written?

Bellerive Royals Series – Interconnected standalones

Fake Crown

Scarred Crown

Heavy Crown

Fallen Crown

Tucker Billionaires – Interconnected standalones

Temporary Love

New Adult Sports

Saving Us

Fake Crown

Donaghey Brothers Series – Romantic suspense

Retribution

Resurrection

Redemption

Little Falls Series – Small Town Romance

Rival Hearts

Mending Hearts

Healing Hearts

Guarded Hearts

First Date Challenge – loosely linked to the same world – for maximum enjoyment, read after Book 2

Adult Contemporary Romance

When Stars Fall

Miss Matched

About Wendy Million/W. Million

Wendy Million is a high school teacher whose award winning contemporary romances about strong women and troubled men have captivated her loyal readers.

Writing as Wendy Million, she is the author of the romantic suspense series *The Donaghey Brothers,* as well as the contemporary second chance romances, *When Stars Fall*, and *Miss Matched*.

Writing as W. Million, she's the author of the *Bellerive Royals* series, the *Little Falls* series, and the *Tucker Billionaires* series.

When not writing, Wendy enjoys spending time in or around the water. She lives in Ontario, Canada with two beautiful daughters, two cute pooches, and one handsome husband (who is grateful she doesn't need two of those).

Acknowledgements
My Personal Love Notes

I wrote most of this series a long time ago, and so I'm sending a special shout-out to readers on Wattpad and Radish who read early drafts of these ideas and characters. Your feedback was invaluable in shaping these characters and this world.

A special thank you to Angela from Proof Positive, whose thoughtful comments and attention to detail is always incredibly helpful.

Thanks to my cover designer, Shannon Passmore, who's patient with my tweaks and changes. Covers are probably one of the most stressful parts of this job for me and she makes it infinitely easier.

As always, a heart-felt and genuine shoutout to my family—my husband, my girls, and my dad. All of you help me maintain some balance, so I don't burn out, but you also give me the space to do what I love.

9 781990 754159